Three Great
Hardy Boys®
Mysteries

The Hardy Boys®
in

The Secret of the Caves

The Secret of
Pirates' Hill

The Secret of the
Old Mill

by
Franklin W. Dixon

This Hardy Boys Three-in-One
was first published in 1994 by Diamond Books,
77–85 Fulham Palace Road, Hammersmith,
London W6 8JB.

Published pursuant to agreement with
Grosset & Dunlap, Inc., New York USA.

The Hardy Boys® Mysteries

THE SECRET OF THE CAVES

The Secret of the Caves was first published in the UK
in 1972 by William Collins Sons & Co. Ltd.

Frank leaped towards the ledge and grabbed the shotgun.

.1.

Telescope Hill Trouble

"Don't kid me, fellows," chubby Chet Morton said, moving his metal detector about the Hardys' front lawn. "You can find all kinds of things on the beaches with this gadget."

"Like what?" blond-haired Joe asked, winking at his brother Frank.

"Lost jewellery, money, gold-plated pens—"

Chet was interrupted by the arrival of a tall, broad-shouldered youth.

"Hi, Biff!" Frank called out. "Chet's trying to find a treasure."

Biff Hooper examined the new device and raised his eyebrows. "I know just where you can use this, Chet. You might find a lot of valuable stuff."

"Where?"

"At the Honeycomb Caves. My grandfather told me a freighter was sunk off the point during a hurricane. Lots of stuff was washed up."

"Just what I told you," Chet said, with a supercilious glance at the Hardy brothers.

Frank, eighteen, and Joe, a year younger, looked sceptically at their enthusiastic friends.

"There are a lot of important things to be found!"

9

Chet burbled. "How about the four of us going on a trip together?"

"To the Honeycomb Caves?" Joe asked.

"Sure. Why not? It's only fifty miles down the coast. Good swimming and fishing there, too."

"I'll explore the caves for hidden jewels," Joe said dryly, "while you and Biff pick up a million dollars' worth of rusty nails."

"It's a deal," Biff said, laughing. "Let me try that gimmick, Chet."

The stout boy removed the earphones from his head and handed Biff the long thin tube with a metal disc at the end.

"When you hear a loud clicking," Chet said, "you know that something metallic is under the ground."

His face intent, big Biff moved about the grass with the detector. Suddenly a voice from inside the house called, "Frank! Joe!"

"Okay, Dad, we're coming," Joe answered. He leaped up the front steps three at a time, with Frank at his heels.

Inside, Mr Hardy, a tall athletic man, motioned his sons into his study.

Fenton Hardy's reputation as a sleuth was worldwide. A former crack New York City police officer, he had moved to Bayport to become a private detective. Now his sons seemed destined to follow in their father's footsteps.

"What's cooking, Dad?" Frank asked, as the two boys sank into comfortable seats.

"Another mystery?" queried Joe.

Mr Hardy flashed a smile, then became serious and

opened a dossier before him on the desk. "I've got important news," he said.

"About what, Dad?" Joe asked.

"Telescope Hill."

"Where the U.S. is erecting the Coastal Radar Station?" asked Frank.

"Exactly."

"What's going on there?" Joe asked.

"Trouble. That's all I know so far," Mr Hardy replied. He told his sons that he had been deputized by the U.S. Government to aid in security at the gigantic installation designed to protect the coast of North America.

"To hunt out spies?" Joe asked.

"More likely saboteurs. There have been some strange, unexplained accidents at the site."

"Attack from within?" Frank queried.

"Yes. Perhaps a guard. That's my guess. I'm going to reorganize the guard security system and nip trouble in the bud. I thought you boys might like to help."

"Sure, Dad!" Frank said. "Will we need disguises or anything?"

"Not exactly."

"But," Joe began, "Chet wants us to—"

"That can wait," Frank interrupted impatiently. "Can't you see, Joe, we might be heading into a dilly of a mystery?"

Just then the quiet of the balmy June afternoon was shattered by a wild shriek in front of the Hardys' home. Frank and Joe jumped up, startled.

"Good grief, something's happened!" Frank exclaimed.

Both boys dashed out of the house, followed by Mr Hardy. Chet was jumping up and down on the front lawn, while Biff, looking excited, made the metal disc hover above a spot on the lawn.

"He's found a treasure!" Chet cried out. "This thing's clicking like fury. We've really got something, Frank!"

Several cars passing the Hardy home slowed down as the drivers watched Chet's antics. Then a huge trailer truck, carrying a load of construction steel, came to a halt while the driver honked for the cars to move on.

"More material for the radar installation," Frank thought, as the long vehicle rumbled out of sight down the street.

"Look, it's just about here," Biff said. He took off his earphones and marked an X on the grass.

"Do you expect us to dig up this fine lawn to satisfy your tomfoolery?" Joe said in mock seriousness.

"We just can't let it lie there," Chet protested. "Suppose it's an old coin worth hundreds and hundreds of dollars."

Now Mr Hardy was interested. With a wink he said, "Okay, boys, dig it up. Let's see what good detectives Chet and Biff are."

Chet ran to the garage and returned with a spade. With it he carefully cut the turf, placed it to one side, and probed the dirt with the point of his spade. He hit something hard and metallic.

"What did I tell you?" Chet beamed. "This detector is the greatest. Oh boy, are we going to have fun at Honeycomb Caves!" He dug up a spadeful of dirt, which he deposited beside the hole.

From the soil fell the metallic object. The Hardys recognized it as a tiny toy fire engine, rusted and corroded.

As the others crowded about, Joe picked up the toy and wiped off the crumbling earth which clung to the wheels. "Thanks, Chet," he said gravely, "I lost this fire engine seven years ago when I was ten."

"You were probably trying to hide it from me," said Frank, and laughed.

"Well," said Biff, "we've found Chet's Number One treasure. What's next? A ship's compass at Honeycomb Caves?"

Chuckling, Mr Hardy excused himself, while the boys chatted about the trip.

"I'm afraid we can't go, fellows," Joe said.

"Not this time, anyhow," Frank chimed in. "We have to work on a case with Dad."

"Say, what is going on?" Biff demanded.

"We can't tell," Frank replied. "It's confidential."

"Whatever it is," Chet said, "count me out of any dangerous stuff." Their stout friend bemoaned the fact that every time they were about to have fun, some sort of detective work had to come up.

Chet already had been involved in some deep mysteries which the Hardy boys had solved. But in each case, although reluctant at first, their staunch friend had joined in the sleuthing as an invaluable ally.

"When can you come with us?" asked Biff, evidently as eager as Chet to explore around Honeycomb Caves.

"That depends," said Frank, "on—" His eyes were suddenly diverted by someone walking up the street.

The other three boys turned to see an attractive girl

about their age hurrying along the pavement. She had wavy jet black hair, flashing brown eyes, and a gait that told the world she was in a hurry.

"A new neighbour?" Biff whispered, grinning.

"I've never seen her before," Joe said.

The girl, heels clicking, hastened to the Hardys' front path. There she stopped suddenly, turned towards the boys, and took a few steps forward.

Chet gave a low whistle and rolled his eyes. The girl, although she had a pretty face, wore a sad, worried look. "I would like to speak to the detective," she said nervously.

Joe's face brightened. "My brother Frank and I are detectives," he replied. "May we help you?"

"Don't mock me," said the girl, and her lower lip quivered.

Frank and Joe were taken aback. But they were even more nonplussed when their caller suddenly burst into tears!

·2·

Over the Fence

"HEY, wait a minute!" Joe blurted. "Don't cry!" But tears continued to course down the girl's face.

As the boys looked on in embarrassed silence, Mrs Hardy hurried out of the door, followed by her husband.

"Goodness gracious!" exclaimed Laura Hardy, a slim, good-looking woman. She hastened to the girl and put an arm about her shoulder. "Come inside, dear. Perhaps we can help you."

Frank whispered to Chet and Biff, "Wait here until we find out what this is all about."

Mrs Hardy sat on the living-room sofa beside the young caller. The girl dried her eyes and announced that her name was Mary Todd. She sobbed once more and said, "My father was a friend of yours, Mr Hardy."

"Oh, yes. George Todd of the Redding Machine Company. A fine man. I haven't seen him for years."

"Well, Dad passed away, and Mother too," the girl said.

The Hardys all expressed sympathy. Then Mary explained, "That's not why I'm crying, though. It's about my brother."

Mr Hardy leaned forward in his chair and said, "His

15

name is Morgan, isn't it? As I recall, a very bright boy. A little older than my sons."

Bravely fighting back tears, Mary told the Hardys that her brother, Morgan Thomas Todd, an instructor on foreign affairs at Kenworthy College, had disappeared.

"And I want you to find him, Mr Hardy," Mary said pleadingly. "The police are working on the case, but have discovered no leads."

The girl explained that she was a freshman at Kenworthy College, which had just ended the spring term. Her plan had been to spend the summer with relatives on the West Coast, but since her brother had disappeared several days before, she had cancelled her trip and come to Bayport.

"I just don't know what to do, Mr Hardy," she said. "Please help me."

Frank and Joe looked at their father. What would his decision be? He thought for a moment before speaking. "As I recall, your brother spent some time studying political methods in a foreign country."

"Yes, he did," Mary said, and mentioned the nation, which was unfriendly to the United States. She added that while he was there, Morgan Todd had suffered a fall and injured his head. "He seemed all right when he came back, but now I'm afraid he's lost his memory and just wandered away from the college."

"You mean as the result of his fall?" Mrs Hardy asked.

"Yes. A sort of delayed reaction."

"Fenton, I hope you take the case," Mrs Hardy said earnestly.

The detective now gave Mary a reassuring smile. "Of course I will." He turned to Frank and Joe. "You know I have already accepted an important case, but if you boys pitch in, I can also undertake the search for Morgan."

"Dad, you know we will!" Joe said eagerly.

Mary Todd's face brightened. "Oh, thank you, thank you," she said. "Boys, please forgive me for being such a crybaby."

"That's all right," Joe replied, a little embarrassed.

"Sure," Frank put in. "I don't blame you. Maybe we acted a little too smart. Have you a picture of your brother?" he added.

Mary took a snapshot from her purse and gave it to Frank. "Just don't lose it," she said, smiling. Then she rose to bid them good-bye. "I'll be staying at the Bayport Hotel," she said.

At that moment the doorbell rang. Mrs Hardy answered it and an attractive dark-haired girl walked in. She was Iola Morton, Chet's sister, who was a schoolmate of the Hardys and a particular favourite of Joe's.

"Hello, Iola," Joe said, reddening slightly.

Then Frank said, "Iola, this is Mary Todd."

The two girls smiled and exchanged greetings. Then Iola said, "Joe, what did you and Frank do to my poor brother? He's simply crushed that you two won't go treasure-hunting at Honeycomb Caves."

"You can guess what the reason is," Frank said.

Iola giggled. "A mystery?"

Frank and Joe, after a nod of approval from their father, told her about Mary Todd's problem.

"Oh, you poor dear," Iola said kindly. Her eyes sparkled. "I have an idea! Suppose you stay at our home until Mr Hardy and the boys find your brother."

"Oh, I couldn't impose."

"You don't know my mother," Iola said. "She'll insist that you stay. I hope you don't mind being a little way out in the country. We live on a farm."

"I'd really love it," Mary said. "You're all so wonderful to me."

The two girls left the house together. Frank and Joe followed and quickly briefed Chet and Biff on the missing instructor.

"Another mystery! That settles it!" Chet exclaimed. He turned to the Hardys and said gravely, "Gentlemen, the Hooper-Morton treasure expedition will be forced to take off without you."

"Come on, Chet," Iola ordered. "Get that old jalopy of yours running, destination Bayport Hotel."

"What for?" her brother asked, putting his metal detector in the back of the car.

When Iola told about their new guest, Chet opened the door gallantly with a bow. "The two of you can squeeze into the front seat with me," he said, then gave Biff a big wink and murmured, "Some guys have all the luck."

"That's you, pal." Biff laughed.

At the dinner-table that evening Frank and Joe discussed with their father what steps to take first in both mysteries. The brothers, it was decided, would leave the next day for Kenworthy College, in upper New York State. It was located in a town of the same name, about a six-hour drive away.

"And now getting back to my case at the radar site," Mr Hardy said, "I'll show you around the place tonight."

"Great!" Joe exclaimed eagerly.

Ever since the brothers had been old enough to engage in sleuthing, there had been a great camaraderie among the Hardy "menfolk," as Laura Hardy referred to them. Frank and Joe had first demonstrated their detective ability in an adventure known as *The Mystery of the Aztec Warrior*. Their most recent challenge was *The Wailing Siren Mystery*. By now, crime detection had become the boys' chief avocation.

The three left the house and Frank backed the boys' car down the driveway. The vehicle was old but well kept by the brothers, who preferred it to their father's new sedan.

Frank drove five miles north of the town to an elevated spot overlooking the Atlantic Ocean, and directly below, Barmet Bay.

From the road they could see Bayport hugging the coast, with its many docks stretching like dark fingers into the bay. Frank drove for half a mile farther. Now the road was bordered by a high steel-mesh fence. Presently he stopped in front of a gate guarded by two uniformed men. Mr Hardy got out and showed his badge, then introduced his sons to the guards. "I'd like to show the boys around," he said.

"Okay, Mr Hardy," one of the guards replied, saluting.

The three Hardys tramped along a wooded lane which snaked upwards to the top of Telescope Hill.

"Little did the old pioneers know that their telescope

lookout would be used for this giant radar," Frank said, as they approached the summit.

Here the trees had been felled, and the area was covered with heavy construction equipment and piles of steel framework. Already the radar tower had risen more than a hundred feet into the air, its girders sticking up weirdly into the evening sky.

"Looks like nobody's around," Joe said, glancing about. "Sure is quiet."

"Don't be fooled," Mr Hardy told him. "There's a large corps of watchmen on duty."

"Still, it's a pretty big place to be patrolled one hundred per cent efficiently, isn't it, Dad?" Joe asked.

"You're right."

Just then another uniformed guard walked quietly past the construction equipment twenty yards from them. "Evening, Mr Hardy," the man said.

"Evening, Bill." Fenton Hardy returned his salute, then walked on with his sons. They encountered three more guards before they had circled the hilltop.

Each man was immediately recognized by the detective, although he had met the entire staff only that morning.

On the way back to the gate, Frank left the lane. Walking waist-high through weeds and brush, he observed the fence. "I wonder if they're planning to electrify the fence?" he called out to his father.

Before Mr Hardy could answer, Frank was startled by rustling noises. A dim figure rose up from the brush about ten feet away. Stealthily as a cat, a man raced to the fence.

"Stop!" Frank yelled, and sprinted after him. The

fellow clawed his way to the top of the steel mesh and leaped down with the agility of a panther. He hit the ground with a thud on the other side and bounded off into the woods. Mr Hardy and Joe dashed to Frank's side.

"Jumpin' catfish!" Joe declared. "You've already flushed one of the spy pack."

"I hope not for good," Frank said. "I'd rather have grabbed him."

Suddenly his eye was caught by an object snagged on a bush. Frank plucked it off and triumphantly held out an odd-looking cap. "We've got a clue, anyhow."

The trio examined the cap. It was dark red with a small green peak. There was no label inside.

"I've never seen one like this," Joe commented. "It could be an import."

"Good guess," Frank agreed.

It was growing dark, so Mr Hardy voted against pursuing the intruder. He kept the cap, however, for more careful study.

Next morning Frank and Joe were up early. They hastily packed for the trip to Kenworthy College, then had breakfast with their parents.

"You have a plan mapped out, boys?" Mr Hardy asked.

Frank nodded and laid down his fork. "We'll see the police and the dean, then get permission to examine Morgan Todd's quarters."

"Check carefully on any close associates he might have had," Mr Hardy advised.

"And do be careful," Mrs Hardy added. "Of course,

I know you're perfectly capable of taking care of your-selves."

"You can say that again, Laura," Mr Hardy re-marked as a smile crinkled his eyes.

Joe checked the petrol and oil in their car while Frank loaded the luggage into the boot. "All set."

"Okay." Joe took the wheel and zigzagged through the Bayport streets until they came to the highway which led directly west. Early morning traffic was light, consisting mainly of large trucks heading east towards the radar construction.

The road, level at first, rose in a long curve towards the top of a hill, three miles out of town.

Joe kept far to the right side as a truck crested the hill and headed down. It was pulling a long trailer, on top of which was balanced a huge crane.

As it approached, Frank suddenly cried out, "Joe . . . the trailer . . . it's cut loose!"

The trailer veered towards the centre of the road on a collision course with the Hardys' car.

Joe tried desperately to swerve out of its way. To make matters worse, the huge crane began to topple over.

"Look out!" Frank cried in warning.

·3·

Bouncy Quill

FRANTICALLY Joe looked about for a way to dodge the runaway trailer. He spied a small lay-by and spun his wheel sharply. But before he could reach that haven, the crane hit the top of the Hardys' car with a ripping crash!

Joe clutched the wheel as the car swerved and shuddered, finally coming to rest on the dirt shoulder. Both boys glanced back. The huge crane lay twisted in a ditch, the trailer alongside on its back. Frank and Joe hopped out to look at the damage.

"Wow! Look at this. Pretty close!" Frank said, pointing to a long jagged cut in the roof of the car.

A quarter of a mile down the hill, the truck driver had stopped his vehicle and walked back. He came up to the Hardys and the three talked over the strange accident. As they surveyed the broken crane and the trailer with upturned wheels still spinning, the truck driver said glumly, "More bad luck. We're really getting it on this radar job!"

"What do you mean?" Frank asked. "Have things like this happened before?"

The driver hooked his thumbs into his braces and gave a low whistle. "Happened before! I'll say!" He told the boys that in three days this was the third accident to heavy equipment bound for the radar project.

"So now I've got to make out more papers and reports for the construction company," the driver said, as if this were even more difficult than driving his unwieldy rig.

Joe took out his wallet. "We have to report to our insurance company," he said. "They'll take care of everything."

After Joe and the driver had exchanged information, the boys set off again. As they drove along the highway, the Hardys speculated on the unusual accident. Was this a case of sabotage? Did it have anything to do with their father's assignment, or the intruder they had seen the night before?

"I don't see how it could have been aimed at us personally," Joe said.

"I agree," his brother replied. "Could've been a weak coupling. Or perhaps the trailer brakes didn't hold. The claims investigators will find out."

The brothers stopped for a quick lunch along the way, and arrived at the outskirts of Kenworthy an hour later with Frank at the wheel.

"Keep an eye open for a place to stay," he said as he reduced speed.

They passed several motels, none of which looked particularly inviting.

"Hey, Frank, what about that place ahead?" Joe suggested. A large billboard announced that the Palm Court Motel offered the traveller the latest luxuries.

"Not a bad-looking place." Frank pulled into a

driveway which led to a cottage with a simulated thatched roof. It bore the sign OFFICE. To the left stretched a long, low building made up of the motel units. Before each door stood an artificial palm tree. Frank and Joe got out and looked around. To the right of the office they counted twelve neat little cottages of the same thatched-roof variety. The ubiquitous palm tree stood before each one.

"Kind of corny," Joe remarked.

"But comfortable looking," his brother said. "We might do worse."

In the office they were greeted by a middle-aged man with a thin fringe of hair circling his head an inch above the ears. He stroked his bald head and greeted the boys with a smile. "College students visiting from somewhere else?"

Frank evaded the question and asked the price of a motel room. When he was told, Frank registered for himself and his brother, took the proffered key, then drove the car in front of Unit Seven.

As the boys entered with their luggage, Joe grinned. "Some people are pretty nosey."

"The less people know about our business the better," Frank said, as he put his suitcase on a rack, then opened it.

After they had refreshed themselves, the boys went out, locked the door, and hopped into the car.

"First port of call," Frank said, "will be the police station."

"Good idea." Joe nodded. "Let's learn what the local cops found out."

Police headquarters was in the basement of the newly-built town hall. The chief was out of town, so the boys introduced themselves to the desk sergeant and asked for background regarding the Todd case.

"Morgan Todd just walked out and disappeared," said the sergeant. "Absent-minded professor kind of stuff, you know."

"Any clues at all?" Joe asked.

"Nope, nothing," the sergeant replied. "But we'll probably hear from him in a few days." He leaned forward. "Confidentially, I think he was one of these overworked eggheads. You know, studying all the time. Too much strain!"

The boys did not comment, but thanked the officer and left.

"Talk about jumping to conclusions!" said Joe, when they were in the car again. "That sergeant takes the biscuit!"

They decided next to talk with the dean.

After getting directions from a passerby, Frank drove to the outskirts of town, where the small college nestled on a wooded knoll. Frank stopped in front of the administration building. He and Joe climbed the marble steps and entered the hallway.

They quickly found the office marked DEAN EAST-LAND, and went inside. After telling a receptionist that the nature of their business was confidential, the Hardys were ushered into the official's private office.

Dean Eastland was a tall, spare man with a shock of unruly grey hair. He rose as they entered. "Be seated, young men. You say your mission is confidential? That sounds mysterious."

The brothers took chairs before the dean's desk, and

Frank began by saying that they were trying to find Morgan Todd.

"Yes, yes, good for you," the dean said. "Matter of fact, we're all trying to locate him."

"Our father, Fenton Hardy, has taken on the case," Frank explained, "and we are here to do a little spade-work."

"Ah, yes, yes. I hope you have better luck than we have had," the college official said. "Strange! Very strange indeed!" He shook his head.

"How's that?" Frank asked.

"Well, I mean, the circumstances surrounding his departure." As the boys listened intently, Dean Eastland told how the instructor apparently had prepared an examination for his students, left it on his desk, and disappeared into the night.

"We found the test there next morning," the dean said, "or rather a colleague found it, had it mimeographed, and Mr Todd's students took the examination that day."

The dean picked up a pencil and tapped it on his desk. "But, as you know, Mr Todd never returned. Quite disturbing."

"Who found the exam?" Joe asked impetuously.

The dean looked up in surprise. "Mr Quill did. Cadmus Quill is Mr Todd's colleague and close associate."

Frank and Joe exchanged meaningful glances. They would have to question Cadmus Quill.

"Well, that is about as much as I can tell you, boys," said the dean, rising. "Morgan Todd, I'm afraid, is suffering from loss of memory."

"We'd like to meet Cadmus Quill," Frank said, "and also examine Todd's room if we may, Dean Eastland."

The dean jotted down the address and handed Frank the slip of paper. He walked to the window and pointed across the quadrangle. "Shelly Row is behind that building. It's where we house graduate students and instructors."

The boys thanked the dean and hurried out. As they walked across the quadrangle, they passed groups of students who had just registered for the summer session.

Presently the brothers found themselves behind a short man in his early twenties, noticeable because of his tiptoed bouncy gait and a loud sports jacket. Joe could hardly keep from imitating the peculiar walk as he fell in behind him.

Frank nudged his brother, and as they stepped past the man, Joe could not restrain himself from taking a backward glance at the fellow's intelligent, round face.

Quickly finding Shelly Row, the boys made their way to Number 19 and rang the doorbell. They were so intent on listening for someone inside that they did not hear a person walking up behind them. "Looking for me?" asked a cheerful voice.

Frank and Joe whirled about to face the bouncy fellow with the sporty clothes. "Are you Cadmus Quill?" Frank asked.

"Yes, I am. May I help you?"

The boys introduced themselves, and Quill ushered them into his room. Frank quickly told all that they had learned about the case and asked Quill if he knew anything further.

"I do indeed," he replied, "but the local police think it isn't important!"

"Do you have more facts?" Joe asked eagerly.

"Not exactly," Quill replied. "You might say it's confidential information." He motioned the boys to be seated, then drew up a chair close to them. "Todd was going to be married soon. Did you know that?"

Taken by surprise, the Hardys said No.

Quill told them that Todd had confided in him that he was going to return to Europe to marry a girl he had met while studying in the unfriendly country. "He didn't even tell his sister for fear she might object."

"Then you don't believe he lost his memory," Frank said.

Quill shook his head. "Not at all."

The graduate assistant had no further information to offer, whereupon the Hardys asked if he would show them to Todd's quarters.

"Indeed," Quill said with an officious little smile. "Right next door."

He produced a key and entered the adjoining apartment.

"You see? Everything is neat and orderly," he pointed out. "It's very obvious to me that Morgan deliberately planned to leave."

"What's this?" Frank asked, bending down to look at some mimeographed sheets on Todd's desk.

"I put those there," Quill replied, "—a few of the examination papers which were left over the day after Morgan disappeared."

The young sleuths scanned the room but did not wish to examine it closely with Quill present.

"Thank you," Frank said. "Guess that's all for now. May we come back later and check the room further?"

"Indeed, yes, be my guests," Quill said, and he handed the key to Joe.

As they returned to their car, Frank teased his brother. "Joe, you nearly made a *faux pas* when we first saw Bouncy Quill walking across the campus."

Joe laughed. "He's kind of odd, but I suppose a very smart cooky."

The boys stopped for supper at an inn near the campus, then returned to their motel. Frank opened the door and gasped. Inside was an elderly couple. The man was reading a newspaper while the woman toyed with her hair before the mirror on the dresser.

"Excuse me!" Joe said. "We must be in the wrong room!"

"No, we're not," said Frank. "This is ours—Number Seven."

The woman turned and smiled. "Oh, you must be the Hardy brothers," she said. "The manager moved your luggage out."

"What for?" Frank asked, puzzled and annoyed. "We're registered here overnight."

Then he realized there was no use in arguing. It apparently was not the couple's fault. Frank and Joe hastened to the manager's office. The man smiled broadly. "Well, I've done as you asked. You have a very nice little bungalow and I know you'll enjoy it."

"Wh-what?" asked Joe.

"Your college friends relayed your message," the man said, stroking his bald head.

The Hardys were dumbfounded but listened to the

manager's explanation. "Three boys came here and told me you Hardys wanted one of the cottages where it would be quieter. So we moved you in there bag and baggage." The man added, "It costs only two dollars more a night. You're getting a bargain."

"Where is this cottage?" Joe asked.

"Over there," the man said, pointing to one of the little houses. It was lighted inside.

The boys hastened over, and as they passed the window they saw a stocky youth standing inside. Frank flung open the door. "What's the meaning of this?" he demanded.

The young man whirled round. Frank and Joe saw that he was wearing a black half-mask. At the same time, the cupboard door burst open and out jumped four other masked youths.

"Hey, what kind of a joke is this!" Joe cried out as the intruders jumped both Hardys. They struggled furiously, but the combined weight of the masked boys finally bore Frank and Joe to the floor. They were bound and gagged, then tied securely to two long planks.

Without saying a word, the Hardys' assailants loaded them into an estate car parked behind the cottage. They were driven out of the motel grounds and along the main highway for several miles. Then the driver turned left on to a side road and stopped a mile farther on.

The brothers were lifted out, carried a short distance through some low brush, and laid crosswise on a railway track. Then the masked quintet vanished into the darkness.

Frank squirmed and tugged at his bonds. Joe did too,

but neither boy could loosen the ropes which secured them. Beads of perspiration stood out on their foreheads. Then came a sound which struck terror into their hearts. In the distance they heard the ominous growl of an approaching diesel engine!

·4·

Tricked!

CASTING hopeless glances at each other, Frank and Joe struggled desperately at their bonds while the diesel engine drew closer.

The rumble of the wheels grew deafening. But then, as if by a miracle, the engine throbbed past, leaving only the clickety-clack of freight cars trailing in its wake.

Unscathed but shaken, Frank and Joe continued to work at the ropes which secured them to the planks. By straining until his muscles ached, Frank stretched his bound wrists to where he could dimly see a spike protruding from a railway sleeper. Over and over he snagged the knot upon the spike. Each effort loosened the rope a little more. Finally it fell open.

With his wrists released, Frank tore out his gag and reached over to do the same for Joe.

"Whew!" Joe gasped. "I thought our goose was cooked!"

"It would have been an awful way to say goodbye to mother earth," Frank replied grimly, quickly freeing himself from the plank.

Then he released his brother. The two boys stood up and stretched painfully, massaging their cramped muscles. Twenty yards away the polished rails of another railway line glimmered in the moonlight.

"Look, these tracks we were on are rusty," Frank noted.

"Must be a siding," Joe said, "which isn't used any more."

"A great way to give a guy grey hair at a tender age," Frank remarked.

"It wasn't funny," Joe said, between clenched teeth.

"I'll say not," his brother agreed. "I'd like to find the nut who planned this trick!"

"If I see him first, I'll take care of that joker," Joe said.

After walking along the tracks some distance, the boys came to the highway. There they flagged a friendly truck driver, who readily agreed to drive them to their motel.

Jouncing up and down in the cab beside the driver, the Hardys continued to speculate.

"You suppose what happened to us was just a crazy mix-up?" Joe asked in low tones. "Why should those fellows pick on us?"

Frank frowned. "I have a hunch the whole thing was intended to scare us away from Kenworthy before we could find a good clue."

"Then you think Todd could have been kidnapped?"

"Let's not rule out that possibility," Frank said.

As the truck approached the Palm Court grounds, Joe suddenly chuckled. "If Chet and Biff wanted excitement—they should've been with us tonight. Honeycomb Caves must be pretty tame compared with the Kenworthy capers."

Frank grinned widely. "Chet would've lost ten pounds from fright."

The truck swung over and stopped. The Hardys hopped out, thanking the driver for the lift.

"Sure thing, fellows. So long."

The brothers made a beeline for the office.

"Now to question Baldy," Frank said. He stabbed the buzzer beside the door repeatedly until a light shone inside. The manager, sleepy-eyed and holding up his trousers with one hand, opened the door. He was not in a good mood.

"What do you mean by waking me up at this hour?" he asked crossly. "If you're going to check out, wait till morning, for Pete's sake."

"Somebody else checked us out," Frank said. "We'd like to ask you some questions."

Alarmed by the boys' determination, the manager let them in. There the Hardys learned that the instigator of the room switch was a member of a local fraternity at Kenworthy College.

"I thought these college kids were just going to have some fun with you," the man said.

"The police might give it a different label," Frank replied grimly. "Now, what's this fellow's name and where does he live?"

After the man had jotted down the information, Frank and Joe drove directly to the Delta Sigma fraternity house. Dawn lay like a pink halo on the eastern horizon, but the Hardys' thoughts were anything but heavenly as they rapped on the fraternity house door. No one answered. Joe rang the bell while Frank continued banging.

Finally a young fellow in pyjamas opened up and yawned in Frank's face. "Whatever it is, we don't want any," he said, then started to close the door.

Frank reached for his shoulder and whirled him about. "This isn't any joke," he said. "We're looking for Jack Hale."

"Oh, the president," the youth said, stifling another yawn. "I can't wake him up—he's special."

"I'll say he is," Joe declared.

"But you fellows don't understand." The college boy regarded the Hardys earnestly with his pale blue eyes. "We don't wake the fraternity president until eight o'clock. He doesn't have his first class until nine."

"He's going to have a lesson right now," Frank said sternly. "Get him up!"

The youth shrugged, and padded off in bare feet to the second floor. Listening below, the boys heard shouts and angry words, preceding the appearance of a thick-set youth several years older than the Hardys. In red and white striped pyjamas he thumped down the stairs. When he saw Frank and Joe, he stopped with a startled expression.

"Isn't it kind of early—" Jack Hale started to say.

"Not for a punch in the jaw," Joe declared hotly, and stepped forward with fists cocked.

"Wait a minute, Joe," Frank said. "Let's get some questions answered before you start swinging." He walked over to Hale, who backed away nervously. "I'll put it on the line," Frank said. "What's the idea of leaving us on the railway track? And why did you switch our motel room?"

"Wait a minute, fellows! Hold it!" Hale said. "We

thought you'd guess it was just a little testing job. Anyway, why are you getting so worked up?"

"Yes, why?" the blue-eyed youth put in.

Hale continued, "You two were never in any *real* danger. We had a lookout posted to keep an eye on you in case you needed help. Say, you are going to be Delta Sigma students, aren't you?"

"Of course not," said Joe, his biceps still flexed.

"So you were having us on?" asked Frank. "Who told you to do that?"

Jack Hale looked embarrassed. He cast a fleeting glance up the stairs and seemed relieved when several other Delta Sigma boys moved quietly down behind him.

"I can't tell you who it is," Hale said.

The blue-eyed youth nodded vigorously. "We're honour bound not to reveal his identity."

"We thought you were going to be Delta Sigma men," Jack said. "Honest we did."

"Well, then, you ought to let prospective students in on it too," Frank said. He turned away. "Come on, Joe. Let's get out of here. We have work to do."

Looking somewhat the worse for wear after their strenuous night, the Hardys nonetheless planned another bit of sleuthing before returning to their cottage for sleep.

"Let's examine Todd's room before Quill gets up," Frank suggested.

Joe readily agreed. "At six a.m. Quill's probably still asleep." Joe reached into his pocket. "I have the key to Todd's apartment."

The Hardys encountered a few milk delivery trucks

and one newspaper boy as they made their way to Shelly Row. Joe inserted the key quietly and turned it in the lock. The boys entered. Frank pressed his ear against the apartment wall. Silence.

"He's still in the arms of Morpheus," Frank whispered.

"Okay," Joe said. "Let's look around."

Enough daylight filtered through the two front windows to allow the boys to examine the apartment carefully. While Joe concentrated on objects of furniture, Frank looked through notes and textbooks lying about. But the boys could find no evidence as to where Morgan Todd might have gone.

"I guess the police search was pretty thorough, after all," Joe commented. "What are you looking at, Frank?"

His brother held one of the mimeographed examination sheets in his hand and was scrutinizing it. Joe watched Frank as he scanned sentence after sentence on the white paper. Then a strange expression came over his face. Joe had seen it before when Frank was on the trail of a clue.

"You found something?" Joe asked excitedly.

"I'll say I have!" Frank declared, sucking in his breath. "Wow! Look at this!"

. 5 .

Counter-attack

JOE glanced over his brother's shoulder. "All I see is an exam paper—the fill-in type."

"Yes," Frank replied. "But there's a clue right under your nose."

"I don't get it, Frank. You must have super vision."

"Look. Read the first question, Joe."

" 'Russia's present political system was founded by ——' "

"I don't care about the answer," Frank said. "Now read the second question."

" 'Only —— men from California have been named to the Supreme Court.' "

Joe frowned. "It's still a riddle to me."

Enjoying the game he was playing, Frank asked, "How many questions are there?"

"Eight."

"And the first letter of the first word in each question spells what?"

Joe's eyes quickly roved down the side of the exam sheet. "R-O-C-K-A-W-A-Y." He whistled. "The name of a town!"

"That's it—Rockaway," Frank said. "Todd did leave a clue. And I don't think the police found it, either."

"Good for you," Joe said, slapping his brother on the back. "I guess I'm too exhausted for any deep brainwork."

"We'll have breakfast before we turn in," Frank said. "Then we'll go to the post office and find out from their guidebook how many Rockaways there are in the U.S."

"There's probably at least twenty-five," Joe said with a sigh. "By the time we check on them, Morgan Todd could be in Timbuktu." He yawned deeply, then placed his ear to the apartment wall.

"Hear anything?" asked Frank.

"Bouncy Quill is up," Joe said. "Let's get out of here before he discovers us. He'd be sure to ask a lot of questions."

Because the campus cafeteria was not yet open, Frank and Joe stopped at an all-night café on the outskirts of town. After eating a hearty breakfast, they returned to their cottage.

"Oh boy, now for a peaceful sleep," Joe said. He kicked off his shoes and flung himself on top of the bedspread.

Too exhausted to undress, Frank did the same. The boys slept soundly for several hours.

Frank awakened first and thought he was having a nightmare. A pillow was pressed hard over his face and a powerful hand pinned his shoulder to the mattress.

Trying to cry out, Frank kicked wildly and flung the intruder away from the bed. Someone hit the opposite wall with a thud and crashed to the floor. The noise aroused Joe, who sprang up, wild-eyed, and looked around the room.

"Jumpin' catfish!" Joe glared at the stunned figure

on the floor. "Biff Hooper, what're you doing here?"

Biff aroused himself and shook his head. "Got to clear the cobwebs," he said. "I was only fooling, Frank. You jumped me like a wounded panther."

Frank laughed. "You got off easy, boy."

At that moment Chet sauntered through the doorway, munching noisily on potato crisps. He dipped into a huge cellophane bag and pressed another handful into his mouth. Still munching, he asked, "What's all the racket?"

"Biff making a grand entrance," Frank said wryly. "Sit down, fellows. We'll tell you our latest news. How about some crisps, Chet?"

The stout lad proffered the crinkly bag, and the Hardys helped themselves. As they ate, they briefed Biff and Chet on their findings at Kenworthy College and their harrowing experience of the previous night.

"Wowie!" Biff exclaimed. "You Hardys sure stir things up!"

"And now," Joe said, "we have to find out how many Rockaways there are in the U.S.A."

"I can tell you one," Chet said. "It's near Honeycomb Caves."

"I never heard of it," Frank said in surprise.

"Neither did I," said Chet. "It's a dinky place."

Biff explained that they had driven down the coast early that morning and stopped at a small petrol station a couple of miles north of Rockaway. "We asked the attendant how to get to Honeycomb Caves," he went on, "and he warned us not to go."

"Why?" Frank asked.

"He said awful things might happen to us if we did."

"Something very strange is going on there," added Chet with a great air of knowledge. "It sounded like a real mystery so we thought maybe you'd like to take time out and look into it."

"I knew you'd try to snag us into going to those caves," said Frank, chuckling.

Chet flung out his arms dramatically. "After all, Biff and I thought sure you would've found Morgan Todd by this time!"

"It's not going to be so easy," Frank said. With a wink at his brother, he added, "But thanks for thinking about us. Come on, Joe! Our first stop's the post office." He glanced down at his dishevelled clothes and grinned. "I mean, after the shower."

Fifteen minutes later both boys were in fresh clothes and Joe said, "Okay, let's go."

He was about to step out of the door when he suddenly closed it and motioned to the others. "I think we're in for a fight, fellows, so get ready."

"What's the matter?" Frank asked, and looked out of the window.

Across the broad lawns of the Palm Court Motel strode four youths. In the lead was Jack Hale!

"Delta Sigmas," Joe said tersely. "Maybe the ones who made trouble for us last night. If they think it's four against two, they're mistaken."

"Right!" said Biff, who liked nothing more than playing tackle on the Bayport High football team.

"Okay," said Frank. "You and Chet hide in the cupboard." Then, opening the door, he politely invited the four fraternity men to enter.

"Hi," Jack said with a half-smile. "We have a little surprise for you."

But before he could utter another word, the cupboard door was flung open. Biff bolted across the room, taking a flying leap at two of the college boys. Chet pounced on the third. Only Jack remained standing. His face bore a pained expression.

"We don't want to fight!" he said.

"Then what did you barge in on us for?" Joe demanded.

Biff dragged two of the students to their feet, and Frank said, "Okay, let's smoke the peace pipe. What's up, Jack?"

Embarrassed, the fraternity president said that he had come to offer Frank and Joe invitations to join Delta Sigma should they decide to attend Kenworthy College.

"You're the kind we like," he said. "Plenty of guts!"

"Thanks for the invite," Joe said coolly. "We'll keep it in mind if you tell us who put you up to that low-down trick last night."

Jack looked at the floor and the Hardys could see that he was torn between loyalty to the unknown perpetrator and regard for them.

"Really, I can't tell," he said finally. "You wouldn't want me to rat on a pal."

"No hard feelings," said Frank, though he thought the youth was foolish to protect such a person. Then he introduced Biff and Chet.

"Wow!" said one of the college boys. "We could use you two on the Kenworthy football team."

With that, the Delta Sigmas left.

Frank drove the Bayporters to the post office, located beside the town hall. A helpful clerk passed the postal directory over the counter and Frank thumbed through its pages.

"Hey, look at this," he said. "There are only three Rockaways—one in Oregon, one in New Jersey, and the other on the coast down from Bayport."

"It's certain we won't go to Oregon or New Jersey first," Chet said. "You fellows will investigate the closest one or I miss my bet."

"O genius of a treasure hunter!" declaimed Joe, as he placed the right palm of his hand on his forehead and bowed low. "We, your humble servants, salaam!"

The others guffawed at the sudden look of embarrassment that swept over Chet's face as he cast his eyes quickly round the post office to see if anybody was watching. Seeing no one, Chet joined in the laughter.

Frank handed back the directory to the grinning clerk and thanked him. The boys, still laughing, trooped out of the post office.

"Well, our next destination—Rockaway!" Frank said. He added thoughtfully, "You know, this isn't a bad move. We'll leave here as if we've been stymied on our investigation."

"That's right," Joe said. "So if anyone has been tracking us, they'll think we've given up." As an afterthought he added, "We ought to thank Cadmus Quill and the dean before we leave."

"Let me go too. Maybe I won't see the inside of a college again," Chet quipped.

The four drove to the campus, parked, and entered the administration building.

Dean Eastland, as before, was courteous to his callers. After thanking Frank and Joe for their interest in the case, he promised to relay any new information to them.

"By the way, Dean Eastland," Frank said, "would you send us the roster of Delta Sigma fraternity?"

"Of course," the dean replied, and jotted down their Bayport address.

As the boys walked into the hallway they met Cadmus Quill.

"We're going back to Bayport," Frank told him. "I'm sorry we couldn't find your friend Todd."

"Anyhow," said Joe, "thanks for your help, Mr Quill."

"Not at all," replied the instructor as he shook hands with the two boys. "I'm sure there's no need to worry. I feel strongly that he's in Europe—probably already married."

"It's possible," Frank said. "Well, perhaps we'll see you again."

"Come on, fellows," Biff said as they left the building. "If I hang around this college campus any longer I'll be as smart as you are."

"I'm itching for Honeycomb Caves," Chet bantered. "I feel in the need for some ready doubloons."

As the boys hastened back to the Hardy car, Frank had the feeling that Cadmus Quill had followed them out of the building. When he slid behind the wheel he glanced into his rear-view mirror.

There stood Quill on the steps, gazing at them intently. Then he turned back to the door.

Suddenly, above the sound of the starter motor,

Chet let out an Indian war whoop and yelled, "On to Rockaway!"

Frank, with his eyes still on the rear-view mirror, saw Quill stiffen and spin around.

· 6 ·

The Toppled Tower

CADMUS QUILL stood on the steps and stared at the boys with a startled look on his round face.

"That remark hit home!" Frank thought. He got out of the car and ran up to Quill before he had a chance to retreat. "You seem interested in Rockaway," Frank said bluntly, hoping to catch him off guard. "Do you know somebody there?"

Quill smiled. "I thought for a moment," he replied casually, "that your friend had said *Far* Rockaway, in New York. I have an uncle who lives there."

Frank was momentarily at a loss about how to pursue his line of questioning. This gave Quill time to turn on his heel. He strode off, saying, "I have a lecture to prepare. Good luck to you!"

Frank returned to the car, and as the boys drove back to the motel he discussed with them Quill's peculiar actions.

Joe spoke up. "That uncle bit doesn't ring true. Quill is keeping back something, I'll bet."

"Why should the name Rockaway strike him?" Chet wondered.

"Who knows?" Joe said. "Maybe he discovered the Rockaway clue in Todd's exam."

"I don't get it," Frank said, as he parked in front of the cottage. "Quill knows we're detectives. If he did find the Rockaway clue, why didn't he tell us?"

"Maybe he wants to follow it himself," Joe replied.

"This Cadmus Quill will bear watching," remarked Biff, now thoroughly caught up in the excitement of the mystery.

Chet suggested that while the Hardys were packing, he and Biff would take his jalopy to a service station. "We want to check it out before starting the trip to Rockaway," Chet said.

The brothers entered their quarters. While Joe tossed his belongings into his suitcase, Frank telephoned Bayport. Mr Hardy answered.

"Frank," he said, "I'm glad you called!" The boy was surprised at his father's clipped tone.

"What's the matter, Dad?" he asked.

"I'm afraid you and Joe will have to come home right away. It's urgent, and I'd rather not take time to explain it."

"Okay, Dad. But just one thing," Frank added quickly. "We're suspicious of a fellow named Cadmus Quill. Will you get us a confidential report on him, please?" Mr Hardy promised and Frank hung up. "Something's gone haywire in Bayport," he said to his brother, then repeated their father's message.

While Frank packed his belongings, Joe hustled over to the motel office to pay their bill. He returned to the car just as Frank was stowing the luggage into the boot. At the same moment, Biff and Chet drove up.

"All set for the big adventure at Honeycomb Caves!" Chet sang out exuberantly. "Joe, Frank, I bet I get better mileage than you boys on the way to the coast."

When the Hardys did not smile at the boast, Biff sensed something was wrong. "What's the matter, fellows?"

"We can't go with you—at least not now," said Frank.

"Sorry to leave you in the lurch like this," Joe added, as he slid behind the wheel.

Frank told them about their father's cryptic message.

"Well, if you're needed in Bayport, I guess that's that," Chet commented.

"We'll join you as soon as we can," Frank promised.

"We'll be camping on the beach," Chet said.

Grinning, Joe started the car. "So long, and don't join any fraternities!"

Joe held the speedometer needle at the maximum speed allowed, and the countryside flashed by. When they hit the turnpike, Frank took turns with his brother at the wheel. Now, with greater speed, the miles melted past.

"She purrs like a kitten," Frank said. "A great car, Joe."

"Good thing we had the engine tuned," Frank remarked as the wind whipped through his hair.

After a quick stop for lunch, Joe drove away from the roadside restaurant.

"Want to listen to the news?"

"Okay. What country's having a war today?"

"Maybe someone has landed on Jupiter," Frank said as he clicked on the high-powered transistor.

The first word to hit their ears was "Bayport." Joe took his foot off the accelerator and Frank turned up the volume. The newscaster's report sent a shiver up their spines: *The radar tower on Telescope Hill had toppled over in a high wind!*

"This must be the emergency Dad meant," Frank said. "Come on. Let's go."

Joe guided the car expertly along the motorway, and, slightly under six hours since they had left the town of Kenworthy, the Hardys pulled into their driveway.

As the boys carried their luggage in at the back door, Mrs Hardy met them.

"Hi, Mother," said Frank. "Where's Dad?"

"At the radar site. He didn't have time to tell you all about it on the phone."

"We heard the report on the car radio," said Joe.

"Your father wants you to go right over," Mrs Hardy said.

The boys carried the suitcases to their rooms, splashed cold water on their faces and hurried back to the car.

As they neared the construction site, traffic was slowed by the large trucks plying back and forth to the installation.

Finally they reached the gate. Frank parked the car, and he and Joe approached the guard. The brothers identified themselves.

"Our father is waiting for us inside," Frank said.

With a nod of recognition the security man admitted them. Briskly Frank and Joe trotted up the incline which led to the top of Telescope Hill.

Joe gave a low whistle as they neared the toppled tower. It had cut a jagged scar in the woodland and lay twisted and broken. A number of men were inspecting it. Mr Hardy, with a magnifying glass in one hand, was examining a girder at a point about five feet from the ground, where the steel superstructure had snapped off.

"You made good time," the detective said as his sons ran up. He added quickly, "I'm sorry, but I won't need you after all, boys. I found what I was looking for, soon after I summoned you."

"What's that, Dad?" asked Frank.

"Look here," the detective said, and handed him the magnifying glass.

The young sleuth studied the break in the steel. "I'll say you found something! Here, take a look, Joe."

The younger boy also was amazed as he noticed that the break was smooth and clean except for a burr at the edge of the girder.

"This was cut almost all the way through to weaken the structure," said Joe, "but I don't see any saw marks."

"It was probably done with an electronic cutter," Mr Hardy remarked. "I've already reported this to the government men. Their chief engineer agrees with my theory."

"And the high wind finished the job?" asked Joe.

"Exactly," his father replied. He added that the saboteur had cut the line so straight and deep that the girder had been snapped off like a crisp cracker.

"We're up against a daring and well-equipped ring of saboteurs," Frank commented, as the three walked alongside the fallen tower.

"But I wasn't sure of that at first," Mr Hardy said. "That's why I needed you. I wanted you to do some undercover work to help me find out whether it really was sabotage." He added that he had not revealed the nature of his urgent request for fear someone might have tapped his phone line. "I didn't want anyone to find out what I suspected."

"Any information on Cadmus Quill?" Joe asked, as they passed beneath a tall pine tree, the top of which had been sheared off by the tower.

"Nothing yet," Mr Hardy said. "A very reliable agency is checking into it. They'll send me the report in code."

Suddenly the detective yelled, "Look out!" and gave Joe a push which sent him sprawling headlong on to the grass. Simultaneously a huge chunk of metal thudded to the ground inches from his body.

"Good grief! Where'd that come from?" Frank cried, looking up into the tall pine.

"A piece of the tower must have broken off and got stuck in the branches," Mr Hardy said. "You all right, Joe?"

The boy picked himself up, took a deep breath, and grinned. "Being a detective can be dangerous!" he said. "Thanks for the assistance."

The three Hardys went through the main gate. "Our car is parked close to yours, Dad," Frank said.

A short time later father and sons entered their house together. After a late dinner with Mrs Hardy, the tired sleuths turned in.

When the boys came down for breakfast the next morning they found their father already up.

"There's a letter for you, boys," he said, pointing to the hall table.

Frank picked up the long heavy envelope. "It's from

Dean Eastland," he said. "Must be the fraternity roster."

As he spoke, the doorbell rang and Joe hurried to answer. It was a telegram for Mr Hardy.

"The report on Quill," Joe said eagerly.

"Bring it into my office," his father said, leading the way.

The detective opened the telegram and studied the mysteriously coded message. Taking a pencil and pad, he unscrambled the code letter by letter. His sons looked on intently over his shoulder. The information was concise. "Cadmus Quill. Good student. Good family. Good reputation. Likes to travel. Made an extended tour of study abroad three years ago."

"But look at the country he studied in!" Frank said excitedly.

Joe whistled. "The same one Todd visited last summer!"

"Dad," Frank exclaimed, "do you know what this could mean?"

·7·

The Palais Paris

"I GET it!" Joe burst out. "Both Quill and Todd were brainwashed into helping a foreign power!"

Mr Hardy spoke up. "Frank, what's your opinion?"

"My theory," Frank said, "is that maybe Todd and Quill had opposing views about this unfriendly country. Joe's jumping to conclusions and maybe I am too, but—"

Frank dropped into a thoughtful silence.

"Go on," Mr Hardy encouraged him. "You may be on the right track."

"If Todd was against the country and Quill for it, maybe they had a quarrel."

"Which could have led to Todd's disappearance?" Joe asked.

His brother nodded. "And whoever ordered the fraternity to trick us in order to scare us off," he added, "is in on the plot." Frank was still holding the letter from Dean Eastland. "Maybe this will give us a clue." He slit open the envelope and withdrew a printed pamphlet.

Frank's eyebrows shot up. "Oh—oh!" he exclaimed. "Here's our answer!" He slapped the booklet down on his father's desk and pointed to the words on the cover:

Delta Sigma Fraternity—Cadmus Quill, Faculty Adviser. "He probably was behind the trickery."

Mr Hardy glanced at Frank and said, "That certainly fits in with your theory."

"Yes," Joe agreed. "I think the police ought to question Quill."

Mr Hardy also thought this would be a good idea, so Frank telephoned the police chief at Kenworthy. He told the officer what he had just learned. The chief thanked him and promised to call the Hardys back after he had interrogated Quill.

Later, just as the family was sitting down to breakfast, the phone rang. Frank answered. "Oh, hello, Chief," he said. "Any luck with Quill?"

Mr Hardy and Joe jumped up from the table when they heard Frank exclaim in astonishment:

"He did? . . . All right. Thanks a lot . . . You'll keep us posted? . . . Right . . . Goodbye."

"What's the scoop?" Joe asked eagerly.

"More mystery," Frank said. "Now Quill has disappeared!"

Joe gave a low whistle. "Kidnapped?"

"Maybe."

Mr Hardy's brow furrowed. "You boys could be close to the truth about that foreign country's being involved," he said. "Maybe both Todd and Quill were whisked away because of some political information they gleaned."

Frank went on to report that the Kenworthy police had issued a seven-state missing person alarm for Cadmus Quill. "Only when he's found," Frank added, "can we tell whether Quill is friend or foe."

Various aspects of the case were discussed by the detective and his sons during the meal. What move to make next was the question. Mr Hardy said that since sabotage was definitely indicated at the radar site, he could free his sons to concentrate on the Todd matter.

"I vote we look for Quill," Joe suggested, as Mrs Hardy sliced a broad wedge of home-made coffee cake for Frank.

"Umm! Great as usual, Mom," Frank remarked, having disposed of a generous bite. "What do you say, Dad? Shall we follow up the Rockaway clue?"

"Maybe Joe has a point," Mr Hardy replied. "I have a definite feeling that if you find Quill you'll find Todd."

Joe grinned at his brother. "Lucky our bags are still packed."

The boys had gone to their room to bring down the luggage when the phone rang. Fenton Hardy was first to pick up the receiver in his study.

The caller was Chet Morton who said that he wanted all three Hardys to hear his story.

"Hold on. I'll get Frank and Joe on the other wires."

In a few moments Frank was at the hall phone, and Joe at the upstairs extension. "Are you all there now?" Chet's voice was edged with excitement.

"Right," Joe said. "What's up?"

"Maybe *you* can tell *me*," Chet said. "What is this guy Quill anyhow? A maniac?"

"Quill?" Frank echoed as his father and brother gasped in amazement. "Have you seen him?"

"Seen him! I'll say so," Chet replied. "I think he's out of his head."

"Come on, boy! Give us the lowdown!" Joe prompted.

"Quill forced our car off the road on the way to Rockaway, that's what!" Chet said.

"Did he follow you all the way from the college?" Fenton Hardy put in.

Chet said that must have been the case. "After a while Biff noticed somebody trailing us."

"How did you know it was Quill?" asked Frank.

Chet told of stopping for a traffic light. The other car had lingered several lengths behind. "But we recognized his moonface!" Chet said triumphantly.

Several miles farther on, as he and Biff rounded a curve, Quill's car had cut them off.

"My old jalopy scraped against a tree," Chet went on. "Biff got a bump on the head, but otherwise we weren't injured. It ruined the paintwork, though."

"I'm sure glad it wasn't any worse," Frank said.

"Did Quill keep on going?" Joe asked.

"Yes. In the direction of Rockaway. Say, why don't you fellows come down here and protect Biff and me?"

"Not a bad idea," said Frank. "Where shall we meet you?"

"We'll go on to Rockaway and set up our tent on the beach," Chet replied.

"Okay," Joe put in. "Get there as soon we can."

After Mr Hardy added his approval to the plan, the Hardys said goodbye and hung up.

The three detectives were perplexed about Biff and Chet's brush with Cadmus Quill. "Why would he pick on them?" Joe mused.

Frank shook his head. "My hunch is Quill thought you and I were in that car, Joe!"

Mr Hardy added a word of caution. "Don't take unnecessary risks, boys. Your enemies are dangerous."

As the brothers were about to leave, their mother said, "Oh, by the way, I have an errand I'd like you to do."

"Anything for you, Mother," said Frank, kissing her on the cheek.

"Well, it's really for Aunt Gertrude."

Joe rolled his eyes. "Oh—oh. Is Aunty coming for another visit?"

When Mrs Hardy nodded, Joe remarked, "It's just as well we're leaving for Rockaway now. Aunt Gertrude wouldn't approve of this mystery, I'll bet!"

Miss Gertrude Hardy was actually a great favourite with the boys despite her tart tongue and frequent predictions of dire mishaps overtaking her sleuthing nephews.

Frank chuckled. "What's the big deal for Aunt Gertrude?"

"Get her a spinning wheel."

"But—" Joe gulped. "Where're we ever going to find one?"

"Perhaps at the Palais Paris," Mrs Hardy replied with a twinkle.

"Wow!" Joe exclaimed. "Sounds real fancy—what is it?"

Mrs Hardy explained that there was a new and very attractive French restaurant on the main highway near Rockaway. "I understand," she added, "that the restaurant has an antique shop connected with it. It's

only a few miles from where you're going. I checked it
on the road map."

The boys grimaced slightly at the idea of having to
bargain for an old spinning-wheel, but assured their
mother they would pick one up if available.

"Wonderful," said Mrs Hardy. "I think your aunt
will be here by the time you return."

Frank and Joe hurriedly stowed their luggage in the
car. Their parents came to say goodbye. "Watch out
for those saboteurs at the radar site, Dad," Frank said.

"I intend to. Good luck yourselves."

Both boys hugged their mother, shook hands with
their father and hopped into the car.

"The camping equipment is already in the boot,"
Joe said. "Have we forgotten anything, Frank?"

"We're all set," his brother replied, giving the circle
sign with his thumb and forefinger.

The morning was grey and foggy as the boys set off
with Joe at the wheel, but an hour later the sun shone
through and burned off the mist.

The coastline now assumed roller-coaster proportions
as they approached the Honeycomb Caves area. The
highway was about two hundred feet above sea-level.
A short plateau extended to the lip of the palisades to
the left of them before dropping down abruptly into
the Atlantic Ocean.

"The caves are below these cliffs somewhere," declared Joe, motioning towards the coastal side. The
sea, hidden most of the time by a thick stand of woods
and undergrowth, occasionally flashed through in
brilliant glimmers.

Presently they approached a rambling, attractive

building with stone trim and a wide porch. "There's the Palais Paris," said Frank, pointing to a sign on a lamp-post announcing the fashionable restaurant. It was set thirty feet back from the right side of the road with a neat parking area beside it. The lanes, marked with white paint, were nearly filled with expensive new cars.

"A good crowd for lunch," Joe remarked, as he pulled in and parked.

The brothers got out and walked towards the entrance to the antique shop located next to the restaurant in the same building. As they passed the open door, Frank noted the well-dressed patrons seated at the tables. There was also a sign tacked to a post beside the door. It read: WAITRESSES WANTED.

"A ritzy place, I'd say, Joe," he remarked. "And if they have a big selection of antiques we ought to be able to find Aunt Gertrude her spinning-wheel."

The boys entered the shop and looked round. The broad floorboards were pegged, giving the place an old-fashioned appearance. Several long tables were filled with ancient-looking articles such as candle moulds, clocks, pewter pieces and bed-warmers. From the low ceiling hung a black iron pot and several oil lamps.

"Hey, over there, Frank!" Joe pointed to one corner of the room, where a spinning-wheel was suspended on two hooks fastened to the ceiling.

"Just what we're looking for." Frank walked over to inspect the wheel. Joe followed.

"Why have they got it hanging in mid-air?" he wondered.

"For the effect, I guess," Frank replied. He looked about for a sales assistant. Meantime, Joe tried to lift the wheel from its supporting hooks.

A resounding *crack* made Frank whirl about, just in time to see the spinning-wheel fall to pieces over Joe's head. They landed on the floor with a clatter.

"Leapin' frogs!" Frank exclaimed. "How'd that happen?"

"I don't know," Joe said. "I only touched it."

The noise brought a woman running from the back of the shop. She was tall, with dark eyes and black hair which was pulled back into a knot. "Oh, what have you done!" she cried with a pronounced French accent, putting her hands to her head.

"Nothing!" Joe protested. "The old wheel just came apart like matchsticks."

"We wanted to buy it," Frank said. "It must not have been very well made."

"That piece was valuable," the woman declared indignantly. "It was not for sale." She wrung her hands. "It was for show only—to set off our beautiful antique display."

Joe was embarrassed. "I'm sorry," he said. "Maybe we can put it back together again." He picked up the large wheel and the spindle, still intact.

"*Non!*" The woman's eyes flashed. "You do not get away so easily. I am the manageress here. You will have to pay for this wheel."

Joe groaned. "Why didn't I keep my hands off it!"

"You will pay!" the woman repeated. She hastened into the back of the shop and returned seconds later with a tall, burly, well-muscled man.

"Marcel," she said, "you will know how to handle this."

"These the kids?" he growled.

"Yes," the woman replied. "They refuse to make good for this spinning-wheel which they have so carelessly broken."

Joe opened his mouth to object, but Frank nudged him to silence. The muscular man advanced on them threateningly. In a low voice he rumbled, "I advise you to give us the money and be on your way!"

·8·

The Old Man's Warning

FRANK, although angry, wished to avoid a fight. He and Joe were on a sleuthing mission—this must come first. "How much do we owe you?" Frank asked the belligerent man. At the answer, Frank shook his head. "We don't have enough money, but I'll leave my watch for security."

Marcel sniffed. "Let's see it."

Frank slipped off the handsome stainless-steel timepiece which he had received the Christmas before. "It's a good Swiss make," he said.

As Marcel examined the watch, Joe took twenty dollars from his pocket. "How about twenty dollars and the watch?" he asked. "That should be enough for a broken old spinning-wheel."

Marcel glanced at the woman and she gave a barely perceptible nod.

"Okay," he said. "But don't come around here again breakin' up our antiques."

"We'll be back," Frank said, "with the thirty dollars to redeem my watch."

The shop manageress grudgingly produced a cardboard carton into which Frank and Joe placed the

63

spinning-wheel parts. Then they put the box in the boot of their car.

As Frank drove off, he said, "Something phoney going on here. That spinning-wheel was only slapped together."

"Looks like the whole shop might have been set up in an awful hurry," Joe remarked. "I'll bet most of the other stuff is junk too."

"I wonder how Aunt Gertrude's going to like her antique," Frank said, with an ear-to-ear grin.

"I hate to think!" Joe said wryly, taking a road map from the glove compartment.

After studying it for a moment, he announced, "We're not far from Rockaway now. Boy! It's really a small speck on the map!"

Frank laughed. "I hope we don't miss the place."

Presently he drove down a long hill, and the Hardys found themselves in Rockaway. It was nothing more than a small crossroads village on the shore adjacent to a fishing pier. The brothers soon came to the camping site on the beach and parked. They spotted Biff and Chet sunning themselves before their tent. As the Hardys parked on the shoulder of the road, their friends hurried over.

Frank and Joe got out and looked at Chet's damaged jalopy.

"Wow! That's a bad dent!" Joe said. "Cadmus Quill didn't pull any punches."

"You can say that again!" Biff retorted.

"I think he's got it in for all of us!"

"Have you looked for him around here?" Frank asked.

"Look for yourself," Chet replied with a sweep of his hand. "There's nothing but a couple of stores and a few shacks."

True, Rockaway could hardly be called a town. It was a sleepy little place, quite picturesque and redolent of fish. A weather-beaten building stood across the street. Above the door was a large sign: TUTTLE'S GENERAL STORE.

"Let's stock up on grub," Frank said. He and Joe took rucksacks from their car and the four boys headed for the store.

A venerable man with whiskers was seated behind a counter. He was intently scrutinizing a newspaper.

The old gentleman put aside the newspaper and regarded them through his thick-lensed spectacles with grave curiosity, as though they were some new specimen of humanity.

"You're Mr Tuttle?" Frank ventured.

"Yup. What can I do for you?"

"We'd like to know how far it is to Honeycomb Caves."

The man's eyes widened. "Honeycomb Caves!" he repeated in a high, cracked voice. "You lads going to pass by there?"

Chet spoke up. "No, we're going to camp in the caves and do some beachcombing." He told of his metal detector and how they hoped to locate some washed-up treasure.

Mr Tuttle leaned over the counter. "You— you're goin' to camp in Honeycomb Caves!" he exclaimed incredulously.

"Why, yes," Joe said.

The storekeeper shook his head solemnly. "You're new in these parts, aren't you?"

"From Bayport," Frank offered. "This is the first time we've been down this way."

"I thought so," returned the bewhiskered man with a great air of satisfaction, as though his judgment had been verified.

"Tell us," Frank said patiently, "how much farther do we have to go to reach Honeycomb Caves?"

"It's a matter of five miles by the road. Then you'll have to walk a bit."

"Is there a place we can pitch our tent?" Chet asked.

"Oh, yes. A fisherman lives nearby—name of John Donachie. He might allow you to camp near his cottage. But if I was you, I wouldn't do no campin' thereabouts. That is," Mr Tuttle added, "unless you stay away from the caves."

"We'd like to explore them," Joe said.

The old fellow gasped. "Explore 'em! Lads, you're crazy!"

"Is it against the law?" Chet inquired.

"No, it ain't. But it's against common sense."

"Why?" asked Biff.

"It just is," the storekeeper retorted, as though that explained everything.

"You mean the caves are dangerous?" queried Frank, enjoying the conversation.

"Maybe, maybe," returned their informant mysteriously. "If you take my advice, you'll stay away from 'em."

Joe rested his elbows on the counter. "Can't you at least tell us the reason?"

Mr Tuttle seemed to relish the boys' attention. "Well," he went on, "some mighty queer things been happenin' down there lately. A fisherman I know was scared near to death. There's been some peculiar lights around the caves and shootin' too."

"Shooting!" Frank exclaimed.

"Guns goin' off!" the storekeeper said emphatically, as if they had failed to understand him. "Two men already tried to find out what was goin' on there and got shot at."

Frank pricked up his ears. He wondered whether either of these men was Cadmus Quill. The boy described the college assistant to the old fellow and asked if he had seen such a man.

"Naw. These were local citizens. But they won't go back to those caves again, I'll tell you."

Still mumbling his disapproval, Mr Tuttle nonetheless supplied the boys with the provisions they needed. These were packed into the rucksacks which the boys slung over their shoulders.

They returned to the camping site and ate lunch. Then they took down the tent, stowed it into Chet's car, and set off in two vehicles, following the directions the storekeeper had given them.

They retraced their route over the highway, then turned to the right down a steep rutted lane that ended on the open seashore near the fisherman's cottage.

The small house was built at the base of the hill two hundred yards from where the beach ended abruptly against towering cliffs. The waves battered against the sheer wall of rock. The quartet could make out a

68   THE SECRET OF THE CAVES

winding path leading up the hill directly behind the cottage.

"I know what they call this place," Chet said gravely.

"Does it have a name?" Biff asked.

"Sure. Fish Hook."

"Fish Hook? Why?" Biff asked, neatly falling into Chet's trap.

"Because it's at the end of the line." Chet guffawed and slapped Biff on the back.

Biff groaned. "You really hooked me on that one, pal."

"Okay," said Joe. "Let's cut the comedy and see if we can park here."

The boys approached the door of the cottage and knocked. It was opened by a stocky, leather-faced man of middle age. He had a look of surprise on his good-natured countenance.

"Mr John Donachie?" Frank asked.

"Correct. What can I do for you boys?" he inquired.

"May we leave our cars here for a while?" Frank asked.

"Sure. For an hour or so?"

"Perhaps for a few days," Frank replied.

The fisherman's expression changed instantly to one of concern. "You're not goin' over to the caves, are you?"

When Frank said Yes, the man shook his head gravely. "You'd best be goin' back home," he warned. "There's strange doin's in the caves these days. It's no place for boys like you."

The fisherman was joined by his plump, rosy-faced wife who repeated the admonition.

Frank felt his spine tingle. His hunch persisted that Cadmus Quill might be mixed up in the mysterious occurrences at Honeycomb Caves.

"What's been going on there?" Frank pressed.

"Lights mostly and shootin'."

"Haven't any people been seen?"

"Not a livin' soul."

"That's strange," Chet said.

"Strange ain't the word for it," declared the fisherman. "It's downright spooky, like ghosts or somethin'."

"Have you been down to the caves yourself, Mr Donachie?" Frank asked.

"Just call me Johnny." The fisherman said that a few days before, his boat was washed ashore there in a squall. "When I got back in the sea again," he went on, "I saw a couple o' lights down near the caves. Next I heard two or three shots and then a yell."

"A yell?" Frank asked.

"The most awful screechin' I ever heard," the fisherman said.

"Well, that proves *somebody's* there," Biff remarked.

Despite the Donachies' warnings, the boys were determined to set out.

"Can you show us the quickest route?" Joe asked.

With a resigned look, the fisherman led the boys a short distance along the beach and pointed to the path leading up the hill. "You'll have to follow that to the top of the cliffs. From there look for a deep ravine. That'll take you down to the caves."

The campers thanked the couple, and with knapsacks and blanket rolls over their shoulders, began the ascent. The hill was steeper than it looked and it was more than an hour before the boys reached the summit.

Here a magnificent view awaited them. Far below lay the fisherman's cottage like a toy house. The ocean was a flat blue floor.

Venturing close to the edge of the cliff, Joe peered over. He saw a sheer wall of rock with a few scrubby outcroppings of gnarled bushes.

"No wonder the caves can't be reached by skirting the shore," Joe said. "The only way along the base of the cliff is by boat."

Chet looked up at the sky. "Come on, fellows," he said. "We can't afford to lose any time. We're in for a storm." The breeze bore to their ears the rumble of distant thunder.

"Chet's right," Joe said. "These squalls come up suddenly. Let's move!"

Without further ado, the boys hastened along the faint trail that led among the rocks. They could see no sign of the ravine, but judged that it would be almost invisible until they came upon it.

A few raindrops hit the faces of the boys as they plodded on. Flashes of lightning zigzagged across the darkening sky, followed by a terrific thunderclap. Then rain started falling heavily.

The wind rose, and far below, the surf boomed and crashed against the base of the cliff. The foursome stumbled on, scarcely able to follow the path in the gloom. The wind howled, lightning flashed, and thunder crashed constantly.

With Frank in the lead, the boys plunged forward into the streaming wall of rain. Chet and Biff were next and Joe brought up the rear. On and on they went, heads bent to the storm. Would they ever find the ravine?

Suddenly Frank came to a stop and looked behind. "Where's Joe?" he shouted above the clamour of the gale. The others looked about. Joe had vanished!

·9·

The Cavern

"Where on earth did Joe disappear to?" exclaimed Biff.

He, Frank and Chet peered through the teeming rain, but the gloom was so intense that it was impossible to see more than a few yards away.

"We'll have to go back," Frank decided quickly. "Joe probably sat down to rest and got lost when he tried to catch up with us."

The trio retraced their steps over the rocks, keeping close together. They shouted again and again, but in the roar of the storm they knew there was little chance that Joe would hear them.

"Perhaps he fell down and hurt himself," Biff suggested. "He may be lying behind one of these big rocks where we can't see him."

"Maybe he fell over the cliff!" said Chet, voicing the thought for all of them. For a heartsick moment the boys just stood there, faces pale and streaming with rain. Suddenly, above the roar of the storm, they heard a faint cry.

"Listen!" Frank exclaimed.

Breathlessly, they waited.

Again came the cry. "Help! Help!"

The three boys ran to the edge of the cliff, stopped and peered down. Over to one side, about four feet below, they spied a dark figure.

It was Joe, clinging to a small bush growing out of the sheer cliffside. "Hurry!" he called in a strained voice.

"Hang on! We'll get you!" Frank shouted. But his heart sank when he saw that Joe was beyond his reach.

"There's only one thing to do," he said to Biff and Chet. "You two hang on to me while I lower myself over."

"You'll never make it," Biff protested, as Frank shrugged off the gear he was carrying. "You'll both be killed."

"It's the only chance, and I'm going to take it!" Frank flung himself down and began to edge forward until he was leaning far over the edge. Biff and Chet seized his ankles and braced themselves.

Bit by bit, Frank lowered himself head first. He dared not look down, for he was hanging at a dizzy height. "A little more!" he called out.

He swung lower, gripped Joe's wrists, and secured a tight hold. "Ready, Joe?"

"Okay," was the hoarse reply.

"Haul away!"

Chet and Biff began dragging Frank back. There was a double weight now, but the Hardys' staunch friends were equal to it!

Inch by inch the boys were hauled nearer safety. It seemed ages to Frank before he was over the top again.

At that moment, with his brother just below the rim

of the cliff, Frank felt Joe's wrists slipping from his grasp.

But Chet and Biff scrambled forward and seized Joe's shirt. Together the three pulled him over the edge on to the rocky ground.

For a moment the boys were too exhausted to say a word.

"Boy, that was a narrow squeak!" Chet said solemnly.

"We'll stick closer together after this. How did it happen, Joe?" Frank asked.

"I stopped to tie my bootlace. When I looked up again I couldn't see you at all, so I began to run. I didn't realize I was so near the edge of the cliff. Then some of the rock must have broken off under my feet, because everything gave way and I felt myself falling."

When Frank and Joe had recovered from their gruelling experience, they got to their feet and the adventurers resumed their journey over the rocks. This time no one lagged behind and all stayed well away from the edge of the cliff.

In a short time Frank gave a cry of relief. "The ravine!" he yelled.

Through the pouring rain, just a few yards ahead, the others discerned a deep cut in the rocks, and they all scrambled down into it.

Far below, they could dimly see the beach and the breaking rollers. Slipping and stumbling, the Bayporters made their way down the steep, winding ravine.

Joe was first to reach bottom.

"Look! A cave!" He pointed right towards the base of the cliff. There, but a short distance from the breaking waves, was a dark hole in the steep wall of rock.

Frank took a flashlight from his pack and led the way into the dark mouth of the cavern. In its gleam he saw that their shelter was no mere niche in the face of the cliff, but a cave that led to unknown depths.

"Looks as if we can start exploring right here and now," he said.

"Explore my neck!" grumbled Chet. "Let's build a fire. I'm wet clear through!"

"What do we do for firewood?" practical Biff inquired.

This had not occurred to the others. They glanced at one another in dismay.

"That's right," Joe said. "There's not much wood around and it's soaked by now, anyway."

Frank moved farther back into the dark cave with his flashlight. Suddenly he exclaimed in mingled astonishment and delight. "Well! Can you beat this, fellows?"

"What?" called Joe.

"Firewood!"

"Where?"

The others came hastening over to Frank.

"Look!" He cast the flashlight beam against the cave wall to his left.

In the centre of the circle of radiance, they saw a neat pile of wood.

Joe whistled in surprise. "That didn't get here by accident—someone stacked it."

Frank stepped over and picked up one of the sticks. "Good dry driftwood. We'll have a roaring fire now."

"I wonder who piled it in here," Biff remarked.

Chet shrugged. "Why worry about that?"

"Probably the mystery men who are doing all the yelling and shooting," Biff said. "We'll be in for it if this is *their* cave we've stumbled on."

He, Chet and Joe began carrying wood over to the centre of the cave. Frank, meanwhile, set down the flashlight, took out his pocketknife, and whittled a particularly dry stick until he had a small heap of shavings. Over these he built a pyramid of driftwood. Then he took a match from his waterproof case and ignited the shavings. They flared up brightly.

Anxiously the boys watched the small blaze. Frank had been afraid that lack of a draught might cause so much smoke that they would be almost suffocated. To his relief, the smoke spiralled upwards and was carried off. "Must be an opening in the roof," Frank observed.

Soon the fire was burning briskly. As its warmth penetrated the cave, the boys took off their drenched clothes and spread them about the blaze, then wrapped themselves in the heavy blankets they had brought with them.

The rest of the afternoon the rain continued unabated. The clothes dried slowly. Once Biff went to the cave mouth and looked out at the wind-lashed sea.

"Do you think the water comes in here at high tide?" he asked.

"No," Frank replied. "The cave floor was dry when we came."

At dusk Chet produced the frying pan, and the fragrant odour of sizzling bacon soon permeated their refuge. The boys never enjoyed a meal more than their supper in the cave. The driftwood blazed and crackled, casting a cheerful glow which illuminated the rocky ceiling and walls of the underground chamber. With crisp bacon, bread toasted brown before the fire, hot chocolate, and jam, they ate ravenously, and at last sat back with deep sighs of sheer content.

Although part of the floor of the cave was rocky, much of it was sand, which provided a fairly comfortable resting-place. The boys were tired after their long journey, so they stretched out in their blankets and were soon drowsily chatting, while the fire died lower and lower. At last it was only a glow in the dark and the voices ceased.

An hour passed. Two hours.

Suddenly Joe was awakened. He was just about to turn over and go to sleep again, wondering vaguely what had aroused him, when he heard a footstep close by.

He raised himself on one elbow and peered into the gloom, but could see nothing.

When he heard a rustle, he spoke up. "Is that you, Frank?" The words rang out clearly in the deep silence.

Instead of the reassuring voice of his brother, Joe heard a muffled exclamation and scurrying footsteps. Someone was running across the floor of the cave!

·10·

A Terrifying Loss

"Who's that?" demanded Joe, scrambling to his feet.

There was no answer.

"Fellows! Wake up!" Joe exclaimed, as he stumbled about in the darkness, trying to find his flashlight.

"What's the matter?" came Chet's sleepy voice. "It isn't morning yet. Let me sleep."

"Wake up! Someone's prowling around here."

"Maybe it was Biff," came Frank's voice. "Biff, you here?"

There was a deep sigh. Then Biff said drowsily, "Of course I am, why?"

Frank switched on his flashlight and played the beam around the cave. Biff and Chet sat up in their blankets and blinked. "What's wrong?" Biff demanded.

Joe told about the intruder.

"Did he go out the front way?" Biff asked.

Joe shook his head. "No. He seemed to go farther into the cave."

"Well, then," Frank said decisively, "we'll go and look for him."

The boys hurriedly dressed, and taking flashlights, followed Frank deeper into the stygian cave. Thirty paces ahead they were confronted by an arch in the rock, an opening that seemed to lead into a tunnel. They walked into it cautiously, and Frank kept his light focused on the floor to make sure no pitfalls lay before them.

The tunnel was about fifteen feet in length and six feet high. As the floor was of solid rock, they were unable to find any footprints indicating that someone had passed that way.

The tunnel led to another cave. "Maybe there's a regular chain of caves!" Joe exclaimed as the boys stepped out into a massive underground chamber.

"I guess ours is only the beginning," Chet remarked.

In the glow of their flashlights the foursome saw that the huge room in which they now stood had a number of dark openings in the walls. These were, presumably, tunnels leading into caves beyond.

Frank frowned. "There are at least a dozen different passages out of here. The prowler might have taken any of them."

"Let's tackle the biggest," Biff suggested.

"Good idea. If we don't get anywhere, we'll try the others."

The largest tunnel was straight ahead. The boys crossed the cavern and Frank led them into the dark passage. Seconds later he exclaimed softly, "Look!"

"What?"

"A footprint."

Clearly discernible was the imprint of a boot in a patch of wet sand.

"We're on the right trail," Joe said quietly. "Come on!"

With increasing excitement, the searchers pressed

forward and in a few moments emerged into another cave. This was an enormous underground vault, the largest they had yet seen. Even the four flashlight beams failed to reveal all of the rocky walls and ceiling.

As they started to cross it, Biff's light went out. He muttered in annoyance and tried to coax a gleam from the silvery tube. No luck.

"Take mine," Frank offered, but Biff declined. "Stay close, then," Frank said, as they continued across the huge cavern.

The floor of the cavern was piled high with rocks, evidently from cave-ins over the years. In other parts it was pitted with gullies and holes. In trying to avoid these, the boys gradually became separated.

Biff stumbled along behind. He felt the loss of his flashlight, but said nothing, relying on the radiance provided by the others.

Soon, however, the three lights became widely scattered. Biff found himself in total darkness.

He stood uncertainly for a moment, then called out, "Hey, fellows, wait for me!"

He took a step forward and stumbled. As he fell, he groped wildly for a firm rock, but there was nothing there.

With a cry of terror, Biff hurtled down into blackness.

For a moment the other three boys froze in their tracks. Then they shouted for Biff, time and again, but there was no answer. They searched frantically among the rocks and crevices, but found no sign of him.

In the glow of the flashlights they looked at one another anxiously and listened in vain for a faint cry.

There was no sound but the echoes of their own voices.

"We won't give up!" Frank vowed. "We'll search every pit and hole in here!"

With desperate patience they scoured the cave, but at last were forced to admit that it was no use.

"This place is too big," Chet said dejectedly. "We need more light." He sat down on a rock and buried his face in his hands.

"I have an idea," Frank offered. "Let's build a fire. That'll help."

Chet brightened. "Good idea!"

"Come on," Frank said. "We have lots of wood left in the outside cave."

"That's not a bad stunt!" Joe declared hopefully. "With a roaring bonfire we'll be able to light up the whole place enough to see what we're doing."

The boys retraced their steps into the outer cavern where they had slept. They filled their arms with wood and were about to re-enter the tunnel when Joe noticed something that made him drop his wood on the stone floor with a clatter.

"What's wrong?" Chet asked.

"That's funny," Joe returned. "I was sure we left our supplies right near this woodpile."

"We did," Frank assured him.

Joe turned his flashlight on the place where the greater part of their supplies had been stacked. A loaf of bread and a tin of sardines lay on the rock, but that was all.

"They've been stolen!" Frank exclaimed.

"By that prowler, I'll bet!" Joe said. "He probably

hid himself until we passed, then sneaked back here and stole our food."

"We can't worry about that now," Frank said grimly. "Let's go!"

Swiftly Joe gathered up his firewood and the boys returned to the big vault.

Hastily the fire was built and soon the flames flared high. The companions were surprised at the number of holes and crevices now revealed.

"It's a wonder we weren't all killed," Chet said. "We were prowling around this chamber without any idea of the real danger."

Methodically the boys resumed their search, investigating each opening, deep or shallow. But in spite of the extra light and all their shouting, their efforts were in vain.

"I'm afraid it's no use," Chet said, gulping. "It's as if Biff was swallowed up."

"We need help," Frank said tersely. "We'll go to the village and get some men with ropes and searchlights."

Disconsolately the boys turned back. But as they did, Chet let out a bloodcurdling cry.

On the wall of the cavern flickered the huge shadow of a hand!

·11·

No Trespassing!

THE ghostly shadow caused the boys' hearts to pound until they saw the reason for it. A hand was reaching up from one of the pits, and the bonfire's glow threw its silhouette on the cavern wall.

"Biff!" Joe cried out.

Only a groan answered. The Hardys and Chet leaped towards the faltering hand as it groped for the lip of the pit. Frank grasped it and together the boys pulled Biff out. He lay dazed for a moment.

"You're hurt!" said Joe, bending down to examine a large egg on Biff's left temple.

"I'm all right now. A little dizzy yet, but it isn't serious."

"What happened?"

"I fell into the pit and struck my head against the rocks. When I came to, I was lying beneath an over-hang. I must have been out for a few minutes."

"A few minutes!" Chet exclaimed. "We've been hunting for you for over an hour."

Biff looked incredulous and shook his head in dismay when told about the stolen supplies.

"Boy! What a mess we're in," he said, as his companions helped him out of the cavern.

They returned to the outer cave and fell fast asleep. When morning came, a diligent inspection of their quarters failed to reveal any clues as to the thief.

"We're out of luck, that's all," Frank concluded. "Our light-fingered friend fooled us neatly."

"At least the storm is over," said Biff, who was feeling better.

From the cave they could see the sun shining on the blue waters of the sea. As Chet unlimbered his metal detector he moved it over a rocky part of the floor. "Hmm. That's funny," he said.

"Did you find a pirate's chest?" Joe grinned.

"No. But I hear a buzzing noise. Maybe this thing's broken." He moved outside and began to swing the disc back and forth over the beach.

All at once Chet dropped his detector, fell to his knees, and dug furiously in the sand. His astonished companions watched from the cave entrance.

Finally the stout boy pulled something out and held it aloft in his right hand. "Ha! I told you!" he shouted.

"What is it?" Biff asked, as he, Frank and Joe hurried over.

"A pistol. Probably a pirate's. Or maybe from the sunken ship."

"By golly, Chet, I have to hand it to you," said Frank, as he examined the piece and wiped wet sand from it. "Hey, wait! This isn't old."

"You're right!" Joe burst in. "It's hardly rusted at all." He handled the weapon. "Looks like a Smith and Wesson."

"But see the marking," Biff said. "Made in Spain."

Chet looked wisely at his companions. "What do you make of it, boys?"

"Perhaps this very pistol caused all the shooting we've heard about," Biff offered.

Chet beamed. "Well, fellows, I guess *I* found a mystery. Want to solve it?"

"And leave the trail of Todd and Quill?" Joe asked. "Nothing doing!"

"Just a minute," Frank put in. "How do we know Cadmus Quill didn't drop the pistol?"

"Wow!" Joe clapped a hand to his forehead. "That's a pretty wild guess for you, brother."

"You're dreaming, Frank!" Chet chimed in.

Biff, too, thought Frank's guess was farfetched, and added, "Enough of deductions. How about some chow? I'm famished." He looked hopefully up the ravine, but Chet, for once, was more excited about detecting than eating.

"Please, fellows," he begged, "let's go a little way up the beach yet. Who knows what I'll find!"

"Okay," Frank agreed. "Only a quarter of a mile. Then we turn back."

The sandy shore wound about the face of a great bluff of black rock, and when the boys had skirted this precipice they were confronted by a dark opening at the base of the cliff just a few yards away.

"Another cave!" Frank exclaimed.

Chet gave a cheer and ran ahead with his detector.

When they were just in front of the entrance the boys halted with exclamations of surprise.

Tacked on a board stuck in the sand beside the cave mouth was a tattered sheet of paper. Scrawled in heavy black letters were the warning words *No Trespassing.*

The companions looked at the sign in astonishment, then Chet grinned. "By order of the Rockaway chief of police, no doubt. Maybe somebody put it here for a joke," he said. "Let's take a peep inside."

Frank was first to reach the cave and peer inside. Then he turned back to the others. "This sign isn't a joke," he said quietly. "Somebody does live here!"

Curiously the boys crowded into the mouth of the cave. In the gloom they could see a crude table and a mattress with blankets. On a ledge of rock was an improvised cupboard consisting of an old soap carton containing canned goods and other provisions.

"Well," Chet declared, "we have a neighbour who might offer us some grub."

"We certainly have," Biff said, looking down the beach. "And if I'm not mistaken, here he comes now."

Along the shore strode a tall, grey-haired man wearing a blue shirt and overalls, the legs of which were tucked into high rubber boots. The man, oblivious to the boys, held a bugle in his left hand. He stopped, looked at the sea, and blew a loud, clear call. Then he wiped his lips with the back of his hand and continued towards the cave.

When he spotted the four boys he stopped short, blew another flurry on the bugle, and hastened up to the Bayporters.

"I'm Commander E. K. T. Wilson, Queen's Navy, retired," he announced. "You should have saluted, but I guess you didn't know."

To make up for this breach of etiquette, the boys

saluted smartly. This appeared to gratify the man immensely.

"You're landlubbers, eh?"

"I suppose so," Frank admitted with a smile.

"Well, we can't all be sailors. It isn't often people come to see me."

"Do you live here?" Joe asked, indicating the cave.

"This is my home when I'm ashore. I'm resting between cruises just now. What are your names?"

The boys introduced themselves.

"Glad to meet you," returned Commander Wilson. "I get used to being alone, but it's a pleasure to have visitors."

"It's lonely enough here," Frank agreed.

"Isn't bad. Not half as lonely as the time I got marooned in the South Seas."

The boys looked at him with new interest.

"You were really marooned?" Chet asked.

"Aye. It was when I was in command of a destroyer cruising the South Seas a good many years ago. We landed for water on a little island that you won't find on any map. It was a hot day—very hot. Must have been over a hundred degrees in the shade. So while my men were loading the water on my ship I sat down in the shade of a cactus tree. Before I knew it, I was asleep."

"And they went away and left you?" Joe put in.

"They did."

"But you were the captain!"

"I guess they thought I was in my cabin, and of course none of 'em dared disturb me. When I woke up, the ship was gone."

"Ee-yow!" Biff exclaimed.

"Well, sir, I didn't know what to do. I was like this here fellow Robinson Crusoe that you read about. But I had to make the best of it, so I fixed myself up a little house and lived there for nearly six months, all by myself."

"Didn't the ship come back for you?"

"They couldn't find the island again. Anyway, the quartermaster who took charge of the ship didn't want to find me, I guess. He wanted my job."

"Did you have anything to eat on the island?" Biff asked.

Chet interrupted. "Speaking of food, Commander, could you help us out with some breakfast?"

"Sure, me hearties. Growing boys should eat plenty. Now what was I talking about? Oh, well, doesn't matter."

A wink passed around the circle of friends as the man went inside and returned with a slab of bacon. Chet volunteered to start a fire, and got it going quickly as the old man cut strips of bacon and put them into a frying pan.

"How about a swim while we're waiting?" Frank suggested.

"Let's go!" Joe shouted.

The boys skinned off their clothes and ran into the surf. Joe swam beside his brother. "Frank, Wilson doesn't sound much like an Englishman."

"I don't think he has all his marbles," Frank replied.

"Do you think Wilson helped himself to our supplies?"

"I didn't see them in his cave," Frank said, adding,

"He seems harmless. I'd like to ask him some questions, though."

"And could I go for some crisp bacon! Race you back to shore!"

Using the Australian crawl, the brothers streaked over the wave tops and hit shore together. There Biff and Chet joined them, and after they dressed, the refreshed quartet trotted up to Commander Wilson, who sat near the fire. The frying pan lay at the sailor's side—empty, and Wilson was chewing on the last piece of bacon. He looked up.

"Who are you?" he asked bluntly.

"The Hardy boys," Frank began in surprise. "And what—"

"Well, beat it! Scram! I don't want you around here!"

· 12 ·

Undercover Work

COMMANDER WILSON's gruff order to leave caused the four boys to stare at him in wonderment.

"But, Commander," Joe protested, "you—"

"Don't 'Commander' me!" the man said, rising to his feet and shaking his fist at the boys. "I want to be left alone! That's why I'm a hermit."

Frank shook his head. "No use arguing, fellows," he murmured. "Come on."

They strode away across the sand, with Chet muttering about the loss of a good meal.

"That old sailor's a real lulu," Biff said, disgruntled. He glanced at Frank. "What'll we do now?"

"First thing is to get some food."

"And where is the food?" Biff asked sarcastically.

"Maybe we can grow mushrooms in the cave," Joe quipped.

Chet trailed behind. The headphones were clamped to his ears, and once more he swung his metal detector back and forth over the sand.

"If you have strength enough," Frank told Biff, "we can climb up the ravine, cross the cliffs, and go back down to Johnny the fisherman's place. Maybe he'll give us chow, or else we can drive back to Rockaway for more supplies."

"Bright prospects!" Biff grumbled. "I thought I could do some fishing today. It's great after a storm." Then suddenly Biff recalled that his fishing gear had been stolen with the rucksacks. "Doggone it!" he exclaimed. "That burns me up! I'll bet that Commander Wilson took our stuff and stashed it out of sight!"

"I doubt it," Frank said. He turned and called to Chet, who was now a hundred paces behind. "Come on, hurry up!"

Chet waved and nodded, but still continued to swing his detector. Then he gave an excited bellow.

"Sounds like the mating call of a walrus," Biff commented.

"He may have discovered another weapon," Joe said, as they hastened back to their stout pal.

"Hey, fellows, there must be a whole arsenal underneath here," Chet said. "You should have heard the terrific noise in my ears."

All four boys dropped to their hands and knees and dug like fox-terriers in a bone yard. Biff was first to reach something solid. He tugged and yanked, finally coming up with a rucksack!

"Look!" Biff cried out. "It's mine!" He brushed the wet sand from the knapsack, opened it quickly, and pulled out his collapsible fishing gear.

The other three quickly recovered their supplies, a little damp, but none the worse for their burial in sand.

Chet unscrewed the lid of his canteen and took a

long swallow of water. "I told you this metal detector would pay off," he said.

Biff grinned. "I could kiss you, Chet, for finding my tackle."

Chet stepped backwards in mock horror. "Please, please, not here," he said, and the others roared with laughter.

As their own cave was not far from the spot, the boys hastened back and took out the rations. A fire was quickly started and Chet presided over the frying pan filled with crisp bacon. "Phooey on the commander," Chet said smugly.

"Which reminds me," Frank put in, "I'm not finished with that old codger yet."

"What more could you learn from him?" Joe asked. "He's as nutty as a fruitcake."

"Maybe he is, maybe he isn't," Frank replied. "In either case, I'd like to study him a little closer and ask some more questions."

Joe looked thoughtful as he spooned a portion of scrambled eggs into his tin plate. "Do you think he might have seen Cadmus Quill or some other mysterious prowlers around here?"

As Frank broke off a piece of crusty bread from a long loaf, he said that was exactly his idea.

"Well, you fellows go about your sleuthing," Biff said. "I'm going fishing."

"Where?" asked Chet.

"From the top of the cliff," Biff replied. "I can heave my line a mile out from that point. Maybe I'll catch something big where the water's deep."

"I'm with you," Chet said. He turned to the Hardys

and added, "If you fellows run into trouble with Wilson, just call us."

During the rest of the meal the boys talked about the thief who had buried their supplies in the sand.

"If he didn't keep them for his own use, what was the point of stealing 'em?" Biff mused.

"To get us away from here," Joe said promptly. "Somebody doesn't want us around."

"Like Commander Wilson," Biff said. "What do you think, Frank?"

The young sleuth shrugged. "There might be one man or two—maybe a whole gang operating around here. But we'll find out sooner or later."

"You'd better find out sooner," Chet declared, "else we'll be starving again."

"If you mean somebody's going to steal our supplies a second time," Joe said, "you're mistaken." He told of having seen a small crevice fifty yards away at the base of the ravine. "We'll hide our stuff there until you two get back with the whale you're going to catch."

When the fire had been put out and their camping place tidied up, the four adventurers hid their rucksacks and parted.

Frank glanced over his shoulder to see Chet and Biff trudging up the ravine, as he and Joe trotted towards Wilson's cave. They saw the old sailor standing in front of his cave, sketching something in the sand with a slender stick. When he saw them approach, he quickly rubbed the sole of his boot over the sand and hailed the brothers. "Hello there! Have you come to visit me?"

Frank and Joe exchanged glances, and walked up to the man. "Why, yes," said Frank. "Do you remember us, Frank and Joe Hardy?"

"Of course I do. Where did you go after I invited you to breakfast?"

"Why, we came—" Frank began.

"Didn't see hide nor hair of you. Thought you went back to Bayhill, or Portside, or wherever you came from. Where are your two friends?"

"They went fishing," Joe replied.

"Where?"

"To the top of the cliffs."

"Dangerous. Mighty dangerous. I hope they come back all right," Wilson said.

He shook his head, clasped his hands behind his back, and walked in circles before his cave.

"Commander Wilson," Frank began slowly, "have you seen any people prowling around Honeycomb Caves?"

Wilson stopped short and looked Frank squarely in the eyes. "I'm alone. A hermit. That's what I am. I haven't seen anybody. Nobody comes near me. They think I'm queer."

Joe described both Todd and Quill. "Have you seen anyone resembling them?" he persisted.

"No. But come to think of it, there *was* a fellow—"

The Hardys looked alertly at the old sailor. Had he seen one of the missing men?

"Yes, go on," Frank encouraged. "What did he look like?"

"The first one you mentioned."

"Todd?"

"Yes. I once knew a fellow like that. He was second mate on my cruiser in the Philippines."

Joe turned aside and made a wry face as the man continued:

"Come to think of it, his name was Todd. Yes, it was," the commander went on. "He shipwrecked me deliberately and I had to climb a pineapple tree until the natives stopped beating their drums and went home."

Joe leaned close to Frank and said in a low voice, "He's off again. What'll we do now?"

As Commander Wilson rambled on, Frank edged closer to the mouth of the cave and glanced inside. He gave an involuntary start as he saw something he had not noticed before. But before he could whisper to Joe, Wilson wheeled about. "A man's cave is his castle," he said tartly.

Frank tried to manage a grin. "Well, I guess we'd better be going, Commander," he said. "Those fellows must have caught a fish by now."

Without saying a word, the old salt went into his cave. The Hardys continued down the beach again. When they had gone a dozen yards, Frank seized Joe's arm and pulled him behind a large rock.

"What's the matter, Frank?"

"Joe, I saw a cap in Wilson's cave—the same foreign style that was dropped by the fellow at the radar site!"

"Do you think there's some connection?"

Frank suggested that they hide and watch the old fellow's cave. "You notice he got mighty excited when I looked into his quarters."

"I'll bet he's got something in there he doesn't want us to see," he said, peering over the rock. Suddenly he hissed, "Watch it! Here he comes!"

The two boys crouched low. Joe poked his head around the boulder for a quick look. "Frank, he's going down the beach the other way—probably to look in our cave."

"Now's our chance to explore his," Frank said. "Is he out of sight yet?"

"Yes."

Frank and Joe scrambled out of their hiding-place and dashed into Wilson's cave.

"Boy, is it deep!" Joe exclaimed. "It goes away back!"

"And look here," Frank said, picking up the cap from the floor. "This could be more than a coincidence."

"Wow! He's got an arsenal too!" whispered Joe. He pointed to a shotgun lying on a rock ledge.

"So that's where the mysterious shooting came from," Frank guessed. "And how about this?"

He picked up a dog-eared notebook from beside the gun and leafed through it.

"It's a code book! Let's take it to the light so we can study it."

The boys had been well schooled in cryptography by their father. Eagerly the two moved nearer the mouth of the cave.

All at once the interior darkened and Commander Wilson stood at the entrance! "Spies! You're all spies!" he boomed. "Give me that book, you—you young pirates!"

As Frank and Joe stood tongue-tied, Wilson lunged towards the stone ledge.

"Look out!" Joe cried out. "He's going for the shotgun!"

·13·

A Straight-Line Clue

FRANK dropped the code book and leaped to intercept Commander Wilson before he could reach the shotgun. But the old man was as agile as an athlete! He dodged and twisted out of Frank's way like a piece of spring steel and grabbed the weapon.

"Frank! Run!" Joe shouted, as he ducked towards the front of the cave.

Realizing it was now impossible to cope with Wilson, Frank dashed after his brother. But as the two boys reached the cave mouth, there was a loud explosion. Frank stumbled and fell to the ground.

"You killed him! You killed my brother!" Joe cried out. He bent down over the prostrate form. But instead of finding blood on the back of Frank's red shirt, Joe saw a large, round white patch. At the same time Frank shook his head, got to his knees, then stood up.

"Are you all right?" Joe asked. Out of the corner of his eye he saw the smoking shotgun in Wilson's hand. The old man had a gleeful expression on his face.

"I'm okay," Frank said. "Let's get out of here!"

The boys retreated halfway to the water's edge before stopping.

"The blast knocked me down," Frank said, reaching about gingerly to touch his back. "What was the gun loaded with?" He removed his shirt and the brothers examined it closely. "Joe! This looks like flour! It *is* flour!"

"So that's what Wilson used for ammunition!" Joe said. "Now I know for sure he's off his head."

With mixed feelings of embarrassment and chagrin, Frank donned his shirt and the Hardys looked back as Wilson emerged from the cave. Again he shook his fist.

"That's what you spies get for snooping around Commander Wilson's cave!" he shouted. "You have some nerve trying to read the code book of the Queen's Navy!"

"We were only looking at that funny cap," Frank called back. "Where did you get it?"

"In Rockaway, of course—where I get all my supplies," Wilson said. "That's where I go when the Queen's Navy forgets to send the supply ship."

Shaken by the weird incident, the brothers headed for their cave.

"That cap will bear some investigating," said Joe.

"You're right," Frank agreed. "If they're sold at the general store in Rockaway, maybe the Bayport prowler bought his there too."

"Look who's coming," said Joe. They glanced up to see Chet and Biff scrambling down the ravine towards them. Biff had a monster of a fish slung across his shoulder.

"Hi, fellows!" Chet called out. "Look what we caught!"

Joe grinned. "It's almost as good as a whale!"

Puffing and beaming, Chet and Biff hastened up to the Hardys. The sea bass which Biff carried weighed more than thirty pounds.

"Will we stuff ourselves today!" Chet said gleefully, then added quickly, "And I discovered a mine, too."

"A gold mine, I suppose," Joe said.

"I don't know what kind," Chet said seriously, "but my detector picked up some funny noises."

"Chet's right," Biff said. "*Something's* buried up there. Fellows, you ought to go and hear for yourselves. I'll show you the place."

"Okay. You win," Frank said sceptically.

"I'll cook some of the fish while you're gone," Chet said. He added wistfully, "I wish we had some flour to sprinkle on it."

Frank gulped and Joe pounded him on the back.

"Did I say something wrong?" Chet asked.

"Oh, no!" Frank said hastily. "Give us the detector, Chet."

Joe took the device and in a few minutes the three boys were clambering up the ravine towards the top of the cliff.

When they reached it, Joe donned the earphones and held the detector several inches off the ground. "Over there," Biff directed. Joe went towards the spot. A moment later he winced as a clicking chattered like a machine-gun in his ears.

"No kidding, there is something underneath here," he said. "Listen for yourself, Frank."

Frank complied, then moved the detector from right to left. "That's strange," he muttered. "This mine, or whatever it is Chet discovered, runs in a straight line."

"Maybe a water pipe," Biff said. "Wouldn't that be a joke!"

"A water pipe from where to where?" Joe countered. "Why put a drain underground at a place like this?"

"Whatever the thing is," Frank said, "it lies east to west, apparently from near the coastline to the highway."

"I've got an idea," Joe said. He moved to a clump of pine trees growing several hundred yards back from the precipice and selected the tallest. "Give me a boost, Frank."

After getting a lift from his brother, Joe shinned to the first branch, scrambled to the top of the tree, and looked intently westward.

"What do you see over there?" Frank called up.

"You'd be surprised!" said Joe.

"Come on," Biff said. "You're tracing an imaginary line. What does it point to?"

"The Palais Paris," Joe replied. In a few moments he was back on the ground. "Frank, I have a strange feeling about that place. Let's investigate it."

"Not this minute," his brother replied. "I'd like to do some digging."

"But with what?" asked Joe.

"I'll get some tools," Biff volunteered. "Johnny the fisherman will lend us his." He hastened off and returned presently with a shovel and pick-axe over his shoulder.

The boys took turns at wielding the pick and shovel. Rocks and dirt flew up out of the hole they fashioned. But they reached three feet down without striking metal.

Biff leaned on the shovel and ran his thumb along his brow like a windscreen wiper. "We might dig all day and not find anything," he said. "Frank, do you suppose it *is* a metallic substance which makes the detector click like that?"

"I'm not sure," Frank replied. "It might be an electrical conduit. Let's check in Rockaway."

"Okay." Joe chuckled. "As soon as we've eaten that feast Chet's preparing for us."

The boys left the tools near the edge of the cliff where they could find them, then retreated down the ravine to the cave. Chet had made a spit, on which large chunks of the freshly caught sea bass were grilling over hot coals.

"Smells great, Chet," Joe said. "Let's eat and be on our way."

"We're going back?" Chet asked in dismay.

"To Rockaway for the time being," said Frank, and told what they had observed on the cliff-top.

"Then I did find a good clue, eh?" Chet asked proudly. "First the pistol and now this. What would you fellows do without me?"

"We'll make an operator out of you, like Dad's assistant, Sam Radley," Frank said.

"Just so long as it isn't dangerous," Chet said, and passed out portions of the succulent fish. Frank, Joe and Biff had to admit it was one of the finest meals they had ever tasted.

"It's great brain food," said Chet. "I think we're going to need it on this case of yours," he added with a wink at the Hardys.

"Don't worry," Biff said. "They'll get to the bottom of this—some day."

The banter flew back and forth until the meal was finished. Then Chet put out the fire and the boys packed for the return trip. Camping in the salty sea air seemed to give them extra energy. They sang their way along the top of the cliff, where they picked up the digging tools and made the long descent to the fisherman's house.

Mrs Donachie came out to greet them. "Oh, I'm so glad all you boys returned safely from those awful caves," she said.

"We're still in one piece." Joe grinned. "Is Johnny here? We're returning his tools."

"He's out fishing," the woman said. "I'll tell him you stopped by."

The boys said goodbye and headed for their cars. "Come back when you please," Mrs Donachie called after them.

The Bayporters waved goodbye and drove quickly back to Rockaway, where they pulled up in front of the general store. Frank led the way inside.

Mr Tuttle, the proprietor, was sitting behind the counter, his chair tipped back. "Well, what did I tell you?" he greeted them, shaking his head vigorously. "You got into trouble at the caves, so you came back!"

"Who said anything about trouble?" Chet demanded.

"Well, you've got somethin' on your minds." The

whiskered man squinted. "I can tell by the way you barged in here."

"To tell you the truth," Frank said, "we have. I wonder if you could direct us to the town engineer's office. We'd like to study some public maps and surveys."

The old fellow raised himself expansively and snapped his braces. "Seein' that I'm the mayor of Rockaway," he said, "I can show you to the archives." With a flourish of his right hand, he indicated a door at the back of the store.

"In there?" asked Joe.

"That's the office of the mayor *and* the town engineer," the storekeeper said.

The boys followed him into the room. To their surprise they found it neatly arranged, with a desk, a filing cabinet, and large survey maps on the walls. These showed the adjoining countryside, complete with service lines of all kinds.

Frank and Joe studied the maps carefully as Biff and Chet looked over their shoulders.

"No, I can't see any electrical conduits or water pipes," said Frank as his finger followed the area from the cliffs to the Palais Paris. "Joe, you may have a good hunch about that place. I've got an idea."

When Mayor Tuttle asked about their interest in the maps, Frank deftly turned the question aside, saying what a good camping site they had in Rockaway.

After buying more supplies, the boys drove to the camping site.

"Hey, Frank, what's this big idea of yours?" Joe asked impatiently.

Frank grinned. "Gather round and listen. It may work." He said that Joe and Chet would be dispatched to Bayport, while he and Biff continued sleuthing in Rockaway. "Your mission," he told his brother, "will be to get Callie and Iola to apply for waitress jobs at the Palais Paris."

·14·

Startling News

JOE whistled. "A great idea, Frank. The girls can be our undercover agents."

"Exactly," Frank said. He turned to Chet. "Maybe you can convince Iola she should do this for Hardy and Sons."

"I think she'd do it just for Joe," Chet said, and guffawed.

"All right, all right," Joe said, "let's go." He called over his shoulder. "Find out about that cap, Frank!"

He and Chet hopped into the jalopy and drove away. Two hours later they pulled into the driveway of the Morton farmhouse.

Iola and Mary Todd hastened out to greet them. Mary, although happy to see the boys, had a wistful air. Joe realized she was disappointed that her brother had not been found, and wished he had good news for her.

When the four young people had gathered in the cool spacious living-room, Joe asked Iola, "Will you get Callie Shaw to come right over?"

"I'll phone her now. Why?"

"Tell you later."

While they waited for Callie, tall frosty glasses of lemonade were served by Iola, who grew more curious with each cool sip. Twenty minutes later Callie Shaw arrived. She was a good-looking blonde girl whom Frank Hardy often dated.

"Hi, everybody," she said, her eyes sparkling. "Why the mysterious summons?"

"Yes, Joe Hardy," Iola put in. "Don't keep us in suspense any longer.

With a dramatic gesture Joe began. "We have something exceptional to ask you girls."

"I know! You want us to go on a picnic at the caves," Callie said hopefully.

Joe shook his head. "We want you and Iola to apply for waitress jobs at the Palais Paris."

"So you can spy on what's going on there," Chet burst in.

Dumbfounded, the three girls listened intently to the story of the boys' adventures.

"You mean you want us to help you on a detective case?" Iola said happily. "Oh, we'd love to!"

A determined look crossed Mary's pretty face. "If Callie and Iola are going to help you boys find *my* brother, I want to help too."

"But—but—" Chet started to protest.

"No buts about it," Mary said emphatically. "All three of us girls will be detectives!"

Mary's enthusiasm amused Joe and Chet. But Callie and Iola were delighted to have her join them in applying for waitress jobs at the Palais Paris.

"We'll call ourselves the three musketeers!" Iola said proudly.

"Ugh!" said Chet. "I can just see you now duelling with steak knives."

Iola gave her brother a withering look, then turned to Joe with a bright smile. "What do you want us to do when we get there? Shall we go under assumed names?"

"To answer your second question first," said Joe. "You and Callie give your names, but I don't think Mary should use her last one—just in case these people have read about her brother's disappearance."

"All right," Mary said promptly. "I'll call myself Mary Temple."

"Good," Joe replied. "In answer to your first question, Iola—if and when you get to be waitresses, just keep your ears and eyes open for anything suspicious going on at the Palais Paris."

"And not too much giggling either," Chet said, with a brotherly wave of his hand.

"Of course not, silly!" Iola retorted. "When do we start?"

"First thing tomorrow," Joe said. "We'll meet here at eight o'clock."

"Meantime"—Iola's eyes twinkled—"we gals can practise balancing trays."

Afterwards, Joe rode to Bayport with Callie in her sports car. "I'll pick you up in the morning," she said, pulling up at the Hardy home. " 'Bye, now."

Joe was disappointed to learn that his father was out of town. "Your dad won't be back until sometime tomorrow," said Mrs Hardy. "By the way, did you boys find a spinning-wheel?"

"Well—er—yes," Joe replied. "But it needs a little work. We'll fix it up, though, Mom." He added apprehensively, "Aunt Gertrude hasn't arrived yet?"

"No, but I expect her any day."

Joe quickly briefed his mother on their recent adventures, including the cap clue and the plan to return to Rockaway. "There's a phone at the general store in case you want to reach us," he said. Joe had supper and retired early. Right after breakfast he took enough money from the brothers' safe to cover the balance on the spinning-wheel and retrieve Frank's watch.

Promptly at eight o'clock Joe and Callie arrived at the Morton farm, and the five young people set off in Chet's jalopy. Iola sat next to Joe as the teenagers drove happily along the highway to Rockaway.

Frank and Biff met them at the camping site, somewhat surprised to see Mary Todd.

"I have news for you," Frank said. "Old Man Tuttle doesn't sell those foreign caps."

"I told you Wilson was nutty," Joe commented.

It was then decided that Biff should drive the three girls to the restaurant. Frank explained, "The Palais Paris people already know Joe and me. They might get suspicious if we show up with you."

"Well, I don't see why we girls can't drive alone," said Iola. "We have our licences with us."

Although the Hardys knew that Callie and Iola were good drivers, they insisted that Biff go along as a precautionary measure.

"There may be a bunch of gangsters hiding out there," Chet quipped. "And Biff can take care of *them*, eh pal?"

"Single-handed!"

"And don't forget—you are Mary *Temple*," Joe emphasized. The girls waved as Biff drove them away in Chet's car.

"Do you suppose they'll all get jobs?" Joe asked, as he, Frank and Chet watched the car disappear round a bend.

"Even if only one is hired," Frank said, "we'll have an undercover agent on the spot."

"She can always check on those phoney antiques," said Chet, as he pulled up a stalk of grass and nipped it between his teeth. "So, what do we do now?"

The boys were strolling past Tuttle's General Store. Chet answered his own question. "I could go some ice-cream."

"Okay." Joe grinned. "It's hot and we'll have to wait, so why not fuel up, eh, Chet?"

"We can ask Mr Tuttle about Commander Wilson, too," Frank suggested.

Chet treated them to ice-cream on a stick. In between bites, the boys questioned the storekeeper.

"Mr Tuttle," Joe spoke up, "do you know anything about that ex-sailor hermit who lives at the caves? His name is Wilson."

The mayor gave Joe a sideways look. "Hermit? Lives in a cave? Never saw the likes of such in my town, and never heard of a soul *livin'* down there."

The trio said goodbye and left. Chet said, "Let's go to the car. There's a good jazz programme from Bayport."

But as they approached the car, Mayor Tuttle raced out after them. "Hey, come back!" he called excitedly.

"Oh—oh, what now?" said Frank, turning.

The old man went on urgently. "The telephone," he said. "Somebody's calling you—your father."

Frank dashed back inside, followed by Joe and Chet.

He ran to the public booth and picked up the receiver. "Dad, this is Frank. What's up?"

The reply creased a furrow between his eyes. "Leapin' lizards!" he exclaimed. "Okay, Dad. We'll get over there right away. Thanks for calling."

Frank stepped out of the booth, and faced the other boys, who were bursting with curiosity.

"Tell us what happened," Joe demanded.

"Remember that rundown on Cadmus Quill?" Frank said. "Well, Dad learned something else. Guess what—the Palais Paris is owned by a corporation, with Cadmus Quill listed as secretary!"

Joe let out a long whistle. "Then something fishy *is* going on around there," he said. "The girls might be in danger! Let's go!"

Chet sprinted as fast as the Hardys and all three bolted into the car together. Joe spun the rear wheels in his haste to get away!

In the meantime, Iola, Callie and Mary were being ushered through the restaurant of the Palais Paris to the manager's office at the rear. In order to avoid being conspicuous, Biff Hooper had parked Chet's car at the far end of the car-park. Biff himself crouched down out of sight on the floor of the back seat.

The girls were greeted by a suave-looking slender man with a small black moustache. "Mesdemoiselles," he said, rising from his desk, "do I understand that you wish to work as waitresses at the Palais Paris?" The manager spoke with a French accent. He added quickly, "Ah, *pardon*. I am Pierre Dumont."

"Yes, Mr Dumont," Callie Shaw spoke up. "A friend of ours saw your sign. We would like to apply for jobs."

"You speak French?"

"*Oui*," Iola replied. "We've studied it in school."

"*Très bien.*" Pierre Dumont nodded. "And you have had restaurant experience?" He turned his glance to Mary and asked quickly, "What is your name?"

"Mary Todd—Temple!" she said, flustered.

"Todd-Temple," the manager said, lifting his eyebrows. "An English name, I presume."

"Yes, yes," Mary stammered.

Mr Dumont murmured, "One moment, *s'il vous plaît.*" He pressed a buzzer. The girls stood nervously. A moment later the door opened and a muscular, brawny man entered.

"You wanted somethin', boss?"

Mr Dumont drew the man aside and whispered.

"Got yuh, boss," the man said, then hurried outside.

The manager once more turned his attention to the girls. "So sorry. Now—if you will leave your names with me," he said, "I shall let you know. I have had several other applicants."

He handed a pad across the table and the girls wrote their names, addresses and phone numbers.

The three applicants thanked the restaurant manager and left his office. On the way through the restaurant, Callie, who was last, glimpsed three well-dressed men pushing open the swing doors to the kitchen. Their voices floated back and Callie caught a few words in a foreign tongue. "That's not French," she thought, surprised.

When the girls were outside, Mary whispered, "Oh, what an idiot I am for giving my real name."

"Don't worry," Callie said.

"Do you think Mr Dumont was suspicious of us at all?" Iola mused. "He kept looking at me funnily."

"It's just your imagination because we're playing detective," Callie said.

The girls were nearly at the jalopy when Pierre Dumont hastened from the restaurant towards them. Iola whirled. "He's after us. Run!"

·15·

A Growing Suspicion

THE frightened girls raced towards the car, but their speed was outmatched by Pierre Dumont. He overtook them halfway across the car-park.

"Wait!" he commanded. "Why are you running away?" He extended a handbag towards them.

"Oh dear," said Mary. "It's mine. I must have left it on your desk. Thank you."

"I return it with pleasure, mademoiselle," Dumont replied. With a slight bow, the manager walked away.

Callie sighed with relief, and the girls hastened towards Chet's car.

"Biff! We're here!" Iola said in a loud whisper.

No reply.

"What happened to our chauffeur?" Callie said, and opened the car door. She looked into the back seat and gasped.

Biff Hooper lay in a heap on the floor, with an ugly welt on the back of his head!

"Biff! What happened?" Iola cried. "Come on, girls. Let's lift him up." It took the combined strength of all three to lift big Biff onto the back seat.

"Thank goodness he's breathing!" declared Mary Todd, her hands trembling in fright.

While Callie chafed Biff's wrists, Iola patted his face gently until the youth opened his eyes.

"Ow, my head," Biff said, wincing. He touched the welt and winced again.

"Someone gave you an awful whack," said Iola. "Did you see who it was?"

"I didn't see anything but stars!" Biff commented wryly.

"There's something very odd going on around here," Iola, said with a determined set of her chin. "I'm going right back to talk with Mr Dumont."

"Wait a minute," Callie said, putting a restraining hand on Iola's arm. "If Dumont is in on all this, as I think he is, it won't do us any good. Let's report to Frank and Joe, quick."

"I think that would be better," Biff said. "Boy, am I groggy!"

"I'll drive back," Callie said. She hopped into the front seat while Mary and Iola remained in the back, on either side of Biff. Callie started the car, drove out of the car-park, and soon was whipping along the highway towards Rockaway. She slowed down slightly for a right-hand curve. At the same instant a hedgehog plodded into the road. Desperately Callie swerved towards the centre of the road to avoid the creature. Just then another car sped towards them from the opposite direction.

Callie gripped the wheel and turned it hard. The cars passed with less than an inch to spare. With squealing brakes, both vehicles pulled over and stopped.

Frank, Joe and Chet hopped out of the Hardys' car and ran over to the girls and Biff.

"Whew!" said Joe. "That was a close call."

"I'm sorry," Callie said. "I—I didn't want to hit that poor animal."

"Forget it," said Joe. "What's the matter with you, Biff?"

"I'm all right now," the tall boy said, stepping out of the car with Iola and Mary. "Somebody conked me on the head. That's all."

"What!"

The girls told what had happened at the Palais Paris, and Mary said, "I don't trust that Pierre Dumont, in spite of his fancy French manners."

A quick comparison told the Hardys that the burly man to whom Dumont had whispered must have been Marcel.

"He might have been the one who hit you, Biff," Frank said. "Maybe Dumont ordered him to case the car and when he spotted you hiding in the back he let you have it."

When Callie told about the three men speaking in a foreign tongue, Frank and Joe exchanged meaningful glances.

"Good for you, Callie," Frank said. "But think hard, can't you identify the language?"

"No. I couldn't even guess," Callie replied.

"Let's go back and have a look-see," Joe said. "Besides, Frank, I brought along enough money to bail out your watch."

Chet transferred his gear, including the detector, to his jalopy, then took the wheel and followed the Hardys' car to the Palais Paris. By this time the carpark contained many cars.

"They must have really good food here," Iola commented.

"I hope it's better than their antiques," Joe said.

All three girls said they would like to see the antique shop.

"Okay," Joe said. "But don't try to buy anything. It'll fall apart!"

When the woman shopkeeper saw the Hardys she frowned, hastened into the back room, and reappeared with Marcel. Frank gave the girls a questioning glance. A nod from Iola told him it was indeed Marcel whom Dumont had summoned during their interview.

The muscular man did not bat an eyelid when he noticed Biff.

"Well," Marcel growled at the Hardys, "what do you want?"

"I came back to claim my watch," Frank said.

As Joe opened his wallet and took out the money, the woman reached under the counter.

"Thanks," Frank said, after the exchange was made. "Now all we have to do is put the spinning-wheel together."

Marcel smirked. "Tough luck."

"By the way," Joe said suddenly to the saleswoman, "where can we find Cadmus Quill?"

Her dark eyes darted to Marcel before she replied, "Cadmus Quill? I have never heard of him."

Marcel thrust his head forward menacingly and said, "All right. You got your watch, so scram out of here."

"But the girls want to look at your antiques," Frank persisted.

"Some other time," Marcel said, jerking his thumb

towards the door. "We don't want you kids in the way of the payin' customers."

Several patrons, having finished their luncheon, had wandered in and were looking about the shop.

"Okay," Frank said to the others. "Let's go."

When they reached the cars, Frank said, "Joe, I don't think you should have mentioned Quill."

"I thought I might catch them off guard," Joe replied.

"I think you did—trouble is, now they'll really be suspicious of us," Frank said, "provided Dad's report of Quill's connection here is correct."

"Where do we go from here?" Joe asked.

The young detectives held a hasty conference. "I suggest we pack up and go back to Bayport," Frank said. "Joe and I should talk with Dad and then decide on our next move."

The Hardys made a speedy trip to Rockaway for their gear and rejoined the others.

Biff rode in the Hardys' car with Frank and Joe, while Chet chauffeured the girls in his jalopy. Five miles later they stopped at the Hamburger Haven, piled out of the cars, and occupied counter stools.

After the girls had ordered, Chet boomed, "Three hamburgers for me, a double order of chips, and a thick chocolate malted drink."

While they chatted over their refreshing luncheon, the young detectives were amused by a small boy tumbling on a grassy plot outside the window. As Joe paid for the meal, the youngster ran up, crying.

"What's the matter?" Iola asked.

"I lost all my pennies," he said. "They dropped out of my pocket."

"Don't worry. We'll find them for you," Chet said importantly. He winked at Frank. "You see what I mean when I say that everybody should have a metal detector?"

"Okay, Sir Galahad," said Frank, "do your good deed for the day."

Chet hastened to his car. The others saw him frown. Then he ran to the Hardys' car and rummaged through it.

"What's the matter, Chet?" Biff called.

"My metal detector! It's gone!" Chet cried out in dismay.

·16·

Deadly Clicking

"YOUR detector *must* be in one of our cars," Joe said. "Come on. Let's look again."

But despite a thorough search of both vehicles, Chet's prized possession could not be found.

"There's only one answer," Chet said. "My metal detector was stolen while we were parked at the Palais Paris."

"You're telling me!" Biff put in. "That place is a jinx for us."

"I think Chet's right," Frank agreed. "Joe, you, Chet and I will go back to the restaurant. Biff can drive the girls to Bayport in the jalopy and take our gear too."

"Okay," Biff said. "But be careful of those monkeys at the Palais Paris. You know what one of 'em did to me."

Callie and Iola were reluctant to leave the Hardys, but conceded it was best that they return home with Biff.

"After all, we don't know how long the search will take," Iola said.

"Besides," Callie remarked with a twinkle, "I think we girl detectives have had enough excitement for one day!"

"Too much!" Mary declared.

After the girls and Biff were on their way, Frank, Joe and Chet hopped into the Hardys' car and drove directly to the Palais Paris.

Frank parked and the three boys entered the restaurant and walked briskly to the manager's office. They could see Dumont through the open door. He beckoned. "*Entrez.* Come in."

"We'd like to talk to you," Frank said seriously.

Dumont smiled. "No doubt you are seeking jobs," he said. "I am sorry to say that we do not have any—at present, that is. But you may give me your—"

"We don't want to work here!" Chet broke in tartly. "All I want is my metal detector. It was stolen from my car!"

"Metal detector? Ah, so that's what it is. You say stolen? *Ma foi!* Indeed, such is not the case."

Chet's eyes bulged as Dumont rose, walked to a small cupboard, and pulled out the missing detector.

"That's mine, all right," Chet said as the man handed the device over. "Where did *you* find it?"

"Precisely where you left it."

"It was left in the car," Frank said tersely. "Who swiped it? Do you know?"

A pained expression crossed Dumont's face. "It was not 'swiped,' as you Americans say," he retorted. "The detector was left standing in a corner of our antique shop."

Chet scratched his head and looked perplexed. "That's funny. I don't think I carried it in there—or did I?"

Now even the Hardys were stumped. Chet was so

fond of his new gadget he might conceivably have taken it inside. Frank gave their stout friend a questioning look. "Well, I can't remember taking it from the car, but I couldn't say for sure," Chet said. "Well, anyhow, thanks a lot, Mr Dumont," he added. "Mercy buckets, as you French say."

The manager rubbed a forefinger over his black moustache. "*Merci beaucoup*," he corrected, smiling. "Feel free to visit us any time."

The boys went outside and hurried towards their car. "He seemed like a nice enough guy," Chet remarked. "Compared to that Marcel character, anyhow."

Frank and Joe did not reply. Both were deep in thought about the strange incident. If Dumont had had the metal detector stolen, then why would he return it so graciously?

"As Shakespeare says, there's something rotten in Denmark, Joe," said Frank, as he slid behind the wheel.

"Denmark alias Palais Paris," Joe muttered.

Chet put his metal detector on the back seat, then sat in front between the Hardys. "Come on, Frank," he urged. "Let's see if we can catch up with my jalopy."

"Relax," Frank said. "I'm not going to break any speed limits."

"You can say that again," Joe replied. "We've had enough hard luck for one day."

The boys enjoyed the cool offshore breeze as they headed north towards Bayport along Shore Road. After ten miles, Frank stopped for a red light at an intersection. The engine purred quietly. All at once Joe's keen ears detected another sound.

Something was clicking on the back seat!

Joe jerked his head round. Nothing there but the metal detector. The boy reached back to turn it off. To his astonishment, the switch was already in "off" position.

"Frank!" Joe said tersely. "Quick! Pull over!"

The light had just shown green and Frank drove across the intersection and stopped on the shoulder of the road. "What—"

"Get out! Hurry!" Joe cried, opening his door and diving on to the ground. Frank did the same, and Chet followed a split second later.

Boom! A thunderous roar rent the air!

For a moment the Hardys lay half-stunned. Then Joe looked up. Smoke poured from the back of the car, which was a shambles. Frank raised his head and groaned at the sight. The brothers slowly got to their feet, but Chet remained face down in the dirt. The Hardys hastened to his side.

"Wh-what happened?" Chet asked in a weak voice, turning his head slightly.

"That detector of yours was booby-trapped," Joe said. He bent down to pick up the twisted metal, still warm from the blast.

Carefully Frank helped Chet get up. He swayed uncertainly, unable to regain his balance. "Everything's going in circles," he said. "Boy, I'm—I'm woozy!"

The Hardys sat him down beside the road, and flagged the first car that passed.

"Get help. We need the police and an ambulance!" Frank commanded.

"In a jiffy!" The driver sped off and the brothers placed Chet gently on a grassy spot beneath an oak tree.

"Jumpin' catfish!" Joe declared. "Our car's a wreck, Frank. What'll we do?"

"Have it towed back to Bayport for repairs. Hey, wait a minute!" Frank lifted the shattered boot lid. In the carton lay the pieces of spinning-wheel. These had not suffered any damage. Frank took out the carton.

Chet was very quiet. He merely stared at the sky until a siren sounded in the distance. First to appear on the scene was a state trooper car with two officers. It was followed by an ambulance, its red light blinking rapidly.

The brothers quickly identified themselves to the policemen, who recognized the Hardy name immediately. The officers gave their names as Starr and Dunn.

"What happened here?" Trooper Starr asked.

"An explosion," Frank said, pointing to the car. "Joe and I are okay, but our friend may be hurt."

Chet was lifted to a stretcher and placed in the ambulance. "We'll take him to Bayport Hospital," the driver said.

Frank and Joe tried to cheer their pal. "You'll be fine, Chet," said Joe. "Just relax and obey the doctor's orders."

"We'll see you soon," Frank added.

Chet attempted a grin. "You sleuths will have to get along without me, I guess."

The ambulance doors were closed, and with siren wailing, it sped north along the highway.

Trooper Dunn then radioed for a vehicle to tow the damaged car to a repair shop in Bayport. "It won't be here for another hour," Dunn told the boys. "No use your waiting. We'll take you home after we hear your story."

Frank and Joe briefed the troopers about the strange disappearance of the metal detector at the Palais Paris and the officers promised to make an investigation. They took the detector as evidence. Then at top speed, Trooper Starr drove the boys—and their spinning-wheel—to their front door.

Mr Hardy himself came out and shook hands with the officers, old friends of his. After Starr and Dunn had driven off, the detective and his sons went into the living-room. Frank took the wooden pieces from the carton and put them on the floor.

"Dad, we've had a terrible time," Joe began.

"I know something about it," Mr Hardy said. "Mr Morton phoned me. You'll be glad to know that Chet is suffering only from shock and has been taken home."

"Thank goodness!" Frank said.

"Now come up to my study and we'll go over the whole situation," Mr Hardy said.

Mrs Hardy brought glasses of lemonade, and the three sleuths discussed every angle of the Todd-Quill case, while sipping the cool beverage.

"I'm convinced the Palais Paris is involved in some way," Frank concluded.

"It would seem so," Fenton Hardy agreed. "Tell me more about this Commander Wilson."

The boys took turns at relating their weird experiences at the Honeycomb Caves.

"E. K. T. Wilson's just plain loony," Joe stated flatly.

"I wouldn't agree with you one hundred per cent,"

his father said. "If Wilson is as insane as he seems, I think he would be in an institution."

"You mean maybe he's not crazy at all?" asked Frank. "It's an act?"

Their father thought that this was a possibility, however remote, and advised his sons to pursue the Wilson angle with all their power.

"I'll tell you why, boys. Your enemies are on the run!"

"You really think so?" Joe asked.

"Absolutely. They're desperate. The booby-trapped detector proves it. When they find that you three escaped, the criminals will show their hand again. Mark my words. So be extra careful."

Fenton Hardy went on to say there were no new developments in the radar station case. "Things have been quiet," he said. "Too quiet."

"Like the calm before the storm," Joe said.

Just then the Hardys' doorbell chimed. The boys heard their mother answer it and exclaim, "Gertrude Hardy! I'm so glad to see you!"

Frank and Joe exchanged wry grins. "Speaking of storms," said Frank, "Aunt Gertrude has arrived."

The detectives broke off their conference and went down to greet the visitor. Gertrude Hardy was a tall, angular woman with a strong personality. She was most emphatically not in favour of her nephews following in the footsteps of her famous brother.

"Chasing criminals is no pastime for young boys" was one of her favourite expressions. But beneath her peppery manner, Aunt Gertrude held a warm affection for Frank and Joe, and they for her.

"Hi, Aunt Gertrude!" Joe said.

"Good to see you again," said Frank.

Without any ado whatsoever, Aunt Gertrude pulled a hatpin from her bun, removed her flowered hat, set it on the sofa, and demanded, "Where's my spinning-wheel?"

"Why—why—Aunt Gertrude—" Joe began.

"Don't stall," Miss Hardy said sternly. "Your mother just told me that you purchased a spinning-wheel."

"We did," Frank said.

"Well, where is it?"

Joe feebly pointed to the spindles and other accessories lying on the floor.

"That? That's my spinning-wheel?" Aunt Gertrude gasped.

· 17 ·

A Bold Warning

WITH the withering directness of a district attorney, Aunt Gertrude questioned her nephews about the broken spinning-wheel. Mr and Mrs Hardy did a magnificent job of suppressing smiles as their relative relentlessly pursued her cross-examination.

"You say you broke it, Joe? How?"

"It was hanging from the ceiling and I touched it."

"Now, Joe, refresh your memory!" Aunt Gertrude said. "A spinning-wheel on the ceiling! Bosh!"

Frank sprang to his brother's defence. "But it was only on display," he explained. "It wasn't for sale."

"Sakes alive! Then why did you buy it?" Aunt Gertrude said.

"We had to," Joe said. "There was this big husky fellow, Marcel—"

Aunt Gertrude threw up her hands. "What imaginations!" she exclaimed.

"It's the truth, every word of it," Frank insisted. "We can prove—"

"Oh, I believe you." Aunt Gertrude tossed her head vigorously. "Although the whole thing is beyond me!" Without another word, Miss Hardy scooped up the pile and marched from the room into the kitchen. In a moment her footsteps could be heard descending to the basement.

Frank and Joe looked at their parents and shrugged in embarrassment.

"Don't worry," Mrs Hardy smiled. "Your Aunt Gertrude really appreciates what you boys have done."

A telephone call to the Morton home that evening revealed Chet was progressing nicely. "His hair was singed a little at the back," Mrs Morton told Frank. "But otherwise he's pretty much recovered from the shock. Why don't you and Joe come over and see him tomorrow morning?"

"Fine. We will."

Before going to bed, the brothers went to the kitchen for a snack. Aunt Gertrude was there. Still embarrassed about the spinning-wheel, Frank and Joe grinned sheepishly. But their aunt seemed to be in good spirits and handed them her personal cheque for fifty dollars in payment for the antique.

"Junipers!" Joe said. "That's swell of you, considering the condition it's in."

Thoroughly rested after a good night's sleep, the brothers had breakfast and got ready to visit their stout friend. Frank took a few moments to call Biff. "Sorry I can't join you fellows today," Biff said. "Too much work around the house. But in case of an emergency don't hesitate to holler. And tell Chet to keep his chins up."

Mr Hardy had given his sons permission to use his car, but as they were about to step out of the back door, their mother stopped them. "Aren't you taking Chet some flowers?"

"Flowers?" Joe said. "Oh, Mom, of course not."

"Well, you should take the patient something," Mrs Hardy persisted.

"You're right. How about a fruit basket?" Frank suggested.

Their mother nodded approvingly. "A good idea— cater to Chet's appetite."

"He takes pretty good care of that himself," Joe said. "All right, we'll stop at the store on our way."

The boys drove to the heart of Bayport, where they stopped at a fancy food shop. There the proprietor made up an attractive basket of fruit, covered with transparent plastic and topped by bright red ribbon.

As they drove out of town over the country road to the Morton farmhouse, Frank and Joe discussed their next step in solving the mystery of the missing Morgan Todd.

"Dad thinks we should investigate Commander Wilson further, so we'll do it," said Frank. "Remember Todd's riddle of the word *Rockaway*. We still have more sleuthing to do around Honeycomb Caves."

"When do we start?" Joe asked impatiently.

"As soon as we visit Chet." Frank turned off the road into the driveway of the Morton home and parked. Between them, the Hardys carried the large fruit basket into the house. They were met at the front door by Mary Todd.

"Oh, how gorgeous!" she said, admiring the colourful gift.

THE SECRET OF THE CAVES 131

Mrs Morton came downstairs and greeted the boys warmly. "I think Chet can see you now," she said, adding that Iola was out shopping.

Mary and the brothers mounted the stairs to the second floor. "I hope he's feeling very much better," Frank said.

"He's quite comfortable," Mary·said. "That poor, brave boy!"

When they entered Chet's room, Frank and Joe looked about, amazed. His bed was flanked by two bouquets of flowers. On the bedside table lay a half empty box of chocolates and a quart bottle of raspberry squash, four-fifths consumed.

Reclining on three fluffed pillows lay Chet, with a cherubic look on his round face.

"Hi, fellows," he said feebly with a wave of his hand. "How's tricks?"

"Jumpin' catfish!" Joe exclaimed. "You got the best trick of all. How about it, Frank, let's get ourselves blasted too?"

"It isn't any fun," Chet said, and with a look of pain held his hand to his forehead.

Instantly Mary Todd sprang to his side with a cool, damp cloth which she placed over his brow. "You poor dear," she said, and Joe gulped.

Frank stifled a grin. "We're going back to the caves," he announced. Chet's reaction was startling. He whipped off the compress and sat up.

"You are? Take me along, will you? That fishing was great!"

"We're not going fishing—not for fish, that is," Frank said.

"More sleuthing? Ugh!" Chet groaned and sank back on the pillows.

"Well, now that you're a celebrity," Joe said teasingly, "enjoy it while you can, Chet, old boy."

This seemed to revive the chubby patient. "May I have another drink of squash, Mary?" he asked. His young nurse nimbly moved to the other side of the bed and poured a glass of the sparkling beverage. Chet drank it and lay back again. "Yes, I guess I am a celebrity, fellows. The reporter got my personal story this morning."

"Reporter?" Frank said quickly.

"Yes," Mary put in, "from the *Bayport Times*."

"Mary made a big hit with him," Chet went on with a grin. "He asked a lot of questions about her, too."

"Wait a minute," Joe said. "What was this fellow's name?"

"Otto Lippincott." Mary supplied the answer.

"I never heard of anyone by that name on the *Times*," Frank said.

Frank excused himself to make a phone call and hurried downstairs. He returned ten minutes later, his face flushed with excitement.

"There is no Lippincott who works for that newspaper," he said. "Chet, you've been duped."

Disappointment, then indignation, crossed Chet's face. "Do you mean that guy was a phoney?" he blurted.

"Nothing else but. He came here to fish for information," Frank replied.

Joe turned to Mary and asked, "How much did you tell this man?"

"Oh, have I done the wrong thing again?" Mary wailed.

"Well, maybe," Frank declared. "But it's too late to worry over spilled milk. From now on I advise both of you to keep mum on anything you know."

Just then the front door slammed and Iola's cheerful voice floated up the stairs. "Frank, Joe. Are you here?"

Joe blushed a little. "Yes, Iola, come on up."

Quick footsteps sounded on the stairs and Iola hurried into Chet's room. In her hand she held a white envelope. "I found this in the mailbox," she said. "No stamp or anything. It just says 'Chet Morton.' "

"Another well-wisher, I suppose," Chet said importantly, and took the envelope. He tore off one end, blew into the slit, and removed the note.

"Good grief! Listen!" He read, " *'Get Hardys off case or your life will be in danger.'* "

Iola gasped and clutched Mary's hand. "Oh, this is terrible!" she cried out.

Frank frowned and bit his lip. "I didn't want to get your family involved, Chet."

"What'll we do?" Joe asked.

Frank's mind worked rapidly. "We'll get Sam Radley to stand constant guard on the house here," he said. "After dark tonight we'll smuggle Mary to our house. Mother and Aunt Gertrude can stand watch over her there."

"I'll say!" Chet said. "I wouldn't want to be the one to cross your Aunt Gertrude's path."

A telephone call to the Hardy home confirmed Frank's protection plan, and Sam Radley, who fortunately was in town, told the boys he would report to the Morton farm.

When Mr Hardy's operator arrived about noon, Frank and Joe excused themselves and returned home.

Frank telephoned Bayport Police Headquarters and notified Chief Collig about the impostor and the threat Chet received. Collig promised to dispatch a squad car to patrol the area during the night and relieve Radley.

"What about Honeycomb Caves?" Joe asked, after his brother had finished the call.

"We'll tackle them tonight," Frank said. "As soon as we have Mary safely here."

"Shall we go in the *Sleuth*?"

Frank mulled over the question. Finally he shook his head. "Going by water is a good idea, Joe, but these crooks are keeping close tabs on us and would probably recognize our boat."

"How about using Biff's?" Joe suggested. "He says the *Envoy* just got a new engine and it's in great shape."

Frank phoned Biff immediately and arranged to use his speedboat for the brothers' sleuthing adventure.

The Hardys thanked their pal, who kept his craft in a boathouse half a mile from the Hardys'. After supper Frank and Joe packed their gear to have it in readiness. Then they drove out to Chet's place.

"Is Mary ready to come with us?" Joe asked Iola, as they stepped into the hall.

"Just about."

The Hardys heard footsteps on the stairs and glanced up to see a slim, handsome young man descending. He wore dungarees, work jacket and farm hat.

"Hey!" Frank cried out. "That's not a guy, that's a gal!"

Mary Todd grinned in her disguise. "Iola and I thought up the idea. Like it?"

"Terrific." Joe nodded approval. "You two have the true detective spirit."

Chet, who appeared fully recovered, now came downstairs.

"I thought you were still shell-shocked," said Joe, with a sly look at their stout friend.

"Without a nurse I'm better already," quipped Chet. Then he took on a serious demeanour. "Now look, fellows, be extra careful of Mary, won't you?"

With a promise that they would, the Hardys left the Morton house and drove Mary to their own home.

Aunt Gertrude and Mrs Hardy received the girl kindly, and showed her to the second guest room.

Biff Hooper arrived minutes later and drove the brothers to his dock. In a few minutes the two sleuths and their gear were aboard the *Envoy*. Joe started the engine.

"I checked the running lights," Biff said. "Everything is okay."

The Hardys thanked him and shoved off, with Joe at the wheel. The *Envoy* knifed through the waters of Barmet Bay, its shore front twinkling with lights. As the boys passed the boathouse where the *Sleuth* was kept, Frank called out, "Throttle down, Joe. What's that light over there?"

Joe brought the *Envoy* about and saw a light flickering from the window of their boathouse. "Jeepers! I don't know!" He extinguished the running lights and crept quietly over the dark waters.

As they neared the boathouse Frank suddenly exclaimed in alarm. Smoke was seeping out from beneath the door. Their boathouse was on fire!

·18·

Searchlight

THE wailing of a police siren drifted across Barmet
Bay, followed by the clanging bells of a fire engine.
Now the window glass of the Hardy boathouse broke
with the heat, and flames licked out, illuminating the
water.

With one hand on the steering wheel, Joe reached
over for the fire extinguisher clamped on the side of the
Envoy. Throttle open, the craft leaped through the water
until Frank called out:

"Joe! Slow down."

"Why? Our whole boathouse will burn up."

"The fire department will take care of it." Frank
had hardly spoken before an arch of water was
sprayed against the building and the flames were being
quenched.

As Joe slackened speed and circled about, Frank
explained, "This blaze could have been set for two
reasons. One, to keep us from using the *Sleuth*, and
two—"

"I get you already," Joe said. "A diversionary
action!"

"Exactly." Frank nodded. "If our enemies are up to

something tonight, they'll want to pin us down in Bayport."

By now the smoke too had abated, and firemen raised the door of the boathouse. In the glow of their lanterns, the brothers could see that the *Sleuth* was still afloat.

"She may not be badly damaged," Frank said. "At any rate, we can't stop to see now. On to Honeycomb Caves, Joe."

Unfortunately, the *Envoy* did not have a ship-to-shore radio, as did the *Sleuth*. The brothers therefore could not communicate with their home, but knew that Mr Hardy would be notified of the boathouse fire soon enough.

Joe snapped on the running lights again, and the *Envoy* purred through the rolling waves as its pilot guided the craft expertly along the coast he knew so well.

After the *Envoy* passed a blinking buoy marking the entrance to Barmet Bay, the run south was nearly a straight line. But even with smooth sailing, it was nearly two a.m. before the great cliffs loomed in shadowy silhouettes on their starboard side.

Joe throttled back, and the *Envoy* rocked in the waves as the young detectives discussed their next move.

"Let's cruise past the caves as close as we can get," Frank said. "After that, we can put in at John Donachie's dock."

Frank took turns with his brother at the wheel, and, guiding the *Envoy* silently towards shore, the boys studied the Honeycomb Caves. The half-moon illuminated the shore just enough to make the dark cave openings look like the baleful eye sockets of a skull.

The craft ran parallel to the shore, and as they neared Commander Wilson's cave house, Joe chuckled. "I'll bet the old boy is sawing wood right now— For Pete's sake, Frank!"

The brothers were startled by a brilliant finger of light which suddenly shot from the cave mouth across the water.

"A giant searchlight!" declared Frank.

The bow of the *Envoy* nearly touched the edge of the powerful beam, and Frank turned hard on the wheel to reverse his course. The light moved away from the boat, giving its churning wake a chance to settle in the darkness unseen. Frank and Joe bent low, hoping the wave troughs would conceal the *Envoy*. Then the light disappeared as suddenly as it had swept the green sea.

"Junipers!" said Joe. "That was a close squeak!"

"Came right from Wilson's cave!" Frank exclaimed. "Dad hit it on the nose. Wilson's not nutty at all. He's as sane as we are, and up to something sinister."

"Do you suppose he picked us up on radar, or heard our engine?" Joe pondered as Frank made a big circle and headed for the fisherman's dock.

"It might have been a signal," Frank said. "And we just happened on it by luck."

"A signal for what," Joe asked, "or to what?"

"Maybe a ship lying offshore, or men waiting in a small boat. Who knows?"

"How can we find out?"

Frank replied with determination, "Maybe Johnny Donachie can help us. If he'll take us fishing with him tomorrow, we can lie low offshore and spy on the caves with binoculars."

"Great idea," Joe said approvingly. "Too bad we'll wake him up in the middle of the night."

When the *Envoy* docked at Johnny's pier, Frank and Joe got their first good look at the fisherman's craft. It was a little more than thirty feet in length, with a cabin sticking up like an inverted cheese box.

"A pretty old tub," said Joe, as he hopped out of the *Envoy* and made fast.

"Looks sort of top-heavy," Frank said. "But if it suits Johnny Donachie, it's okay with me."

The brothers walked up to the dark house. Frank took a deep breath and knocked on the door. Seconds later a yellow light blinked on and a sleepy voice sounded behind the closed door. "Who's there?"

"Frank and Joe Hardy."

The door opened a crack and the fisherman looked out.

"Thunderation!" he said, opening the door to admit the boys. "What brings you out at this hour?"

"We're doing some more detective work," Joe replied. "Did you see the light down the coast tonight?"

The fisherman said that he had noticed a glow in the night sky several times. "It's weird. That's why I stay away from that spooky place."

"We have a favour to ask," Frank said. "Will you take us fishing tomorrow?"

"Sure, don't see why not. Hey, you boys must be tired. We have an extra room."

"Thanks, but we can sleep in our boat," said Frank.

By this time Mrs Donachie had been awakened and insisted that the Hardys stay for the rest of the night.

Secretly Frank and Joe were glad to accept and slept soundly until they were aroused for breakfast.

After they had eaten, the boys covered the *Envoy* with a tarpaulin, then joined Johnny on his boat, which bore the faded name *Lena*. The fisherman started the noisy engine, and with a *clink-clunk-clink-clunk* the old craft limped seaward.

At Frank's request, Johnny headed down the coast parallel to the caves but far enough out to avoid suspicion. Frank and Joe crouched behind the gunwales, keeping their binoculars trained on shore.

Half an hour elapsed. Suddenly Joe straightened. "I see some people!" he said.

"Me too. And look. Isn't that Wilson up there?"

"Moving around like an athlete!" Joe observed.

The commander and three other men were carrying boxes into the cave mouth.

The boys' arms ached from their steady surveillance. At last, two hours later, Wilson reappeared. He sat in front of his cave for a while, then moved off to the cavern in which the Hardys had stayed and appeared to examine it briefly before returning to his own headquarters.

"Frank, we have to get ashore and find out what's going on," Joe said.

"That may come sooner than we expect," his brother replied, glancing up into the lowering sky.

The waves became a deeper green and the lacy tops were flicked off by the freshening breeze.

"Fishin's over for the day," Johnny told the boys. "We got to go back."

"How about a little longer look," Joe coaxed, seeing Wilson stride along the shore.

"These storms come up awful fast," Johnny said. "We'd best be puttin' back." But the Hardys finally coaxed the fisherman to remain for a short while in order to spy on Wilson. Almost immediately, the fishing boat began to lurch as the waves grew higher.

"Can't stay another second," Johnny said. "It's gettin' dangerous."

With a *clink-clunk* the old motor-powered *Lena* chugged slowly back towards the fisherman's wharf.

"Can't you give her more speed, Johnny?" Joe called out as the waves grew taller and the wind whistled about their ears.

"Six knots is the best she can do."

They were halfway to their destination when a huge wave crashed upon the deck, nearly washing Joe into the sea. But the boy clung to a railing post until Frank dragged him into the safety of the cabin.

The old tub now listed badly. "We'll never make it!" Johnny said gloomily, as the rough sea bullied the boat about and rain lashed the waves.

Just then Joe looked towards shore and exclaimed, "Frank! Is that the *Envoy* I see?"

Frank raised his binoculars. "It sure is. Well, what do you know? Johnny, your wife's coming to our rescue."

Minutes later, Mrs Donachie came about in the *Envoy*. Joe threw a line to her and, with the sea heaving about them, the woman towed *Lena* to shore. When both craft had been moored at the dock, they hastened inside the house, soaking wet.

Frank shook his head. "I've got to hand it to you, Mrs Donachie. You certainly have a lot of courage."

"And skill too," Joe said admiringly.

The woman pushed back wisps of damp hair and replied with a smile, "What do you expect from a fisherman's wife?"

By early evening the rain had ceased and the skies were clear. After a hearty supper John Donachie pushed his chair back from the table, lighted his pipe, then said, "Now that the storm's over, are you boys takin' the *Envoy* back to Bayport?"

Joe shook his head. "Frank and I want to get closer to those caves and see what's going on."

"At night?" The Donachies looked fearful.

"Yes. As soon as it gets dark enough," Frank said.

"We should be back before daybreak," Joe added, testing his flashlight.

After many admonitions to be careful, the boys disappeared along the trail in the darkness. The climb to the top of the cliffs was arduous, but the way was clear in the moonlight.

"Here's the ravine," Joe said finally, and the brothers made their way down to the sandy beach. There they stopped for a moment to get their bearings.

"We'll have to crouch low and stay as close to the cliff as possible," Frank advised. "I'll lead the way."

The Hardys passed the mouth of their old cave and crept stealthily towards Wilson's cavern. Suddenly Frank pulled Joe back into a crevice of rock. "Good grief!" he whispered. "Look out there!"

Three hundred yards offshore a small red light winked like the eye of a sea monster. But even in the gloom the boys recognized a conning tower.

"A submarine!" Joe exclaimed.

·19·

A Raft of Trouble

THE magnitude of the mystery they had uncovered hit Frank and Joe like a stunning blow. This was it! Commander Wilson was a fraud, a cover-up for some sort of gang receiving supplies and men by secret submarine at the Honeycomb Caves.

Another light winked from in front of Wilson's cave. Slowly the sub surfaced, its whaleback silhouette standing out in the darkness.

"They've contacted each other," said Joe. "If we only had a boat."

"I have an idea," Frank said. "We'll swim out to the sub." He stripped down to his shorts and Joe did the same. "We might make it if Wilson doesn't turn on the big searchlight."

The brothers concealed their clothes behind a rock, then waded into the surf. They dived into a wave and, with strong overhand strokes, rapidly swam towards the submarine. Silently the Hardys came up to the undersea craft, and treading water, clung to the hull.

Tensely the boys waited. A few moments later the hatch opened. Frank and Joe held their breaths as six men piled out, dragging a large rubber life raft. They flung it into the water with a *plop*, and stepped inside, where two of their number manned paddles.

Hearts thumping wildly, Frank and Joe pressed back against the sub, their faces barely showing above water, ten feet away from the raft.

The men spoke a strange foreign language, but suddenly one said sternly in English, "Do not use the mother tongue. It is dangerous. We are now in America!"

Frank decided on a bold strategy, and nudged his brother. "Come on!"

Swiftly the boys pushed off and swam underwater to emerge silently right behind the raft. They reached up and gripped it with one hand, scissor-kicking so as not to be a drag on the rubber craft as the paddlers guided it across the waves towards shore.

The brothers glanced back, to see the conning tower of the sub disappear beneath the waves.

"Ah, there's Wilson's light!" came a voice from the raft.

"Yes, our calculations were correct," said another man. "We will show these Americans!"

Finally Frank and Joe felt their toes touch bottom. When the men hopped out, the boys swam underwater away from shore, then surfaced and once more trod water. This time their eyes fell upon a most unusual scene. In the glow of the light inside Wilson's cave, they saw the commander greet each of the new arrivals, pumping their hands as they stepped inside.

But there was something different about Wilson. His

face looked younger. And . . . his hair was now black.

"Wilson's no old man. That was a grey wig he was wearing!" hissed Joe. "He used face make-up too."

"There's no time to lose!" Frank said, and both boys swam to the beach. The only evidence of activity was the dim glow coming from the cave mouth. Now and then it faded as if those inside were milling about.

The Hardys quickly got their clothes and slipped them on. "If we only had some help," Frank said, as they inched closer to the entrance of the cave. From within came the hum of voices.

They halted and looked about in the darkness. "I think they would have posted a sentry," Frank said. "Do you see anybody, Joe?"

Joe flashed his light up and down the beach, but could see no one. "What now, Frank?"

"Into the cave. We've got to see what this is all about."

The brothers listened, but the voices had receded. Only muffled sounds emerged from the cavern. Clutching their flashlights, Frank and Joe slipped inside. At first the interior looked much the same as the first time they had seen it. The shotgun lay on the ledge, the code book was still in evidence, and the food supply was stashed as it had been previously.

But as the boys penetrated deeper, their mouths fell open in wonderment. To the rear of the cave was a thick electrical conduit which snaked back into the cavern. Tiptoeing forward, Frank and Joe finally came to a thick wooden partition with an iron door.

"Good grief!" Joe declared. "Frank, this is set up like a hidden city."

"I think those men might be spies, or saboteurs," Frank whispered. "Maybe they're connected with the trouble at the radar site."

"But what about Quill and Todd?" Joe asked. "How do they fit into all this?"

"I don't know yet. But we've found the mine that Chet discovered," Frank said. "That metal conduit. And it makes a beeline to the Palais Paris."

"I could just smell something phoney about that whole place," Joe declared, moving closer to the iron door. "Frank, let's go in!"

"Okay, I'm game. But we'd better stick close together."

Joe's hand reached for the door handle. Suddenly a voice behind them froze the boys into immobility.

"Hardys, you're through!"

The boys wheeled about. Joe gasped. "Cadmus Quill!"

The short, bouncy college instructor leered at them. Behind him stood four henchmen.

"You're trapped!" Cadmus Quill said.

Frank whispered to his brother and Joe nodded. As Quill and his strong-arm men advanced, the boys uttered a bloodcurling war-cry and charged like half-backs! Joe tackled two of the men, bowling them over. They scrambled to their feet and grabbed Joe. He twisted frantically to escape their grip. Frank doubled Quill with a blow to the solar plexus, then dashed past the other two men towards the cave mouth. They darted after him.

Frank's plan was working! With speed born of desperation, the boy leaped towards the ledge and grabbed the shotgun. Then he aimed it overhead, close to the electrical conduit.

Frank pulled the trigger. There was a deafening blast and a shower of sparks. The lights went out and an acrid pall of smoke filled the cavern.

·20·

Loyal Pals

THE sudden blast and blackout threw the Hardys' assailants into confusion. The next moment, youthful shouts were heard from the entrance, and two flashlights illuminated the cave.

"Frank! Joe! What's going on?" came Chet's voice.

"Wow! They need help!" cried Biff.

Quill and his four thugs, seeing the reinforcements, dashed to the iron door and jerked it open. The four young sleuths raced after them, but were too late. The fugitives disappeared inside, the door clanged shut, and a bolt clicked fast. The brothers, then Biff and Chet, tried the handle to no avail.

"How did you know we were here?" Frank asked.

"Chet and I got to thinking about you two working on this case all alone," Biff said. "So we drove down to Johnny Donachie's. We missed you by minutes."

"So we climbed up the cliffs and down the ravine," Chet added.

"And made it here just in time," Joe said. "I don't think we could have scared them off much longer without you."

"That isn't all," Biff went on. He said that before they had left Bayport, Mr Hardy had alerted the State

Police to search the Palais Paris. "Some of the cops are on their way to the caves too."

The boys heard scuffling sounds coming from behind the iron door.

"Sounds like somebody running," Joe said.

"And stumbling about in the dark," Frank added.

The brothers reasoned that the short-circuited conduit had also blacked out the area beyond Wilson's cave.

Just then the rumpus inside was accompanied by frantic shouts. The bolt clicked, and as it did, Frank and Joe grabbed the handle and held it tightly.

"We've got them trapped, and we're going to keep them that way!" Frank declared.

The melee within grew in intensity. It was punctuated by a shot. Someone groaned. Then came banging on the iron door.

"Frank and Joe, if that's you, open up!"

"Dad!" Joe exclaimed, hardly daring to believe his ears.

"Open up, boys. We've caught the gang."

The brothers let go the handle and stepped back as the door swung inward. Several great searchlights illuminated the chamber and Fenton Hardy stepped out. He was followed by six policemen, each of whom had a manacled prisoner in tow. One of the prisoners the boys recognized as E. K. T. Wilson. He glowered at them balefully.

"Great going, Dad!" Frank exclaimed. He now reported the submarine incident and had just finished when two state troopers dashed in through the beach entrance. They were officers Starr and Dunn. "Have you got them all rounded up?" Trooper Dunn asked.

"I think so," Fenton Hardy replied. "But there's one man still missing—Morgan Todd. We think he's around here somewhere."

Upon learning of the sub, Trooper Starr switched on his portable radio transmitter and broadcast an urgent request to intercept the undersea prowler.

Revelations came so thick and fast that Frank and Joe were dazed by the hornets' nest which they had uncovered. At Fenton Hardy's direction, the troopers took up positions at the mouth of the cave while the rest of the party pressed deeper into the passageway behind the iron door.

The gradient was up, and as the boys marched along they could see that the tunnel was man-made. The walls and ceiling bore the marks of excavating tools, and here and there the passage was shored with planks.

Finally Fenton Hardy led the young sleuths to a flight of concrete steps. They ascended to a metal door, opened it, and found themselves in the kitchen of the Palais Paris!

There, on the floor and manacled back to back, sat Dumont and Marcel. They glared at the Hardys with hate-filled eyes.

"They're the ones who did this to us!" Marcel said bitterly. "If they hadn't come snooping—"

"Shut up!" Dumont snapped. "Fool!"

"It's okay for you, big shot," Marcel complained. "You've got plenty of dough to help you. But not me!"

Police Chief Collig of Bayport and two of his men stood by with drawn pistols as three other gang members were flushed from upstairs rooms at the Palais Paris.

"I think we have them all rounded up now, Fenton," Collig said.

"Good work. The Federal men will be here any minute."

A sound of sirens from a distance reached their ears. They howled like banshees as they drew closer, then petered out in front of the Palais Paris. Car doors banged shut, and ten Federal agents burst into the restaurant.

Dumont and Marcel were pulled to their feet, and stood in line with the rest of the prisoners as the government men entered the kitchen.

"You've done a splendid job for us, Fenton," said a tall man with hair greying at the temples.

Mr Hardy turned to his sons. "This is Special Agent Alberts," he said, and made the introductions. Then the detective added, "Actually, my sons and their friends cracked this case. My credit is secondary."

"Well, you all did a magnificent job," Alberts told the four boys.

"But we still haven't solved the mystery of the missing Morgan Todd," Frank said.

"You found Morgan Todd all right," Agent Alberts said, grinning at the young detectives.

"*What?*" they chorused.

The tale which the Federal men unfolded nearly defied imagination. The Hardys' warning about the sub had been relayed instantly to the Navy, and Coast Guard. Destroyer depth charges in the area off the caves had forced the craft to the surface.

"The Navy has caught a nice prize," Alberts said. "And your friend Todd, who'd been imprisoned on the sub, is aboard one of our destroyers this moment, safe and sound."

Hearing this, Joe dashed to the telephone and called the Hardy home. He spoke to his mother, who relayed the good news to Mary. He could hear Mary's cry of delight, and then sobbing, as she broke down and wept with joy.

A police van carried the prisoners to Bayport for further interrogation. Biff Hooper went back in the *Envoy*, while the Hardys, Chet and Agent Alberts returned in a police car. It was then the boys learned the true magnitude of their case.

"Morgan Todd was the key to the whole mystery," Mr Hardy told them. The young instructor had, while abroad, stumbled upon bizarre information. The foreign country in which he was studying had set up a spy and saboteur centre in the Honeycomb Caves. Also, they had engineers working on a project designed to nullify the effect of the new U.S. Coastal Radar Station at Telescope Hill.

"A device was to be raised out of the cave area at night," Agent Alberts said, "that would have jammed the radar signals."

"But where does the Palais Paris come in?" asked Frank.

"That was a front," Mr Hardy said. "The gang's engineers constructed the tunnel to lead directly from the Palais Paris to the shore, and enlarge the caves."

"And credit for that discovery goes to Chet," Frank

said, slapping the stout boy on the shoulder. "His metal detector did the trick!"

"And the U.S. Government," the Federal agent said, "is going to reimburse you, Chet, for your detector, and also for repairs to your car, Frank and Joe."

Alberts went on to explain that Morgan Todd, being cautious and conservative, had decided to conduct a solo investigation of the caves before turning over his information to the U.S. Government.

"I'll bet that's where he made a mistake," Chet commented.

"Right. Cadmus Quill, who had been brainwashed by the foreign spy ring into being a traitor, helped to kidnap Todd. But before they carried him away that night, Todd begged them to allow him to prepare the examination for his students."

"A pretty clever fellow," Mr Hardy conceded, "to leave that Rockaway tip. And you boys did a grand job in discovering it."

"Commander Wilson had me fooled," Joe said wryly, as the car neared Bayport.

"Dad had the right angle on him," Frank said.

When the limousine pulled up in front of the Hardy house, Alberts said he would drive Chet home. They would all meet Chief Collig for a conference at Bayport Police Headquarters at ten o'clock the next morning.

It was nearly daylight when Frank and Joe fell asleep. They awakened later to learn that all of Bayport was buzzing with the excitement of the great coup the boys had pulled off.

Frank and Joe went to headquarters with Mary Todd. In Chief Collig's office they were joined by

Chet, Biff, Iola and Callie. Then two Federal agents
appeared with Morgan Todd. He and his sister flung
themselves into each other's arms in a fond embrace.

Morgan Todd shook hands vigorously with the
Hardys. "I can't thank you enough for saving my life!"
he said warmly. Todd revealed that the submarine was
to have taken him to a remote part of the world, where
he would have been incarcerated for the rest of his
life.

"We have some other interesting details too," Alberts
said. "Commander E. K. T. Wilson was a phoney, of
course. In his younger days he was an actor, who
defected while in the service of his country on a foreign
tour of duty."

"That nutty bit of his nearly paid off," said Joe,
"with that shooting and all."

Frank grinned. "Good thing he overdid it somewhat,
at least enough for Dad to catch on."

Chief Collig reported that Wilson, under relentless
quizzing, had admitted losing the pistol on the beach
the night he had prowled about the boys' cave. As for
the stacked wood, it had been left there by picnickers
months before. An expert on explosives, Wilson had
been called by Dumont to booby-trap the metal
detector.

When Iola Morton asked if there would be any
international complications as a result of the Hardys'
victory, the agent said, "The State Department has
already successfully negotiated the matter."

It was also revealed that Pierre Dumont, the spies'
chief man in the U.S., came from a French-speaking
part of the world and had applied for U.S. citizenship.

Marcel had worked under him abroad and was merely a strong-arm dupe. The woman shopkeeper at the Palais Paris was found to be innocent of any wrong-doing.

"And what about the foreign caps?" Joe asked.

"A careless mistake on the saboteurs' part," Fenton Hardy answered.

The boys learned that the henchman who had dropped his cap at the radar site had also posed later as the newspaper reporter. The same foreigner also had set the boathouse on fire.

Mr Hardy smiled proudly. "You boys were really on the ball!"

"And I'd say that the U.S. Government is in debt to all of you who worked on this case," Agent Alberts added.

The *Bayport Times* had already bannerlined the Hardys' feat, and the telephone rang with congratulatory messages all day.

That evening Mrs Hardy was hostess at a get-together in the detectives' home. Happy, excited voices filled the living-room as Laura Hardy and Aunt Gertrude served refreshments. In the midst of the gaiety a telegram was received by the Hardy boys. It came from Kenworthy College and stated that the fraternity had expelled Cadmus Quill. The message also contained an apology to the Hardys, and congratulations on their patriotic efforts.

Then Joe turned on the record-player. Chet, usually bashful with girls, asked Mary Todd to dance, and soon the living-room was a blur of motion as the young people gyrated to the latest steps.

"I guess your brother wasn't planning to get married after all," Chet said.

"What!"

"Oh, nothing. Just another one of Quill's lies."

When the music was over, Mrs Hardy smilingly called for attention. The young folks gathered in a circle, and Aunt Gertrude emerged majestically from the kitchen, carrying a spinning-wheel.

Frank and Joe gasped in surprise. "Is that the one we bought?" Joe burst out.

Aunt Gertrude pursed her lips and looked proud. "Indeed it is," she said. "I put it all together myself. And I might add it's a rare antique you two found!"

When the claps and cheers died down, Frank Hardy spoke up. "Then you *are* in favour of our detective work," he said.

Aunt Gertrude's answer could not be heard amid the laughter that followed, nor could the boys foresee that their next big adventure would be *The Secret of Pirates' Hill.*

The Hardy Boys® Mysteries

THE SECRET
OF PIRATES' HILL

The Secret of Pirates' Hill was first published in the
UK in 1972 by William Collins Sons & Co. Ltd.

·1· *Underwater Danger*

"DON'T forget, Frank, any treasure we find will be divided fifty-fifty!" Blond, seventeen-year-old Joe Hardy grinned. He checked his skin-diving gear and slid, flippers first, over the gunwale of their motorboat.

"I'll settle for a pot of gold," retorted Frank.

He was similarly attired in trunks, air tank and face mask, and carried a shark knife. The brothers had anchored their boat, the *Sleuth*, off a secluded area of beach. It ran beneath a low, sand-dune-covered, rocky promontory called Pirates' Hill. The only other boat in sight was that of an old fisherman out for an early morning catch.

"Here goes!" said Frank as he plunged into the cool waters of the Atlantic. Together, the boys swam towards the bottom.

Suddenly Joe clutched his brother's arm and pointed. Twenty feet in front of them and only a short distance from the surface was another skin diver in a black rubber suit and a yellow-trimmed cap. The barbed shaft of a spear gun he held was aimed in their direction!

As the man pulled the trigger, Joe gave his brother a hard shove, separating the boys. The arrow flashed between them and drifted away.

"Wow, what's that guy trying to do?" thought

Frank. Had he mistaken them for fish? Or was he just practising?

The diver made no attempt to come forward and explain or apologize. Instead, he swam off.

"That's strange," Joe said to himself.

Motioning for his brother to follow, he swam towards the diver to find out what he was doing. But not wanting to be questioned, the spearman, with powerful strokes, shot to the surface.

Pointing, Joe indicated to Frank, "Up and after him!"

As the brothers popped above the waves, they looked about. The *Sleuth* lay twenty feet away and the old fisherman was still in the same spot. But the spearman was nowhere in sight.

Frank and Joe lifted their face masks. "Where did he go?" Frank called.

"I can't figure it out," Joe replied, treading water and gazing in all directions. "Let's ask that fisherman."

The boys swam to their motorboat and hung on to the gunwales. Frank called out, "Ahoy there! Did you see another skin diver around here?"

"What's that?" The old fellow, who was wearing a cap which shaded most of his wrinkled face, appeared to be deaf.

Frank shouted, "Did you see a skin diver wearing a black outfit?"

The man laid his pole in the bottom of the boat and cupped both hands over his ears. "Who had a fit?" he called.

"Never mind!" Joe shouted. With a wink at his brother, he said, "Guess he didn't see anybody."

Conjecturing that the stranger might have swum

slightly beneath the surface and taken off towards shore, Frank and Joe decided to resume their diving.

"Down we go," Joe said, as he readjusted the straps that held the air tank on his back. "But keep your eyes open for that spearman."

"Right."

Again the boys submerged. There was no sign of the other diver.

"He sure got away from here fast," Frank thought to himself. "I'd like to know who he is and what he thought he was doing!"

Long, strong strokes with their rubber-finned legs forced the boys downwards through seaweed gardens. Small fish swished in and out among the fronds. Seeing no interesting objects to salvage, Frank signalled Joe to head for deeper water. Air bubbles rippled steadily upwards.

Suddenly a giant form appeared before Frank. A black shark? Frank unsheathed his knife and faced the huge fish. Just then the monster swerved and Frank got a better look at it.

"A tuna!" he told himself, relieved.

As Frank turned to see if his brother was watching, he felt a sudden jar and his face mask was nearly ripped off. Frank clawed desperately to put it in place. "What's going on?" he thought as unconsciousness swept over him.

Joe, who had seen the whole episode, was horror-struck. Another shaft from a spear gun had zipped through the murky deep. From the vast number of bubbles rising through the water, Joe realized that his brother's air hose had been pierced. Water was flooding in!

With powerful strokes, he reached Frank. Towing the limp form with one hand, Joe headed for the *Sleuth*'s anchor line, dim in the distance. Working his fins as violently as possible, he fought his way towards it for what seemed an eternity.

Finally Joe reached the rope and pulled himself to the surface. When both boys bobbed into the air again, Joe tore off Frank's headgear, holding his face above the waves. Then he pushed his brother inside the boat and scrambled after him.

"Frank!" Joe cried out, laying his brother in a prone position and feverishly applying artificial respiration.

Minutes passed before Frank stirred. Joe continued his treatment until he heard a moan, then a feeble question.

"Ugh—where—what happened?"

"We were shot at again and you were hit!" Joe said, helping his brother sit up. "This time it was deliberate."

"The same diver?"

"It must have been."

"Probably hiding behind an underwater rock," Frank concluded.

At that moment the boys heard the fisherman call out, "Something wrong over there?"

Joe shook his head and the old fellow continued his fishing.

"That devilish skin diver must be a phantom," Frank said, after filling his lungs with deep draughts of air.

"I still can't figure him out," Joe mused. "Say, do you suppose he's looking for sunken treasure and wanted to keep us away?"

"I never heard anybody talk about sunken treasure

off Bayport," Frank said.

"No," Joe agreed. "Well, pal, I think you've had enough for one morning. Let's go home."

Waving at the fisherman, he pulled up anchor and started the motor. Two miles away on Barmet Bay was the boathouse where the boys kept the *Sleuth*. As they turned towards the bay entrance, Joe grinned ruefully. "I wish we could have kept that spear for a clue," he remarked, "but it passed clean through your air hose and disappeared."

"Better luck next time."

"What!" Joe exclaimed. "Better no next time at all!" Then he said, "We wouldn't know that fellow even if we should meet him again."

"I did notice one thing," said Frank. "He wore a yellow band round his black swim cap."

"Pretty slim clue. You feeling okay, Frank?" Joe asked, observing how pale his brother was.

The older boy said he had fully recovered from the shock. "Say, look!" he soon added. "Someone's waiting for us at the dock."

Drawing closer, they saw that the man was about thirty-five years old, stockily built, and had wiry, black hair. He stood motionless, his legs braced apart, looking intently at the approaching boys. Joe ran the *Sleuth* inside the boathouse and the brothers stepped ashore.

"Good morning," the stranger said. "My name's Clyde Bowden. I'm from Tampa, Florida. I assume you're the Hardys?"

"That's right," Frank replied, as the trio exchanged handshakes. "What can we do for you?"

"A detecting job."

"That's for us!" said Joe excitedly, but Frank added cautiously, "Let's hear about it first."

The Hardys, star athletes at Bayport High, were the sons of Fenton Hardy. Once a crack detective with the New York City Police Department, Mr Hardy was now an internationally famous private sleuth. The brothers often helped their father on cases and also had solved many mysteries of their own.

Their first big success was *The Mystery of the Aztec Warrior*, and only recently they had had a hair-raising adventure in tracking down *The Secret of the Caves*. Now they seemed to be heading for another mystery.

"How did you know where to find us?" Joe asked.

"I just left your home on Elm Street," Bowden replied. "Your mother said I might meet you here. I understand you're amateur sleuths."

"Yes," said Frank. "While we change from skin-diving gear into clothes, suppose you tell us about your case?"

"I hear that you fellows, as well as your father, do a pretty clever job of detecting," Bowden began.

"Mother didn't tell you that," said Frank, smiling. "She never brags about us."

"No. As a matter of fact, I heard it from your postman."

Frank and Joe grinned at each other as the three left the boathouse, then listened intently as Bowden explained the case. He was searching for an early eighteenth-century cannon known as a Spanish demi-culverin. It was supposed to be in the vicinity of Bayport.

"A Spanish cannon in Bayport?" Joe asked unbelievingly.

"I have reliable information it's around here," Bowden answered. "Although I'm not in a position to tell you how I know about the cannon, I'm certain that with your help I can find it."

As they walked towards the Hardy home, Frank asked the man for the dimensions of the cannon. Bowden described it as being nine feet long and weighing one and a half tons. "It fires an eight-pound shot," he added.

"What do you want the old cannon for?" Joe asked.

Bowden smiled. "Believe it or not, I'm helping to outfit the pirate boats in the famous Gasparilla Exposition in Tampa this year," he replied. "All the details, including the guns, must be authentic."

"That's very interesting," said Frank, as they turned a corner towards the town square. "I should think that the type of cannon you're looking for would be found somewhere around the Caribbean rather than this far north. Many Spanish ships were wrecked—"

Frank stopped speaking as a deafening boom suddenly shook the air.

"What was that?" Bowden gasped, paling.

"It came from the square," Frank replied. "Sounds like trouble. Come on. Let's find out what has happened!"

· 2 · A Suspicious Client

WITH Bowden following, Frank and Joe ran towards a crowd in the town square. They stood round an old

Civil War mortar on a pedestal. White powder smoke drifted from the muzzle.

"Somebody fired the old gun!" Joe cried out in astonishment. "Do you smell that powder?"

"It must have been an accident," Frank said excitedly.

As the brothers made their way through the crowd they saw local police officers Smuff and Riley being questioned by the onlookers.

"What happened?"

"Who set it off?"

"Was anyone hurt?"

Before the policemen could reply, a booming voice sounded and a grizzled old man, dressed in a Minute Man's outfit, complete to tricorn hat and leggings, walked up to the mortar.

"I cain't understand what all this here fussin' is about," he drawled.

Officer Riley stood erect and demanded, "And who do you think you are in that rig?"

The old man's weather-beaten face beamed. He said that he was Jim Tilton, a retired National Guard artillery sergeant. He had been asked by Police Chief Collig to manage the Independence Day cannon salute. "An' I think I look 'propriate for this job," he added.

"But this ain't the fourth of July!" Riley protested. "It's only the first. Why should you come round here bombardin' the town without warnin'?"

The old-timer raised his hands good-naturedly. "I'm mighty sorry I caused so much fuss. After all, I wasn't usin' a ball. I just had some powder an' waddin' in her."

Tilton showed a letter to the officers. It was from Chief Collig and the Fourth-of-July Committee, permitting Tilton to test the mortar.

"Well, there was no harm done," Riley said, "but I should have been notified. But anyway, we know the gun is ready—we and everybody for five miles around!"

Reassured, the crowd dispersed as Officers Smuff and Riley herded them off. Sergeant Tilton remained, talking with a few men. The Hardys moved closer for a better look at the old sergeant and the equipment he had been using.

Bowden also edged forward and stared with keen interest at the various markings on the gun. He told the boys that this was a Federal piece.

"It was cast at the same arsenal that turned out the famous 'Dictator,' " he said. "That was a thirteen-inch mortar used against Petersburg, Virginia, in the Civil War."

"Land sakes," Tilton remarked in surprise, "you know a lot! An' here I am, a veteran of that famous battle between the *Monitor* an' the *Merrimac*, an' I didn't never suspect anything like that about this ol' hunk o' iron."

Everyone laughed and Joe quickly calculated that for Tilton's tall tale to be true he would have to be well over a hundred years old.

As the sergeant began to clean the barrel of the old weapon, Bowden turned to Frank and Joe. "My offer to you," he said in a low voice, "is one thousand dollars if you find the Spanish cannon."

Frank and Joe were amazed. A thousand dollars for an old gun to be used in a pageant!

Sensing their thoughts, Bowden quickly added, "I'm a man of means and can well afford it."

He explained that he had already combed Bayport proper. The boys' responsibility would lie in searching the surrounding areas and nearby towns. Bowden said he was staying at the Garden Gate Motel on the state highway and could be reached there if anything developed.

"We don't charge for our sleuthing," Frank informed the man.

Bowden was astonished. "You've solved all your cases for nothing?"

Joe nodded. "If we should help you," he said, "it will be on that basis."

"Okay. But I'll make it worth your while somehow!" Then, seeing Tilton preparing to leave, Bowden hastily excused himself. "I have a few questions to ask this old codger. See you later."

"Okay, Mr Bowden," Frank replied. "We'll think about your request and let you know."

The Hardys crossed the square and headed for the police station to report the underwater attack on them. They went directly to Chief Collig, a solidly built man in his late forties. He often co-operated with the Hardys on their cases, and now listened intently to their latest adventure.

"This is serious," he said. "I'll tell the harbour patrol to look for a skin diver wearing a black suit and a swim cap with a yellow stripe."

The boys thanked him and left. As they walked up Elm Street on which they lived, their conversation turned to Bowden.

"It seems that we're back in business!" Joe remarked.

"Let's take on the case. It could be interesting."

"I'm a little worried about it," Frank replied. "The whole setup seems a bit phony."

"Your imagination, Frank. Bowden's okay."

Joe was naturally impulsive and always ready for action. Frank reminded him of the many times they had met people who had seemed to be above-board yet had turned out to be dishonest.

"But we'd still have fun looking for the cannon," Joe insisted. "What could we lose?"

"Nothing, maybe."

At the rambling stone house in which they lived, the boys were greeted by their petite mother and their tall, angular Aunt Gertrude—Mr Hardy's sister—who spent most of her time at his house. When she heard of Clyde Bowden's offer, Aunt Gertrude exclaimed tartly:

"A thousand dollars for finding an old piece of junk! There's something underhand about such a deal. Mark my words!"

Mrs Hardy's face wore a worried frown. "I wish your father were here to take the case," she said, "instead of being in Florida."

"Florida!" Joe exclaimed. "Frank, Dad could check on Bowden's credentials. Let's phone him!"

Mrs Hardy said the detective could be reached only by telegram at an address in Miami. Frank wrote it down and hurriedly sent a wire.

"A reply may take several days," Joe remarked. "I hate to wait. Why not make a start on Bowden's case? We can drop it when we like."

"Okay, but let's not get in too deep until we hear from Dad."

"I'll let Bowden know," said Joe. He dialled the

Garden Gate Motel. Bowden was not in, so Joe left a message for him. Then he turned to Frank. "What say we advertise in the newspaper for information about the demiculverin?"

"Good idea." A query was placed in the classified section of the *Bayport Times*, which had a wide circulation in the smaller outlying towns.

"Now we're getting some place!" Joe exulted. "Say, maybe Aunt Gertrude can help us."

"How?"

"As newly elected president of the Bayport Historical Society," Joe said, "she might know of some ancient cannon in the vicinity."

Their aunt had gone to the kitchen to start preparing lunch, so the boys went out there and put the question to her. After a moment's thought, Miss Hardy said, "I know of one cannon."

"Where is it?" Joe asked eagerly.

"Let me see—I think it's on the back lawn of a museum in Greenville."

"Do you know what type it is?" Frank asked.

"I think maybe pre-Civil War," their aunt replied. "Possibly Spanish. I'm not sure."

"We'll take a look," said Joe.

After lunch the boys drove to the Greenville Museum. Frank parked in front alongside the hedge, and the two walked through a gate to the spacious lawn at the back.

The cannon, a long-barrelled six-pounder, stood in the centre of the plot. Joe read the plaque fixed to the piece.

"It's a Spanish gun!"

Frank joined him and read the inscription on the

bronze plaque. It stated:

"*Pasavolante*, meaning fast action. Made in Toledo, Spain. Often called *cerbatana*, after Cerebus, the fierce dog of mythology. *Pasavolante* in modern Spanish means peashooter."

"Do you suppose this could be the peashooter that Bowden is searching for and he just got the name wrong?" Joe asked.

"I doubt it," Frank answered. "Bowden seemed sure it was a demiculverin."

"False clue," Joe sighed.

As the brothers started back across the lawn, they noticed a tall, slender man, with a swarthy complexion, entering from a side gate. Bare-headed and wearing a black cotton motorcycle jacket, he moved hurriedly towards the gun.

The boys looked back at him as they walked. Now the man was kneeling at the *pasavolante*. Frank and Joe saw him rise and run to the far side of the cannon to scrutinize it.

"Maybe he's trying to locate a demiculverin too," Joe remarked. "Let's go back and ask."

Retracing their steps, they had covered only a few feet when the man suddenly ran for the side gate by which he had entered.

"He must be goofy," Joe remarked.

The brothers turned back to the road. Then they heard a motorcycle roar into action.

The swarthy stranger, wearing goggles, sped round the corner, directly towards the boys!

·3· *A Motorcycle Clue*

As THE motorcycle roared down on them, Frank and Joe leaped aside and stumbled headlong into the hedge. The driver missed them by inches!

"Sorry!" he shouted and sped off.

The boys angrily picked themselves up.

"Did that lunatic mean he was sorry he didn't hit us?" Joe stormed.

"I'd like to get my hands on him!" Frank said. "Look at my trousers!" The sharp twigs of the hedge had made a long tear in them.

"Did you get his licence number?" Joe asked.

"No," Frank answered ruefully. "But the motorcycle looked like a foreign make. I saw the letter K on the rear bumper."

"If I ever see that fellow again, he'll have some explaining to do as to why he nearly hit us," said Joe. "And I'd like to ask him about his interest in the old cannon, too."

"He certainly acted as if he was afraid he might be noticed," said Frank.

At home they hurried into the kitchen. Aunt Gertrude was removing a batch of biscuits from the oven. She exclaimed, "No need to charge in here like a herd of buffalo!"

"We smelled the biscuits and couldn't wait to have some," Joe said with a grin, as he reached for the tray of hot ginger snaps.

This subtle flattery softened the maiden lady's stern demeanour. "Well, have one," she said. "But eat too fast and you'll get indigestion."

"Indigestion!" Frank cried out. "What did you do? Bake rocks in 'em?"

Aunt Gertrude gave her nephew a withering look. Although she would be the last person to admit it, she enjoyed the boys' teasing. But to hear her scold and correct them, a listener might think Frank and Joe were the bane of her existence. Aunt Gertrude's peppery manner, however, concealed a great depth of affection for them.

"Frank!" she sputtered. "You've torn your trousers!"

"Had a little accident," he admitted, and told her of the motorcyclist.

"I knew it!" Miss Hardy declared. "Hoodlums are after you again. Stay away from them!"

Frank suppressed a chuckle while Aunt Gertrude took another tray of biscuits from the oven. "You wouldn't want us to let 'em run around loose, would you?" he teased.

"Well, don't say I didn't warn you." His aunt sighed. "Trouble, trouble," she added to herself.

"What trouble?" Frank asked.

"The Bayport Historical Society," Aunt Gertrude replied. "What would you do with a case full of swords?"

Frank nearly choked on a biscuit. "Swords!"

"Yes, cutlasses. I'd like to keep them."

"Please, Aunty, start from the beginning," Joe begged, "and tell us about it."

Aunt Gertrude explained that the Society had recently received a gift from the estate of Senator

Entwistle. It included some lovely old costumes dating from 1812 and a case of cutlasses.

"I argued with our members," Aunt Gertrude went on, "but they insist that we present the cutlasses to the museum at the state capital."

"Too bad," said Frank, then asked, "Is it your job to have them shipped?"

"Yes," she replied. "But the cutlasses are to be moved to the basement temporarily. The museum isn't ready to receive them."

"And you'd like us to help you," the boys said in unison.

"Yes. Tomorrow evening."

"We'll be there."

Frank and Joe went to their room to plan the next move in locating the cannon.

"We can't do anything out of town today," said Frank, glancing at the table clock between the boys' beds. "It's almost time for dinner."

"There's something we *can* do," Joe spoke up. "Visit the motorcycle shops in Bayport and find out the name of the foreign make with a K."

"Good idea, Joe. We may even learn the identity of that fellow who nearly ran us down."

"What are we waiting for? Let's go!" Joe urged.

The boys had better luck than they had anticipated. The first dealer they called on explained that the letter K indicated the motorcycle was the Kesselring, a German make.

"You don't see many of them around," he said. "But they're becoming more popular."

"Do you sell them?" Frank asked.

"No."

"Who does?"

"Nobody in Bayport. And no one in town owns one, either."

"Do you know where the nearest agency is located?" Frank asked.

"Yes," the dealer replied. "In Delmore."

"The penitentiary is there," Joe remarked.

The man nodded. "The dealer mostly sells bikes, but he took on the Kesselring motorcycle agency because he is German."

The Hardys exchanged glances. Had the man they had seen on a Kesselring bought his motorcycle in Delmore? The boys thanked the dealer and rode off in their convertible.

"What say we drive over to Delmore in the morning and talk to that agent?" Joe suggested.

"We'll do it," Frank agreed. "The main road there is still closed. The detour leads past the Entwistle place where the cutlasses came from."

At home the boys were greeted by the aroma of fried chicken that their mother was preparing.

"You're just in time," she said, smiling.

The boys washed, then followed Mrs Hardy and Aunt Gertrude to the table.

"Any word from Dad?" Frank asked.

"No," Mrs Hardy replied. "But we should hear something soon."

Joe asked his aunt about the Entwistle mansion. She had heard it was deserted. "And it's such a beautiful place. A Society member hinted that there might be some valuable pieces, which the executors didn't find, in the house. He said Mr Entwistle was eccentric. They say tramps stay there sometimes."

That evening the boys decided to take a look at the Entwistle mansion.

"Maybe we can find out if there's really anything in the old place," said Frank, as they drove along the detour road towards the old estate.

"Yes—" Joe began, then broke off as the noisy approach of a motorcycle reached his ears. The next moment he exclaimed, "Hey, Frank! That sounds like the Kesselring cycle!"

His brother listened intently. "You're right. Hope he comes this way."

But the Hardys were disappointed when the sound of the motorcycle grew fainter.

"He must have turned down a side road," Joe said. "Let's try to catch up with him."

Frank was about to agree when both boys saw something that made them gasp.

"That red glow in the sky!" Joe exclaimed. "It's right where the Entwistle mansion is!"

"The place must be on fire!" cried out Frank, stepping harder on the accelerator.

Soon they came within sight of the grounds. On a knoll stood the huge house. One wing was a mass of flames!

"We must get the fire department here before the whole place goes up!" said Frank.

He backed the car round, and in a few minutes the boys reached a farmhouse, where they put in a call to Bayport reporting the fire.

Then they sped back to the scene of the blaze. Getting out of the car, they heard sirens wailing. Minutes later, several fire engines halted before the burning mansion. Shouts of firemen filled the air while they fought to restrict damage to the wing that was being consumed.

Finally, after half an hour's battle, the flames were quenched and the bulk of the big house stood unscathed. Chief Tally, after investigating the charred ruins, returned to his car. A good friend of the Hardys, he greeted the boys with a weary smile. Frank told him they had heard that articles of value might be hidden in the house.

"Could be," the fire chief said. "We suspect an intruder was ransacking the place and dropped a lighted cigarette."

Joe told him of hearing a motorcyclist racing away near the Entwistle place. "He might be the one who was here," he said.

Chief Tally smiled. "You boys are always on the job but this is the quickest I've ever received a clue. If you find out anything else about this rider, let me know."

Frank then told him about the man on the Kesselring who had nearly run the boys down. "The machine we heard tonight had the same kind of roar," he said.

"Thanks. I'll keep the information in mind." The chief nodded, then turned to speak to two firemen who would remain at the mansion, and the boys returned to their convertible.

"Frank," said Joe as they drove home, "if that rider is a housebreaker, he may be interested in the cannon for no good reason."

The boys slept well, but early the next morning the telephone awakened them. When Frank reached the hallway to answer it, he heard his mother talking on her bedroom extension. The door was open and she waved him in.

"Fenton, here's Frank now," she said. "You tell him." She turned to her son, excitedly. "That man Bowden is a fake!" she announced.

• 4 •   *New Tactics*

"DAD! Hello!" Frank said. "How are you? . . . That's good. What about Bowden?"

"The man isn't known here in Tampa, Frank."

"Then he was lying about his pageant work?"

"Definitely. No pirate ship with a demiculverin has been entered in the Gasparilla event."

Frank whistled. "I've been suspicious of Bowden from the start. But you don't think we should stop looking for the cannon, do you?"

"No. There's a mystery connected with it. Furthermore, I'm working on a case—swindlers—that Bowden may be mixed up in. Apparently he's using an assumed name."

"Shall we notify the police or shadow him ourselves?" Frank asked.

Mr Hardy advised them to do neither. Instead, he said to stay friendly with Bowden and not let him know they had uncovered his lie.

"It's the best way to get at the truth," he said. "And let me know if I can be of any more help. I'd like to speak to your mother again."

Frank dashed to tell his brother the news.

"Hot-diggety-dog!" Joe cried, hopping out of bed.

"Frank, this is going to be fun. We pretend to play along with Bowden, but all the time we're trying to find out what he's up to!"

"Which problem should we tackle first—Bowden or the motorcyclist?" said Frank.

"Let's combine them in one trip. We'll go to the motel first, then on to Delmore," Joe suggested.

"Okay."

During breakfast with Mrs Hardy and Aunt Gertrude, they related their plan, and when they finished eating, made for the door. Aunt Gertrude stopped them and handed Joe a book.

"You boys might as well employ your time profitably while you're riding along. Joe, read this aloud while Frank drives."

Her nephew glanced at the book. "Why, this is great, Aunt Gertrude! It tells about the various types of artillery. Where did you find this book?"

"In your father's library." She chuckled. "I thought it might give you a clue to that demiculverin you're trying to find."

The boys hugged her, then kissed their mother.

"We'll be home in time to move those cutlasses," they promised.

As the brothers rode off, Joe consulted the index of the book. Then he turned to a section on culverins and read aloud:

"It derives from the Latin word *colubra* [snake]. Culverins were highly esteemed for their range and effectiveness of fire. Their thick walls, long bores, and heavy powder charges made them the deadliest of fieldpieces."

"Fieldpieces!" Frank interrupted. "Why would

Bowden want a fieldpiece on a pirate ship?"

Joe grinned. "Maybe he doesn't know any better. Score one for us!"

Half a mile farther along the highway, Frank pulled up in front of the Garden Gate Motel. The clerk was not at his desk when the boys entered, but a maid told them Bowden was in Cabin 15.

The brothers walked down a long row of rooms.

"There it is!" Joe said, spotting the number. He knocked on the door. There was no answer, so he tried again. Still Bowden did not come.

"Say, this looks like a note," Joe said, eyeing a folded paper pinned below the doorknob.

"Maybe it's for us," Frank suggested.

He and Joe peered at the printed message and opened their eyes wide in amazement. It read:

> *Bowden! Clear out before it's too late!*

"Wow! His enemy!" Frank exclaimed.

"Sounds as if he means business, whoever he is," Joe whispered.

In hushed tones the brothers discussed the threat. Why did Bowden have such a deadly enemy? Was it because of the demiculverin?

"This may drive Bowden away," Joe remarked. "Then we'll lose track of him."

Frank shook his head. "I doubt it. He wants that cannon too badly. Well, let's go to Delmore and stop here on our way back."

The detour they had to make took the boys past the farm of their friend Chet Morton. Chet was eighteen, roly-poly, good-natured, and loved to eat. Solving mysteries with the Hardys always gave him the jitters. Despite this, he was a loyal assistant and on more than one occasion had saved them from dangerous predicaments.

"Let's stop a minute," Joe suggested, seeing Chet's sister Iola near the swimming pool.

Frank grinned knowingly. Joe and Iola dated frequently. The boys parked in the driveway and approached the pretty brunette.

"Hi!" she said.

"Hi, yourself!" Joe said. "Where's Chet?"

Iola pointed into the pool. Their stout friend was under water, wearing flippers and a snorkel. He travelled slowly, the snorkel moving like the periscope of a miniature submarine.

"Ahoy!" Joe yelled, as the brothers ran to the water's edge.

Chet moved about like a walrus. Finally he emerged and removed the face mask and flippers.

"Hi, fellows!" he called. "This business is difficult. Can't get down deep enough."

"What's the trouble?" Joe asked. "That extra fat making you too buoyant?" he teased.

"Now, listen here," said Chet, "just because I know good food when I see it—"

He smacked his lips as if imagining he was about to taste something delicious. Then he changed the subject, telling them he was going to take lessons in skin diving from the same man who had taught the Hardys.

"Swell," said Joe.

"I can't start, though, until I earn enough money to buy all the gear."

"Don't let that worry you," Frank spoke up. "I'll lend you my outfit."

"Thanks. And now bring me up to date on everything that's happened lately."

The Hardys had just finished telling Chet and Iola about Bowden, the mysterious cyclist, and the skin-diving attack, when a car drove in. At the wheel sat Callie Shaw, an attractive girl with blonde hair and sparkling brown eyes. She was Iola's chum and Frank's regular date.

Callie alighted, and after greeting everyone, said, "I'm glad you're all here. I wanted to talk over plans for our Fourth-of-July beach party. Tony Prito is coming with us too."

Tony, a schoolmate and fellow athlete at Bayport High, had been through many adventures with the Hardys.

"Let's have a clambake like last year," Frank suggested.

"And lobster," Joe added. "Tell you what, Chet. You can put on my diving gear and get us some lobsters."

"Not me," said Chet. "I wouldn't tangle with that human devilfish who shot at you fellows."

Iola looked worried. "Do you think he's still lurking around?" she asked.

The Hardys doubted this. "He knows we're looking for him, so he'll probably keep out of sight," Joe reasoned.

Suddenly Frank grabbed Joe's arm. "Look over there! Someone's spying on us!"

He had seen an intruder peering from behind a tree near the road. The quick glimpse of a black jacket led Frank to believe that the man might be the wanted motorcyclist!

"Come on, Joe!" he whispered, setting off.

Instantly the man dodged from behind the tree and started to run. The chase was on!

Having the advantage of a head start, the man managed to keep ahead of them. Then he jumped on a parked motorcycle and sped off.

From the silhouette of the rider and the sound of the motor, there was no doubt in the Hardys' minds as to the spy's identity.

"It's the rider we're looking for!" Joe exclaimed.

Together, the brothers ran back to their car and hurried after the suspect. They had covered nearly two miles before they caught sight of the man. Reaching the crest of the next slope, he looked back. Sensing that his pursuers were getting closer, the rider revved his machine and shot out of sight into the curving downgrade.

"Faster!" Joe urged. "He's getting away!"

Frank bore down and their car whined round the curve in hot pursuit of the Kesselring. Once again in the open, where the highway stretched out for miles, the boys could no longer see the motorcycle.

"He's turned off!" Joe said in disappointment. "But where?"

Frank's brow furrowed. "He couldn't have reached this point," Frank replied. "He must have swung into that dirt road we just passed. Let's go back!"

Screeching to a stop, he made a U turn and sped to the side road. Joe cried out, "I see a single skid track going in there! That's the place!"

Frank swung the car across the road and they plunged onto the rough, narrow, dirt lane. Fresh motorcycle tracks were clearly evident. Dust filled the air, choking the boys as they sped along.

"Stop!" Joe cried suddenly. "The track ends here!"

The car parked and locked, they ran back to where the tracks turned off into the pine woods.

"He couldn't go far through here on his machine," Frank said, as they pressed on excitedly.

"You're right!" Joe whispered a moment later. "Look!"

· 5 ·   The Stakeout

AHEAD of the Hardys in the deep woods stood a cabin. The Kesselring motorcycle was parked near the front door. Quietly the brothers moved into position for a better view of the one-room building. This must be the suspect's hide-out!

"End of our search," Joe whispered exultantly.

The brothers moved forward. Frank signalled Joe to cover the rear of the cabin while he went to the front door. It was open and the place appeared to be deserted. Frank strode inside. The rider was not in sight and there was no place where he might be hiding.

"He gave us the slip," said Frank as Joe joined him.

"But not for long," Joe declared. "He'll return for his cycle."

Frank suggested that they pretend to leave, then double back and stay in hiding until the man returned.

"Suppose he finds out our car is still on the road?" Joe said.

"We'll have to take that chance," his brother declared.

The boys walked off in the direction of their convertible, but five hundred feet beyond the cabin they turned and quietly made their way back. Hiding behind clumps of brush, they began their vigil. Fifteen minutes went by. Thirty.

Suddenly the quiet of the morning was broken by the crackling sound of approaching footsteps. The Hardys tensed. The person was approaching from behind them. They shifted their position.

"Get ready, Joe," Frank whispered.

The steps grew louder and a man appeared through the brush. The boys pounced on him, and they all fell on the ground. Frank and Joe sprang up immediately to look at their victim.

"Bowden!" Joe gasped.

"For heaven's sake, what ails you guys?" the man stormed, picking himself up.

"We—we thought you were someone else," Joe replied.

"Who?" Bowden demanded.

"We don't know," Frank answered.

"That's ridiculous," Bowden declared scornfully.

"Maybe," said Frank, wondering if Bowden had a rendezvous with the occupant of the cabin. "Why are you here?" he asked.

"I might ask you the same thing," Bowden retorted.

"That's easily answered," Frank said, pointing to the motorcycle. "We want to talk to the man who owns it."

"Do you know him?" Joe asked Bowden.

"Never saw the thing before," he answered.

"Now tell us what brings you here," Frank went on.

"A tip about the demiculverin." Bowden glanced about apprehensively. "It may be buried near here."

Both boys surmised this was another phony story. Bowden was carrying no digging tools, nor was he dressed in work clothes.

"Oh, I know I don't look like a digger," he said, as if reading their thoughts. "I was just looking for a likely place to excavate."

"Who gave you the tip?" Frank asked.

"I can't tell you that. The information was given to me in confidence."

Frank was tempted to ask Bowden why he wanted a fieldpiece for a ship. But recalling his father's admonition, he merely said:

"Sorry we knocked you down, Mr Bowden. And tell us if you need help to dig here."

Joe followed Frank's cue to be pleasant. "We went to the motel to see you this morning," he said. "Frank and I thought we'd talk to you a little more about the cannon you want us to find."

Frank broke in. "We saw the warning note on your door." He watched Bowden closely.

"Warning note?" the man repeated, showing real surprise. After Frank explained, Bowden suddenly laughed. "I guess those kids at the motel were pulling a joke on me. They were playing cops-and-robbers when I left." He glanced at his wrist watch. "I must get back."

He strode off in the direction of the road. Joe turned to Frank. "Do you believe that cops-and-robbers story?"

"No. there wasn't a child around that motel. I think

one of us ought to follow Bowden and send the police
up here."

"Good idea. You go; I'll stay," Joe offered.

"Pick you up later."

While Joe concealed himself to stake out the cabin,
Frank cautiously followed the suspect. Presently
Bowden got into a car parked some distance ahead of
the Hardys' and rode off.

"Wonder where he's going," Frank said to himself.
"I'll bet we interrupted a meeting."

He climbed into the convertible and started it.
Keeping a discreet distance behind Bowden, so that he
would not become suspicious, he trailed him. Frank
was disappointed when the man went directly to his
motel and entered his cabin. He did not come out.

"I'll phone Chief Collig," Frank decided, and drove
on to the next gas station to make the call.

He quickly dialled headquarters and talked with the
officer. The police chief agreed to send two men to the
woods at once to relieve Joe.

"Good work," he added.

Frank returned to the woods and proceeded
cautiously to the cabin in case the suspect was hiding
nearby. Joe was not in sight. But after Frank gave
several birdcalls which they used as signals, Joe
emerged from behind a tree.

"Anything doing?" Frank asked.

Joe shook his head, then Frank told him about
Bowden and Chief Collig. Ten minutes later the boys
were relieved by two plain-clothes men who took over
the watch.

The Hardys hurried through the woods and drove on
towards Delmore. It was nearly noon when they arrived

in that town. Passing the massive stone walls of the state prison, they turned into the business section of town and located the motorcycle shop.

"Good morning," said the short, smiling proprietor who introduced himself as Mr Braun. "You wish to rent or buy a bike?"

"We're interested in your Kesselrings," Frank replied. "Do you sell them?"

"Yes, I have the agency. But I haven't sold one of those motorcycles in a long time. One's been standing in my basement for weeks. Would you like to see it?"

Frank and Joe looked at each other. Was their clue going to lead nowhere?

Joe said, "Yes, I'd like to see it."

Mr Braun opened a trap-door in the floor, flicked on a light switch, and the three descended a flight of wooden stairs. The man walked round a high pile of cartons, then suddenly exclaimed:

"*Ach, Himmel!*"

"What's the matter?" Frank asked.

The proprietor clapped a hand to his head. "My Kesselring! It's gone! Stolen!"

Mr Braun excitedly added that he had been on a vacation for two weeks and had just returned. The Kesselring had been there when he left.

"*Ach*, what will I do?" he wailed. "I never should have closed my shop!"

Frank laid a hand on the man's shoulder. "You may get the motorcycle back this very day," he said. He told of finding a machine at the cabin, and that policemen were now at the spot waiting to capture the thief. The dealer was overjoyed at the news.

Frank at once telephoned this latest development to

Chief Collig, while Mr Braun thanked the boys repeatedly. Then they said good-bye and left. After a quick lunch at a nearby snack-bar, the Hardys returned to their convertible.

"Joe, I have a hunch," said Frank. "That motorcycle thief might be a recently-released inmate of the penitentiary. Mr Braun's shop in Delmore would be a likely place for him to rob. Let's ask Warden Duckworth some questions."

"Good idea."

The warden was an old friend of Mr Hardy, and the boys had once assisted him in solving a prison break. Reaching the penitentiary, Frank called him from the main gate phone. A guard accompanied them to Warden Duckworth's office, where the official greeted them cordially.

"What brings you 'way out here from Bayport?" he asked.

Frank told him their suspicions and said, "We'd like to find out the names of men released from here within the past two weeks."

Warden Duckworth rose, walked to his filing cabinet, checked the records, and returned with some forms. "We've let six men go," he replied. "Four old-timers and a couple of young fellows. All had served their time."

"We can forget about the old-timers," Frank said. "The man we suspect is probably in his twenties. Who were the young ones?"

"One is Bob Chidsie, a car thief. The other, Hal Latsky, a safecracker."

"May we see their pictures?" Frank asked.

"Certainly." Duckworth handed over the record cards, to which small photos were attached.

"That's the motorcycle thief!" Joe said immediately, pointing to Latsky.

Frank looked thoughtful. "Don't forget, Joe, we've never seen this fellow close up without his goggles. Warden, could you tell us something more about him?"

"Yes—" The man studied Latsky's card for a moment. "Besides safecracking, he's an explosives expert. Also, he has an unusual hobby—the study of ancient cannon!"

• 6 •   *Profitable Sleuthing*

AT THE mention of Latsky's interest in ancient cannon, Frank cried out, "That convinces me, Warden! Latsky is the man we're after."

Once more the Hardys telephoned Chief Collig, who was even more amazed than before at the brothers' sleuthing. "We'll have you on the force yet!" he said jokingly.

He told them of the stakeout in the woods. Having learned from Braun the serial numbers of the stolen motorcycle, the chief had short-waved them to his men at the cabin. They had then made positive identification of the vehicle.

"It's the stolen Kesselring all right," said the police chief. "The thief hasn't returned yet, but we'll maintain a round-the-clock surveillance for as long as we need it. Braun has agreed to co-operate by leaving the motorcycle there awhile as bait for the thief. He might try to get it back."

Before the Hardys left, Warden Duckworth gave them pictures of Latsky. "Give these to Chief Collig," he requested.

On the way to Bayport the boys discussed the strange turn of events. If Latsky were the motorcycle rider, was he trailing the Hardys because they were searching for an old cannon? Did he know Bowden, and had the two planned a meeting in the woods? Or were they enemies, both looking for the old demiculverin?

"I'll phone Warden Duckworth and see if he can tell us anything about Bowden," said Frank.

At home, Frank immediately put in the call. The warden said he had no released prisoner on his list named Bowden, nor had he ever heard Latsky mention anyone by that name.

"I'll ask the guards and prisoners, though," Warden Duckworth promised. An hour later he called back. "If Latsky knows anyone named Bowden, he never mentioned it here."

"Thanks, anyway," said Frank, and hung up.

He was disappointed not to have uncovered another clue but turned his attention to Aunt Gertrude who had just come in the front door. She was waving three letters.

"I picked these up from the box at the newspaper office," she said, handing them over. "You forgot all about your ad. I suppose these are some answers from cranks. Well, hurry up and open them. I'm entitled to know what's inside!"

Frank smiled as he tore open the first envelope. Joe came to read over his brother's shoulder.

The writer of the first note was the amusing old artillery sergeant who had set off the mortar in the town square the day before. Sergeant Tilton said that he lived up the coast near Pirates' Hill. He had once heard of an old cannon on the hill, but it had been buried by sand in a storm many years ago—long before Tilton's birth.

"That's a swell lead!" Joe exclaimed enthusiastically.

Both boys agreed that the message should be investigated.

The second letter came from Mr Maglan, the retired custodian of the Bayport Historical Society. Frank opened it.

"Wait till you hear this, Aunty." He chuckled.

"Why, what is it?"

"Mr Maglan says three old cannons have been stored in the cellar of the Historical Society's building for thirty years! The new custodian, Mr Lightbody, evidently doesn't know about them."

"What!" exclaimed Miss Hardy. "Cannons in the basement!"

Joe roared with laughter. "Why, Aunt Gertrude, you've been sitting right above three loaded guns all these years without knowing it. I always thought you knew everything about the Bayport Historical Society building."

The boys' aunt did not laugh. "This is serious. Suppose there is powder in them! Why—"

Frank assured her that thirty-year-old gunpowder would be damp and harmless. Aunt Gertrude merely said "Humph!" and then reminded her nephews tartly about carrying the cutlasses to the basement. "Mr Lightbody says they're in the way."

"We'll go right after supper," Joe said. "And we'll investigate those old cannons as well."

The third note was of more serious import. Letters of the alphabet had been cut from newspapers and pasted on the paper to form words.

The message bore no signature—nor a mark to indicate one. It read:

Look for the cannon at your own risk. If you're smart you'll drop Bowden's case.

"Wow! Things are getting complicated!" Joe exclaimed. "The camps are lining up."

"Yes," Frank agreed. "And the writer must have found out we put that ad in the paper."

When Mrs Hardy heard about the threat, she became alarmed. Both she and Aunt Gertrude appealed to the boys to drop the case, at least until their father returned from Florida.

"We can't stop now," Frank protested. "Joe and I are onto some good leads. And Dad wants us on the case. But we will be careful."

Both women sighed. Then Aunt Gertrude said, "Well, Laura, I suppose with three men against us—and one of them my brother—we'll have to give in. But I want to go on record as saying that if you boys get hurt, you can't blame—"

The ringing of the telephone interrupted Aunt Gertrude's tirade. Joe grabbed up the phone and everyone waited tensely.

"Maybe it's Fenton," Mrs Hardy whispered.

Frank noticed Joe's jaws tighten as he listened to the message. It could not be their father.

"Frank," Joe whispered, "come here! It's Bowden. He wants to talk to you, too."

His brother put his ear close to the phone. "Hello," he said, "this is Frank."

Bowden's voice sounded scared. "Listen! You've got to help me! I've been threatened!"

"By whom?" Frank asked. "Those kids again?"

"No, no. This is for real!" Bowden's voice was shaky and faint. But suddenly it became strong again. "Fr-ank! Joe!" he cried out.

"Were you threatened by someone named Latsky?" Frank demanded.

There was no answer.

"Mr Bowden?" Frank said questioningly.

Still there was no response, but suddenly the Hardys heard a thud and the noise of a phone dropping onto a hard surface.

"Hello! Hello!" Frank kept saying.

There was dead silence for another moment. Then a strange voice said ominously:

"You Hardy boys! Drop the cannon search at once! This is your last warning!"

The threat ended with a sharp click in the Hardys' receiver as the intruder in Bowden's cabin slammed down the telephone.

Frank whirled to face his brother. "It sounds as if Bowden has been attacked! Probably by the person who just gave us that final warning!"

Joe started for the door. "Let's hurry over to Bowden's motel. We may catch the guy."

Frank thought it best to get help to Bowden immediately. "He may be seriously injured. I'll notify the desk clerk at the Garden Gate."

With frantic haste, Frank dialled the motel office number, but the line was busy.

"Come on!" Joe urged impatiently. "We can get there in a few minutes if we hurry."

When they reached the motel, Frank parked in front of Cabin 15. The door stood ajar and the brothers burst inside.

Bowden lay face down on the floor, unconscious. Blood trickled from the back of his head!

· 7 · *Mysterious Attackers*

As JOE and Frank rushed over to Bowden, the man groaned slightly and moved his arms. Frank turned him over.

"I'll get some water," Joe offered, and hurried to the bathroom for it.

He filled a glass and sprinkled some of the water against the prostrate man's neck and face. Bowden shook his head dazedly as he regained consciousness, and the boys helped him to his feet.

"How did you—?" he stammered, recognizing them. "Where's—? Oh, my head!"

Frank assisted Bowden to the bed, where Joe applied an antiseptic bandage he had found in the bathroom medicine chest. Then they began to question him. Bowden said he had not seen his attacker.

"I hadn't locked my door," he explained. "Somebody must have sneaked up from behind and hit me with a blackjack!"

"Latsky?" Frank queried, watching Bowden narrowly.

"Never heard of him," he replied.

"Who threatened you?" Joe asked.

"I don't know. An unsigned note had been shoved

under my door. It's right—" Bowden looked towards the telephone stand. "Why—" he sputtered. "It's gone! It was right there!"

"Your attacker must have taken it," said Joe.

Frank telephoned the desk clerk to report the assault. The clerk said he had not seen anybody prowling around, and promised to notify the local police at once.

As Bowden's condition improved, the brothers tried to ferret out more information from their mysterious client. "Where did you say you live in Tampa?" Joe inquired.

"I didn't say. Why do you ask?"

Joe explained that he thought Bowden's family or friends should be notified in case of serious trouble.

"Forget it," Bowden replied with a wave of the hand. "I haven't any family."

The man's reluctance to tell where he lived seemed to confirm Mr Hardy's suspicion that Bowden might be mixed up with a group of swindlers. But the brothers gave no sign of this.

"About the demiculverin," Frank went on. "I read that it's a fieldpiece and not used on ships."

Bowden was startled for a moment but regained his composure by pulling out a cigar. Lighting it, he said, "I admire your thoroughness. But I didn't want the cannon for a ship, only for a pageant—as part of the shore batteries."

"Oh," Frank said nonchalantly, "then the demiculverin isn't too important."

"What?"

"If it's just for a dummy shore battery, you can rig up a wooden one," Frank added.

"But—but, boys!" Bowden's face grew red with

excitement. "I must have the old cannon. Everything has to be authentic."

He laid a firm hand on Frank's arm. "You must help me! I'll double the reward. How about two thousand dollars?"

"It's not the money, Mr Bowden," Frank replied. "It's just that—"

"All right, I'll co-operate better," he said pleadingly.

"For example?"

"I can't reveal all my secrets, but I feel certain the cannon will be found along the shore here," Bowden declared.

"We'll do our best," Frank promised.

When the police arrived, the boys told them all they knew about the attack on Bowden but said nothing about the threat to themselves. Then they left.

"What do you make of it?" Joe asked his brother as they drove away from the motel.

"This mystery is getting more complicated by the minute," Frank replied. "Bowden has an enemy all right, and he's lying when he says he doesn't know who."

On the way home the boys noticed another convertible following them. In the rear-view mirror, Frank saw that the slender, good-looking young man who was driving was alone.

"Do you think he's trailing us?" Frank asked, as the car remained fifty feet behind the Hardys' for about half a mile.

"Why don't you find out? Slow down and see if he'll pass," Joe suggested.

Frank did so. The other driver pulled out and zoomed ahead. As he passed the Hardy car, he stared hard at the boys.

"Did you recognize him, Frank?"

"Never saw him before."

When the brothers arrived home, Aunt Gertrude told them that the Historical Society had just decided to hold a special meeting that evening. "You can drive me to the meeting and carry the cutlasses to the basement while you're there," she said.

After supper Frank and Joe accompanied Miss Hardy to the meeting place.

As Miss Hardy alighted, she pointed to a basement window which was open. "Such carelessness!" she exclaimed. "I must speak to Mr. Lightbody! Frank— Joe, please close it when you're in the basement. Humph! The whole place'll be full of stray cats!"

Her nephews grinned, followed their aunt to the front of the building, and went inside.

"The cutlasses are at the rear of that corridor," Aunt Gertrude said, pointing. "Carry them down to the basement and don't disturb our meeting!" Then she walked briskly into the auditorium.

"How about a look at the heavy artillery while we're there?" Joe said.

They looked about for the custodian to show them the basement entrance, but could not locate him. "I guess we can find our way," Frank said.

He walked over to a door and pulled it gingerly. Instead of leading to the basement, it opened into the auditorium.

Aunt Gertrude was on the dais, gavel in hand. "The meeting will come to order," she said with authority, and the ensuing bang made it plain that she meant every word.

As the members quickly quietened, Frank saw the

custodian seated in the front row. He was a small, thin man with grey hair and wispy moustache. The boys decided not to bother him.

"Let's try this door," Joe said, walking across the corridor. He turned the knob. The door yawned open into pitch darkness.

"This is the basement entrance, all right." He reached inside for the light switch and flicked it on. There was no response.

"I guess the bulb's burned out," Joe said. "I'll get a flashlight from the car, Frank."

He hurried outside and brought back a powerful flashlight which the boys carried in their car at all times. As Joe beamed it down the steps, Frank lifted the case of cutlasses to his shoulder.

"Lead the way, Joe."

Joe preceded his brother slowly down the cellar steps. "Careful, Frank," he warned. "They're steep."

The next moment Joe pitched forward. A blow on the side of his head had knocked him unconscious.

"Joe, what's happened?" Frank cried as the flashlight flew forward and rolled under a table.

In the feeble light Frank missed his footing and lost his balance. The case of cutlasses fell from his shoulder and landed with a jangling crash. Frank banged his head full force on the case and blacked out.

His outcry and the crash of the case threw the Historical Society meeting into an uproar. Mr Lightbody jumped to his feet.

At the same time Aunt Gertrude pounded her gavel for order. "Keep calm. I'll find out what's wrong downstairs. Come, Mr Lightbody! Vice-President, please take the chair!"

Miss Hardy charged to the basement door ahead of the custodian and felt her way down the steps. "Frank! Joe!" she called.

Groping in the darkness, she found the flashlight which was still lit. Waving it around, she gasped.

Dashing for the open window was a man in a motorcycle jacket, a mask over his face.

In his arms were five cutlasses, which had been hurled from the case. The sixth lay on the floor. Beyond it were the two brothers, motionless.

Quickly sizing up the situation, Aunt Gertrude reached down for the free cutlass, at the same time crying, "You scoundrel! What have you done to my nephews?"

With a flailing motion, she slapped the man's back with the broad side of the cutlass. He shoved her back.

"Oh, no, you don't!" she cried out.

Thwack! She hit him again. Terrified, the man dropped the five cutlasses with a din heard in the meeting room upstairs and leaped to the sill. As he started to crawl through the window, Aunt Gertrude whacked him again!

· 8 ·   *The Battle of Bayport*

With the intruder gone, Miss Hardy turned her attention to Frank and Joe.

"Where's the electrical panel, Mr Lightbody?" she asked.

"Under the stairs." He found it and reported that the

basement switch had been pulled, probably by the intruder. The custodian flicked the handle up and the place was flooded with light.

"What happened?" someone called out from the top of the stairs. "Do you need help?"

"Call the police," said Miss Hardy, as she began to chafe her nephews' wrists and the backs of their necks. They soon regained consciousness.

The only injuries the boys had sustained were bruises on their heads. Joe surmised that he had been hit with a blackjack.

After Aunt Gertrude had given a brief description of the assailant, Frank said tersely, "Sounds like Latsky. Let's check for clues to make sure."

As they searched, Mr Lightbody said the basement windows were always locked. The intruder must have forced one open.

Chief Collig arrived in a few minutes and heard the complete story from Aunt Gertrude. "Frank and Joe think it was Latsky," she concluded.

The officer agreed. But a search outside the building revealed no clues except footprints.

"Let's look for fingerprints, boys," Chief Collig suggested. With his kit from the patrol car they searched the basement with no results.

"Latsky must have worn gloves," the officer decided.

"I didn't notice," Aunt Gertrude and Mr Lightbody said together.

An instant later Frank leaned down and cried out, "Here's a button from the fellow's jacket!" On the floor near the open basement window lay a triangular black button imprinted with a motorcycle wheel. "It *was* Latsky!"

Chief Collig dropped the button in his pocket. As he started to leave, the officer said, "The motorcycle rider hasn't returned yet to the cabin. But I'm hoping he may show up there soon."

After Collig had gone, Joe turned to his aunt. "We haven't thanked you for saving us and the cutlasses." He chuckled. "You won the Battle of Bayport, Aunt Gertrude!"

"Oh, tosh!" she said, starting upstairs. "Mr Lightbody, lock and bar that window. Frank and Joe, put those cutlasses back in the case."

When Mr Lightbody and the boys came up a few minutes later, Aunt Gertrude was surrounded by members of the Historical Society, praising her for winning the "Battle of Bayport."

"It was nothing," she insisted. "Now we'll resume the meeting."

All the members followed her inside the auditorium except Mr Lightbody. "Boys, I can tell you about a real Battle of Bayport."

He explained that in reading pirate lore, he had learned that in 1756 a buccaneer ship had attacked two armed merchantmen off Bayport. One of the trading vessels had been sunk with all the officers and crew lost. The other merchantman had managed to sail away.

"The pirate ship," Mr Lightbody continued, "had had so much of her sail raked by the cannon of the merchantmen that she was unable to give chase. Instead, for some unknown reason, she sent a landing party ashore. Some time later the party returned aboard and the pirate ship limped off."

"Where did this happen?" Joe asked.

"Off Pirates' Hill," Mr Lightbody replied.

"The hill is really named after that incident."

Frank and Joe eyed each other with a smile. Maybe there *was* a basis for Jim Tilton's account of the cannon buried in the sand!

"That's quite a story," said Frank. "And now we'd like to see the old cannons in the basement."

Mr Lightbody led the way down another stairway and unlocked a door to a dusty, vaultlike room. Three old weapons, green with age, were set up in a row on oak mounts.

"All three are British pieces," the custodian said. "They're a *minion*, a *saker*, and a *pedrero*. And they are all made of cast bronze."

"What queer names!" Joe exclaimed. "Do they mean anything special?"

"The *saker* was named after the saker hawk, one of the fiercer birds used in falconry. The *pedrero*—you notice that it's longer than the others—is relatively lighter because it was used to hurl stone projectiles. Its walls are thinner than those of other guns. The *minion* is the smallest."

"They have beautiful decorations," Joe observed.

The pieces were covered with flower-and-leaf designs. Atop the *saker*, at its balance point, was a handle in the shape of a dolphin.

"This handle," Mr Lightbody explained, "was used for lashing or lifting the piece. And cannon like these often had colourful nicknames set in raised letters on the barrel. For instance, *The Terror*, *The Angry One*, or *The Avenger*."

"This first one is marked *The Wasp*," Joe remarked. The other cannons bore no names. "Thanks, Mr Lightbody."

He locked the door and led the way upstairs. Reaching the hall, Frank whispered to Joe, "That clue to the demiculverin petered out. Let's try Pirates' Hill next."

"Right. We'll go there tomorrow."

Just then Aunt Gertrude, followed by the other Society members, came from the meeting room. The boys' aunt was beaming.

"The Society has just voted to present us with one of the cutlasses," she told them.

Frank and Joe grinned in delight. "Great!" said Frank, and Joe added, "It'll be a swell souvenir of the Battle of Bayport! Let's take the one you used to scare off the thief!"

He ran downstairs to get it.

The Hardys returned home directly and Joe made a rack for the prized cutlass. Frank hung the weapon on the stairway wall.

"Looks good," Joe remarked. "I think Dad will like it."

As the brothers prepared for bed, they discussed the masked thief's reason for wanting the cutlasses. Frank and Joe could come to no conclusion and finally they fell asleep.

Next morning after breakfast the boys made plans for their trip to Pirates' Hill.

"Bowden seemed pretty sure the demiculverin's somewhere round there," Frank mused. "I'm going to try getting some more information from him before we leave."

He went to the phone and called the Garden Gate Motel. As Joe stood by, he saw an expression of disbelief cross his brother's face. A moment later Frank hung up.

"Bad news," he said. "Bowden checked out early this morning!"

Joe stared at his brother as if dazed. Then he asked, "Florida?"

"He left no forwarding address."

As soon as the boys collected their wits, they decided to postpone their trip to Pirates' Hill and instead try to find Bowden. They would go the rounds of local petrol stations, hoping to find that Bowden had stopped at one of them and might have left a clue to his destination.

They visited one after another without result. As the brothers were about to return home in dismay, Joe said:

"Frank, there's a petrol station about two miles out of town on Route 7. Bowden may have stopped there."

The boys headed for the place and a few minutes later pulled in. A boy was in attendance and they told him to fill their tank.

"Say," said Frank to him, "did a man stop here this morning in a green coupé?"

"Yep," the attendant replied.

"Was he about thirty-five years old, stocky build, and did he have wiry black hair?"

"Yep."

Frank said they were trying to find him and wondered where he had gone. "Did he happen to tell you?"

"Yep. Said he had a big business deal over in Taylorville."

Elated, the Hardys grinned and thanked the boy. They paid him and hurried off.

"Our luck has changed!" Joe remarked.

"I hope we can make Taylorville before Bowden pulls out of there too," Frank said.

At Taylorville, the Hardys began a systematic search for Bowden's car, going up one street and down another. After they had exhausted the business area, they started on the residential section.

"I see it!" Joe cried out presently.

Bowden's green coupé was parked in front of an old-fashioned house which advertised that luncheons and dinners were served there.

"Maybe he's eating," Joe remarked. "What say we park our car round the corner so he won't spot it?"

Frank agreed this was a good idea and kept going. He pulled into a secluded, dead-end street and locked the convertible. As they walked back towards the restaurant, Frank suddenly grabbed his brother's arm. "We'd better duck. Here he comes!"

"Where?" Joe asked.

"From that house down the street—the big white one."

The brothers ducked at the back of a hedge and watched the suspect. He went directly towards his car but did not get in. Instead, Bowden turned into the walk which led to the restaurant and disappeared inside.

"What a break!" said Frank. "Joe, you watch the restaurant. I'll go over to that big white house and see what I can find out about Bowden's activities."

"What'll I do if Bowden suddenly comes out?" Joe asked.

"Run for our car and give two blasts on the horn. I'll come out and join you, so we can follow him."

Frank hurried across the street, planning his campaign at the neighbouring house. "I'll pretend to be a salesman," he told himself.

A thin, white-haired man answered his ring. Smiling,

Frank asked if he were Mr Chestnut. When the man shook his head, Frank asked if he knew where Mr Chestnut lived.

"Never heard of anybody by that name round here," the elderly man said. He chuckled. "But you came close, son. My name's Ash."

Frank laughed, then said he was a salesman and wondered how he was going to find Mr Chestnut.

"Sorry I can't help you, young fellow." Mr Ash smiled. "And I can't buy anything from you. I just spent all my money. A salesman was here a few minutes ago and sold me some stock."

Frank's heart leaped. He was learning more than he had bargained for!

· 9 ·   *Pirates' Hill*

WITHOUT seeming to be too inquisitive, Frank asked Mr Ash, "Was it oil stock you bought?"

The elderly man shook his head. "It was mining stock. The Copper Slope Mining Company. Ever heard of it?"

Frank said that he had. As a matter of fact, his father owned some of the stock. So Mr Bowden was not selling phony stock!

"I'll bet Dad will be surprised at this," he thought, then said aloud, "Where could I find the salesman if I should want to buy some stock?"

Mr Ash told him the man's name was Bowden and he was staying at the Garden Gate Motel in Bayport.

"That's where he told me to phone him if I wanted any more stock."

Frank was amazed and almost blurted out that Bowden was no longer at the Garden Gate Motel. He thanked Mr Ash, then joined his brother, telling him what he had learned. Joe was also amazed and puzzled. The stock was high grade, but the transaction seemed strange.

"We'll wait to trail Bowden," Frank stated.

It was not long before the suspect came out of the restaurant and got into his car. Frank and Joe dashed round the corner and hopped into their convertible. The trail led towards Bayport, and when they reached the town, Bowden not only turned into the Garden Gate Motel, but went to Cabin 15, unlocked it, and stepped inside.

"Well, can you beat that!" Joe said.

The boys parked and spoke to the clerk who had given Frank the information about Bowden's leaving. The man looked at Frank in surprise.

"I thought you said Mr Borden on the phone," he explained. "Sorry. Mr Bowden is still in Cabin fifteen."

The boys went to see him and held a casual conversation about Pirates' Hill, saying they were going to start searching that area the next day. Did Bowden have any suggestions for them?

"No, I haven't," he replied. "But I'm glad to hear you're going to start work. I don't know how long I can wait around here."

"Are you thinking of leaving soon?" Joe asked as casually as he could, hoping for information.

"Oh, not right away," Bowden answered. "But it's

taking a lot of my valuable time to stay here trying to find that demiculverin."

"I understand," said Frank. "Well, we'll let you know what we find out."

Since it was too late to search on Pirates' Hill that day, the boys went home. They gathered various kinds of tools together which they would use for their digging and put them in the car.

"We'll have to take time out from the picnic to make a search," said Frank.

Shortly after breakfast the next morning, the Hardy phone rang. Frank answered the call. It was from Mr Lightbody. In a highly excited voice the curator cried out:

"The Historical Society's building was broken into late last night. The cutlasses have been stolen!"

"Stolen!" Frank cried out unbelievingly. "How did the thief get in?"

Mr Lightbody said a rear door of the building had been forced.

"Joe and I will be right over," said Frank.

The whole family was upset by the news. Aunt Gertrude declared she was going along.

"I feel a personal responsibility for those cutlasses," she said.

She and the boys set off at once. By the time they reached the Historical Society building, Chief Collig was there.

"This certainly is unfortunate," he said. "I can't understand how a thief got in so easily."

"Don't forget Latsky is a safecracker," Joe reminded the chief.

"Wait a second," Frank said. "Let's not jump to

conclusions. We don't know for certain that it was Latsky who broke in here the second time."

Chief Collig agreed with the boy. He said he would put extra men on the case and notify the state police to be on the lookout for Latsky.

"Neither he nor anyone else has shown up at the cabin in the woods," the officer reported. "I had a hunch the man would come back, but apparently I was wrong."

Hearing this, Frank asked worriedly, "But you're not going to take the stakeout away, are you?"

"No, but I believe the fellow knows we're watching the place and won't return."

Just then the old mortar boomed in the town square. Frank and Joe smiled at each other. They had completely forgotten that it was Independence Day! They had planned to watch the parade, then start off for the picnic.

It was eleven o'clock when they reached home to pack their car. Mrs Hardy had left two large cakes for them—a chocolate and an angel cake. Joe put them into the convertible while Frank consulted a book on tides in the Bayport area. Coming out to Joe, he said:

"I guess we can't take the *Sleuth* after all. The water will be too shallow near Pirates' Hill. It will be low tide in the middle of the day."

"How about asking Tony to take us in his *Napoli*?" Joe suggested. "It draws much less water than the *Sleuth*."

"Good idea, Joe. I'll call him."

"Sure, we can take the *Napoli*," Tony said. "I'll meet you at the dock."

The Hardys headed first for the Morton farm. Chet

and Iola were waiting with several baskets of food which included lobsters and a sack of clams. Their next stop was for Callie Shaw, then they drove directly to the waterfront.

"Hi!" cried Tony, grinning at his friends. The *Napoli* was chugging quietly at her berth.

"I'm glad you asked me to go along," he said. "It would be a dull day for me without a date."

As the motorboat skimmed along the bay towards the ocean, Callie suddenly began to laugh. The others looked up and followed her eyes to the stern. There stood Chet, a black patch over one eye and a bandanna round his head.

"Yo-ho-ho!" he sang out. "I'm the pirate of Bayport Bay and I'll show you in a few minutes where a vast treasure is hidden!"

The others roared with laughter and Iola added, "A skin-diving pirate! You'd better bring up a real treasure or you'll forfeit all second helpings as punishment!"

When they reached the end of the bay and turned up the coast, the young people watched for Pirates' Hill. Minutes later they saw it in the distance. The hill was a desolate hump of sand-covered stone jutting into the sea. There was not a house in sight, except one small cottage about half a mile beyond the crown of the hill.

"That must be Sergeant Tilton's place," Frank remarked.

Tony stopped the *Napoli* some distance off-shore and said he was going to test the depth with a pole before going any closer towards land.

"Say, how about my trying out the diving equipment now?" Chet asked. He removed the bandanna and eye patch. "I want to find that treasure for you."

Grinning, Frank helped Chet adjust the equipment.

"I think I'll put my gear on, too, in case Chet runs into trouble," said Joe.

He quickly strapped his air tanks into position and the two boys stepped to the gunwale.

"Hold it!" said Tony. "A guy in a motorboat over there is waving at us frantically. Wonder what's up."

"Who is he?" Frank asked.

"I've never seen the fellow before," Tony replied as the boat bobbed alongside.

Frank called out to the newcomer, a fisherman about fifty, and asked him what was wrong.

"I'm glad I got to you folks in time," the stranger replied. He spoke excitedly. "I just spotted a giant sting ray near here while I was fishing."

"A sting ray!" Frank echoed in surprise. "Thanks for telling us. We'll stay out of the water."

Tony pulled a pole from the bottom of the motorboat and asked Frank to test the depth from the prow of the *Napoli*. Then slowly he steered the boat shore-wards.

All this time Joe had been casting his eyes over the large expanse of water. There was no sign of the sting ray. Finally he said aloud:

"Do you suppose that man was trying to scare us away from here?"

"What do you mean?" asked Callie.

"Well, funny things have been going on lately," said Joe. "That fellow could have some reason for not wanting us to go into the water."

He found binoculars in a compartment and trained them on the other boat which by now was a good distance away. The craft lacked both a name and Coast Guard identification number.

"That fisherman isn't alone!" Joe exclaimed. "I just saw another man's head pop out from under the tarpaulin!"

"Can you see his face?" Frank asked.

"No. He's getting up now, but his back's turned to us."

The Hardys and their friends looked at one another questioningly. Someone had been hiding from the group. Why? And who was he?

· 10 ·   A Spy

"LET's see who those two are!" Joe urged.

"You mean go after them?" Tony asked.

When Joe nodded, Tony made the *Napoli* skim across the water. Joe kept the binoculars trained on the mysterious fishermen. Suddenly they seemed to realize that the young people were heading directly towards them. Like a flash, the man who had remained hidden before dived under the tarpaulin in the bottom of the boat.

The other man started the engine. Then, in a roar which carried across the waves, the boat raced off.

"Wow!" Chet exclaimed. "Some speedy craft!"

"I'll say it is!" said Frank. "That's no ordinary fishing boat!"

The *Napoli* was fast but not fast enough to overtake the other boat. After a chase of a mile, the other craft was out of sight.

"Guess it's hopeless," said Tony in disgust. He turned back to Pirates' Hill.

The young people continued to discuss the men's strange actions until they were back at the beach. Then Chet said, "Let's forget the mystery. If I don't eat pretty soon—"

Joe grinned and finished the sentence for him. "You'll faint, fall in the water, and a man-eating shark will make away with you."

Everyone laughed but Chet. He frowned and added pleadingly, "What's a picnic for, if you don't eat?"

"We'll take care of that," his sister promised.

With the *Napoli* anchored in a scallop-shaped cove, they waded ashore, carrying the baskets of food. The waves lapped the beach gently.

"This is an ideal spot for a beach party," said Callie enthusiastically.

She and Iola took charge and gave orders to the boys. Frank and Tony were to collect driftwood, while Chet and Joe gathered plenty of seaweed. In a few minutes they returned, their arms full.

"What'll we do with this?" Joe asked.

"Those rocks over there will make a good place for the fire," said Callie.

She found a natural pit among the rocks. Into it the boys piled the driftwood and started a fire. Soon there was a roaring blaze. Then Frank heaped more rocks into the fire.

When the stones were glowing red and the flames had died out, the boys placed a layer of seaweed over them. Then the girls laid the lobsters and clams in rows on it and piled several more layers of the stringy green kelp over them.

"I can hardly wait," Chet groaned hungrily, as the tantalizing aroma reached his nostrils.

While the food was steaming, the rest of the lunch was brought out. The meal started with tomato juice and small sandwiches of ham and chicken. As they ate, the Hardy boys brought their friends up to date on Bowden, Latsky, and the search for the demiculverin.

"Later today, Joe and I want to climb to the top of Pirates' Hill and take a look for the cannon," Frank told them.

"We'd better go now," said Joe, grinning. "After this picnic we won't be able to climb!"

A few minutes later the clams and lobsters were ready. The young people gathered round the pit as Joe cleared away the hot seaweed.

"Right this way, folks!" he called out. "First plateful of juicy sizzling hot clams goes to Miss Iola Morton!"

One by one the picnickers came forward and piled their plates. Every clam and lobster disappeared. Then a huge water melon was cut into sections and served along with Mrs Hardy's cakes.

Forty minutes later Chet rolled over on the sand. "I can't move!" he moaned.

"Neither can I!" Joe echoed, sprawling full length on his back. "Girls, that was the greatest meal I ever ate!"

The next hour was a lazy one. Chet was soon snoring and the others stretched out for a rest. But finally they got up and walked to the water's edge. Chet was the last to join them.

"How about my doing that skin diving now?" he suggested.

"Okay," said Frank, and helped his chubby friend into the equipment.

"Isn't anybody coming with me?" Chet asked.

"I'll follow you," said Joe, and started putting on his flippers.

Chet waddled into the sea, and quickly made his way to deeper water, but he did not submerge.

"Chet's so buoyant he can't go down," said Frank. "Joe, you'd better weigh him down some more. Take an extra lead-filled cartridge belt with you and put it on him."

Joe grabbed the belt and splashed into the surf. Reaching Chet, he attached the extra equipment. Almost at once the stout boy vanished beneath the water. Joe, too, submerged.

Ten minutes later Chet emerged, and swaying from side to side, sloshed to the beach. He removed his face mask and grinned.

"Brought you some souvenirs, girls," he said, and laid a large handful of unusual shells streaked with mother-of-pearl on the sand.

"Oh, they're beautiful!" Callie exclaimed.

Iola clapped Chet on the shoulder. "I'm proud of you, brother. Hope there's a pearl among these."

"How far down did you go?" Tony asked him.

"About twenty feet," Chet stated proudly. "I'll go deeper next time. And here's something else I found."

From one of his belts he brought out what looked like part of a rusty ice pick.

Tony grinned. "I suppose a whale dropped this. He likes his drinks cold and chips off the icebergs with it."

Chet ignored him. "I don't think this is a new ice pick," he retorted. "It's old and valuable."

"Sure," said Tony. "It probably belonged to that famous pirate Edward Teach."

"Do you think so?" Chet asked innocently. "I'm going to keep it as a souvenir!"

The picnic group played baseball for twenty minutes, then Frank said, "It seems to me Joe should have come back by this time."

Everyone looked out over the water. Chet scanned the area with the binoculars which Callie had brought ashore in the picnic basket. There was no sign of the diver. Frank became uneasy.

"I'm going to look for Joe," he announced.

Putting on his gear, he hurried into the water and soon was lost to sight. Frank swam up and down the coast off Pirates' Hill but did not see Joe. A sinking feeling came over him. Suppose his brother had been stung by the ray!

Then a more alarming thought struck Frank. He suddenly recalled the black-garbed skin diver who had deliberately aimed a spear at the boys earlier that week. Perhaps the man had returned!

Frank struck out faster and peered around anxiously. Suddenly above him he saw a swimmer whose body extended upright. He was clinging to a boat.

"Joe!" he thought, and hurried towards him.

His brother was grasping the gunwale of the *Napoli*, his face mask removed. Frank pulled up alongside of him and removed his.

"Good grief!" Frank cried out. "You gave us a scare. Where have you been?"

"Sorry, old man," Joe replied. "I was lying in the bottom of the *Napoli*."

"Why?" Frank asked in amazement.

"I've been spying on a spy," Joe replied. "Look up to the top of Pirates' Hill! See that figure silhouetted up there? He's been watching every move you've been making on the beach!"

· 11 · *Strange Footprints*

"THAT man's doing more than looking at us," said Frank, staring at the lone figure on the summit of Pirates' Hill. "He's digging!"

From where the Hardys were clinging to the *Napoli*, it certainly looked as if the man were turning up the sand. He held something resembling a blunt shovel.

"He didn't have that before," said Joe. "Maybe he thinks it's safe now for him to dig for whatever he hopes to locate."

"You mean, because we didn't climb the hill?"

"Yes."

"Well, let's climb it now and find out just why he *is* there!" Frank urged. "It's possible he's burying something, not taking it out."

The brothers donned their masks and swam underwater to shore. They told the others about the man and their desire to see him closely.

"I suggest we separate and start looking for driftwood," Frank said. "Then Joe and I will quietly leave you and sneak up the hill."

The others promised not to alert the man by looking up. Joe indicated a circuitous route to the top which would not be seen from above.

"You take that way, Frank. I'll wander down the beach and go up from another direction. We'll try a pincer movement on the fellow."

"Okay. I wonder if he's Latsky."

"Maybe he's Bowden."

The picnickers began gathering the wood, calling out in loud voices which they hoped would carry to the mysterious man.

"A prize to the one bringing in the most unusual shaped piece of driftwood," Callie offered.

"Bet I'll win!" Chet yelled.

Minutes later the Hardys were on their separate ways up the dune. They slipped and slid in the heavy sand. Progress was slow, but finally both boys reached the crest. Frank and Joe were about three hundred feet apart as they poked their heads above the top and looked around.

The man was nowhere in sight!

"Where'd he go?" Joe asked in disgust. "Do you suppose we scared him off?"

Frank shrugged. "There ought to be footprints. Let's see where they go."

The boys searched and finally found them. The prints were large and far apart, indicating that they had been made by a tall man.

"They go off across the dune in the direction of Sergeant Tilton's house," Frank noted. "But the marks can't be his—he isn't that tall."

The marks might belong to Latsky or Bowden, the brothers decided. Mystified, the boys followed the prints. Suddenly Joe grabbed Frank's arm.

"If it was Latsky, and if he was the one who stole the cutlasses, maybe he was burying them here until the police alert is over."

The boys turned back and dug with their hands as best they could round the area where the stranger had been standing. But nothing came to light.

"Let's go," Joe suggested. "We're giving that man too much of a head start."

The Hardys hurried along the trail of fresh prints in the otherwise smooth sand. The tracks veered suddenly and headed directly for Sergeant Tilton's cottage!

"Maybe we're closing in on the cutlass thief!" said Joe tensely. "This may be his hide-out!"

"You don't mean Tilton?"

"No. But the thief may be boarding with him."

As the boys approached, Frank exclaimed. "The footprints lead right to the door!"

Watching to see if anyone might be looking from a window, Frank and Joe walked up and knocked at the door. There was no answer. Frank knocked again. This time someone within stirred. Footsteps sounded and a moment later Sergeant Tilton opened the door. He was dressed as an officer of the Revolutionary War.

"Well, this seems to be visitors' day round here! Welcome! Come in, boys!"

"Did you have another visitor?" Frank asked, feigning innocence after he had recovered from the surprise of Tilton's appearance.

"Yep. He's gone now."

Sergeant Tilton explained that only a short time

before, a stranger had also stopped at the cottage.

"Where is he now?" Joe asked quickly.

"Oh, he seemed to be in a hurry," Tilton replied. "He was just askin' the best way back to Bayport."

"Who was he?" Joe prodded, trying not to appear too eager to find out.

"Don't rightly know," Tilton answered. "He never said."

"What did he look like?" Frank asked.

"Tall young man. Right nice face. Kind o' greenish eyes an' brown hair. Say, why are you two fellows so all-fired interested in this guy?"

The Hardys laughed. Then Frank said it was because of their advertisement for information about cannon which he had answered.

"So if any people are going to dig for it on Pirates' Hill," he added, "Joe and I want to be the ones."

Tilton chuckled. "Can't say I blame you."

Frank now told Sergeant Tilton about Mr Lightbody's account of the Battle of Bayport. "Do you think there could be any connection between that battle and the cannon you think is buried somewhere up here?"

"I sure do," Tilton replied. "There were some crooked dealin's between those old pirates an' certain folks on land in those days. I figger mebbe somebody ashore was tryin' to sell the cannon or trade it fer the buccaneers' loot."

The artillery sergeant suddenly grinned impishly. "Guess you wonder why I've got this getup on," he said. "I like to dress up in different uniforms. I've got a collection of 'em up in my pirate den. D'you want to see 'em?"

"Pirate den!" Joe exclaimed.

"Yes sirree!" the elderly man replied. "Just follow me."

Though the Hardys felt they should hurry off and try to overtake the young man they wanted to interrogate, they were tempted by Tilton's invitation. Furthermore, they might pick up some valuable information among his treasures.

"All right," said Frank.

Sergeant Tilton led the boys to the kitchen. From an opening in the ceiling hung a rope ladder. The old man grabbed it and thrust his foot into the first rung.

"Up we go!" He laughed. "This is a real gen-u-wine freebooters' cave I got fer myself up here."

Frank and Joe clambered up after the elderly man, who disappeared into the darkness of the room overhead.

Tilton switched on a ship's lantern in a corner of the room. The first thing the boys noted in its dim glow was a pair of cutlasses. For a moment they wondered if the weapons could be part of the stolen collection. But just then Tilton blew a cloud of dust off them, in order to show the cutlasses to better advantage. They had definitely been in the den a long time!

"Look at those treasure chests!" Joe cried out. "And all those guns!"

The room contained an amazing collection of corsair relics. Coins, rusted implements, old maps, pirate flags and costumes, and faded oil paintings of famous buccaneers decorated the walls and tables. On a rack in one corner hung a variety of old Army uniforms.

"This is great!" said Joe, and Frank added, "I wish

we had time to examine each piece. I'd like to come again, Sergeant Tilton."

"You're welcome any time," the man said.

The boys preceded him down the ladder. As the Hardys were about to leave, the man said, "You know, I plumb forgot to mention something to you. Mebbe it's just my fancy, but it seems kind o' strange at that. The young fellow what was here a little while ago—he's lookin' for a cannon, too!"

"He is!" Frank exclaimed. "Did he say what kind?"

"A Spanish demiculverin," Tilton replied.

Instantly the Hardys were sure that they should talk to the stranger. They *must* find him!

"Thanks a lot, Sergeant Tilton," Frank said. "You've been a big help."

"Don't mention it, young fellow," the artilleryman said heartily. "An' hurry back fer a real visit."

Frank and Joe smiled and nodded. Then, following the large footprints that led away from Tilton's cottage, the boys hurried on. The marks led down the side of one dune and up another, but Frank and Joe did not spot their quarry.

At last they reached a point as high as the one on which Tilton's house was situated. Suddenly Joe stopped and gripped Frank's arm. He pointed to a figure in a depression between dunes.

"There's our man!"

· 12 ·   *A Friendly Suspect*

"DON'T let that man get out of sight!" Frank urged, running in a westerly direction through the tall grass on top of the dune.

"He'll have to evaporate to get away this time!" Joe declared, matching his brother step for step. "The fellow's just walking, so we can catch up to him easily."

But this was difficult. He was taking long, fast strides. They ran faster and finally seemed to be nearer the stranger. He was now in full view, only three hundred yards away.

"We might call to him," Joe suggested.

"No," Frank advised. "If he doesn't want to talk to us, he may run and we won't catch him."

At this moment the stranger entered the first of a series of deep dips in the sand. The abrupt rise of the knoll between him and the boys blocked the man from view temporarily.

"Oh!" Joe cried out suddenly.

Unfortunately, at that moment, his right foot had slid into a hole in the sand. As he pitched forward, the boy felt a searing pain in his leg.

"Ouch!" Joe cried out. He got up, grimacing.

Frank had turned at his brother's outcry and now came back. "Hard luck," he said. Kneeling beside Joe, he felt the injured ankle joint. "You've sure wrenched it. Better not step on that foot. Lean on me."

"Okay," said Joe, annoyed at himself. "That ends our little posse. We can't catch him now."

"Never mind," said Frank. "Put your arm round my shoulder," he suggested. "We'll attend to your ankle back at the beach."

With Frank helping him, Joe hopped clumsily through the hot sand. In their concern over Joe's ankle, both boys had stopped looking for the man. Now they peered across the wind-swept sand hills, but did not spot him.

"I hate to lose that fellow but it couldn't be helped." Frank sighed.

Moving as fast as Joe's injured ankle would permit, the brothers presently neared the picnic spot. A fire was blazing. The Hardys smiled to see Chet holding two forks in each hand, cooking frankfurters.

"Our friend must have a vacuum for a stomach," Joe remarked. "*Where* does he put so much food?"

Frank did not reply. He was gazing intently at a strange young man who was watching Chet and chatting pleasantly with the girls. The man, about twenty-eight years old, was very tall, and had a determined, jutting jaw. Under his left arm he carried a small canvas sack.

"Joe," said Frank excitedly, "unless my eyes deceive me, the man we were chasing has walked right into our camp!"

"You're right! And carrying his collapsible shovel too."

"One thing's certain," said Frank. "He's not trying to avoid us. But of course he may still be hoping to find out whether we came here to look for a cannon as well as to have a picnic."

"We'd better be careful!" Joe warned.

As the brothers drew closer, Iola handed the stranger

a frankfurter on a roll. A moment later she looked up and saw the Hardys. "Why, Joe, what happened to your foot?" she cried out solicitously and ran towards him.

Joe explained that he had twisted it. He himself was too interested in the stranger to care much about his throbbing ankle.

"I'm sorry you wrenched your ankle," Iola said, adding, "This is Tim Gorman."

"Hi!" said Joe, shaking hands with the easy-mannered stranger.

"And this is Frank Hardy," Iola continued.

Frank, too, shook hands with Gorman, then the brothers exchanged meaningful glances. Tim Gorman was the man who had passed the brothers in a car the day before yesterday and had gazed so intently at them!

The stranger must have guessed their thoughts, for he soon mentioned the incident. "I was looking for someone with the same kind of car as yours," he explained. "Sorry I seemed so rude."

Frank and Joe nodded. At the same moment Callie remarked, "Tim Gorman tells us that he has just been to see Mr Tilton."

"Yes," the visitor said, "I had a very interesting talk with the old artillery sergeant."

"We know that," Frank told him. "We were up there too."

"And I just about broke my leg trying to catch up with you on the dune!" Joe declared. "You certainly crossed it in a hurry."

"Really? Why didn't you call?" Gorman replied. "I didn't see you."

The Hardys' suspicious attitude softened considerably.

Frank steered the conversation back to Sergeant Tilton. Gorman talked freely, laughing about the amazing pirate den in the attic and the talkative old man's preposterous stories. But he did not mention the cannon, nor give any inkling of why he had been on Pirates' Hill.

Finally Joe bluntly said, "We understand you're looking for a cannon."

Gorman's face clouded. "I suppose Tilton told you that," he said, his jaw set and his eyes flashing. "That man talks too much. I asked him to keep it to himself and he told me he would."

"Is it a secret?" Chet asked.

Their visitor looked annoyed, but he regained his composure quickly. "I suppose you might say so," he replied, looking off into space as if trying to decide whether or not to reveal it.

A sudden quiet descended upon the group. The Hardys' friends waited for the brothers to carry on any further conversation.

Tim Gorman relaxed a little and said, "I may as well admit that I'm looking for a cannon." He paused. "But I'd rather not discuss it."

"As you wish," said Frank politely. "But we might be able to help each other. Joe and I have been reading about cannons."

"They sure have," Chet spoke up. "They know a lot about them."

Gorman smiled and said, "That's very interesting. But, after all, we're perfect strangers. I feel it best that I keep my business to myself. Perhaps later on I could discuss the situation with you. For the present I'd prefer not to."

The pleasant way in which he made the latter statement and the smile which went with it tended to disarm all of the group except Frank and Joe. Though Gorman was friendly, they still felt he was somewhat suspect. Not once had he mentioned a demiculverin, though that was, according to Tilton, what he hoped to find. He also did not reveal the contents of the canvas sack.

"We'll probably see one another from time to time," Gorman announced. "I'm staying in Bayport. Perhaps later I'll be in a position to discuss the cannon with you."

The others made no comment. Tony Prito, however, asked Gorman if he would like to go back to Bayport with them in the *Napoli*.

"Thanks," Gorman answered affably. "But my car is parked on the shore road."

He started to say good-bye to the picnickers then suddenly stopped and stared at an object in Iola's hand. It was the ice pick Chet had found.

Gorman stepped forward. "Where did you get that?" he asked intently.

Chet proudly informed Gorman of his underwater discovery as Iola handed over the pick. Gorman examined it closely.

"Is it an antique ice pick?" Chet asked him.

Gorman swung about, his face flushed with excitement. "This is not an ice pick. It's a gunner's pick! There *was* a cannon near here!"

·13· *Overboard!*

TIM GORMAN's announcement sent a thrill of excitement through the Hardy boys. There was no question now that a cannon had been on Pirates' Hill. But what was more important, was it still buried deep under the sand? Or had the old cannon by this time been washed into the sea?

Frank spoke first. "Have you any idea, Tim, what kind of cannon it might have been?"

They waited impatiently for the young man's answer, but were disappointed in it. "There's absolutely no way of telling," he replied.

The brothers wondered if it could have been a demiculverin, but did not mention this.

Chet had walked up to face Gorman. "How did you know this was a gunner's pick?" he asked.

"Like Frank and Joe, I've been reading a good deal about artillery," the young man replied. He turned the pick over in his hands and continued, "This is part of an eighteenth-century gunner's equipment. It's one of eleven important tools a gunner needed."

"How was this pick used?" Chet inquired.

Gorman explained that by the eighteenth century, powder bags had come into wide use, replacing the loose powder which had formerly been ladled into the bore of a cannon.

"This made it necessary to prick open the bag so the priming fire from the vent could reach the charge."

"Then what?" Chet asked expectantly.

77

"That's where the gunner's pick came in. It was plunged into the vent far enough to pierce the bag. It's sometimes called a priming wire."

Callie suddenly chuckled. "It sounds complicated to me. I'd need several lessons to get this through my head."

"I would too," Iola confessed.

Gorman smiled. "I'll be glad to give you girls cannon instruction any time you say."

Chet and Tony chuckled, but the Hardys shot the man dark looks. They did not want their friends dating any person who was a suspect!

Callie and Iola guessed the boys' thoughts. To tease them, Iola said, "We'll let you know, Tim."

"Don't forget," Gorman said, grinning. "Well, I must be off now."

He shook hands with everyone and said good-bye. When he was out of sight, the boys discussed the man's contradictory manner.

The girls did not agree with the boys. "I think he's charming," said Iola.

Callie added, winking at her friend, "And *so* good looking. But you boys needn't be jealous," she added impishly.

"Who's jealous?" Joe stormed.

The girls giggled. Then they became serious and all discussed the possibility of the demiculverin being hidden on Pirates' Hill.

"You'd better dig for it pretty soon or Gorman will find it first," Callie advised.

"Let's start right now," Frank urged.

Acting as leader he assigned the others to various spots and for an hour the beach and hillside were beehives of activity. Various small objects were dug up but there was no sign of a cannon.

"I guess we'll have to quit!" Tony called out to Frank. He explained that he had promised to be home for supper by seven and take his parents in the Napoli later to see the fireworks.

"We're all going to see them," said Iola. "Sorry you can't join us, Tony."

The tools were collected and carried out to the boat with the picnic baskets. After everyone was seated, Tony set off for town. Frank and Joe sat alone in the prow for a while discussing Gorman. Frank was convinced the young man was above board, but Joe was still suspicious.

"He may just be a very smooth operator," Joe remarked. "Why, he might even be in league with Latsky!"

"What gives you that idea?" Frank asked.

"He certainly knows a lot about the history of ancient artillery."

The boys were interrupted in their discussion by a call from Callie. "Oh, look, everybody!"

The Napoli had turned into the bay and was running close to shore where an area of the water had been roped off for the evening's display of fireworks. A small grandstand had been erected along the bank. In the water two large scows contained the set pieces and the rockets which would be sent skyward in the evening's celebration.

"Looks as if it'll be a good show," Tony remarked.

Chet proposed that his group come early in the Sleuth and anchor near the two barges to get an excellent view of the performance.

"Suppose we meet at the dock at eight-thirty," Frank suggested. "The fireworks start at nine."

This was agreed upon. Iola suggested that when they arrived in Bayport they should transfer the picnic baskets to the *Sleuth* and use the food that was left for a late snack.

"That's using your head, Sis," Chet said approvingly.

Iola had stood up to see the set pieces of fireworks. As Tony steered back to the centre of the bay, she sat down on the gunwale of the boat. She began to croon, "Sailing, sailing over the bounding main," and the others joined in.

When the song ended, Frank sang lustily, "Oh, my name was Captain Brand, a-sailing—"

Suddenly the *Napoli* hit something in the water. The boat gave an abrupt lurch, causing Iola to lose her balance. She fell, banging her head on the gunwale, then toppled into the water.

"Oh!" Callie screamed. "She's hurt!"

Everyone jumped up as the boat rocked dangerously. Instantly Joe kicked off his sandals and dived overboard as Iola disappeared under the waves thirty feet astern of the *Napoli*. With strong strokes Joe reached the spot and surface-dived, while Tony circled the boat back at reduced speed.

As the group watched with worried expressions, Joe's head popped to the surface for a second. He sucked in air, then went under again.

Without a word to his chums, Frank donned his skin-diving gear and was about to plunge over the side when his brother appeared again. This time he had an arm round the girl.

Iola was limp. Apparently she had been unconscious before falling into the water.

She was pulled aboard and Chet applied first aid. There were a few anxious moments before Iola's eyelids opened and she began to breathe normally. Frank told her what had happened.

"You sure you feel okay?" Chet asked solicitously.

"Yes—thanks to you and Joe," Iola said gratefully.

As soon as Tony was sure Iola was all right, he dived overboard to inspect his craft. Fortunately it had not been damaged by the large log which was now floating nearby. Tony climbed aboard and reported this to the others.

"It was a close squeak," Joe remarked.

As the *Napoli* proceeded to the Hardys' dock, Iola insisted that she felt fine. But she did promise to go home at once and rest until it was time to attend the fireworks display.

At the dock, Chet transferred the picnic baskets to the *Sleuth*. Then they said good-bye to Tony and drove off. They went directly to the Mortons'.

At eight-thirty Frank and Joe drove their mother and aunt over to some friends with whom they were to attend the fireworks display and spend the evening. Then the boys went to their dock where Chet and the girls were waiting. Soon the group was aboard the *Sleuth*, heading out to the area where the fireworks were to be displayed. Nearing it, they could hear spine-tingling band music from the grandstand on the shore.

Frank guided the *Sleuth* close to the roped-off area. Floodlights set up on the scows made the scene as bright as day.

As Frank turned off his motor, Joe, seated beside him, suddenly grabbed his brother's arm.

"What's up?" Frank asked, turning. He noticed a worried look on his brother's face.

"The man in charge of the display is the one who warned us about the sting ray!"

Frank gazed ahead and nodded. "I wonder if the fellow who was hiding in the bottom of his boat is here too."

"They're going to start!" Chet called.

A moment later there was a swish and whine as the first rocket was set off. It shot high into the dark sky above the harbour and a fountain of cascading diamonds burst into life. Ohs and ahs echoed from the onlookers.

A second and a third rocket swirled heavenwards. Red and blue sparkles gleamed brilliantly after the sharp explosions.

"This is wonderful!" Iola cried out.

"Oh, they're going to set off one of the figures!" Callie said excitedly. "Look, it's a man pedalling a bicycle!"

A twenty-foot figure, sputtering a yellow-white smoke, appeared to be cycling across the barge.

"There goes another figure!" Chet cried in delight as a multicoloured clown began to dance with slow, jerky motions.

Just then a hissing sound attracted the attention of the Hardys and their friends. The next moment a terrified shriek went up from the girls.

A rocket had been fired horizontally and was streaking directly towards the *Sleuth*!

• 14 •   *The Elusive Mr X*

TERRIFIED, everyone sprawled flat, as the rocket skimmed over the waves like a guided missile!

Whack! The boat shook as the rocket glanced off her bow. A thundering blast followed when the missile exploded ten yards off the starboard side.

Streamers of white light ribboned across the motorboat, but the hot rocket itself sizzled on the surface of the water and then died out in a cloud of acrid smoke.

"That was too close for comfort!" Joe cried out, jumping up.

Frank leaped to the wheel as Chet and the girls peered over the gunwales towards the barge.

"That was no accident!" Frank stormed. "I'm going after the man who set off the rocket!"

"Start the engine!" Joe shouted.

The motor roared to life and the propeller kicked up white foam as the *Sleuth* shot ahead and ducked under the rope of the danger zone.

Closing in rapidly on the barge, the Hardys noticed that one of the Bayport Police Department launches was approaching from the opposite side. Its two powerful spotlights were raking the fireworks platform and the officers were shouting that there was to be no more firing.

"Look!" Joe cried. "That one man isn't paying any attention!"

A stranger to them, he grabbed a lighted torch from the head man and went to a rocket.

"He'll blow us all up!" Callie cried in terror.

A second later the young people saw him run from fixture to fixture, touching his torch to the fuses of the entire remaining display.

Frank did not wait. He put the *Sleuth* in reverse, and the motorboat ran rapidly backwards.

The next moment, the bay shook with the din of the exploding fireworks. Rockets burst forth in all directions with thunderous detonations.

The danger of being struck by the flying rockets also drove the police launch back from the barge towards the centre of the bay. There were anxious moments as the bombardment continued.

Hot fragments from the bursting rockets sprayed the deck and cockpit of the *Sleuth*, but finally Frank got beyond their range.

The din aboard the barge ended as abruptly as it had begun. One glowing wheel continued to turn slowly, but the rockets had spent themselves.

"What a crazy thing to do!" Joe exclaimed.

"Thank goodness we're all right!" said Callie. "Frank, you're a wonder!"

"I'm nothing of the sort," he replied, "and I'd like to punch whoever set off those rockets."

"Not so easy," Chet declared. "All the men on the barges are now swimming to shore."

"I can try!" Frank declared.

He turned the boat and headed for the beach. The stranger who had caused the uproar was not in sight but the man who had warned them of the sting ray was still in the water. Frank drew alongside of him and throttled the engine.

"Climb in!" he called.

The man pulled himself aboard. At the same time the police launch picked up several other swimmers. Not one of them was the man the Hardys wanted to interrogate. But they began to question their own new passenger.

"Who was the man who started that explosion?" Joe demanded.

"I don't know."

"What do you mean? You were in charge of the fireworks, weren't you, Mr—er?"

The man scowled. "The name's Halpen. I was only in charge of the timing," he answered. "The fellows lighted the fuses when I told 'em to. I don't know the name of the guy who disobeyed orders. He just came round before we were ready to start, and I supposed somebody had hired him. It wasn't any of my business."

Frank was not satisfied with the explanation. He hailed the captain of the police boat and asked if he might speak to the men they had picked up.

"Sure thing, Frank," said the officer.

Frank asked them the name of the worker who had set off the rockets. No one knew.

Their own passenger grunted. "I guess the guy just butted in for a good time," he remarked. "Unless," he went on, "he was an enemy of yours."

"If he was, we didn't know it," Joe retorted quickly.

"But he sure is now. He's in for a lot of explaining when we catch up with him!" said Frank grimly.

At the moment there seemed little possibility of this. The man had disappeared and the boys assumed he had swum up the shore line and come out on the beach some distance beyond the crowd.

"I'm getting cold," said Halpen. "Put me ashore, will you?"

"Okay, but first I want to ask you a few questions," Joe spoke up.

"Well, make it snappy!"

"Who was the man hidden under the tarpaulin in your boat the other day?" Joe shot at him.

Halpen's jaw sagged, his composure gone completely. He did not answer at once. When he did, they felt sure that it was not the truth.

"So you saw him, eh? You have good eyesight. Well, he was a stranger to me. His boat capsized and I picked him up. He didn't tell me his name."

"But why did he hide under the tarpaulin?" Joe persisted.

"Afraid of the sun," Halpen answered bluntly. "And he fell asleep."

Frank asked, "Why did you race off in your speedboat when we tried to overtake you?"

Halpen glared at the boy. "You're a wise guy, aren't you? I wasn't running away, or that stranger, either. It was late. My wife was waiting for me. And now, take me to a boat so that I can get to my car."

The Hardys felt frustrated, but there was nothing more they could do. Frank let the man off, then proceeded towards his own dock.

Iola grimaced. "I don't believe one word that man said."

They all agreed. Joe said he would find out who Halpen was and what he did for a living.

"I'll bet it's nothing much," Chet spoke up, opening one of the picnic baskets. "Who wants a sandwich and some soda?"

Everyone did and soon all the food had been consumed. Chet said that he was still hungry, so at the Hardy dock they left for a spot frequented by teenagers which bore a sign:

Bill's Burgers
Biggest on the Bay

Immediately the Hardys' friends went to phone their families that they were all right. Then Joe called the chairman of the fireworks committee, Mr Atkin. He had just reached home.

"Halpen's harmless but a ne'er-do-well," Atkin said in answer to Joe's question. "He manages to get along somehow, doing odd jobs. He once worked in a pyrotechnics factory and understands fireworks. He's had the job of setting off the Bayport rockets and set pieces for the last several years. I can't understand what happened tonight."

"It scared the wits out of us," said Joe, then asked if Halpen owned a speedboat.

"Oh, no. But he manages to borrow boats from people he knows."

Joe now inquired how many men had been engaged to set off the fireworks display.

"Let's see," said Mr Atkin. "Five. Yes, there were five."

"I counted six," the boy told him.

"What!" the man exclaimed. "Then one of them was there without being hired. He probably was the one who caused a near tragedy."

"I'm sure the mysterious Mr X was to blame," Joe agreed. Returning to the group, he told them that so far Halpen's story fitted. "It's a puzzle, though. I don't trust the man."

Frank remarked that he was more worried about the mysterious man who seemed to have aimed a rocket at them.

"You think he did it on purpose!" Callie exclaimed fearfully. "But why? He couldn't have known we'd be there."

"Of course not," Frank agreed. "But when he did spot us, he grabbed the opportunity."

Chet leaned across the table, his eyes bulging. "You mean that guy's mixed up with the cannon gang and wanted to bump us off?"

"It's hard to decide," Frank replied.

At midnight when the Hardys returned home, Mrs Hardy and Aunt Gertrude were worriedly waiting.

"We saw the wild ending of the fireworks display and have been disturbed ever since," said the boys' mother, "even though we called the Mortons and learned no one was hurt. Thank goodness you're really all right."

"But no credit to you two," Aunt Gertrude spoke up tartly. "It's shameful how you always attract danger. If I were your mother—"

"But, Aunty, we're here in one piece, so what's the difference," Joe interrupted. "Now if we had come walking in here minus our heads—!"

"Oh, stop your nonsense!" their aunt ordered. She started up the stairs, calling, "Good night, everyone. You'd all better get some sleep."

The next morning, while the boys were dressing, Frank said they should get in touch with Bowden before searching further. "Since both he and Tim Gorman are looking for the demiculverin, I'd like to know if they're acquainted."

"Let's go!"

"We'll tell him Chet found a gunner's pick on the shore, but don't mention Pirates' Hill."

"Right."

After breakfast, the boys phoned Bowden and asked if they might call on him. "Sure, come on over," he replied. "I'll be waiting for you."

The man seemed a bit less friendly than usual when they arrived. Was he suspicious of them? But when the boys had told their story, he smiled. "You're making progress, I can see that. Keep it up. Time is precious."

Bowden had no news. The police, he said, had no clues to the person who had left him the warning note and later attacked him.

Presently Frank asked, "Do you know a man named Tim Gorman?"

Bowden was visibly disturbed by the question. "Gorman!" he exclaimed, his face flushing. "I'll say I know him, but I'm not proud of it."

"What do you mean?" Joe asked.

"He's no good!" Bowden told the boys that Gorman went about posing as a naval man and was wanted by the police for swindling.

"That's hard to believe," Frank said.

Joe, on the other hand, arched his eyebrows and gave his brother a look, as if to say, "I told you so."

Bowden asked the boys how they happened to know Gorman. Guardedly Frank told of meeting him on the beach. Bowden listened intently. He interrupted the narration several times to ask about details. There seemed to be something he wanted to know, but would not ask point-blank.

Finally, he blurted out, "Did Gorman mention the cutlass?"

·15· *An Alias*

BOWDEN's unexpected question caught Joe off guard. Instead of giving a counter query which might have netted the boys some valuable information, he asked bluntly, "One of the stolen cutlasses?"

Joe's thoughtless remark made Frank wince, and his brother immediately realized his mistake. Their father certainly would not approve of such careless detective work! If Bowden had anything to hide concerning the stolen cutlasses, he now was forewarned.

"Stolen? No, of course not," the man said flatly.

"Then what cutlass are you talking about?"

"Forget it."

Joe, annoyed at his own blunder and Bowden's reluctance to talk, said grimly, "Mr Bowden, we can't have you playing hide-and-seek with facts and still do a good sleuthing job for you."

The man smiled patronizingly. "No need for you to get hot under the collar. Gorman's obsessed with finding a miniature cutlass—says it's a lost heirloom or something of the sort. He puts the question to any new acquaintance."

The Hardys felt this was an unlikely story. "Are you sure?" Frank asked.

"Positive. But he may pretend it's a real one just for effect. Gorman's not given to telling the truth."

Frank and Joe suppressed smiles at this remark. Neither was Bowden noted for sticking to the facts! The boys then took their leave, saying they planned to continue their search for the cannon. Bowden waved good-bye from the motel entrance, urging them to speed up their work.

"I wish Dad would hurry back from Florida," Frank remarked, as they rode along. "This case is getting knotty."

Joe nodded. "It sure is—as knotty as a pine board!"

Frank grinned. "I wish we could look through one of those knots and see the answer." Then, after a few moments, he added thoughtfully, "Joe, this case had me baffled until just now. But I believe I have the answer."

"What is it?"

"It migh sound far-fe'ched," Frank replied, as the car hummed closer to Bayport, "but the combination of cannons, cutlasses, and the story about the pirates' fight all lead in one direction."

Joe smiled. "I get it. You mean hidden treasure."

"Right."

His brother's face broke into a wide grin. "If there's treasure around this territory, let's locate it!" he said with enthusiasm.

"We'll have to dig up more clues, though, before we can dig up any treasure," Frank said.

Since the boys had to go near their home to take the road to Pirates' Hill, Frank suggested that they stop and see if there was a letter or phone message from Mr Hardy. He turned onto Elm Street and pulled into their driveway.

The Hardy telephone was ringing persistently as the brothers entered the house. "Nobody's home," Frank said. "Grab it, Joe."

The boy picked up the instrument in the front hall.

"Yes. This is Joe Hardy. . . . Who? I didn't get the last name. . . . Oh, Smedick. Why do you want to see us, Mr Smedick?" Joe listened for a moment and added, "All right. Frank and I will come immediately."

Joe hung up and turned to his brother. "A guy with a strained voice, named A. B. Smedick, wants to see us at the Bayport Hotel. Room 309. It has something to do with the cannon mystery. Let's go!"

"Who is he?" Frank asked cautiously.

"He didn't explain."

"We'd better watch out. This may be a trap. I suggest we stay in the hall and talk to this fellow."

Frank left a note for his mother telling of their change in plans. A few minutes later the boys parked their convertible in a car park near the hotel. The elevator in the lobby took them to the third floor and the young sleuths stepped out. Joe buzzed 309 and the boys waited. Presently the door opened. The brothers gasped. Tim Gorman stood there!

"What's the idea of this?" Joe asked.

"Please step in," Gorman invited. "I'll explain."

"We prefer staying here," said Frank coolly.

Quickly Gorman reached into his coat pocket, extracted a wallet, and took out a paper and a card. He handed them to Frank.

"This one is my honourable discharge from the Navy," Gorman said, "and the other my naval identification card."

On the card the boys saw the small photograph of the man in a Navy uniform. Joe inspected it closely to see if any touching up had been done.

It was Gorman, all right, beyond any doubt. The paper was a statement of the man's honourable

discharge from the United States Navy two years
earlier.

"Please come in," Gorman said, and the brothers
entered the room. Their host locked the door and they
all sat down close together.

"I'm using the name of Smedick here for protection
against certain people in Bayport who would like to see
me harmed. They know me by name only."

Without explaining further, he went on, "I've investigated you boys thoroughly and know you're trust-
worthy. I'm very eager to have you help me solve a
mystery."

"We're pretty busy right now on another case," said
Joe, who still felt sceptical about the man.

Gorman looked disappointed. "I'm sorry to hear
that. I really need your help."

Frank suggested that Gorman tell them what the
mystery was. Perhaps they could work on it along with
their other sleuthing.

Fully expecting to hear that the man was looking for
a demiculverin on Pirates' Hill, the brothers were surprised when Gorman pulled a pad and pencil from his
pocket and wrote:

> *Meet me tomorrow at 2 P.M. in the brown shack on the
> dune a mile north of Pirates' Hill. I'll tell you then.*

The boys read the message. Frank nodded but Joe,
suspicious, took the pad and wrote:

> *How do we know this isn't some kind of trap?*

Gorman seemed disturbed by the boys' lack of faith
in him. But he smiled at the Hardys and wrote a note
suggesting that they use the word Collado—the name

of a Spanish artillery expert of 1592—as a challenge, and, for a countersign, the name of Hotchkiss, an American artillery expert.

Joe looked annoyed. "How many people will know about this?" he asked aloud. "And before we go any further, suppose you tell us what you know about cutlasses."

The boy's remark hit Gorman like a bomb-shell. He sat bolt upright in his chair, and his face flushed. "Please, not now," he said in a strained voice. "To-morrow. I'll tell you then. I'll be waiting for you."

He rose, took a lighter from his pocket, and burned the notes. Then Gorman walked to the door, unlocked it, and ushered the boys out.

"I'll see you tomorrow," he said, closing the door.

The Hardys did not speak until they reached their car. Then, as they drove, Joe burst out, "What do you make of all this?"

Frank said his curiosity was aroused and he would like to go to the cabin. "But I'll watch out for any double-crossing."

Joe declared he was going to check with the Navy Department in an effort to learn what Gorman had been doing since his discharge. "Do you realize he didn't tell us, Frank, and the man could have become a real phony since that time?"

"You're right. But I doubt that the Navy Department can give you much help on that score."

Nevertheless, he turned towards their house so that Joe could put in a phone call to Washington and make his request to an officer. He made the connection, but the answer, though polite, was discouraging.

"It takes us some time to make a check once a man has been discharged. It might take weeks."

Joe thanked the officer and hung up. 'You were right, Frank," he admitted. "I guess we'll have to carry on without the information. Well, let's get started for Pirates' Hill."

"Let's borrow Dad's magnetometer," Joe added. This was an electronic mine detector for locating metals under sand. "Shall we drive or take the *Sleuth*?"

"Both," his brother answered. "This gear is heavy. Let's drive to our dock and go on by boat."

Once more Frank left a note for Mrs Hardy, while Joe got the magnetometer, then they drove off in the convertible. Joe, thoughtful a few minutes, said, "Frank, we might even unearth the pirate treasure if there is one!"

"Sure," his brother said, grinning. "But we'd better stick to looking for the demiculverin."

The day was overcast and the brothers found the bay fairly choppy. Frank tied a rowboat to the stern to avoid wading ashore with all their gear. By the time Joe anchored the *Sleuth* off Pirates' Hill, a rough surf was churning onto the beach and the rock ledges.

"Let's do our searching systematically," Frank said. He proposed that they mark off sectors and work along the beach and the dunes, moving slowly up the hill.

They worked steadily until one o'clock. The magnetometer had indicated nothing of importance. The boys sat down to rest and eat the sandwiches they had brought. It was ebb tide and the beach was deserted.

As soon as he and Joe had finished eating, they resumed their work with the magnetometer. Whenever it indicated a metal object under the sand, the boys dug hopefully. As time passed they discovered a battered watch, a charm bracelet and a cheap ring, along with a tobacco tin and an old, rusty anchor.

"Say, we could open a second-hand store," Joe quipped.

"And a junk yard, too."

By five o'clock the beach and part of the hill were full of excavations but the boys had not found any artillery. Unfortunately, the magnetometer short-circuited. It would take some time to repair it, they knew. Weary, they gave up the search.

"At this rate it'll take us all summer to cover Pirates' Hill," Frank remarked, flopping down on the sand to rest.

"Yes, and Bowden's in a hurry," Joe answered with a grin.

They rowed back to the *Sleuth* and started homewards. Soon after supper the Hardy phone rang. It was Chief Collig calling the boys.

"I have some important news for you," he told Frank, who had answered.

"What's up, Chief?"

"First, I want to tell you that we still have the stake-out posted at the cabin in the woods, but no one has showed up yet."

"Too bad," said Frank.

"That's not the only thing I called you up about, though. The departmen has been working on the fire-works case. Since you fellows are interested in finding that phony helper I thought you'd like to know we've traced him to a rooming house."

"Where?" Frank asked.

"Right here in Bayport. His name is Guiness. He

skipped out just before we got there, but we picked up a clue that may help us locate him. Patrolman Smuff found it in a wastebasket in Guiness's room."

Frank gripped the phone excitedly. "What is it?"

"An address on a scrap of paper," the chief replied. "It reads *A. B. Smedick, B. H.*"

· 16 ·   *A Surprising Search*

STUNNED by the information, Frank echoed in amazement, "A. B. Smedick, B. H.!"

"Right," said the police chief. "What do you think B. H. stands for?"

"I'm sure that it means Bayport Hotel," Frank replied. "We spoke to such a person there."

"What! Well, then, maybe you can tell us where Smedick is now. He checked out."

Frank, amazed, said he had no idea. "Joe and I are to meet him tomorrow afternoon along the shore. He probably won't show up. But if he does, I'll try to find out where Guiness is."

"Do that," said Chief Collig and hung up.

Frank rushed to tell his family the news.

"That man who tried to blow us up is either an enemy or a friend of Gorman or Smedick or whatever our Navy man's name is," Frank reeled off in a single breath. He related quickly the message from Chief Collig.

"It sounds to me," their aunt said firmly, "as if everybody connected with this Pirates' Hill mystery is a criminal. You should quit the case."

"And not apprehend any of them?" Joe protested. "Oh, Aunty, we can't stop now!"

"Dad will be disappointed in us if we don't solve this mystery," Frank added. He turned to Joe. "At this point I can almost share your suspicions about Gorman."

Joe grinned. "I thought you'd agree sooner or later, but it took the police to convince you."

"Hold on! I didn't say I'm entirely convinced. I'll let you know after we talk to Gorman at that shack tomorrow afternoon."

"If he shows up," Joe added.

Next morning it was raining heavily. Closing the bedroom window, Frank remarked, "No wonder the bay was kicking up yesterday. This storm was on its way then. It doesn't look as if we'll be able to do any searching at Pirates' Hill today."

During breakfast the boys decided to do some morning sleuthing on the stolen cutlasses. Perhaps they would give an important clue.

"Perhaps they have turned up at some of the curio shops and pawnbrokers by now," Frank observed. "Let's look at those places."

The boys' first stop was a curio shop near the Bayport railroad station. The owner lived alone in two rooms in the rear of the store. Frank gave the old-fashioned bell-pull several tugs. A few moments went by before the proprietor appeared at the door. There was soap lather on his chin.

"Step right in, boys," he said eagerly. "You're early. Just look around while I finish shaving." He returned to the back room.

"This man has got a lot of interesting looking weapons," Frank said presently, after walking round. He eyed an old-time flintlock hanging on the wall. "But," he added, "none of them has any special mark such as the authentic pieces have. These must all be imitations."

"Shall we leave?" Joe asked his brother. "We're probably wasting our time."

Though his voice was low, it carried to the rear of the shop. The proprietor came running out, pleading with the boys not to go until he had shown them the weapons.

"Sorry, we're looking for antique cutlasses," Frank told him.

"What difference does the age make," the man asked, "if you want a cutlass? If you don't have much money, I can rent you a sword."

Joe grinned. "If you can rent me a white Arabian horse along with the cutlass, it's a deal."

The dealer, realizing that he had been trying a little too hard to sell, smiled and told the boys to come back some other time.

"Well, score zero for us on that call," Joe sighed as they climbed into their car.

The Hardys drove across town to a shabby antique shop, owned and operated by a Mr Dumian.

"Yes, I have cutlasses," the dealer replied to Frank's question. He eyed the boys with curiosity over his bifocal glasses. "It's funny you're wanting them. Recently a boy named Gil Fanning—about eighteen years old—sold me five cutlasses. Told me they were family relics."

"Is he a local boy?" Frank asked, interested.

"Yes. He lives in Bayport," Mr Dumian answered.

"On Central Avenue. I paid him twenty dollars apiece —a pretty steep price, but they were the real thing. Beautiful cutlasses."

"May we see them?" Frank asked eagerly. The thought that they might be the Entwistle relics caused his heart to beat faster.

"I'm sorry," the dealer replied. "Right after Fanning brought the weapons in, a swarthy-looking fellow in a black motorcycle jacket came into the shop and bought every one!"

The Hardys shot chagrined looks at each other. It appeared that Latsky had beaten them to the draw! Furthermore, the Hardys were dumbfounded by the appearance of Latsky at the shop—assuming that the man in the leather jacket was he. It certainly looked now as if Latsky were not the person who had taken the cutlasses from the Historical Society's building. Could Gil Fanning have been the thief?

"That's not all," the man continued. "Last evening, just as I was closing up shop, a stout boy came in here looking for cutlasses. And now when you fellows come in asking for the same thing, I begin to wonder if there—"

"Did this stout fellow give his name?" Joe broke in.

"Yes," Mr Dumian said, turning to a spike of notes on his desk. "He wanted me to get in touch with him if any more cutlasses came in. Here it is." He tore a slip of paper off the spike and handed it to Frank.

The paper bore the name Chet Morton!

"Chet Morton! We know him," Joe burst out. "What would he want with the swords?"

"Search me," said Mr Dumian.

The boys thanked him and left the shop. Once outside, they decided to talk to Gil Fanning, then go and ask Chet why he wanted cutlasses.

"What a muddle!" Frank exclaimed, as the brothers went into a drugstore to look up the name Fanning in the Bayport telephone directory. One was listed at 70 Central Avenue.

Frank and Joe drove there in the downpour and found that Gil, an orphan, lived with his grandparents. Tearfully the elderly woman said the boy had not been home for a week.

"He's always been hard to manage," she said, "but we knew where he was. This is the first time he's ever stayed away without leaving word."

"Have you notified the police?" Frank asked.

"Oh, no," Mrs Fanning replied. "Gil phoned he'd be back in a while—had a job. We were not to worry." Suddenly she asked, "But why are you here? Is our boy in some kind of trouble?"

"Not that we know of," Frank answered. "Mrs Fanning, did you give Gil permission to sell any of your heirlooms?"

"Cutlasses," Joe added.

A frightened look came over the woman's face. "You mean swords? We never had any swords. You must be mistaken."

"No doubt." Frank smiled, not wishing to disturb the elderly woman any further. "Well, thank you," he said. "I hope Gil returns soon."

Frank and Joe left, puzzled by the information. Where was Gil Fanning?

The rain was now torrential. Driving carefully, Frank made for Chet Morton's. Presently he came to a sharp bend in the road.

"Better slow down," Joe advised. "This is like a hurricane!"

Hugging the right side of the road, the boys suddenly heard and saw through the torrential rain a car racing into the curve from the opposite direction. It swung awkwardly and skidded, then sped almost side-on towards the Hardys' car!

"Look out!" Joe yelled.

Frank swung to avoid a collision. But in doing so, the convertible veered towards a deep ditch!

· 17 ·   A Missing Pal

THE boys felt a terrific lurch as the wheels on the right side of the car dropped into the soft, rain-soaked ditch. The car tilted dangerously, and Frank fought hard to get it back on the road.

Just when it seemed as if the car could not possibly stay upright, the muddy front wheel leaped onto the hard surface. Then the rear one pulled up.

"Golly!" Joe exclaimed. "I thought we were goners!"

Frank heaved a sigh, then muttered angrily, "That crazy driver ought to have his licence revoked!" He hopped out to inspect the wheels, but no damage had been done.

As he started off again, Joe said, "Say, do you suppose he tried to force us into the ditch on purpose, hoping we'd overturn?"

"You mean the driver was one of our enemies?" Frank smiled ruefully. "If he was trying to cause an accident, he nearly succeeded."

On reaching the farmhouse, Frank and Joe learned from Iola that about an hour ago Chet had taken his flippers and snorkel, and gone to their swimming pool to practise skin diving.

"Chet still wants to buy an outfit like you boys have," said his sister. She smiled. "He says he can't earn enough money for it by working on the farm, so he's going to look for another job."

Frank and Joe chuckled. Their stout friend had never shown any interest in work. Over the years Chet had had to be cajoled by his family and the Hardys to finish jobs he had started. Seldom had he been known to look for work!

"Chet sure must want that diving equipment bad," Joe remarked.

Iola said her brother was intensely interested in skin diving. "Ever since he found that gunner's pick, he's had a great desire to dive for treasure."

Frank and Joe told Iola about their search the day before, then went to the pool to talk to Chet about his visit to the antique store. They wanted to know why he was looking for cutlasses.

To their surprise, Chet was not in sight. At the edge of the pool lay his snorkel and flippers. The Hardys walked round the pool, peering down into the water. Chet was not there.

"He must be off earning some money," said Joe with a grin.

The brothers returned to the farmhouse and told Mrs Morton and Iola that Chet was not around. Both looked concerned. Mrs Morton said that Chet never left the farm without saying where he was going.

"Perhaps he went off with that boy who was here,"

Iola suggested. She told the Hardys that about half an hour ago a youth about Chet's age had strolled in and asked for him. They had directed him to the pool.

"Who was he?" Frank asked.

"We'd never seen him before," Iola answered. "He said his name was Gil. He didn't give his last name."

At this announcement Frank and Joe stared questioningly at each other. Was he Gil Fanning, the boy who had brought the cutlasses to Mr Dumian's shop to sell?

"What's the matter?" asked Iola, noting the boys' puzzled expressions.

Frank told her and Mrs Morton the whole story. Both of them looked worried and Mrs Morton said, "Oh, dear, I hope nothing will happen to Chet!"

Frank and Joe tried to reassure her that he knew how to take care of himself, but secretly they, too, were greatly worried.

"If the boys went off together walking, they probably haven't gone far," said Frank. "We didn't pass them on the road, so they must have headed in the other direction. We're driving that way, Mrs Morton, so we'll look for Chet."

"If you don't find him, will you please telephone?" Mrs Morton requested. "If Chet isn't home within an hour, or if I don't hear from him, I'm going to call the police."

The Hardys hurried off. As they rode along, their eyes constantly swept the landscape, hoping to catch sight of their chum. They went for three miles without passing a car or seeing anyone walking along the road. Presently they came to a combination country store and petrol station.

"I'll go in and phone," said Frank, getting out of the car.

Joe decided to go along, eager to learn any news of Chet. The Hardys spent fifteen minutes trying to get the Morton home. The line was constantly busy!

"I hope it's Chet calling his mother," Frank said.

But when he finally reached Mrs Morton, he was disappointed. Their pal had not returned home and the family had not heard from him. They, in turn, were disappointed that the Hardys had not seen Chet, and Mrs Morton declared that she was going to get in touch with Chief Collig at once.

When the conversation ended, Frank turned to Joe. "What do you think we should do? Keep hunting for Chet, or go on to the shack?"

"Let's go on," Joe replied. "Chief Collig will do everything possible, and we might pick up a clue to Chet's whereabouts by keeping our date."

Frank agreed. They bought two bars of chocolate from the old man who ran the store, then went outside. As they approached their convertible, Joe gasped and grabbed Frank's arm.

"Oh, no!" he cried out, pointing to the two rear tyres. Both were flat!

The brothers rushed over to the car. Not only were the tyres flat, but to their dismay there were huge slashes in them!

"Someone deliberately cut our tyres!" Joe exclaimed.

Frank's face turned white with anger. "Now, what do we do?" he exclaimed.

It was evident that whoever had done the mischief had come there quietly. The boys did not recall hearing a car go past. They wondered whether the tyre slashing

had been the malicious mischief of some prankster, or
whether one of their enemies was pursuing them and
doing everything possible to keep the boys from
meeting Gorman.

"We have only one spare," Joe remarked with a
groan. "Where can we get a second?"

"Maybe the storekeeper sells tyres," suggested Frank,
and returned to the shop.

Fortunately, the old man kept a few seconds in his
cellar. Frank found one that fitted the car and brought
it upstairs. The kindly shopkeeper, feeling sorry for the
boys and disturbed at what had happened, sold the
tyre to them cheaply. Working together, they soon replaced the slashed tyres.

"It's 'way after two o'clock," Frank remarked, as
they went to wash their hands. "I wonder if Gorman
will wait."

Joe reminded his brother that the stranger might not
be at the shack at all. He still mistrusted the man and
was sure a trap had been laid for the Hardys.

"Maybe," said Frank. "Anyway, we'll approach
with caution."

Two miles farther on they reached a side road which
they figured would take them near the shack. It was a
sandy, single-lane drive which twisted through the
scrub pines. In places it was so narrow that the rain-
soaked branches brushed against the side of the car.

Presently the road ended and Frank braked the convertible to a stop.

"There's the shack!" Frank pointed to their right, as
he put the car keys in his pocket.

The ramshackle old building, badly weathered and
sagging, stood between two dunes. The boys trudged

towards it through the wet sand, a fine spray from the wind-swept sea stinging their faces.

"What a dismal place!" Frank exclaimed.

Joe smiled grimly. "Perfect spot for a trap!" he muttered.

"I don't believe Gorman's here," Frank said as the boys pushed on, their hearts pounding with excitement. "There's not a footprint leading to the place!"

As they approached the shack, the boys were amazed to see that the front door was wide open. They concluded no one could be inside, for certainly any occupants would have closed the door against the terrific wind.

Nevertheless, Frank cried out lustily, *"Collado!"*

The boys stood outside, waiting for an answer. The countersign which Gorman had suggested was not given nor did anyone appear.

"It's apparent Gorman's not here," said Joe. "And if this is a trap, we're not going to walk into it. Let's go!"

At that moment the boys heard a muffled cry from inside the shack. Someone must be in trouble!

Their minds intent on helping the person, the Hardys forgot that they had planned to be cautious. Without a moment's hesitation, the boys rushed into the building.

The next instant they were seized by two masked men!

·18· *Mixed Identities*

AMBUSHED by the two masked men, Frank and Joe fought like wildcats. The assailants were much heavier in build and held the boys with grips of steel. Neither man relaxed his vice-like hold for a moment, despite a hard, occasional punch which the Hardys managed to land.

As the boys fought desperately, the face masks slipped off the men—strangers to the Hardys.

Joe wrested his right arm free and sent a vicious punch to his adversary's jaw. The man fell back, groggy. Joe could escape.

"Here I come, Frank!" he yelled.

But in the same instant a kick from the other desperado sent Joe sprawling. In a flash his own antagonist was on top of him. There was little punch left in him but his great weight held the boy down. With the man sitting on his chest and holding his arms, Joe could hardly breathe.

At this point Frank was giving his opponent a rough time. The man was now gasping for breath. "I'll get him really winded," the boy thought, wriggling even harder to break loose.

"Hold still or I'll finish you for good!" the man threatened.

"Just try it," Frank grunted defiantly.

He gave another violent twist and almost broke loose. But the man retained his powerful hold. An unexpected downward swipe with his stiffened hand caught Frank on the back of the neck and the youth slumped to the floor.

The man turned his attention to Joe and helped his pal pin the young sleuth to the floor. He bound and gagged him, then trussed up Frank and tied a handkerchief across his mouth. The men held a whispered consultation, then one of them went into a back room. He returned a moment later dragging something in a canvas sack. He slid it into a corner and both men left the shack by the front door. The boys heard a muffled groan.

A human being was in the sack!

The Hardys concluded it must be Gorman. He, too, had been ambushed! Were the attackers enemies of Gorman working on their own or were they in league with Bowden? Or perhaps Latsky?

Desperately, the boys tried to loosen their bonds. Frank found that by wriggling his jaw and rubbing the gag against his shoulder he could loosen it. At once he cried out:

"Gorman!"

As the bundle in the corner moved feebly in reply, both boys were horrified to see their assailants rush back into the shack. They had heard Frank's outcry. Without a moment's hesitation, they knocked both boys unconscious.

Some time later Joe revived. He was amazed to find that he was outdoors and dusk was coming on. He saw Frank not far away and on the other side of him the person in the canvas sack.

"We're in a gully," Joe thought, as he struggled to rise.

His arms were still tied behind him and the gag was

in his mouth. Every part of his body ached. He was lying face up in a puddle of rain water and was soaked.

Frank, still unconscious, was also bound and gagged. His position was precarious: he lay in a deeper part of the ditch with rushing water only inches from his face. The stream, swollen by heavy rain, was tumbling along in torrents.

"Frank will drown!" Joe thought in horror. "I must get him out of here!" He struggled desperately and finally by twisting and turning, slipped his own gag off. But his bonds held firmly.

"Frank!" he shouted. "Sit up! You'll drown!"

At first there was no response, then his brother made a feeble effort to rise. Frank raised his head a few inches and tried to pull himself up, but he lacked the strength. Exhausted, he slumped back into an even more dangerous position.

"I must rescue him!" Joe told himself.

He dragged his body through the mud to Frank. Rolling onto his side, he was able to clutch his brother by one leg with his tied hands. Getting a firm hold, he pulled Frank inch by inch from the threatening stream.

It was an agonizing task. The sharp gravel on the edges of the gully scraped Joe's cheeks, but he finally dragged his brother to a safe spot. He managed to remove the gag, but the knots on Frank's bonds defied him. And Frank could not get his brother's untied.

"We'd better give up," said Joe, "or I may be too late to save Gorman."

"Go ahead," Frank said feebly. His own arms had no feeling in them.

The canvas sack lay only slightly out of water. "Those thugs must have figured on having the three of us drown in the stream. They evidently sent us rolling down the bank, but we didn't go far enough."

Redoubling his efforts, Joe crawled to the sack and tried to secure a hold similar to the one on his brother. But the embankment here had a slimy, muddy surface. With each attempt to haul the sack away from the water, Joe slipped. His own body, instead of catching on the coarse gravel to give him traction, went backwards.

"I'll never get Gorman out this way!" Joe groaned. "I'll have to get my hands free."

The bonds were as tight as ever. Joe decided to crawl back to Frank and have him work on the knots again. Halfway to his goal, he heard the sound of an approaching car. Apparently there was a road above the gully!

"Help! Help!" Joe cried out.

The car went by and the boy's heart sank. He yelled even louder. Then, to his immense relief, he heard the car slow down. Then it stopped.

A door slammed, and Joe continued his cries for help. Someone came running and a man leaned over the rim of the gully.

Bowden!

"Joe Hardy!" the man cried out. "Good grief! What happened to you?"

"Come down here, quick!" Joe yelled, "and untie me! And we must get the others out!"

Bowden slid down the embankment.

"There's a penknife in my pocket," Joe told Bowden. "Get it out and cut me loose."

Bowden did so, and together he and Joe freed Frank and assisted him to his feet.

The canvas sack moved. Bowden jumped back, startled. "For Pete's sake, what's in there?"

"It's—" Joe started to say, when Frank gave his brother a warning look.

"We don't know," Frank spoke up, "but it's probably a man. Two thugs knocked Joe and me out. They must have put all three of us here."

He and Joe went to the sack. Both were wondering what Bowden's reaction was going to be when he and Gorman faced each other.

With the penknife Joe slashed the cords that bound the sack and yanked it open. A cry of astonishment burst from the Hardys. *The prisoner was not Gorman! He was Chet Morton!*

The stout boy, bound and gagged, and wearing only bathing trunks, gazed at his rescuers stupidly. He was weak and in a state of shock.

"Chet!" the Hardys exclaimed, removing his bonds.

As their pal took in great draughts of fresh air, Bowden asked, "Is he a friend of yours?"

"Yes," Joe replied. "We must get him home at once."

"I'll take you there," Bowden offered.

"Thanks. Where are we, anyway?" Frank asked him, slapping and swinging his arms to restore the circulation.

"On the shore road about ten miles from Bayport. Say, where did you fellows get slugged?"

"Somewhere up on the dunes," Frank replied offhandedly. He felt in his pocket. "The car keys are gone. I suppose those guys stole our bus."

Bowden preceded the boys up the steep embankment. Frank and Joe assisted Chet, who could hardly put one foot in front of the other.

"You'll feel better, chum, as soon as we get you something to eat," Joe told him.

Chet nodded. "Awful hungry," he admitted.

Out of earshot of Bowden, Frank whispered to Chet, "We thought you were Gorman."

"Yes," said Joe. "That guy double-crossed us." He looked at Frank. "I guess you're ready to admit now that Gorman is a phony!"

· 19 ·   Chet's Kidnap Story

As THE three boys followed Bowden to his car, the man's denunciation of Tim Gorman came back to them. Bowden probably was right, but where did he himself fit into the picture? The Hardys wondered if there were any significance to the fact that he happened to be passing this spot when the boys were in the gully.

"The less we say the better," Frank warned the others.

Joe got into the car's front seat, ready to grab the controls should Bowden drive off the main road and lead them into any more trouble. But the man drove along normally and in silence.

Suddenly Joe cried out, "There's our car just ahead!" It had been pulled into the side of the road. "Our attackers didn't steal it after all."

Bowden stopped and waited as the Hardys examined the car. The keys were in it. No one was inside, the boot contained only the two damaged tyres, some tools, and two pairs of old swim trunks. It started at once and purred softly.

"Well, thanks again, Mr Bowden," said Frank, as the three boys transferred to the convertible. By this time it was almost dusk. "We'll have to show our appreciation to you by working harder than ever to locate the demiculverin."

Just then they were startled by a sound that resembled a low, muffled groan.

Frank looked round quickly. "What was that?"

"Just the wind in the trees, I guess," Bowden replied as he waved and drove off.

"Well one thing seems certain," Frank said, pulling out onto the road. "I'm sure that Bowden knew nothing about the attacks on us."

"Maybe not," said Joe. "On the other hand, he may have employed those thugs and was driving out here to see if they had followed orders."

"If you're right," said Frank, "he sure got a surprise. And say, what about Gorman? I guess he didn't come to the shack after all."

"But sent those thugs instead," Joe said.

"Listen, you just said it was Bowden."

"Sure I did. I don't know what's going on. I'm completely baffled. Chet, tell us what happened to you. When were you brought to the shack?"

"Shack? Was I in a shack? To tell you the truth, I don't know where I was."

"Don't you remember hearing me call out to Gorman?" Frank asked.

"No. I was unconscious a long time." Chet paused, looking into space. "Here's the story. It all began when I put an ad in the paper."

"For what?" Joe asked.

"Skin-diving equipment. I wanted to buy some second-hand. You know how I like to pick up a bargain."

"Yes, we know," Frank said, smiling. "Get on with your story, Chet."

"Well, this morning a fellow my age came out to the farm to see me."

"Called Gil," Frank said. "Iola told us when we went to see you. What was his last name?"

"Gosh, I don't know. I didn't ask him," Chet said. "I was too excited."

"You mean about getting the skin-diving equipment?" Joe asked.

"That's right. You see, he told me he represented a man who was willing to sell his equipment cheap."

"What happened then?"

"I was out at our pool when he arrived. His car was parked down the road and he offered to drive me to the man's house to look at the gear. Since he was in a hurry, I hopped in without waiting to change."

"What then?" Frank asked.

"This fellow was a crazy driver, believe me," Chet went on. "He was off like a racing driver. On the highway we missed a car by inches as we came into a sharp turn."

The Hardys looked at each other and whistled. "So you were the one in that car that nearly hit us!" Frank exclaimed.

Chet gulped. "It all happened so fast I didn't have time to see who was in the car. My gosh, what if we had crashed!"

"Where did this Gil go then?" Frank prodded.

Chet said that the boy had finally stopped the car in a wooded section which he said led to the house. "As soon as I stepped out, a stocky, masked man jumped from behind a tree. In a flash he had me tied up and blindfolded."

"Then what?" Frank asked.

"While I was lying there in the rain, he said, 'What did you do with the cutlass?'

"'Which cutlass?' I asked. And fellows, what do you think he did? Kicked me and said, 'You know which cutlass I mean.'

"I told him that I had been to an antique shop to buy one but had arrived too late. The man didn't have any left. I sure didn't want to tell him about the one you fellows have."

"I'm glad you didn't," said Joe. "Chet, we were at that shop and heard the story. We think the fellow who bought all the cutlasses was Latsky."

"Honest? Good grief! That sure complicates things."

"Why did you go to the shop?" Frank asked.

Chet smiled wanly. "I was hoping to get a clue for you fellows on the cutlass Gorman and Bowden know about."

"Good try," said Joe. "Go on with your story."

Chet scowled angrily at the recollection. "When I wouldn't tell that guy anything, he flew into a rage. I don't know what he hit me with but he sure put me out. From that time on I don't remember a thing until you found me in the gully."

Just then the car reached the side road which led to the shack where Frank and Joe had been ambushed. Frank turned into it.

"Hey, where are you going?" Chet asked. "I thought you were going to get me something to eat. I'm weak."

"Ten minutes won't make any difference," Frank replied. "I've just had an idea."

"Well, it had better be good," Chet grunted.

Frank said it was possible that the figure in the canvas sack at the shack had not been Chet. Why would his attackers have bothered to take him there and carry him off again?

"The prisoner was probably someone else—maybe even Gorman," Frank declared, "and he may still be there."

"So we're about to make a rescue," Joe spoke up. "But I'll bet you the person is not Gorman."

"Listen, f-fellows," Chet quavered, "I d-don't want to be c-captured again."

"You won't," said Frank. "You'll take the car key and hide in the boot. You can act as lookout and give us the old owl whistle if anyone approaches."

Frank parked in the same spot as before. The brothers put flashlights in their pockets and got out. The area ahead was in semi-darkness, with the shack standing out like a black block silhouetted against the sky.

The Hardys moved cautiously, in order not to step in the footprints that came away from the shack. Mingled with them were drag marks, no doubt made by the unconscious boys' feet as they were removed from the building.

"You take the front of the shack, Joe, I'll go round the back," Frank suggested, as the boys approached it.

The brothers separated. Finding no sign of an occupant, they finally beamed their flashlights through the windows. The shack was empty.

In swinging his flashlight back, Joe became aware of something interesting in the sand a few feet away. Quickly he summoned his brother and pointed out a depression in the damp sand.

"Someone was lying there," he said, "face down."

"Well, it wasn't Chet," Frank surmised. "Or Bowden or Latsky." From head to toe the length was a good six feet.

"Look!" Joe exclaimed. "There's an initial here!"

The boys bent over a spot near the face mark in the sand. Scratched faintly was a letter.

"It looks like a *C*," Joe commented.

"Or perhaps a *G*," Frank said. "It could stand for Gorman."

The boys assumed that the man, bound and gagged, had made the impression with the tip of his nose. A more careful search of the area on the beach side of the shack revealed footprints and drag marks that indicated he had first been taken into the shack, probably in a sack, then later pulled down to the beach and carried off by boat.

The boys trudged back to the shack and again looked at the impression of a face in the sand. Frank felt sure it belonged to Gorman.

"I wish we could make sure," Joe said.

"I think we can," Frank replied, looking down. "Let's make a mould of this face."

The Hardys often made plaster moulds of footprints and handprints. They kept the equipment for doing this in their workshop over the garage.

"We'll have to come back and do it later," Frank said. "In the meantime, we'll protect this impression in the sand."

He went inside the shack and looked about for something to use. In one corner was an old box. Carrying it outside, he placed the box firmly over the sand impression so that the wind would not disturb it.

"Let's go!" Joe urged.

As they started back across the sand towards their car, the stillness was suddenly shattered by the mournful hoot of an owl. Chet's signal that something had gone wrong.

The Hardys broke into a run!

· 20 ·   *An Impostor*

THE hooting was not repeated and the brothers wondered if Chet were in trouble. They raced to the convertible. No one was in sight.

Joe pulled up the lid of the boot which was open an inch. Chet, inside, looked relieved.

"Did you hoot?" Joe asked him.

"I sure did. A couple of guys were here. I heard them coming through the woods, so I gave the signal."

"Where are they now?" Frank demanded.

"Both of them ran back through the woods when they saw you coming."

"Who were they?"

Chet said he did not know. It was too dark to see them well, but neither was the man who had knocked him out. From Chet's description the Hardys concluded they might be the men who had attacked them in the shack.

"They didn't use any names," said Chet, "but they talked a lot." He added that upon seeing the car, they had seemed worried, wondering how it got there. "They decided that perhaps the police had brought it as a decoy. Just then they saw you coming and beat it." Chet laughed softly as he climbed out of the boot. "I guess they thought you were the cops!"

"It's a good thing they did," said Frank, "or we might have had another battle on our hands."

As the three boys drove home, Chet was very quiet. Joe teased him about it. "So weak from hunger you can't talk?" he asked.

"I'm worried, fellows," Chet said. "I wasn't going to tell you, but maybe I should."

"What's bothering you?"

"When our attackers find out we're still alive, they're really going to make it tough for us!"

Frank declared they could not make it much tougher, but agreed all of them should be on the watch for trouble.

Chet gave a gigantic sneeze. "Those guys'll kill us one way or another," he complained. "But I'll probably die of pneumonia."

Joe wrapped a blanket round Chet's shoulders, but he sneezed all the way to the farm. By the time they pulled into the Morton driveway he was feeling chilled.

"Sorry," said Frank, his conscience bothering him a bit that they had not brought their pal home sooner.

"Look!" Joe exclaimed as they pulled up behind a police car. "Chief Collig's here now."

Mrs Morton and Iola were overjoyed to see that Chet was safe. Callie, who was spending the night, and the officer expressed their relief also.

Chet's mother at once insisted that he take a hot shower and go to bed. She prepared a light supper, topped off with steaming lemonade.

In the meantime, the police chief, a'ong with Callie and Iola, listened in amazement as Frank and Joe related their experiences.

Chief Collig agreed that the case had become serious. "Take it easy, fellows," he advised. "I'll notify the state police about that shack. I'm sure they'll want to station a man there."

"Joe and I plan to make a plaster cast of an impression we found in the sand by the shack," Frank told him. "It might be a good clue."

"I doubt that it will work," said the chief. "But good luck. When do you plan to do it?"

"Very early tomorrow morning."

"I'll tell state police headquarters."

The chief said he himself would put more men on the case and station a plain-clothes man near Chet's farm. As he left the house, Mrs Morton bustled into the living-room to report that Chet had finally stopped sneezing. "He'll be asleep in a few minutes," she said.

Before Frank and Joe left they telephoned their home. Mrs Hardy answered and was happy to hear that the boys had suffered no ill effects from their experiences that day.

At home, Aunt Gertrude greeted them at the back door with rapid-fire words of advice about staying away from mysterious shacks.

"We might never have seen you again!" she told her nephews. "I've read about gangsters putting victims into barrels of concrete and throwing them into the sea."

"Ugh!" said Joe, then added with a grin, "That sure would be concrete evidence against them, wouldn't you say, Aunty?"

"Oh, tush!" she said, and went to the stove to remove a panful of warm milk, which she poured into glasses for the boys. "When you've finished this and the supper your mother has prepared, go to bed and get a good night's sleep."

"I guess we'd better," said Joe. "Frank and I have a date at six tomorrow morning." He told her what it was.

Both Aunt Gertrude and Mrs Hardy sighed, and the boys' mother said, "I suppose it won't be dangerous for you to go if a state policeman is there."

"I'll call you," Aunt Gertrude offered.

Next morning at five-thirty she roused her nephews. "Hurry!" she commanded. "Breakfast is ready and cold eggs and toast are no good."

The brothers dressed quickly and went downstairs to find that their mother and aunt had prepared hot cereal, scrambled eggs, and cocoa.

"The sooner you solve this mystery, the better!" Aunt Gertrude said. "It has me on pins and needles."

"Too bad," said Joe. "But I think we'll be closer to a solution when we make this death mask."

"What are you saying? Goodness! Oh, dear! I didn't know someone was—"

The brothers laughed and calmed their aunt's fears. Then, becoming serious, Frank said he hoped the person whose face had made the impression in the sand was still alive.

Joe, pushing back his chair, said, "I'll carry the equipment from our lab, Frank, while you get the car out."

Shortly after six o'clock the boys started off, promising to report back home by lunchtime.

"I shan't be here," said Aunt Gertrude. "I'm going over to the state museum to a lecture. While there I'll explain about the cutlasses. The trip will take me until ten tonight."

"Happy landing, Aunty!" Joe said, smiling.

It was a pleasant ride in the fresh morning air and the sun had risen when the boys arrived at the dunes. At once they were challenged by a state trooper who stepped from the woods. Frank showed his driver's licence and introduced his brother. The man gave his name as Williams.

"Chief Collig said you might come," the officer told them. "Go ahead. There's another officer, named Winn, at the shack."

Lugging the equipment for making the mould, the Hardys walked over and introduced themselves to State Trooper Winn. He said no one had been there since he had come on duty.

The box was still in place over the imprint of the face in the sand. Joe lifted it. The impression was intact.

"That was a good idea," Trooper Winn said. He watched intently as the boys worked.

First, Frank used a spray gun and covered the impression with a quick-hardening fluid. While he was doing this, Joe mixed the plaster in a pail. Then he carefully poured it into the sand.

"When that sets, I hope we'll have a replica of the face, clear enough to be recognizable," Frank remarked.

When the mould was hard, Frank lifted it from the sand and turned it over. The result was an indistinct blob. Only the chin line was clear.

"Tough luck," the trooper said. "The sand dried out too much during the night."

"Still, I'm certain it's Gorman!" Frank said, pointing out the solid, jutting jaw. "He's a victim of those phonies!"

Quickly Joe explained the circumstances to the trooper. "He was attacked by thugs working for higher-ups," he stated.

"Will you tell all this to Williams?" the officer requested. "He'll send out an alarm over the radiophone in his car."

"Let's go!" Frank urged.

The brothers gathered their implements and hurried back to the car. Frank told Trooper Williams of their discovery and he notified state police headquarters from his car, well hidden in the woods, to start a search for Gorman. When he finished speaking, Williams let Frank use the radiophone to contact Chief Collig. The officer said he would order a local search at once for Gorman.

"I'll let you know if we have any luck, Frank," the chief promised.

Frank joined his brother, then the Hardys said good-bye to the trooper.

"What do you say we stop at Chet's?" Joe proposed as they reached the main road.

"Good idea. I'd like to know how he is. And he'll want to hear the result of our experiment."

They found Chet in bed. There was no doubt he had a cold, but fortunately there was no sign of pneumonia.

"Maybe it pays to be fat," he said, smiling. "Keeps the cold out."

The Hardys stayed with him an hour and told him of their morning's activities.

"Golly," Chet exclaimed, "where do you suppose Gorman is?"

Frank shrugged. "A prisoner some place of either Bowden or Latsky. I hope the police find him soon. It may solve a lot of problems."

Joe, eager to continue his own sleuthing, rose and said, "Take it easy, Chet. We'll let you know if anything new turns up."

It was noon when the brothers reached home. Mrs Hardy had a delicious luncheon ready and suggested afterwards that they rest awhile. But the boys were eager to continue their search for the demiculverin.

"I'd like to stay out on the dunes until it's too dark to dig," said Joe. "Let's take some supper with us."

Frank agreed. They kissed Mrs Hardy and said they hoped to be back by nine. Working in the damp sand proved to be a hot, arduous task and just before they ate, the brothers went swimming. When the sun was about to set, they packed their tools and left.

"Not one clue to that demiculverin," said Joe in disgust.

"But we're not giving up!" Frank declared.

At nine o'clock exactly the Hardys' car hummed up Elm Street and Frank turned into their driveway. The boys noticed a dark-blue saloon parked in front of their home.

"A caller," Joe said. "I wonder who it is."

Pulling up in front of their garage door, the boys got out and and went in through the kitchen entrance.

Mrs Hardy greeted them. "You've just missed a friend."

"Who was it?" Frank asked.

"Tony Prito's cousin Ken," Mrs Hardy stated. "He came for the cutlass, as you requested."

"What!" Frank cried in alarm.

Mrs Hardy explained that when the stranger had come to the door, he had told her that Frank and Joe had been at Tony's house telling them about the cutlass. "Tony phoned and said his cousin would pick it up in a few minutes," Mrs Hardy concluded, "so I wrapped the cutlass in newspaper and gave it to him."

"Mother!" Joe cried. "That man was an impostor! We weren't there and Tony has no cousin Ken!"

Mrs Hardy sank into a chair. "Oh, boys, how dreadful!" she wailed. "I'm so ashamed!"

Frank put an arm round her. "Don't worry. But I guess we'd better find that man, Joe."

The brothers dashed to their convertible and sped after the thief.

"There he goes!" Joe cried as Frank turned the next corner.

The convertible leaped ahead. Five blocks farther on, the driver of the blue saloon, apparently unaware that he was being followed, stopped for a red light. Frank and Joe quickly pulled alongside on his left. The man at the wheel wore a black motorcycle jacket.

"Latsky!" the brothers exclaimed.

On the seat alongside him Joe saw a narrow, newspaper-wrapped package. The stolen cutlass!

As Joe flung open the door and hopped out, the man turned to look at the boys. His swarthy face twisted into an ugly sneer.

"We've got you, Latsky!" Joe cried out, quickly reaching for the door handle.

But the ex-convict was quicker. Revving his engine, he shot across the street against the red light. Joe was flung to the pavement.

·21· *The Wreck*

BRAKES screeched as oncoming cars tried to avoid Latsky. Joe picked himself up and jumped into the car. Frank, gritting his teeth impatiently, waited for the signal to change. When it turned green, he took off in hot pursuit of the fleeing saloon.

"I hope Latsky sticks to the main highways," Joe said, peering ahead for a glimpse of the fugitive. "With his head start, we'll have a tough time catching him if he goes into a side street."

Reaching the outskirts of the older section of Bayport, Frank increased his speed. Suddenly, going over a small rise, the boys saw the red glow of rear lights. A car swung to the left into a T-intersection highway that circled wide to the right, by-passing the outlying residential section.

"It's Latsky!" Joe shouted.

At almost the same moment, the boys heard the wailing of a siren close behind them. As Frank made the turn, Joe glanced back.

"A police car," he said. "I guess the officer thinks we're speeding. Slow down, Frank."

The boy eased his foot off the accelerator and the squad car pulled alongside. Chief Collig was at the wheel. "Where's the fire, boys?" he grinned.

"We're after Latsky," Frank explained, and quickly told of their chase.

"I'll lead the way!" the chief said, and raced off, the Hardys following.

Though the officer drove a special high-powered police car, Joe doubted that he could catch the fleeing car. Latsky had too much of a head start. "Frank," he suggested, "what about the short cut past the old Pell farm? Maybe we could cut back onto the main road and make a road block."

"Great! I'll try it."

Frank turned right at the next lane, roared over a narrow macadam road for a mile, and turned left into another dirt lane. Minutes later he zoomed onto the main highway again.

"Here he comes!" Joe cried out, as two headlights flashed over a low hill behind them. In the distance the whine of the police siren sounded.

Frank slammed on his brakes and angled the convertible across the road, so that the red tail-lights blinked a warning to stop. Both boys jumped out, concealing themselves behind a tree along the roadside.

"Wow!" Joe whispered. "Latsky and the chief must be doing ninety!"

Suddenly there was a squeal of rubber on concrete. Latsky had seen the road block and braked. His car swayed from side to side.

"He's out of control!" Frank cried, as the oncoming car headed wildly for the tree behind which the brothers had taken cover.

As the boys ran, the car bounced off the tree, screeched across the road into a field, and overturned.

"Whew!" Joe gave a low whistle as he and Frank sped towards the wreck, torches in hand.

While they were still some distance from it, they saw Latsky stumble from the car. Dazed for the moment, the man staggered, but quickly regained his balance and sped off into the darkness of woods beyond.

At that moment Chief Collig roared up and stopped. Seeing the torches he got out and hurried across the field. The Hardys were trying to pick up Latsky's footprints.

"Am I seeing things?" the officer cried out. "How did you get here? And what's going on?"

"Short cut," Joe said. "We set up a road block and stopped Latsky, but he ran into these woods."

Swinging the bright beams of their lights in the woods, the trio of pursuers followed the footprints. They led to a wide brook.

"Latsky's clever," Chief Collig remarked. "He must have entered the water and walked either up or downstream."

The brothers offered to take one direction while Chief Collig took the other.

The officer shook his head. "No use. I'll radio from my car and have the place surrounded."

The three left the woods. While Chief Collig went ahead to phone from his car, the Hardys paused to look over the wreck of Latsky's car.

"He's dropped the cutlass!" Joe cried out excitedly as his flashlight picked up the glint of the shining steel blade.

Grabbing it, they hurried to the police car. Chief Collig was delighted that the boys had retrieved their ancient sword, then said, "My men are starting out now to track down Latsky. By the way, that wrecked car was stolen. Too bad."

Soon a tow truck arrived to haul the smashed saloon back to the police garage. The Hardys said good-bye to the chief, and started home to give the cutlass a close examination.

After telling their mother and Aunt Gertrude, who had returned, that they had the weapon, the boys went directly to their laboratory over the garage. Under the powerful work lamp, they found that on one side the blade had the name of the maker, *Montoya*.

"There's probably more," said Joe excitedly, getting out bottles of chemicals with which to clean off the metal. Every inch of the fine Damascus steel blade was inspected for other markings or hidden writings. There were none.

"The maker of this cutlass must have considered it too fine to mark," Joe said. Old as it was, the sword still had a keen edge.

Next, the handle was cleaned. Every seed pearl in the design was intact, and the gold leaf was still in place.

"Let's examine that handle closely," Frank suggested, getting a magnifying glass.

There was a heavy, richly encrusted leaf scroll pattern. The boys scrutinized this to look for any gems or contraband. Until almost midnight they continued the inspection, unsuccessfully.

"I still think there might be something in this handle," Frank said stubbornly. "Let's try that special magnifying glass of Dad's."

"Good idea!" said Joe. "I'll get it."

He ran back to the house and in a few minutes returned with the extremely powerful glass.

Frank focused it over the handle inch by inch. Suddenly, he smiled in triumph. "Look here, Joe!" he exclaimed.

Following Frank's finger, Joe saw a tiny line which had been cleverly worked into the leaf pattern. "Do you think it's an opening!" he asked.

"Yes."

With the thin blade of a knife, Frank tried to force open the crack, but this proved impossible.

"Maybe there's a spring hidden somewhere in the handle," Joe suggested. "Let me try it."

Frank handed the cutlass to him and Joe bent over it intently. He pressed each tiny leaf with no success. The crack did not widen.

"Maybe it has some connection with the blade," Frank mused. "But how?"

"The spring could be rusted after all these years. I'll try hitting it on something," Joe said.

He looked round the laboratory and found a slab of stone left over from a previous experiment. Grasping the handle of the cutlass firmly, he jabbed the tip against the hard surface.

Click! The crack widened a full inch!

The boys were jubilant. Frank knelt and quickly but gently picked up the sword.

"The tip contains a tiny mechanism," he said after a moment's scrutiny. "It extends through the blade all the way to the handle."

He inspected the opening and reached into it with his thumb and forefinger.

"Anything there?" Joe asked, holding his breath.

Frank nodded. Gingerly he pulled out a piece of ancient parchment.

"There's writing on it!" Joe exclaimed excitedly.

Frank smoothed out the parchment so that the boys could read it.

· 22 ·   *Gunner's Tools*

"FRANK, this is written in a foreign language," Joe said, disappointed that he could not read it.

The words were not modern Spanish, but, they thought, possibly an old version of t.

"Whatever it says must be mighty important," Frank concluded, "or the writer wouldn't have hidden the message."

"And Bowden and Gorman and Latsky must think so too," Joe added. He grinned. "Frank, we've beaten 'em all!"

Happy but weary, the boys went to bed, the cutlass safely tucked under Frank's mattress.

At breakfast they showed the old parchment to their mother and Aunt. They were all bending over it excitedly when Chet walked in.

"Wow!" he said when he heard the newest development in the mystery. "You boys sure are good detectives."

"We're not good enough to read this," Frank admitted. "It must be translated right away."

Just then the phone rang. "I'll take it," Joe offered, hoping it would be Mr Hardy.

The other boys stood near as he spoke.

"This is Joe," he replied to the speaker. The caller

spoke for some time. Placing his hand over the mouth-piece, Joe whispered to Chet and Frank, "Come here. It's Bowden!"

He held the receiver a distance from his ear to let the others hear the conversation. Bowden said that Gorman had just been arrested in St Louis while travelling under an assumed name.

"Good grief!" Joe exclaimed, then asked Bowman how he had received this information.

"A friend of mine on the St Louis police force, knowing I was interested, just phoned me," Bowden replied. "I guess we can go about our job of locating the cannon without any further interruption from fakes like Gorman."

The boys were sceptical of the story. It certainly did not ring true.

To Bowden, Joe merely said, "Thanks for the in-formation. We're working on the case."

The man told Joe he would let the Hardys know if anything further developed. He was about to hang up when Chet burst out:

"Tell him we've found the clue in the cutlass!"

Frank gave Chet a warning look, but too late. Bowden's next words were, "I heard what someone just said. Congratulations, Joe!"

Before the boy could make any comment, Bowden went on to say that he had planned to tell the Hardys of the cutlass clue, which he had heard about several months ago.

"I had a feeling, though," he said, "that it might be just an old rumour, so I kept the story to myself. And besides, I figured that being such clever detectives, you and your brother would discover the truth, anyway."

"I see," replied Joe noncommittally. Then he said good-bye and hung up.

Chet apologized for revealing the news about the cutlass. The brothers were disturbed but assured him that by working fast they would get to the bottom of the mystery and no harm would result from Chet's slip.

"Now if only we could think of someone who might translate the message on the parchment," Frank said thoughtfully.

"Let's try our Spanish teacher, Miss Kelly," Joe suggested. "If she—"

At this moment the doorbell rang. Aunt Gertrude went to answer it and was given a telegram.

"It's for you boys," she said, handing over the message to Frank.

"This wire is from Dad!" the boy said, as he unfolded the message. "Say, Joe, it's in code!"

The brothers dashed up to their father's study and removed Mr Hardy's code book from his filing cabinet. Quickly they unscrambled the message. Their jaws dropped as they read:

BEWARE DOUBLE-CROSSING OF BOWDEN!

"Double-crossing!" Frank echoed. "Dad must have further information about Bowden."

"I wish he had told us more," Joe said, as the brothers returned to the first floor with the news of Mr Hardy's message. Instantly their mother and Aunt Gertrude became alarmed.

"After all that has happened," said their aunt firmly, "I think you should leave town for a while. You can take me on a trip in the car."

The boys were fearful they might be forced into

making the trip. Both instantly promised to take extra precautions from now on.

"If Bowden doesn't suspect that we mistrust him," Frank said, "we'll have the advantage."

"Which we hope to hold till Dad returns," Joe added.

Chet whistled. "Well, count me out of any more trouble," he said. "I'm off home. Let me know what that foreign parchment says."

After Chet had chugged off in his jalopy, Frank suggested that they call on Miss Kelly and see about having the parchment translated.

"Let's stop at police headquarters on the way," Joe said. "We'll check Bowden's story about Gorman's arrest."

With the parchment tucked securely in Frank's inner pocket, they drove to the police station. There the sergeant in charge promised to check with the St Louis police about the alleged arrest of Gorman. Before leaving, Frank asked if the man named Guiness who had exploded the fireworks had been caught. The officer shook his head.

"Please let us know what you find out about Gorman," Joe said as they walked out.

Frank drove across Bayport to the small cottage where Miss Kelly lived. She was a pleasant, middle-aged woman, well liked by her students.

"We wondered if you could help us solve a mystery," Joe said, as they all sat down in her cool, attractive living-room.

"By the expressions on your faces I thought you must be working on one," Miss Kelly said. "What is it?"

Frank produced the parchment. "Is this Spanish, and can you translate it? We're stumped."

The teacher studied the scrawled writing for a moment. "No wonder," she said. "This is written in Portuguese—old-fashioned Portuguese at that."

"What does it say?" Frank asked eagerly.

"I'm sorry, but I can't translate it," the woman said slowly. "But a Mrs Vasquez I know might help you."

Handing back the parchment, Miss Kelly explained that the elderly Mrs Vasquez was Portuguese and the mother of a fishing boat captain.

"Mrs Vasquez isn't well and doesn't get up until afternoon," Miss Kelly explained, "but I'm sure if you went to see her after lunch, she would help you. I'll give you her address." She looked in the telephone directory and wrote it down. The boys thanked her and left.

"If we can't get the message translated until after lunch," Joe urged, "let's go out to Pirates' Hill and call on Sergeant Tilton. Maybe he can give us some idea of where to dig."

"Okay," Frank agreed. "We haven't had any luck ourselves." He drove out to the sand dunes.

The boys went directly to Tilton's cottage. Dressed in dungarees and a coonskin cap, the sergeant was working in his small flower garden.

"He probably doesn't have buckskins to match the hat!" Joe whispered.

The man was in high spirits. "Hi there, boys!" he yelled.

"Good morning, Sergeant," Frank replied, "We've come to do some more digging for that cannon."

"I see."

"We thought maybe you could show us where you think it should be," Joe added.

"Well, now, let me see," the man drawled as he came towards them. "Suppose I walk round the place with you." He grabbed up a folding canvas chair.

When they had gone about fifty yards along the dunes, he stopped and scratched his head. "Accordin' to my system of reckonin', the gun must have been located just about—No." He moved a few steps to his left. "Just about here."

While Sergeant Tilton lighted an old pipe and seated himself comfortably on his folding chair, the boys started digging. The ex-gunner told them story after story of his Army adventures while they dug deep through the white sand.

"Hold everything!" Joe called some time later. He was standing waist deep in a hole. "I've found something!"

He bent over and came up with a queer-looking gadget. "What would this be?" he asked, handing it to the sergeant.

Tilton examined it carefully. "This here's a gunner's scraper!" he replied.

"Probably belonged to the same gear as that primer Chet found the other day," Frank whispered to Joe.

Protected by sand, it had withstood the ravages of time better than the primer had.

"The cannon's just *got* to be near here!" Joe declared excitedly.

"That's right, my boy." The sergeant wore a knowing look as he handed the scraper back. Puffing on his pipe, he blew out a small cloud of smoke. "Don't stop diggin', lads."

Ten minutes later Frank uncovered a six-foot long wooden pole fixed at one end with an iron blade. As he handed it to Tilton, the old ordnance man exclaimed, "It's a handspike! You must be gettin' close!"

· 23 ·   *Guarding a Discovery*

THOUGH eager to dig quickly, Frank and Joe paused to stare at the strange-looking pole.

"What was it used for?" Frank asked Tilton.

"To manhandle the heavy cannon," he replied. "With this tool, the gunners could move the carriage, or lift the breech of the gun, so's they could adjust the elevatin' screw."

"Boy! We're getting hot!" Joe exclaimed triumphantly. "The cannon will be our next find!"

Jubilantly expectant, the Hardys dug deeper into the sand. But nothing further came to light.

Finally Frank straightened up with a sigh. "Joe," he said, "it's noon. We'd better stop now. You know we have an errand in town."

Joe had almost forgotten their plan to call on Mrs Vasquez and have the parchment translated. "You're right, Frank." He asked Tilton to keep the spike and pole until they called for them. Then the brothers quickly refilled the hole, took their tools, and started back to town.

After stopping at a diner for a quick lunch, the Hardys drove directly to the dock area, where they easily found Mrs Vasquez's modest home. When Frank explained the boys' mission, her daughter-in-law ushered them inside.

A white-haired old lady with black eyes stared curiously at the Hardys from a rocking chair. She smiled, adjusted her black shawl, and motioned for them to be seated.

"Mother doesn't speak much English," the daughter-in-law said, "but I'll translate for you."

The Vasquezes spoke rapidly in Portuguese, then the old lady leaned back and read the parchment. When she looked up, more words in Portuguese followed between the women.

"What is she saying?" Joe asked eagerly.

"Mama says this message gives directions."

"For what?" Frank's heart pounded.

Again there was a rapid exchange of words in the foreign tongue, then the younger woman smiled. "Directions to a cannon. Is that right?"

"Wow! I'll say it is!" Joe could not contain himself. "Frank, this breaks the case wide open!"

The older boy remained calm. He asked, "Does it say where the cannon is located?"

"Yes. I'll write it all down."

"In English, please!" Joe requested.

As Mrs Vasquez spoke, the younger woman translated and wrote:

On high rock Alaqua Cove due east setting sun first day July is treasure cannon. Demiculverin.

The woman smiled. "Does this mean anything to you boys? Where is Alaqua Cove?"

"That was the old Indian name for Bayport, I think," Frank replied. "Thanks a million. And please, keep this a secret—for a while at least."

"Oh, yes. Mama and I will say nothing until you tell us we can. I'm glad we could help you."

Frank and Joe bowed to Mrs Vasquez, then left. They were grinning ecstatically.

"At last we're going to solve this mystery!" Joe exclaimed jubilantly.

"The time of year is perfect," Frank said. "If we're wrong, we're no detectives."

"Right."

On reaching Pirates' Hill with their digging tools, Joe became uneasy. "I hate to wait until sunset. Can't we start?"

"Sure. I've been here so much in the past few days that I can tell you exactly where the sun will set." Frank pointed to a distant church spire. "Right there." He took a compass from his pocket and moved until his back was east of the spire. "The cannon should be somewhere along this line." He shuffled through the sand.

"The directions said 'high rock,' " Joe reminded him. "There are rocks under this sand. Let's try the highest point on this line."

The boys set to work. For half an hour they dug furiously. Finally, Frank's spade struck metal!

"J-Joe!" Frank exclaimed. "The cannon!"

A moment later they uncovered the curve of a barrel, and judging from its dimensions, they were convinced that this was the Spanish demiculverin for which they had been searching.

"Success!" Joe cried, thumping Frank's back.

Frank wore the broadest grin his brother had ever seen. "This is super!" he exclaimed.

With their shovels the boys quickly concealed the valuable discovery until they could return the next day and uncover it completely. Then, to bewilder any prying eyes, the Hardys decided to make small excavations elsewhere. They wandered off and started to dig at random.

A short time later two figures appeared over the dunes. Chet and Tony Prito!

"We came out in the *Napoli*," Tony said. "Thought you'd be here. We called your mother who said to give you a message."

"About Gorman," Chet added. "The police left word that he's not in St Louis."

"Just as we suspected," said Frank. "I wonder if Chief Collig has any news about Gorman."

"No," said Chet. "He phoned to say that there was no progress on that score. Say, have you fellows had any luck out here?"

Frank, in a low voice, told him about finding the demiculverin. "Yee-ow!" Chet exploded.

Tony congratulated his friends and asked what the Hardys' next move would be.

"We'll dig up the whole cannon tomorrow," Frank replied.

"I wish we could stay here tonight and get an early start," Joe said. "How about camping out to stand guard over the cannon?"

"Swell idea," said Frank. "Remember Dad's warning about Bowden—he may double-cross us. And that could happen any minute."

Tony offered to go back to town and pick up a tent, sleeping bags, and food. "I'll call your folks and tell 'em, fellows," he promised.

The camp on Pirates' Hill was ready by nightfall, the tent pitched on the cannon site. As the stars came out, the Hardys and Chet crawled into their shelter. Tony was to stand guard first and posted himself outside the tent flap.

At ten o'clock Tony became aware of an approaching figure. Instantly he wakened his sleeping pals. They waited tensely until the person was almost at the tent.

"I'll get him!" Joe cried.

The campers lunged out of the shelter and Joe was about to tackle the oncoming figure when they recognized him.

"Sergeant Tilton!" Frank exclaimed.

The boys smiled at the man's clothes. He looked enough like a pirate to be one!

"So it's you," drawled the elderly man. Sergeant Tilton explained that he had spotted their flashlights and come to see who his new neighbours were. "I was just tryin' on this outfit from my pirate collection when I saw the light."

Knowing that the old man was inclined to gossip, the boys decided to keep secret their finding of the cannon. They chatted casually with Tilton, telling him they had set up camp to be ready for some sleuthing early in the morning.

"Well, boys," the sergeant said finally, "I'd better git back to my shack. I suspect you'll all be snorin' soon." Chuckling, he walked off.

The rest of the night passed quietly, with the boys rotating the watches as they had planned earlier. By six o'clock they were preparing breakfast, after which, Frank, Joe, and Tony started work under the tent, with Chet as lookout.

Within an hour the three boys had dug a deep pit and uncovered the entire demiculverin. The old field-piece appeared to be in good condition.

"What a beauty!" Frank exclaimed.

"And look at this number on it!" Joe cried out. On the barrel were cut the numerals 8–4–20. "It must be a code for this type. Let's find out what it stands for."

Leaving Chet and Tony on guard, the Hardys drove home to inspect their father's books on cannons. Joe's hunch that the numerals might be a code was in vain. They read on.

Suddenly Frank exclaimed, "I get it! An eight-pound ball and four pounds of powder."

"And twenty degrees of elevation!" cried Joe.

Hearing the excited talk of the boys, Mrs Hardy looked into the room and asked, "Have you found out something interesting?"

"Sunken treasure!" Joe exulted. "A ball shot from the demiculverin probably marks the spot where the old merchantman was sunk by the pirates in that Battle of Bayport!"

Mrs Hardy was astounded. She started to praise her sons when the front doorbell rang. Frank hurried down to answer it. Opening the door, he blinked in amazement.

Bowden!

As Frank recovered from his surprise, he said, "Come in," and called loudly over his shoulder, "Joe! Mr Bowden's here!"

Joe came down the stairs like a streak of lightning. "What's up now?" he wondered.

Bowden smiled. "Can't stay but a few minutes. Good news travels fast. I understand you've located the cannon I asked you to find!"

The Hardy. were dumbfounded. They stared speechlessly.

"I'll soon pay you for solving my case," Bowden continued. "A truck will come out to the dunes tomorrow to pick up the cannon."

· 24 ·   *Human Targets*

THOUGH looks of dismay showed on the Hardy boys' faces, they did not affirm Bowden's statement that they had located the demiculverin. Neither did they deny it.

"Where did you hear that we'd found a cannon?" Frank asked.

The man's reply proved to be another bomb-shell. "I was out there and your friends told me."

Frank and Joe were too astonished to make an immediate comment. They exchanged quick knowing glances. Whatever Bowden's real reason was for wanting the ancient cannon, they were going to try keeping it from him until they heard from their father or the police.

Bowden smiled. "I now own Pirates' Hill."

As the boys watched, thunderstruck, he took several impressive-looking documents from his pocket and showed them to the boys. One was a certificate of sale, another a government release, and the third a letter with a notary-public seal. This stated that Bowden had a right to anything found on Pirates' Hill.

"They certainly look authentic," Frank said, but realized the papers could be clever forgeries.

Mr Hardy's dire warning to his sons indicated that Bowden was probably a confidence man. It was possible that his accomplices could imitate signatures and even print fake documents.

Suddenly an idea came to Frank. The stock certificates of the Copper Slope Mining Company which Bowden had sold to Mr Ash in Taylorville might be counterfeit!

"I must get in touch with Dad about this," Frank concluded.

"It looks as if the hill is yours all right, Mr Bowden. If there's a cannon on it, there may be other treasures, too."

Frank's assurance pleased Bowden. "I hope you're right. And I'm glad you boys see the whole thing my way. To tell you the truth, I thought you might want the old cannon yourself. Accept my congratulations for a grand job!"

After he left, Frank went into a huddle with his brother and told him about the possibility of the stock being counterfeit. Joe whistled and suggested that they compose a telegram in code to their father telling him this, and mentioning the fact that the cannon had been found and Bowden was claiming it. Frank phoned the message to the telegraph office.

"I hope this information will bring Dad up here," Joe said. "Frank, this fellow is crooked. We can't just hand him the cannon!"

"Of course not. Don't forget, Joe, digging out the sand round the demiculverin so that it can be lifted, and lugging the two tons of iron over the sand will be no child's play. It may take days. Maybe something will happen in the meantime to stop Bowden."

"Let's hope so," said Joe. "Well, what do you say

we do some computing on those numbers we found on the cannon?"

He felt that they would indicate where a ball would land if it was shot from the cannon when the gun barrel was raised to the 20 degrees o elevation. The boys discovered that they were unable to solve the gunnery problem exactly.

Frank suggested that they drive over to see Mr Rowe, head of the mathematics department at Bayport High School. "He's teaching summer school, and I'm sure he'll be there now."

The boys set off for Bayport High and found that fortunately Mr Rowe was having a free period. Intrigued by the problem, he went to work, filling several sheets of paper with calculations. At last he said:

"The cannon ball would land two thousand yards away, if trained and elevated at precisely the angle given in the figures."

Frank and Joe thanked the teacher, then hurried to their car. On the way back to the dunes, Frank remarked that if the demiculverin had not been moved from the position in which the pirates had placed it, and currents had not shifted the ship, the ball should land exactly on the spot where the sunken merchantman rested. "And that's where the treasure will be!"

"If your guess is right," Joe said, "we could get permission from the Coast Guard to fire one ball, locate the spot, and then hand over the cannon to Bowden—with our compliments!"

Frank grinned, but reminded his brother that whatever their plans, they must work fast. "Bowden is not going to let any beach grass grow under his feet!" he warned.

Driving directly to Pirates' Hill, they parked off the shore road as before and ran up the dune to rejoin Chet and Tony.

At the edge of it Joe stopped short. Grabbing Frank by the arm, he cried out, "Well, look over there! Bowden again! We can't lose him!"

At the site of the cannon, he and Sergeant Tilton were talking to Chet and Tony.

"Good-bye to our little plan," Joe said woefully.

"Maybe not," Frank remarked hopefully as they rushed forward.

Chet and Tony dashed up to meet the Hardys and whispered that after Frank and Joe had gone back to town the boys had continued digging. The two men had caught them off guard.

"You can see the cannon very plainly now," Tony said. "Chet and I thought we'd surprise you and dig out all the sand from the front of it."

Frank quickly related Bowden's visit to the house. Tony frowned. "Maybe that gossipy Sergeant Tilton told him we were here. They might even be in league!"

As the group reached the men, the Hardys received only a nod from Bowden, but the genial old sergeant began to talk excitedly. Today he was resplendent in the blue field uniform of a Northern officer of the Civil War. He explained that at Bowden's request he was preparing a charge similar to the one he used to test the mortar in the town square at Bayport.

In spite of Bowden's efforts to signal him to keep quiet, Sergeant Tilton continued, "An' I'm goin' to test the strength o' the barrel fer Mr Bowden. He wants to be sure it'll be safe fer him to fire off durin' that there Exposition in Floridy."

At once the Hardys were suspicious. "Are you sure you aren't planning to shoot a cannon ball off right now?" Joe asked.

The old gunner looked in disgust at the boy. "Of course not. That'd be against the law. I'd have to git permission from the Coast Guard."

"That's right," said Joe, eyeing Bowden to watch his reaction. But the man showed none.

As the boys watched Sergeant Tilton, he prepared the powder charge and fired the gun. A thunderous boom followed. As the smoke cleared, he rushed back to inspect the piece for the presence of any cracks.

"She stood up fine!" he exclaimed. "First rate!"

"Well, thanks, Sergeant," said Bowden. "I guess the cannon will do for the pageant. I'll see you later," he added as he walked away towards the road.

The old man began running his hands along the cannon and talking to himself. "Great piece o' work," he declared. He turned to Frank and Joe. "I'd like to tell you a bit about this."

"We'd like to hear it a little later," said Frank.

The Hardys were eager to try locating the old sunken merchantman. When their friends agreed to help, Frank asked Chet to drive to their boathouse in the convertible and pick up the aqua-lung diving gear. Tony offered the use of the *Napoli* from which to work.

When Chet reached the road where the Hardys' convertible was parked, Bowden was just driving away. As the car gathered speed Chet saw a piece of paper blow out of the window. Picking it up, he examined it curiously.

"Why, it's a stock certificate of the Copper Slope

Mining Company!" he said to himself. "It must be valuable. I'd better return it to Mr Bowden."

Then a thought struck him. "This was the tock Frank and Joe were talking about. It might be phony!"

At once Chet decided to leave the certificate at the Hardys' home for inspection later on. He got into the car and drove back to Bayport.

Out on the dunes, Frank was just saying to the old sergeant, "Tell us about this cannon."

Tilton beamed. "Firing a gun like this here one is a pretty risky thing."

He went on to explain that the demiculverin most likely had been used at some Spanish colonial fort before the pirates had captured it. The normal life of such a cannon was twelve hundred rounds. But in an outpost, where it was hard to get new weapons, a piece like this was always fired many rounds beyond that figure, increasing the danger of explosion with each burst.

"When cracks develop round the vent or in the bore," Tilton said, "you got to be mighty careful. The muzzle sometimes blows clean off 'em!"

"Look!" Joe cried. "It's chained to a boulder."

This convinced the Hardys that they had been right in their deductions. The cannon was placed so that a ball fired from it would strike one particular place in the ocean!

The boys took sights along the gun barrel and checked them with their compass. The barrel pointed due east. This would make it easy to estimate the approximate spot where the treasure should be. They chafed under the necessity of awaiting Chet's return.

"What are you fellows aimin' to do, now that you've got this mystery solved?" Tilton asked them.

"Look for another case, I guess," Joe replied. "Right now we're going for a swim." To himself he added, "And look for the buried treasure!"

"Hm," said Tilton. "I ain't been in the water fer nigh on thirty years."

He climbed off the gun emplacement just as Chet came hurrying across the sand. He was not carrying the diving gear.

"Something's up!" Joe declared.

Puffing, Chet halted in front of the others. "I've got big news. Chief Collig phoned your home, Frank and Joe. Latsky's been captured!"

"Honestly?" Frank exclaimed, hardly daring to believe it was true.

"Great!" Joe cried out. "How?"

"Latsky finally returned to the cabin. Seems he had money buried there and had run out of funds," Chet replied. "The police had no trouble nabbing him."

Joe grinned. "Latsky'll be back in his old cell for a long stretch."

After a brief discussion about him, Frank looked at Chet. "In all the excitement I guess you forgot our diving gear."

Chet laughed and told him it was in the car. The four boys said good-bye to Tilton and went to pick up the gear. On the way, Chet told the others about the stock certificate Bowden had dropped and that Mrs Hardy now had it.

"Swell work, Chet!" Frank thumped his friend on the back.

The diving equipment was carried to the beach. As

the boys waded out to the *Napoli*, Joe reviewed what
they would do. Tony and Chet were to remain aboard
the boat, while Frank and Joe did the diving.

"We'll work by dead reckoning on the first attempt,"
Joe told his pals. "Frank and I will go over the side at
the estimated distance from shore."

"Let's get started," Tony urged.

"Hold on!" Frank said. "I think we're foolish to
leave the cannon unguarded with Bowden loose. No
telling what he may try to pull."

"What do you suggest?" Joe asked.

"That one of us go back and watch. If Bowden
comes, our guard can signal and we'll get to the hill in
a hurry."

"I'll do it," Chet offered. "But how can I signal
you?"

Tony took a large, yellow bandanna and a clean
white rag out of the boat's locker. He handed them to
Chet. "Wigwag with these," he said.

"And be sure to hide behind a dune," Frank
cautioned, "so that Bowden won't see you."

"Gee, I'm really going to be busy," said Chet, as he
sloshed back through the water.

The others climbed into the motorboat and Tony
started the engine. Frank and Joe gave directions to the
site of the sunken treasure, using the church spire as a
landmark and keeping on a course due east. Tony
steered the *Napoli* carefully while Frank and Joe tried
to estimate a distance of two thousand yards from shore.

"Stop!" Frank commanded presently. "Unless all
our reckoning is wrong, the treasure ship must be
directly below us."

There was silence for a few moments as the full

import of the boy's words struck them all. They might be about to make an intriguing find!

"Let's go down!" Joe urged his brother.

The Hardys donned their gear and climbed over the side.

Tony, watching Chet intently, suddenly cried out, "Wait, fellows! Chet is signalling!"

Back on Pirates' Hill their pal had seen Bowden sneaking up to the cannon. As he watched the man, terror struck his heart. Bowden was ramming a charge of powder into the ancient gun. Then he inserted a cannon ball into the muzzle!

All this time Chet was wigwagging. The boys on the water interpreted, "*Bowden here. Look out for—*"

The missile ready, Bowden ran to the back of the cannon and inserted a fuse into the vent hole. Chet's hands were shaking with fright. Bowden flicked on his lighter and held it to the fuse, then stepped back.

"Run!" Chet signalled.

Boom!

With a shuddering detonation the demiculverin sent the deadly ball directly towards the *Napoli!*

· 25 ·   *Divers' Reward*

WHAM! *Smack!*

The cannon ball hit the *Napoli* full force a second after the three boys had flung themselves away from it. Spray and debris flew in every direction.

The Hardys, only a few feet away, were knocked unconscious by the concussion. Tony, unhurt, was worried about his companions. He realized that in their diving equipment they would float and could breathe even if they were unconscious. However, he was afraid that his friends might not have survived the shock.

Catching up to Joe, he was just in time to see the boy move his arms. He was alive!

"Thank goodness!" Tony said to himself.

He told Joe a cannon ball had been fired at them and advised him to dive deep to escape a possible second shot. The boy nodded.

Tony went to find Frank. To his relief, he too had regained consciousness. Tony overtook him.

"Do you think Bowden meant to kill us?" Tony asked.

"It certainly looks that way."

Just then Joe surfaced and the three boys looked at the *Napoli*. One glance told them that it was doomed.

"Too bad," said Frank.

"Yes," Joe agreed. "Guess we'll have to swim to shore. Stick close to us, Tony."

The boys struck out towards the distant beach, but they had not swum fifty yards when they heard the roar of a motor launch.

"A Coast Guard boat!" Joe called out.

The launch circled once, then pulled in closer to pick them up. The young lieutenant in charge, who introduced himself as Ted Newgate, was glad to hear that the boys were all right. He glanced at the ruined *Napoli*.

"We heard two reports o a cannon and came to investigate," he said as the boys were hauled aboard. "What's going on here?"

"Someone on the hill tried to blow us out of the

water," Joe answered. "I want to get to shore as fast as possible and find him."

The powerful marine motor kicked up white foam as the boat headed towards land. Nearing Pirates' Hill, Frank gave a startled cry. "Joe, there's Dad!"

"Where?"

"Over there on the beach with Chief Collig and Chet."

Joe shaded his eyes. "And look who's handcuffed to Collig! Bowden!"

When the bow hit the sand, Frank and Joe hopped out and raced across the beach to greet their father, a handsome, strapping man in his early forties.

"Are you both all right?" he asked.

"We're okay, Dad, but no thanks to Bowden," Frank replied.

The police chief said, "You boys can thank your lucky stars you're still here to tell the story. The charge against Bowden will be assault and battery with intent to kill. And the Coast Guard will have something to say about his firing without permission."

Bowden looked completely beaten. The police chief explained that the man had stolen a cannon ball from the town square the night before, hoping to put it to use someday and locate the site of the sunken merchantman.

"When he spotted you fellows out there, Bowden saw a good chance to eliminate you from the race for the treasure."

Joe glared at the prisoner. "We didn't trust you from the start, but we didn't think you were a killer."

The police chief said Bowden had brought about his own arrest. "If the repercussion from that old cannon hadn't knocked him out, he would have got away before your dad and I showed up. He was armed, so Chet wouldn't have had a chance to stop him. Well, greed will catch up with a guy sooner or later. Bowden will have a long stretch in prison to think this over."

Frank asked his father how he happened to have come to Pirates' Hill. "Because I hoped Bowden was here and I wanted to have him arrested at once for selling fake stock certificates." Mr Hardy smiled broadly at his two sons. "You've helped me solve my own case of bringing a notorious gang of swindlers to justice. I've been tracking this fellow's friends all over the South. His real name is Layng. They've been counterfeiting legitimate types of stock, getting prospects through the mail and selling them phony certificates."

Chief Collig beamed. "I hear you fellows kept playing Bowden along like a hooked marlin!"

Joe inquired when Mr Hardy had arrived from Florida. "Only an hour ago," the detective said. "When your telegram arrived, I came up here in a jet police plane. Chet clinched matters by leaving the stock certificate he picked up when Bowden dropped it. The instant your mother handed it to me I recognized it as a counterfeit."

Hearing this, the prisoner winced, chagrined to think that he had given himself away by carelessly losing the certificate.

Collig started to walk towards the shore road. "We'd better get this man Bowden behind bars," he said.

The others followed. When they reached the police car, Chief Collig phoned headquarters to report he had a prisoner. In turn, the sergeant on duty reported that he was holding a suspect for the Hardy boys to identify.

"Follow me in your car," the chief told Frank and Joe, "and we'll find out who it is."

On their arrival at police headquarters, the brothers were first shown a black skin-diving suit and a yellow trimmed skull cap by the sergeant.

"Good grief!" Joe cried out. "The guy that nearly winged us wore gear like this. Where'd you get it, Sergeant?"

"From that man over there. His name is Guiness."

The Hardys turned to look. "The man who shot the rockets at us on the Fourth of July!" Frank exclaimed. "Say, Guiness," he said, walking over to him, "how did you know we were going to be there that night?"

"I didn't," the prisoner answered, "but my chance came right then and I took it."

Guiness admitted that he was in league with Latsky, whom he had met recently. But the prisoner denied knowing Bowden or anyone named Gorman.

"What about the paper with the name Smedick on it which the police found in your waste-basket?" Frank asked. "Didn't you know Smedick was Gorman?"

Guiness denied this, saying Latsky must have discovered Gorman's alias and dropped the paper on one of his visits to Guiness's room.

"Where is Gorman?" Frank shot at Bowden.

He did not answer, but this fact gave Frank a lead. As events flashed through his mind, an idea came to him.

"You had Gorman attacked at the back of the shack on the beach and you had him taken away in the boat he'd rented to get there. Later, you hid him in the boot of your car. We heard him moan."

Bowden's face went ashen. Frank's surmise had turned the trick. Bowden confessed that he had lied to the boys about Gorman's character. He had had him trailed and ambushed at the shack by henchmen. When the Hardys arrived unexpectedly, it had been necessary for the thugs to attack them too. Worried, they had taken the Hardys to the gully and dumped them. Then they had abandoned the car.

Coming back to the shack they had met Bowden and told the story. Later, Bowden had driven past the gully to check and received a real surprise.

"I had to rescue you because I wanted you to think I was on the level," Bowden said. "That moan you heard in my car was Gorman. I told you it had been made by the wind."

"What about him? Where is he?" Frank persisted.

"Gorman's in good shape," Bowden said. "You'll find him in the room next to mine at the motel, tied up. He's supposed to be sick and has an attendant. No one else goes in."

Chief Collig said he would send two men there at once to release Gorman and bring him to headquarters. While the others waited, more facts came out about the case.

During a prison term, Bowden had met Latsky who knew a lot about ancient cannon, including the story of the Battle of Bayport. Each man determined to find the treasure for himself after being released. It became a bitter race between the ex-convicts, with Gorman against both of them.

"First you had to locate the cutlass with the directions," said Frank.

"Yes," Bowden admitted. "Latsky tried to get the

old cutlasses from the Bayport Historical Society building but failed. Then I took them."

Joe snapped his fingers and said, "I see how it went. When you found none of them contained the parchment, you had Gil Fanning sell them for you. Latsky later purchased the five cutlasses only to find that none of them contained the parchment."

"Yes," said Frank, "and you had Chet lured off to be questioned and slugged and put in the gully with Joe and me."

As he was talking, two officers walked in with Gorman and an eighteen-year-old youth.

Chet gazed in amazement. "That's the fellow who got me in trouble!" the stout boy shouted, doubling up his fists.

"Take it easy," Chief Collig advised. "I'll handle this."

The new prisoner was introduced as Gil Fanning, Gorman's attendant. He said he was a newcomer to Bayport. His parents had died and he was now living with his grandparents. He had needed money, so he had started working for Bowden.

"I—I didn't think I was doing anything wrong," Gil said. "Then first thing I knew, I was in so deep I couldn't get out. It'll kill the old folks when they find out."

Bowden admitted that the boy had been his dupe, and hoped that harsh punishment would not be meted out to him. The ex-convict at first would not reveal the names of his henchmen, but finally he did, and Chief Collig ordered their immediate arrest.

The Hardys turned to Gorman and asked if he felt all right. "Yes," he said, "and I'm glad you fellows uncovered the secret in the cutlass, instead of Latsky and the others."

He told them that the directions to the location of the cannon, according to the legend, had been hidden in the cutlass belonging to the pirates' captain. It had been lost ashore during a scuffle among the pirates themselves.

"Go on! Go on!" Joe urged as Gorman paused.

The former Navy man said he had learned about the treasure and the demiculverin from an ancient diary. "It was written by the wife of the merchantman's captain," he said. "She tried for years to locate the site of her husband's sunken ship."

Gorman said he was a direct descendant of the captain and had the diary in his possession. After an honourable discharge from the Navy he had decided to try finding the sunken treasure.

Joe smiled and asked a question of Bowden. "Was it Latsky who threatened you in the message we found on your door and sent us one?"

Bowden nodded. "He later knocked me out when I was talking to you fellows on the phone."

"And tell me, who was hiding under the tarpaulin in the boat when Halpen warned us away from the sting ray?"

"I was," Guiness replied. "I told Halpen to give you that phony story. And Latsky hired me to dive for the sunken treasure ship. When you boys showed up while I was at work, I thought you were hunting too. So I shot at you with a spear to scare you off."

When the questioning ended, the prisoners were led away and the others left. Mr Hardy invited Gorman to stay at their home until he had recovered completely from the manhandling he had received.

"Thank you. I accept," the young man said, smiling.

"And please forgive Joe and me for suspecting you," Frank spoke up.

"I will on one condition," Gorman replied with a grin. "That you four boys show me where that treasure is and let me share with you whatever the government will let us take."

The Hardys laughed and Joe said, "That won't be hard to take!"

"But first," said Frank, "from whatever we get, I suggest that we buy Tony a new and even better *Napoli*."

The others quickly agreed, then Joe said, "I guess this treasure hunt will be the most exciting adventure we've ever had."

But another was soon to come their way, which was to become known as *The Flickering Torch Mystery*.

Two days later the whole group, in skin-diving outfits, climbed over the side of the *Sleuth* and descended to a depth of thirty feet. There lay the ancient merchantman, its timbers rotted away, and moss and barnacles covering the metal parts.

Cautiously Gorman and the boys swam in and out, removing the debris. At last their search was rewarded. There, in the uncovered hold of the old vessel, lay a vast quantity of gold bullion. Through their masks, the divers beamed at one another triumphantly.

The Hardys and their friends had found the ancient treasure!

THE SECRET
OF THE OLD MILL

The Secret of the Old Mill was first published in the UK in
1972 by William Collins Sons & Co. Ltd.

"The Hardy Boys, so you're the snoopers we've trapped!"

A Narrow Escape

"WONDER what mystery Dad's working on now?" Joe Hardy asked.

His brother Frank looked eagerly down the platform of the Bayport railroad station. "It must be a very important case, the way Dad dashed off to Detroit. We'll know in a few minutes."

Joe looked at his watch impatiently. "Train's late."

Both boys were wondering too about a certain surprise their father had hinted might be ready for them upon his return.

Waiting with Frank and Joe for Mr Hardy's arrival was their best friend, Chet Morton. "Your dad's cases are always exciting—and dangerous," the plump, ruddy-faced boy remarked. "Do you think he'll give you a chance to help out on this one?"

"We sure hope so," Joe replied eagerly.

"Well, if I know you fellows," Chet went on, "you'll get mixed up in the mystery somehow—and so will I, sooner or later. There goes my peaceful summer vacation!"

Frank and Joe chuckled, knowing that Chet, despite his penchant for taking things easy and avoiding unnecessary risks, would stick by them through any peril.

Dark-haired, eighteen-year-old Frank, and blond, impetuous Joe, a year younger, had often assisted their detective father, Fenton Hardy, in solving baffling mysteries. There was nothing the two brothers liked more than tackling a tough case, either with their father or by themselves.

Chet gave a huge sigh and leaned against a baggage truck as though his weight were too much for him. "I sure could use something to eat," he declared. "I should have brought along some candy or peanuts."

The Hardys exchanged winks. They frequently needled their friend about his appetite, and Joe could not resist doing so now.

"What's the matter, Chet? Didn't you have lunch? Or did you forget to eat?"

The thought of this remote possibility brought a hearty laugh from Frank. Chet threw both boys a glance of mock indignation, then grinned. "Okay, okay. I'm going inside to get some candy from the machine."

As Chet went into the station, the Hardys looked across to the opposite platform where a northbound train roared in. The powerful diesel ground to a halt, sparks flashing from under the wheels. Passengers began to alight.

"Did you notice that there weren't any passengers waiting to board the train?" Frank remarked.

At that moment a man dashed up the stairs on to the platform towards the rear of the train. As the train started to move, the stranger made a leap for the last car.

"Guess he made it. That fellow's lucky," Joe commented as the train sped away. "*And* crazy!"

"You're telling me!" Chet exclaimed, as he rejoined the brothers. Munching on a chocolate bar, he added: "That same man stopped me in the station and asked me to change a twenty-dollar bill. There was a long line at the ticket window, so he didn't want to wait for change there. He grabbed the money I gave him and rushed out of the door as if the police were after him!"

"Boy!" Joe exclaimed. "You must be really loaded with money if you could change a twenty-dollar bill."

Chet blushed and tried to look as modest as he could. "Matter of fact, I do have a good bit with me," he said proudly. "I guess the man saw it when I pulled out my wallet to be sure the money was there."

"What are you going to do with all your cash?" Frank asked curiously. "Start a mint of your own?"

"Now, don't be funny, Frank Hardy," Chet retorted. "You must have noticed that for a long time I haven't been spending much. I've been saving like mad to buy a special scientific instrument. After your dad arrives, I'm going to pick it up."

"What kind of hobby are you latching on to this time, Chet?" Frank asked, grinning.

From past experience, Frank and Joe knew that their friend's interest in his new hobby would only last until another hobby captured his fancy.

"This is different," Chet insisted. "I'm going to the Scientific Specialities Store to buy a twin-lensed, high-powered microscope—and an illuminator to go with it."

"A microscope!" Joe exclaimed. "What are you

going to do with it—hunt for the answers to school exams?"

Frank joined Joe in a loud laugh, but Chet did not seem to think there was anything funny about it.

"Just you two wait," he muttered, kicking a stone that was lying on the platform. "You don't know whether or not I'll decide to be a naturalist or even a zoologist."

"Wow!" said Joe. "I can just see a sign: *Chester Morton, Big-game Naturalist*."

"Okay," Chet said. "Maybe even you two great detectives will need me to help you with some of your cases."

The conversation ended with Frank saying, "Here comes Dad's train."

The express from Detroit rolled into the station. The brothers and their friend scanned the passengers alighting. To their disappointment, Mr Hardy was not among them.

"Aren't there any other Bayport passengers?" Frank asked a conductor.

"No, sir," the trainman called out as he waved the go-ahead signal to the engineer and jumped back on to the car.

As the train pulled out, Joe said, "Dad must have been delayed at the last moment. Let's come back to the station and meet the four o'clock train."

"That's plenty of time for you fellows to go with me and pick up my microscope," said Chet.

The boys walked to Chet's jalopy, nicknamed Queen, parked in the station. The Queen had been painted a brilliant yellow, and "souped up" by Chet during one

of the periods when engines were his hobby. It was a
familiar and amusing sight around the streets of Bayport.

"She's not fancy, but she gets around pretty quick,"
Chet often maintained stoutly. "I wouldn't trade her
for all the fancy cars in the showrooms."

"The petrol gauge reads 'Empty,' " Joe observed, as
Chet backed the jalopy from the kerb. "How do you
figure we'll make it downtown?"

Chet was unconcerned. "Oh, the tank's really half
full. I'll have to fix that gauge."

The Hardys exchanged amused glances, knowing
that Chet would soon be so absorbed in his microscope
that he would forget to tinker with the car.

Suddenly Chet swung the Queen around in the
parking area. The rough gravel caught in the tyre
treads and rattled against the rear bumpers.

"Hey! What's the big rush?" Joe demanded. "We
have three whole hours to get back there!"

"Who's in a hurry?" said Chet, adding proudly,
"I'm not driving fast. I just wanted to find out if I
changed the turning circle of the Queen by adjusting
the tie rods."

"Some adjustment!" Joe grimaced. "Think we'll
get to town in one piece?"

"Huh!" Chet snorted. "You don't appreciate great
mechanical genius when you see it!"

In the business centre of Bayport the boys found
traffic heavy. Fortunately Chet found a parking spot
across the street from the Scientific Specialities Store
and swung the car neatly into the space.

"See what I mean?" he asked. "Good old Queen.

And boy, I can't wait to start working with that microscope!" Chet exclaimed as the three boys got out and walked to the corner.

"All bugs beware," Joe grinned.

"You ought to be a whiz in science class next year," Frank said, while they waited for the light to change.

When it flashed green, the trio started across the street. Simultaneously a young boy on a bicycle began to ride towards them from the opposite side of the street.

The next moment a large saloon, its horn honking loudly, sped through the intersection against the red light and roared directly towards the Hardys and Chet. Instantly Frank gave Joe and Chet a tremendous push and they all leaped back to safety. To their horror, the saloon swerved and the young boy on the bicycle was directly in its path.

"Look out!" the Hardys yelled at him.

· 2 ·

Trailing a Detective

THE boy on the bicycle heard the Hardys' warning just in time and swerved away from the onrushing car. He skidded and ran up against the kerb.

The momentum carried the boy over the handlebars. He landed in a sitting position on the pavement, looking dazed.

"That driver must be out of his head!" Joe yelled, as he, Frank and Chet dashed over to the boy.

The saloon continued its erratic path, and finally, with brakes squealing and horn blaring, slammed into the kerb. It had barely missed a parked car.

By now the Hardys and Chet had reached the boy. He was still seated on the sidewalk, holding his head. "Are you all right?" Frank asked, bending down. The boy was about fourteen years old, very thin and tall for his age.

"I—I think so." A grateful look came into the boy's clear, brown eyes. "Thanks for the warning, fellows! Whew! That was close!"

Frank and Joe helped him to his feet. A crowd had gathered, and the Hardys had a hard time keeping the onlookers back. Just then the driver of the saloon made his way through the throng. He was a middle-aged man, and his face was ashen and drawn.

"I'm sorry! I'm sorry! My brakes wouldn't hold. Are you fellows all right?" The driver was frantic with worry. "It happened so fast—I—I just couldn't stop!"

"In that case, you're lucky no one was hurt," Frank said calmly.

The Hardys saw a familiar uniformed figure push through the crowd towards them.

"What's going on?" he demanded. He was Officer Roberts, a member of the local police department and an old friend of the Hardys. The driver of the car started to explain, but by this time he had become so confused that his statements were incoherent.

"What happened, Frank?" Officer Roberts asked.

Frank assured him no one was hurt and said that apparently the mishap had been entirely accidental, and the only damage was to the boy's bicycle. The front wheel spokes were bent and some of the paint was scratched off the mudguard. The car driver, somewhat calmer now, insisted upon giving the boy five dollars towards repairs.

"I'll phone for a tow truck," Joe offered, and hurried off to make the call while Officer Roberts got the traffic moving again.

After the garage truck had left with the sedan, and the crowd had dispersed, the boy with the bicycle gave a sudden gasp.

"My envelope!" he cried out. "Where is it?"

The Hardys and Chet looked round. Joe was the first to spot a large Manila envelope in the street near the kerb. He stepped out and picked it up. "Is this yours?" he asked.

"Yes! I was afraid it was lost!"

As Joe handed over the heavy sealed envelope, he noticed that it was addressed in bold printing to Mr Victor Peters, Parker Building, and had *Confidential* marked in the lower left-hand corner.

The boy smiled as he took the envelope and mounted his bicycle. "Thanks a lot for helping me, fellows. My name is Ken Blake."

The Hardys and Chet introduced themselves and asked Ken if he lived in Bayport.

"Not really," Ken answered slowly. "I have a summer job near here."

"Oh! Where are you working?" Chet asked.

Ken paused a moment before replying. "At a place outside of town," he said finally.

Although curious about Ken's apparent evasiveness, Frank changed the subject. He had been observing the bicycle with interest. Its handlebars were a different shape from most American models. The handgrips were much higher than the centre post, and the whole effect was that of a deep U.

"That's a nifty bike," he said. "What kind is it?"

Ken looked pleased. "It was made in Belgium. Rides real smooth." Then he added, "I'd better get back on the job now. I have several errands to do. So long, and thanks again."

As Ken rode off, Joe murmured, "Funny he's so secretive about where he lives and works."

Frank agreed. "I wonder why."

Chet scoffed. "There you go again, making a mystery out of it."

Frank and Joe had acquired their keen observation and interest in places and people from their father, one of the most famous investigators in the United States.

Only recently, the boys had solved *The Flickering Torch Mystery*. Shortly afterwards they had used all their ingenuity and courage to uncover a dangerous secret in the case of *The Secret of Pirates' Hill.*

"Come on, you two," Chet urged. "Let's get my microscope before anything else happens."

They had almost reached the Scientific Specialities Store when Joe grabbed his brother's arm and pointed down the street.

"Hey!" he exclaimed. "There's Oscar Smuff. What's *he* up to?"

The other boys looked and saw a short, stout man who was wearing a loud-checkered suit and a soft felt hat. Chet guffawed. "He acts as if he were stalking big game in Africa! Where's the lion?"

"I think"—Frank chuckled—"our friend is trying to shadow someone."

"If he is," Chet said, "how could anybody *not* know Oscar Smuff was following him?"

Oscar Smuff, the Hardys knew, wanted to be a member of the Bayport Police Department. He had read many books on crime detection but, though he tried hard, he was just not astute enough to do anything right. The boys had encountered him several times while working on their own cases. Usually Smuff's efforts at detection proved more of a hindrance than a help, and at times were actually laughable.

"Let's see what happens," said Joe.

In a second the boys spotted the man Oscar Smuff was tailing—a tall, trim, well-dressed stranger. He carried a suitcase and strode along as though he was going some place with a firm purpose in mind.

The boys could hardly restrain their laughter as they watched Smuff's amateurish attempts to put into action what he had read about sleuthing.

"He's as about inconspicuous as an elephant!" Chet observed.

Smuff would run a few steps ahead of the stranger, then stop at a store window and pretend to be looking at the merchandise on display. Obviously he was waiting for the man to pass him, but Smuff did not seem to care what kind of window he was looking in. Joe nudged Frank and Chet when Oscar Smuff paused before the painted-over window of a vacant store.

"Wonder what he's supposed to be looking at," Chet remarked.

Smuff hurried on, then suddenly stopped again. He took off his jacket, threw it over his arm, and put on a pair of horn-rimmed glasses.

"Get a load of his tactics now!" Joe laughed. "He's trying to change his appearance."

Frank chuckled. "Oscar's been studying about how to tail, but he needs a lot more practice."

"He probably suspects the man has contraband in his suitcase," Joe guessed, grinning.

The tall stranger suddenly turned and looked back at Smuff. The would-be detective had ducked into a doorway and was peering out like a child playing hide-and-seek. For a moment Smuff and the stranger stared at each other. The man shrugged as though puzzled about what was going on, then continued walking.

Smuff kept up his comical efforts to shadow his quarry, unaware that the boys were following him. Near the end of the block, the man turned into a small variety store and Smuff scurried in after him.

"Come on!" said Joe to Frank and Chet. "This is too good to miss."

The boys followed. Oscar Smuff was standing behind a display of large, red balloons. He was so intent on his quarry that he still did not notice the Hardys and Chet.

Frank looked around the store quickly and saw the stranger at the drug counter selecting some toothpaste. The suitcase was on the floor beside him. As they watched, the man picked up the toothpaste and his bag, and went up to the checkout counter. He took out a bill and gave it to the woman cashier.

Immediately Smuff went into action. He dashed from behind the balloons and across the front of the store. Elbowing several customers out of the way, he grasped the man by the arm and in a loud voice announced, "You're under arrest! Come with me!"

The man looked at Oscar Smuff as though he were crazy. So did the cashier. Other people quickly crowded round.

"What's the matter?" someone called out.

The Hardys and Chet hurried forward, as the man pulled his arm away from Smuff's grasp and demanded angrily, "What's the meaning of this?"

"You know very well what's the meaning of this," Smuff blustered, and grabbed the man's arm again.

"Now, miss"—Smuff turned to the cashier—"let me see the bill this man just gave you."

The woman was too surprised to refuse the request and handed the bill to the amateur detective.

Smuff took the money. The Hardys stepped up and peered over his shoulder. The bill was a five-dollar one. Suddenly the expression on Smuff's face changed to confusion and concern.

"Oh—er—a five—" he stuttered.

He dropped his hold on the man's arm and stared down at the floor. "Awfully sorry," he muttered. "It's been—a—mistake."

Both the man and the cashier looked completely bewildered. The next moment Smuff whirled and dashed from the store.

The Hardys and Chet rushed after him. They were overwhelmed with curiosity as to what Smuff thought the man had done. The boys soon overtook the would-be detective.

"What's up?" Joe demanded. "Looking for somebody suspicious?"

Oscar Smuff reddened when he realized the boys had witnessed his entire performance.

"Never mind," he said sharply. "I'll bet even you smart-aleck Hardys have made mistakes. Anyhow, this is different. I'm helping the police on a very special, very confidential case."

As he made the last statement, Smuff shrugged off his look of embarrassment and assumed an air of great importance.

"Well, I can't waste precious time gabbing with *you* three." Smuff turned and rushed off down the street.

The boys watched his bustling figure as he disappeared into the crowd. "I wonder what kind of case 'Detective' Smuff *is* working on?" Frank mused.

"I do too," Joe said, as Chet finally led the way into the Scientific Specialties Store.

Mr Reed, the shop owner, stood behind the counter. He was a plump, pleasant man with a shock of white hair that stood erect on his head.

"Have you come for your microscope, Chet?" he asked. As he spoke, the man's head bobbed up and down and his white hair waved back and forth as though blown by the wind.

"Yes, sir, Mr Reed," Chet said enthusiastically. "My friends, Frank and Joe, are looking forward to trying out the microscope just as much as I am."

Joe smiled a little sceptically, but Frank agreed with his chum. Chet pulled out his wallet and emptied it of ten- and twenty-dollar bills. "Here you are, Mr Reed. I've been saving for a long time so I could get the best."

"And the best this is." Mr Reed smiled. "I'll get the microscope you want from the stockroom." The proprietor picked up the money and disappeared into the back of the store.

While they waited, Chet pointed out the various instruments on display in the showcase. The Hardys were surprised at how much Chet had learned about microscopes and their use.

After waiting five minutes, Chet grew impatient. "Wonder what's keeping Mr Reed," he said. "I hope he has my 'scope in stock."

At that moment Mr Reed returned. There was a look of concern on his face.

"Don't tell me you haven't got the model," Chet groaned.

Mr Reed shook his head. When he spoke, his voice was solemn.

"It's not that, Chet," he said. "I'm afraid that one of the twenty-dollar bills you gave me is a counterfeit!"

An Unexpected Return

"COUNTERFEIT!" Chet burst out. "*Counterfeit!* It can't be. I just drew the money out of the bank this morning."

The Hardys, nonplussed, stared at the twenty-dollar bill Mr Reed was holding.

"I'm sorry, Chet," Mr Reed said sympathetically. "But just a few days ago all the store-keepers in town were notified by the police to be on the lookout for fake twenties. Otherwise I wouldn't have checked it. I can't understand, though, why the bank didn't detect it."

Frank's mind raced. "Wait a minute!" he exclaimed. "Chet, what about the man you gave change to at the station?"

"You're right, Frank!" Joe put in. "*He* must have passed Chet the phoney twenty!"

"You mean he gave it to me on purpose?" Chet asked indignantly.

"It's possible," Frank said. "Of course it would be pretty hard to prove whether he did it intentionally or not."

"What did the man look like?" Joe questioned Chet. "We got only a glimpse of him running for the train. He was medium height and stocky, but did you notice anything else about him?"

Chet thought for a few seconds. Then he said, "I do remember that the man had a sharp nose. But he was wearing sunglasses and a slouch hat, so I didn't notice much else."

The Hardys tried to fix a picture of the man in their minds. Meanwhile, Chet looked gloomily at the bogus bill.

"What luck!" he complained. "Here I am cheated out of twenty dollars and the microscope."

"I'm sorry, Chet," Mr Reed said. "I wish there was something I could do about it."

"Don't worry, Chet," said Joe. "You'll get the microscope anyway." He turned to his brother. "How much money do you have with you?" he asked. "I have five-fifty."

Frank emptied his pockets, but all he had was three dollars in change and bills.

"We'll lend you what we have," Joe offered. "Eight-fifty."

Although Chet protested, the Hardys insisted, and Mr Reed added, "You can take the microscope along and pay me the balance when you can."

Frank and Joe put their money on the counter, while Mr Reed went to wrap the instrument.

"Thanks. You're real pals," Chet said gratefully.

When the store owner returned with the package, Chet said, "I'll go right down to Dad's office and borrow the balance. We'll get back here later this afternoon. Thanks very much, Mr Reed."

The boys were about to leave when Frank had a sudden thought.

"Mr Reed," he said, "would you let us borrow that

counterfeit bill for some close study? We'll be sure to turn it over to Chief Collig."

"Swell idea," Joe said.

The proprietor, who was familiar with the Hardys' reputation as sleuths, readily assented. Frank put the bill in his pocket and the boys left the store.

They hurried back to Chet's car and drove to Mr Morton's real-estate office several blocks away. The office was on the ground floor of a small building. They entered and were greeted pleasantly by Mr Morton's efficient secretary, Miss Benson.

"Hello, boys. Enjoying your summer vacation?"

"Yes, thanks, Miss Benson," Chet said, eyeing his father's empty desk. "When will Dad be back?"

"Your father's gone for the day, Chet," she replied. "He decided to go home early."

"That's funny," Chet mused. "Dad usually stays until five at least."

"We have time to drive out to the farm before we meet the train," Joe said. "Let's go."

The Morton farm was on the outskirts of Bayport. When Chet swung the car into the driveway, Joe noticed with pleasure that Iola, Chet's sister, was waving to them from the front porch. Dark-haired Iola, slim and vivacious, was Joe's favourite date.

When they told her about the counterfeit bill, she exclaimed, "What a shame!"

Joe agreed emphatically. "And we'd sure like to get a lead on the man who passed it to Chet."

"Sounds as if you Hardys are in the mood for some sleuthing," Iola said, with a twinkle in her eye.

"What's this about sleuthing?" asked attractive Mrs

Morton as she came outside and joined the group.

The boys quickly explained. Then Chet asked his mother, "Is Dad around?"

Mrs Morton smiled. "He isn't here right now, Chet. He's attending to an important job."

Chet looked disappointed until his sister giggled and said, "Dad's not too far away." Iola winked at her mother and they both began to laugh.

"Your father's important job is at his favourite fishing spot," Mrs Morton told Chet.

"Fishing!" Chet exclaimed. "He never goes fishing during the week!"

"He did this time," said Mrs Morton. "I guess the good weather was too much for him to resist."

A few minutes later the boys were in the jalopy and driving down a country road bordered by woods. Half a mile farther, Chet stopped and turned off the Queen's engine. The sound of rushing water could be heard.

"This is the spot," Chet announced, and they started off through the woods.

The boys soon came to a clear, running stream and spotted Mr Morton seated contentedly on the bank. He was leaning against a tree, holding his rod lightly between his knees and steadying it with his hands.

Just as the boys called a greeting to him, the line began to jerk and almost immediately the rod bent till the tip was close to the water. Mr Morton leaped to his feet and shouted, "Just a minute, fellows! I've hooked a beauty!"

Mr Morton was an expert. He let the fish take just enough line to bury the hook properly, then he very gently braked the reel with his thumb.

So intent was Mr Morton on his fishing that he was not aware that his son was now rushing down the slope towards him. Suddenly Chet slipped on a moss-covered rock and fell forward. He lost his grip on the box containing the microscope and it flew towards the water. Joe, behind Chet, leaped forward and grabbed the box.

"Whew!" Chet exclaimed, regaining his balance. "Good work, Joe! Thanks a million!"

The three boys joined Mr Morton, who was busy landing his catch, a fine, small-mouthed black bass. He held up the fish for them to admire. "Isn't it a beauty, boys?" he said.

"Terrific, Dad," Chet replied, still out of breath from his near tumble. "And I have something to show *you*."

He unwrapped the package and held out the microscope. Mr Morton put the fish in his creel, then studied the instrument closely.

"It's a topnotch one, son," he declared. "And just the model you wanted."

"Yes, Dad. Only there's a slight problem connected with it."

"Oh—oh." Mr Morton chuckled good-naturedly. "I should have known from the look on your face. You didn't have enough money, after all. Well, how much do you need?"

"That isn't all there is to it," Chet hastened to inform him, and told about the counterfeit bill.

Mr Morton's face darkened. "I hope we're not in for a flood of phoney bills."

Frank nodded. "Especially since these are very clever imitations."

Chet's father handed over twenty dollars in small bills.

"Thanks, Dad."

"From now on, Chet, be careful about giving change to strangers," Mr Morton cautioned.

"I will," his son promised fervently. "Getting cheated once is enough!"

Chet paid the Hardys the money they had lent him. Then he said to his father, "I sure was surprised when Mother told me you were fishing—in the middle of the week."

Mr Morton smiled broadly. "I've been working hard the past year on the big sale of land to Elekton Controls," he said. "I thought it was time to take an afternoon off and do some thinking while the fish were nibbling."

"Is that the property behind the plant they just finished building?" asked Frank.

"That's right." Mr Morton pointed upstream. "You can just see the top of the main building from here."

"The property you sold has the old Turner mill on it," Joe remarked. "Quite a contrast. A company that makes top-secret control parts for space missiles in a modern building right next to an ancient, abandoned mill."

"I suppose they'll tear the old place down," Frank remarked.

"No, Elekton has decided to use it," Mr Morton went on. "I suggested to them that the old mill would make an attractive gatehouse for the plant's rear entrance. After all, it's a historic place, built by the settlers when this whole area was inhabited by Indians.

The company has renovated the old mill a bit, restoring the old living quarters and adding modern facilities."

"Is someone living there?" Joe asked with interest.

"I understand a couple of their employees are," Mr Morton replied. Then he continued, "They've even repaired the wheel, so it's turning again. Hearing the rushing water and the grinding of the wheel's gear mechanism brought back memories to me."

"About the Indians, Dad?" Chet joked.

"Not quite, son." His father smiled. "But I *can* remember when the mill produced the best flour around here. Your grandmother made many a delicious loaf of bread from wheat ground in the Turner mill."

"That's for me!" Chet said.

Everyone laughed as Mr Morton reminisced further about having seen the mill in full operation when he was a boy. Suddenly he and the Hardys noticed that Chet had fallen silent. There was a familiar, faraway look in his eyes.

Joe grinned. "Chet, you're turning some new idea over in your mind."

"That's right," Chet said excitedly. "I've been thinking that maybe I could get a summer job at Elekton."

Mr Morton exchanged amazed glances with the Hardys at the thought of Chet working during the summer vacation! But, with growing enthusiasm, Chet went on:

"I could earn the twenty dollars I owe you, Dad. Besides, if I am going to be a scientist, I couldn't think of a better place to work."

"Elekton's a fine company," his father said. "I wish you luck, son."

"Thanks, Dad." Chet smiled broadly. "See you later. I have to go now and pay Mr Reed the money I owe him."

On the drive back to town, Chet told Frank and Joe that he was going to apply for a job at the Elekton plant the next day.

"We'll go along," Joe offered. "I'd like to see the plant and the old mill."

"Swell," said Chet.

When they reached the shopping area in Bayport, Chet drove directly to Mr Reed's store. The three boys had just alighted from the parked car when Chet excitedly grabbed his friends' arms.

"There he is!" the chubby boy exclaimed. "Right down the street—the man who gave me that phoney twenty!"

· 4 ·

The Shadowy Visitor

"THERE he goes! Across the street!" Joe said excitedly. "Let's ask him about the counterfeit bill!"

The three boys broke into a run, dodging in and out of the crowd of afternoon shoppers. The Hardys kept their eyes trained on the stocky figure of their quarry.

But their chase was halted at the corner by a red traffic light against them. The street was congested with vehicles and it was impossible for the boys to get across.

"What luck!" Joe growled impatiently.

It seemed to be the longest red light they had ever encountered. When it changed, the threesome streaked across the street—but it was too late. The stocky man was lost to sight. The Hardys raced down the next two blocks, peering in every direction, but to no avail.

Disappointed, Frank and Joe went back to Chet, who had stopped to catch his breath.

"We lost him," Joe reported tersely.

Frank's eyes narrowed. "I have a hunch that man who passed the bogus twenty-dollar bill to Chet knew it was counterfeit. That last-second dash for the train was just a gimmick to make a fast getaway. But his showing up here in Bayport a couple of hours after he took the train out of town is mighty peculiar."

Joe and Chet agreed. "He probably got off in Bridgeport," Frank went on. "That's the nearest big town."

As the boys walked back towards the Scientific Specialties Store, they speculated about the source of the supply of bogus money.

"Maybe it's Bridgeport," Frank said. "That could be one of the reasons he took the train there—to get a new supply, or palm off more."

"You mean they might actually make the stuff there?" Chet asked.

Frank shrugged. "Could be," he said. "I hope no more counterfeit bills are passed in Bayport."

"There probably will be," Chet said ruefully, "if this town is full of easy marks like me."

"Let's keep a sharp lookout for that fake money-passer from now on," Joe said, "and other clues to the counterfeit ring."

"Who knows," Chet put in, "it could turn out to be your next case."

As soon as Mr Reed had been paid, the boys drove to Bayport Police Headquarters. Chet decided to take his microscope into headquarters and show it to Chief Ezra Collig. The keen-eyed, robust officer was an old friend of Fenton Hardy and his sons. Many times the four had co-operated on cases.

"Sit down," the chief said cordially. "I can see that you boys have something special on your minds. Another mystery?"

He leaned forward expectantly in his chair.

"It's possible, Chief," replied Frank, as he handed over the counterfeit bill. Quickly the Hardys explained what had happened, then voiced their suspicions of the man who had just eluded them.

"Have there been any other reports of people receiving fake bills?" Joe asked the officer.

Chief Collig nodded. "Chet's not the first to be fooled," he replied. "Since the Secret Service alerted us to watch for these twenty-dollar bills, we've had nearly a dozen complaints. But we've instructed the people involved not to talk about it."

"Why?" Chet asked curiously.

"It's part of our strategy. We hope to trap at least some of the gang by lulling them into a feeling of false security."

The boys learned that Chet's description of the stocky stranger tallied with what the police had on file.

"He's a slippery one," the chief added. "It sounds to me as if the man wears a different outfit each time he shoves a bill."

"Shoves?" echoed Chet.

"A shover—or passer—is a professional term for people who pass counterfeit money," Chief Collig explained. He rubbed the bogus bill between his fingers. "This is a clever forgery," he said. "Let's see what it looks like under your microscope, Chet."

It took just a minute to rig and focus the microscope. Then, under Chief Collig's directions, the boys scrutinized the faults in the bill.

"Look at the serial number," the chief pointed out. "That's the large, coloured group of numbers that appears on the upper right and lower left portions of the bill."

As the boys peered at the number, Chief Collig made some quick calculations on his desk pad. "Divide the serial number by six," he went on, "and in this case, the remainder is two."

When the boys looked puzzled the chief smiled. "On the upper left portion of the note you'll see a small letter. One that is not followed by a number. That's the check letter, and in this case it's B."

The boys listened as Chief Collig further explained, "If the letter B corresponds to the remainder two, after you have done the division, it means the bill is either genuine—or a careful fake. The same way with the remainder, one. The check letter would be A or G; and with the remainder three, the check letter C or I, and so on."

"Wow! Some arithmetic!" Chet remarked.

Frank looked thoughtful. "In this case, the test of the divisional check indicates the bill is genuine."

"Exactly," Chief Collig said. "And the portrait of Jackson is good. The border, sometimes called lathe or scrollwork, is excellent."

"But, Chief," said Joe, puzzled, "everything you've mentioned points towards the bill's being the real thing."

"That's right. However, you'll see through the microscope that the lines in the portrait are slightly greyish and the red and blue fibres running through the bank note have been simulated with coloured ink."

In turn, the boys peered through the microscope,

observing the points the chief had called to their attention.

Chief Collig snapped off the light in Chet's microscope and pulled the bill out from under the clips that were holding it in place.

He handed the fake bill to Frank and at the same time gave him a genuine one from his wallet. "Now feel the difference in the paper quality," he directed.

Frank did so and could tell immediately that the forged bill was much rougher and thicker than the genuine one.

Just then the chief's telephone rang. He answered it, speaking quickly. When he hung up, Chief Collig said, "I must go out on a call, boys. Thanks for bringing in this bill. If you come across any others like it, or clues that might help the police, let me know. In the meantime, I'll relay your description of the suspect to the Secret Service, and also turn this bill over to them."

Chief Collig rose from his desk, and the boys walked out of the building with him. On the way, Joe said, "I wonder if Oscar Smuff has heard of the counterfeiting racket, and is—er—working on it."

"I wouldn't be surprised." The chief sighed. "That fellow will never give up."

The boys did not mention their encounter with Smuff earlier in the afternoon, but they were fairly certain that Oscar Smuff had trailed the man because he was a stranger in town and had been carrying a suitcase. The aspiring detective undoubtedly had jumped to the conclusion that the suitcase was filled with counterfeit money.

When the chief had gone, Joe glanced at his watch.

"If we're going to meet Dad's train, we'd better get started."

The three boys climbed into the jalopy and drove off. They arrived at the station just as the four o'clock train was coming to a halt.

A moment later they spotted Mr Hardy alighting from the rear car. "Dad!" cried Frank and Joe, and dashed to greet him, followed by Chet.

Fenton Hardy, a tall, distinguished-looking man, smiled broadly. "I appreciate this special reception— and a ride home too," he added, noticing Chet's jalopy.

"Right this way, sir," Chet grinned.

Joe took his father's suitcase and everyone went to the car. As they rode along, the boys gave Mr Hardy an account of the afternoon's exciting events.

The detective listened intently. In conclusion, Frank said, "Dad, does your new case have anything to do with the counterfeiting ring?"

Mr Hardy did not answer for a moment. His mind seemed to be focused on another matter. Finally he said, "No. But I'll be glad to help you boys track down any clues to these counterfeiters. I have a feeling you'll be on the lookout for them!"

"We sure will!" Joe said emphatically.

As they turned into the Hardy driveway, Frank said, "Maybe more leads will show up around here."

Fenton Hardy agreed. "That's a strong possibility."

They were met at the door by Aunt Gertrude, Mr Hardy's unmarried sister. She was a tall, angular woman, somewhat peppery in manner, but extremely kindhearted. Miss Hardy had arrived recently for one of her frequent long visits with the family. In her forth-right manner she was constantly making dire predictions about the dangers of sleuthing, and the terrible fate awaiting anyone who was a detective.

She greeted her brother affectionately as everyone went into the living-room. With a sigh she asked, "Will you be home for a while this time, Fenton, before you have to go dashing off on another case?"

Chuckling, Mr Hardy replied, "I'll probably be around for a while, Gertrude—especially if the boys run into any more counterfeit money."

"What! Laura, did you hear that?" Aunt Gertrude turned to a slim, attractive woman who had just entered the room.

"I did." Mrs Hardy greeted her husband, then urged the boys to explain.

After hearing of Chet's experience, both women shook their heads in dismay. "Well, the sooner those counterfeiters are caught, the better!" Aunt Gertrude declared firmly.

"That's what we figure, Aunty," Joe spoke up. "We'll see what we can do! Right, Frank?"

"You bet."

Chet added, grinning, "With the Hardy boys on their trail, those counterfeiters won't have a chance!"

"And Laura and I will lose sleep worrying," Aunt Gertrude prophesied.

Frank and Joe exchanged winks, knowing that actually she and Mrs Hardy were proud of the boys' sleuthing accomplishments, though sometimes fearful of the dangers they encountered.

"What delayed you today, Fenton?" Aunt Gertrude asked her brother. "Another case, I suppose."

Mr Hardy explained, "There is a special matter I'm investigating, but I'm not at liberty to talk about it yet."

His next remark diverted the boys' attention from the counterfeiters. "Frank and Joe, will you be free tomorrow to see the surprise I have for you both?" he asked. "It'll be ready late in the afternoon."

"We sure will!" his sons exclaimed together. They knew what they hoped the surprise would be, but did not dare count on it.

The brothers tried without success to coax a hint from their family.

"All I can say," Aunt Gertrude remarked, "is that you're mighty lucky boys!" With a deep sigh she added, "But this surprise certainly won't help my peace of mind!"

"Oh, Aunty!" said Joe. "You don't really worry about us, do you?"

"Oh, no!" she exploded. "Only on weekdays, Saturdays and Sundays!"

Before Chet left for home, he reminded Frank and Joe of his intention to apply to Elekton Controls Limited for a job.

Overhearing him, Mr Hardy was immediately interested. "So you want to enter the scientific field, Chet?" he said. "Good for you and lots of luck!"

The detective told the boys that the company, in addition to manufacturing controls, was engaged in secret experiments with advanced electronic controls.

"Not too long ago," he concluded, "I met some of Elekton's officers."

It flashed through Chet's mind that he might ask the detective to make an appointment for him, but he decided not to. He wanted to get the job without help from anyone. Frank and Joe suggested that Chet came for them early the next afternoon.

"I have an idea!" Chet exclaimed. "Let's go earlier and take along a picnic lunch. We'll be right near Willow River. After I apply for a job, we can eat by the water. Then you fellows can help me collect bark and stone specimens."

"Microscope study, eh?" Frank grinned. "Okay. It's a deal."

At supper Aunt Gertrude commented wryly, "There'll be two moons in the sky when Chet Morton settles down to a job!"

The others laughed, then the conversation reverted once more to counterfeiting. Mr Hardy backed up Chief Collig's statement that the bogus twenty-dollar bills being circulated were clever imitations. "I heard that the Secret Service is finding it a hard case to crack," he added.

Frank and Joe were wondering about their father's other case. They realized it must be extremely confidential, and refrained from questioning him.

In the middle of the night, Joe was suddenly awakened by a clattering sound. He leaped out of bed and rushed across the room to the front window. It was a dark, moonless night, and for a moment Joe could see nothing.

But suddenly he detected a movement near the

front door, then saw a shadowy figure running down the path to the street.

"Hey!" Joe called out. "Who are you? What do you want?"

At the end of the path the mysterious figure leaped on to a bicycle. It swerved, nearly throwing the rider, but he regained his balance and sped off into the darkness.

"What's going on?" Joe cried out.

The Bicycle Clue

Joe ran downstairs to the front door, flung it open, and dashed outside. He reached the end of the path and peered in the direction the mysterious cyclist had taken. The person was not in sight.

Puzzled, Joe walked back slowly to the house. Had the stranger come there by mistake? "If not, what did he want?" Joe wondered.

The rest of the Hardy family had been awakened by Joe's cries to the stranger. By this time they were clustered at the doorway and all the lights in the house were on.

"What's the matter, Joe?" Aunt Gertrude demanded. "Who were you calling to at this unearthly hour?"

Joe was about to reply when he noticed a large white envelope protruding from the mailbox. He pulled it out, and saw that his father's name was typed on the front. "This is for you, Dad."

Joe handed the envelope to Mr Hardy. "That fellow on the bike must have left it."

Joe was besieged with questions, and he explained what had happened.

"It's a funny way to deliver a message," Frank commented.

"Very suspicious, if you ask me!" Aunt Gertrude snapped.

Suddenly they all noticed that Mr Hardy was frowning at the contents of the envelope—a plain piece of white paper.

"What does it say, Fenton?" Mrs Hardy asked anxiously.

He read the typed message: " *'Drop case or else danger for you and family.'* "

There was silence for a moment, then Aunt Gertrude exclaimed, "I knew it! We can't get a decent night's sleep with three detectives in the family! I just *know* there's real trouble brewing!"

Although she spoke tartly, the others realized Miss Hardy was concerned, as always, for her brother's safety.

"Now, don't worry, Gertrude," Fenton Hardy said reassuringly. "The boys and I will be on guard against any danger. This note probably is the work of a harmless crank."

Aunt Gertrude tossed her head as though she did not believe this for a moment.

"Let's all look around for clues to the person on the bike," Frank suggested.

Flashlights were procured, and the entire family searched the grounds thoroughly on both sides of the front doorstoop and the walk. As Frank and his aunt neared the end of the front walk, Miss Hardy cried out, "There's something—next to that bush."

Frank picked up the object. "A bicycle pedal!" he exclaimed. "Aunty, this is a terrific clue! I think we have *four* detectives in the family!"

His aunt forced a rather embarrassed smile.

"The pedal must've fallen off the bike Joe saw," Frank said. "That's why it swerved."

Back in the house, the family gathered in the kitchen. They were too excited to go back to bed immediately, and the boys were eager to question their father. They all had biscuits and lemonade.

"What case did the warning refer to?" Joe asked.

"I can't be sure," the detective replied slowly.

Again the boys wondered about Mr Hardy's secret case, and longed to know what it involved. "Maybe the threat is connected with that one," Frank thought. Before the boys went to sleep, they decided to track down the pedal clue early the next morning.

Right after breakfast, Chet telephoned. He told Frank, who took the call, that his sister Iola and her friend Callie Shaw had offered to pack lunch if they could go along on the picnic.

"Swell," Frank said enthusiastically. Callie was his favourite date. "In the meantime, how'd you like to do some sleuthing with us?"

"Sure! What's up?"

Frank quickly told Chet about the excitement of the previous night. "Meet us here as soon as you can."

When Frank and Joe informed Mr Hardy of their plan to trace the pedal, he nodded approval. "I must go out of town for a short while," he said. "But first, I'd like to examine the warning note in the lab."

The boys went with him to their fully-equipped laboratory over the garage. Mr Hardy dusted the note carefully, but when he blew the powder away, there was no sign of a fingerprint.

Holding the note up to the light, Mr Hardy said, "There's no watermark. Of course, this is not a full sheet of paper."

"Dead end, so far." Joe frowned. "If we could only locate the typewriter this message was written on—"

Shortly after Mr Hardy had driven off in his saloon, Chet arrived. "Where to, fellows?" he asked as they set off in the Queen.

"Centre of town," Joe replied.

On the way, the brothers briefed Chet on their plan, which was to make inquiries at all the bicycle supply stores. In the first four they visited, Frank showed the pedal and asked if there had been any requests for a replacement that morning. All the answers were negative. Finally, at the largest supply store in Bayport, they obtained some helpful information.

"This particular pedal comes from a bike made in Belgium," the proprietor said. "There isn't a store in town that carries parts for it."

The boys were disappointed. As Frank put the pedal back in his pocket he asked the proprietor where parts for the Belgian bicycle could be purchased.

"It might be worth your while to check over in Bridgeport," the man said. "I think you'll find Traylor's handles them."

"It's an odd coincidence," Frank remarked, when the boys were back in the car. "We've come across two Belgian bikes in two days."

When they reached the Traylor store in Bridgeport, the young detectives learned they had just missed a customer who had purchased a pedal for a Belgian bike.

"Who was he?" Frank inquired.

"I don't know."

"What did he look like?" Joe asked.

The proprietor's brow wrinkled. "Sorry. I was too busy to pay much attention, so I can't tell you much. As far as I can remember, he was a tall boy, maybe about fourteen."

The three friends knew this vague description was almost useless. There probably were hundreds of boys living in the surrounding area who fitted that description.

As the boys reached the street, Joe said determinedly, "We're not giving up!"

"Hey!" Chet reminded his friends. "It's almost time to pick up the girls."

Within an hour the five young people were turning off the highway on to a side road parallel to Elekton's east fence. A little farther on, Chet made a right turn and followed the dirt road that led to the rear entrance of the plant.

"Any luck sleuthing?" Pretty, brown-eyed Callie Shaw asked the Hardys.

"What makes you think we were sleuthing?"

"Oh, I can tell!" Callie said, her eyes twinkling. "You two always have that detective gleam in your eyes when you're mixed up in a mystery!"

"They certainly have!" Iola agreed, laughing.

When they reached a grove bordering Willow River, which was to their left, Chet pulled over. "I'll park here."

The girls had decided they would like to see the changes which had been made in the old mill. As the group approached Elekton's gatehouse, they were amazed at the transformation.

No longer did the mill look shabby and neglected. The three-storey structure had been completely re-painted and the weeds and overgrowth of years cleared away. The grounds and shrubbery of the whole area were neatly trimmed.

"Look!" said Frank. "There's the mill wheel!"

As the Hardys and their friends watched the huge wheel turning, they felt for a moment that they were living in olden days. Water which poured from a pond over a high stone dam on the south side and through an elevated millrace caused the wheel to revolve.

"Oh!" Callie exclaimed admiringly as she spotted a little bridge over the stream from the falls. "It looks just like a painting!"

About three hundred yards from the north side of the mill was the closed rear gate of Elekton's ultra-modern plant.

"Some contrast between the old and the new!" Joe remarked, as they left the dirt road and walked up the front path to the gatehouse.

Suddenly the door opened and a dark-haired, muscular man in uniform came out to meet them. "What can I do for you?" he asked. "I'm the gate guard here."

"I'd like to apply for a summer job at Elekton," Chet told him.

"Have you an appointment?"

"No," replied Chet. "I guess I should have phoned first."

The guard agreed. "You would've saved yourself time and trouble," he said. "I'm sure there aren't any openings, especially for temporary help."

"Well, couldn't I go in and leave an application with the personnel manager?" Chet asked.

The guard shrugged. "Tell you what—I'll phone the personnel office instead," he offered, and went back into the mill.

While they waited, the five looked around. At the south side of the mill grounds, a slender, greying man who wore overalls was clipping the low hedges.

"Look, Callie," said Iola, pointing towards a spot near the hedges. "Isn't that quaint? An old flour barrel with ivy growing out of it!"

"Charming." Callie smiled.

The girls and boys started over towards the mill for a closer inspection. At that same moment the guard came to the door. "Just as I told you," he called out to Chet. "No openings! Sorry!"

"Too bad, Chet," Joe said sympathetically. "Well, at least you can keep on relaxing."

Despite his disappointment, Chet grinned. "Right now I'm starved. Let's go down to the river and have our picnic."

He thanked the guard, and the young people started to walk away. Suddenly Frank stopped and looked back at the mill. Propped against the south wall was a bicycle. Quickly he ran over to examine it. "This looks like a Belgian model," Frank thought. "Sure is," he told himself. "The same type Ken Blake has."

On impulse, Frank pulled the pedal from his pocket and compared it to those on the bike. They matched exactly. Frank noticed that one of the pedals looked much less worn than the other. "As if it had been replaced recently," he reflected, wondering excitedly if someone had used this bicycle to deliver the warning note.

"And could this bike be Ken's?" the young detective asked himself.

He inspected the front-wheel spokes. None was twisted, but several had slight dents. "They could've been straightened out easily," Frank reasoned, "and the paint scratches on the mudguard touched up."

He felt his heart beat faster as he waved his companions to join him. When Frank pointed out the clues to his brother, Joe agreed immediately.

"It could be the bicycle which was used to deliver the message—"

Joe was interrupted by a strange voice behind them. "Pardon me, but why are you so interested in that bike?"

Frank quickly slipped the pedal into his pocket as the group swung round to face the speaker. He was the man who had been clipping the hedges.

"Because just yesterday we met a boy, Ken Blake, who was riding a bike of the same model. We don't often see this Belgian make around."

For a moment the man looked surprised, then smiled. "Of course! Ken works here—does odd jobs for us around the mill. You must be the boys he met yesterday when he was delivering some copy to the printer."

"Yes," Frank replied. "When we asked Ken about his job he was very secretive."

"Well," the maintenance man said, "he has to be! This plant is doing top-secret work. All of us have been impressed with the necessity of not talking about Elekton at all."

"Is Ken around?" Joe asked nonchalantly. "We'd like to say hello."

"I'm afraid not," was the reply. "We sent him by bus this afternoon to do an errand. He won't be back until later." The man excused himself and resumed his clipping.

"We'd better eat," Iola giggled. "My poor brother is suffering."

"I sure am!" Chet rolled his eyes. Laughing, the picnickers started off.

Joe, who was in the rear, happened to glance up at the front of the mill. He was startled to catch a glimpse of a face at one of the second-storey windows. He stopped in his tracks.

"Ken Blake!" Joe said to himself.

As the young sleuth stared, mystified, the face disappeared from the window.

· 6 ·

A Mysterious Tunnel

PUZZLED, Joe continued looking up at the window of
the old mill.

"What's the matter?" Iola asked him. "Did you see
a ghost?"

In a low whisper, Joe explained about the face which
had disappeared. "I'm sure it was Ken Blake I saw at
that window!"

The others followed his gaze. "No one's there now,"
Iola said. "Of course the glass in all the windows is
old and wavy. The sunlight on them could cause an
illusion."

Chet agreed. "How could Ken be here if he was sent
on an errand?"

Joe stood for a minute, deep in thought. "I can't
figure it out, but I'm sure that it was no illusion. Come
on, Frank. Let's check."

While the others walked down the hill, the Hardys
strode up to the maintenance man, who was still trimming hedges.

"Are you sure Ken went into town?" Joe asked.
"Just now I thought I saw him looking out of a second-
floor window."

"You couldn't have. You must have been dreaming." The man gave a jovial laugh.

Joe was still not convinced. Impulsively he asked, "Does Ken ever run any errands for you at night?"

"No," the man answered readily. "He leaves his bike here and walks home when we close at five-thirty."

"Does anyone else have access to the bike after that?" Frank queried.

"It's kept in an open storage area under the rear of the mill and could be taken from there easily."

Although obviously curious, the man did not ask the Hardys the reason for their questions. He looked at his watch.

"Excuse me, boys, I'm late for lunch." He turned and hurried into the mill.

As the brothers hastened to catch up with Chet and the girls, Frank said, "Another thing which makes me wonder if that bicycle is connected with the warning is the description of the boy who bought the pedal. *He* could be Ken Blake."

"I agree," Joe said. "I'd sure like to question Ken."

"We'll come back another time," Frank proposed.

The group picked up the picnic hamper from the Queen and strolled down a narrow path through the woods leading to Willow River.

"Here's a good spot." Callie pointed to a shaded level area along the bank. "We haven't been in this section before."

Soon everyone was enjoying the delicious lunch the girls had prepared: chicken sandwiches, potato salad, chocolate cake, and lemonade. While they were eating, the girls were the targets of good-natured kidding.

"Boy!" Joe exclaimed, as he finished his piece of cake. "This is almost as good as my mother and Aunt Gertrude make."

"*That's* a compliment!" Chet said emphatically.

Callie's eyes twinkled. "I know it is. Joe's mother and aunt are the best cooks ever!"

Iola sniffed. "I don't know about this compliment stuff. There's something on your mind, Joe Hardy!"

Joe grinned. "How are you on apple pie and cream puffs and—?"

"Oh, stop it!" Iola commanded. "Otherwise you won't get a second piece of cake!"

"I give up." Joe handed over his paper plate.

After lunch everyone but Chet was ready to relax in the sun. Normally he was first the one to suggest a period of rest, even a nap, but now his new project was uppermost in his mind.

"Let's start to collect the specimens for my microscope," he urged his friends.

The Hardys groaned good-naturedly at Chet's enthusiasm, but readily agreed.

"We'll need some exercise to work off that meal." Frank grinned.

The girls packed the food wrappings in the hamper. Then, single file, the group walked downstream, paying careful attention to the rocks and vegetation. Chet picked up several rocks and leaves, but discarded them as being too common.

"Are you looking for something from the Stone Age?" Joe quipped. "Maybe a prehistoric fossil?"

"Wouldn't you be surprised if I found one?" Chet retorted.

They followed a bend in the river and came to a small cove with a rocky, shelving beach. Here the willow trees did not grow so thickly. The shoreline curved gently round to the right before it came to a halt in a sandy strip along the river bank.

"What a nice spot," said Callie. "We'll have to come here again and wear our swim suits."

"Look!" cried Iola. "What's that?"

She pointed to a dark opening beneath a rocky ledge which bordered the beach.

"A cave!" exclaimed Joe and Frank together.

Intrigued, the five hurried along the beach for a closer look. Eagerly the Hardys and Chet peered inside the entrance. The interior was damp, and the cave's walls were covered with green growth.

"This'll be a perfect spot to look for specimens," Chet said. "Let's go in!"

The boys entered the cave. The girls, however, decided to stay outside.

"Too spooky—and crowded!" Callie declared. "Iola and I will sun ourselves while you boys explore."

The Hardys and Chet could just about stand up in the low-ceilinged cave. Frank turned on his pocket flashlight and pointed to an unusual yellow-green fungus on the right side of the cave. "Here's a good sample of lichens, Chet."

Soon the boys were busy scraping various lichens off the rocks. Gradually they moved deeper into the cave. Frank halted in front of a pile of rocks at the rear.

"There ought to be some interesting specimens behind these stones," he said. "They look loose enough to move."

Together, the three boys rolled some of the rocks to one side. To their great surprise, the stones concealed another dark hole.

"Hey! This looks like a tunnel!"

Excitedly, Joe poked his flashlight into the opening. By its beam they could see that the hole appeared to extend into the side of the bank.

"Let's go in and see where the tunnel goes!" Joe urged.

"Okay," Frank agreed eagerly. "We'll have to move more of these rocks before we can climb through. I wonder who put them here and why."

Rapidly the boys pushed rocks aside until the narrow tunnel entrance was completely exposed. Joe crawled in first, then Frank.

Chet tried to squeeze his bulky form through the space but quickly backed out. "It's too tight for me," he groaned. "I'll stay here and collect more specimens. Anyhow, I'll bet some animal made the tunnel and it doesn't lead anywhere."

"I'm sure no animal did this," Joe called back, aiming his flashlight at the earthen walls of the tunnel. "Look how hard-packed the sides are—as if dug out by a shovel."

Frank was of the same opinion. He pointed to rough-hewn wooden stakes placed at intervals along the sides and across the ceiling. "I wonder who put those supports here—and when."

The Hardys crawled ahead carefully. There was just room in the passageway for a normal-sized person to get through.

Presently Joe called back to his brother, "Look

ahead! I can see a sharp bend to the right. Let's keep going."

Frank was about to reply when the brothers were startled by a girl's scream from outside.

"That's Callie!" Frank exclaimed. "Something's wrong!"

Sleuthing by Microscope

FRANK and Joe scrambled through the tunnel and out of the cave. They found Chet and the girls staring at an arrow embedded in the sandy beach.

"It—it almost hit us," Iola quavered. Callie, who was white-faced with fear, nodded.

, Joe was furious. "Whoever shot it shouldn't be allowed to use such a dangerous weapon!" he burst out. "That's a hunting arrow—it could have caused serious injury."

Chet gulped. "M-maybe the Indians haven't left here after all," he said, trying to hide his nervousness.

Joe turned to dash off into the woods to search for the bowman.

"Wait!" Frank called. He had pulled the arrow from the sand. "This was done deliberately," he announced grimly, holding the arrow up for all of them to see. Attached to the shaft just below the feathers was a tiny piece of paper. It had been fastened on with adhesive tape.

Frank unrolled the paper and read the printed message aloud: " '*Danger. Hardys beware.*' "

Chet and the girls shuddered and looked around fearfully, as though they expected to see the bowman behind them.

"You boys *are* involved in a new mystery!" Callie exclaimed. "Your own or your father's?"

Frank and Joe exchanged glances. It certainly seemed as though they were involved, but they had no way of knowing *which* case. Did it involve the counterfeit money? Or was it the case their father could not divulge?

"A warning did come to Dad," Frank admitted. "This one obviously was meant for Joe and me. Whoever shot the arrow trailed us here."

Joe frowned. "I wonder if the same person sent both warnings."

"I still think Ken Blake could give us a clue," Frank said. "But we must remember that anybody could have taken the bike from the storage place under the mill."

Frank pocketed the latest warning, then the five searched quickly for any lead to the bowman. They found none. When the group returned to the beach, Joe looked at the sky. "We're in for a storm—and not one of us has a raincoat."

The bright summer sun had disappeared behind towering banks of cumulus clouds. There were rumbles of heavy thunder, followed by vivid flashes of lightning. The air had become humid and oppressive.

"Let's get out of here!" Chet urged. "This isn't a picnic any more!"

The young people hastened through the woods and up the road to Chet's jalopy. As they drove off, rain began coming down in torrents. The sky grew blacker.

Callie shivered. "It seems so sinister—after that awful arrow."

Chet dropped his sister off at the Morton farm and

at the same time picked up his new microscope. He begged to try out the instrument on both warning notes and the Hardys smilingly agreed, although they had an up-to-date model of their own.

By the time they had said goodbye to Callie at her house, and Chet had driven the Queen into the Hardys' driveway, the storm had ended. The sun shone brightly again.

Immediately the three boys went to the laboratory over the garage. Here Frank carefully dusted the arrow and the second warning note for prints. He blew the powder away, and Joe and Chet looked over his shoulder as he peered through the magnifying glass.

"Nothing. Same as the warning to Dad. The person no doubt wore gloves."

"Now to compare this paper with the first note," Joe said.

"Right," his brother agreed. "You have the combination to the cabinet in Dad's study. Chet and I will rig up the microscope while you get the note from the file."

Frank and Chet focused and adjusted the microscope, making sure it was level on the table. They plugged in the illuminator and checked to see that it did not provide too dazzling a reflection. When Joe returned, Chet took the two pieces of paper and fitted them side by side under the clips on the base.

"Okay. Want to take a look, fellows?"

Frank, then Joe, studied both papers. "The quality and texture are definitely the same," Frank observed.

Next, he lifted the second note from under the clips

and slowly moved the paper back and forth under the lenses.

"A watermark!" he exclaimed, stepping back so that the others could look at the faint imprint.

"Sure is!" said Joe. "A five-pointed star. This could be a valuable clue! We can try to track down exactly where this paper came from."

"And also the arrow," said Chet. "I'll make the rounds of sports stores in town."

"Swell, Chet. Thanks," Frank said.

After their friend had left, the Hardys consulted the classified directory for paper manufacturers.

They made several calls without any luck. Finally they learned that the Quality Paper Company in Bridgeport manufactured paper bearing the five-pointed star watermark. The brothers wanted to go at once to get more information, but realized this errand would have to wait.

"Dad will be home soon," Frank reminded his brother. "We don't want to miss our surprise!"

"Right. And I'd like to tell him about the warning on the arrow."

When Chet returned from a round of the sports shops, he was glum. "I wasn't much help," he said. "The arrow isn't new, and all the stores I checked told me it was a standard model that could be purchased at any sports shop in the country."

"Never mind, Chet," said Frank. "At least giving your microscope a trial run helped us to spot the watermark on the second warning note. We've located a company that manufactures paper with the star watermark."

Chet's face brightened. "Let me know if you find out

anything else," he said, packing up his microscope. "I guess I'll take off—and do some nature study for a change."

After he had driven off, Frank and Joe walked to the house. Their minds once more turned to the surprise Mr Hardy had for them.

"Wouldn't it be terrific if—" Joe said to Frank excitedly. "Do you think it *is*?"

"I'm just hoping." Frank grinned.

Just then a newsboy delivered the evening newspaper. The brothers entered the house and went into the living-room. Frank scanned the front page and pointed out an item about new trouble in an Indiana electronics plant.

"That's where an explosion took place a couple of months ago," Joe remarked. "Sabotage, the investigators decided."

"And before that," Frank added, "the same thing happened at a rocket research lab in California. Another unsolved case."

"Seems almost like a chain reaction," Frank remarked.

Any mystery appealed to the boys, but they did not have much chance to discuss this one. The telephone rang. Aunt Gertrude, after taking the call, burst into the living-room. From the look on her face, Frank and Joe could tell she was indignant, and at the same time frightened.

"What's the matter, Aunty?" Joe asked.

"More threats—that's all!" she cried out. "This time by telephone. A man's voice—he sounded sinister— horrible!"

Mrs Hardy came into the living-room at that moment. "What did he say, Gertrude?" she asked.

Aunt Gertrude took a deep breath in an effort to calm down. " '*Hardy and his sons are playing with fire,*' the man said. '*They'll get burned if they don't lay off this case.*' " Miss Hardy sniffed. "I don't know what case he meant. What kind of danger *are* you boys mixed up in now?"

Frank and Joe smiled wryly. "Aunt Gertrude," Frank replied, "we really don't know. But please try not to worry," he begged her and his mother. "You know that Dad and the two of us will be careful."

When Mr Hardy came home a little later, his family told him about the threatening telephone call. The boys, however, did not mention the arrow warning in the presence of their mother and Aunt Gertrude. They knew it would only add to their concern.

Mr Hardy was as puzzled as his sons. "It's a funny thing," he said. "At this point it's impossible to tell which 'case' the person is referring to. If I knew, it might shed light on either one."

The detective grinned and changed the subject. "Right now, I want you all to come for a drive and have a look at the boys' surprise."

"Swell!" Frank and Joe exclaimed in unison.

While Aunt Gertrude and Mrs Hardy were getting ready, Frank and Joe went out to the car with their father. Quickly the boys related their afternoon's experience, concluding with the arrow incident.

The detective looked grim. "Whoever is responsible for these warnings is certainly keeping close tabs on us."

Mr Hardy and his sons speculated for a few minutes

on the fact that the pedal found in front of the house apparently had belonged to Ken's bike.

"I think Joe and I should go back tonight to the place where we had the picnic," Frank told his father. "In the darkness we'll have a better chance to sleuth without being seen. And there might be some clue we missed this afternoon."

"I suppose you're right," agreed his father. "But be cautious."

As Aunt Gertrude and Mrs Hardy came out of the house, conversation about the mystery ceased. Everyone climbed into the saloon and Mr Hardy drove off. Frank and Joe, seated alongside him, were in a state of rising suspense. Was the surprise the one thing they wanted most of all?

· 8 ·

The Strange Mill Wheel

A FEW minutes later Mr Hardy was driving along the Bayport waterfront.

"Is the surprise here, Dad?" Joe asked excitedly.

"That's right."

Mr Hardy drove to a boathouse at the far end of the dock area and parked. He then invited the others to follow him. He walked to the door of a boathouse and unfastened the padlock.

Frank and Joe held their breaths as Mr Hardy swung back the door. For a moment they stared inside, speechless with delight. Finally Joe burst out, "Exactly what we had hoped for, Dad!" and put an arm affectionately around his father.

"What a beauty!" Frank exclaimed, and wrung Mr Hardy's hand.

Rocking between the piles lay a sleek, completely equipped motorboat. It nudged gently against clean white fenders as the waves from the bay worked their way under the boathouse door.

The boys' mother exclaimed in delight, and even Aunt Gertrude was duly impressed by the handsome craft.

"This is the same model we saw at the boat show," Joe said admiringly. "I never thought we'd own one."

"She even has the name we picked out," Frank observed excitedly. "The *Sleuth*!"

Shiny brass letters were fitted on the bow of the boat, with the port of registry, Bayport, underneath them.

Mr Hardy and his wife beamed as their sons walked up and down, praising every detail of the graceful new craft. It could seat six people comfortably. The polished fore and aft decks carried gleaming anchor fittings, and the rubbing strakes were painted white. The *Sleuth* seemed to be waiting to be taken for a run!

"May we try her out now, Dad?" Joe asked.

"Of course. She's fuelled up."

Aunt Gertrude shook her head. "The *Sleuth*'s an attractive boat, all right. But don't you two start doing any crazy stunts in it," she cautioned her nephews. "And be back for supper."

When the adults had left, Frank and Joe climbed aboard and soon had the *Sleuth* gliding into the bay. The boys had no difficulty operating the motorboat. They had gained experience running their friend, Tony Prito's boat, the *Napoli*, which had similar controls.

Taking turns at the wheel, the brothers ran the boat up and down the bay. "Terrific!" Joe shouted.

Frank grinned. "Am I glad we stuck to our agreement with Dad, and saved up to help buy this!"

For some time the boys had been putting money towards a boat of their own into a special bank account. Mr Hardy had promised that when the account reached a certain sum, he would make up the necessary balance.

Now, as the *Sleuth* knifed through the water, Frank and Joe admired the way the stern sat down in the water when the boat gathered speed. Joe was impressed with the turning circle and the fact that no matter how sharp the twist, none of the spume sprayed into the cockpit.

"Wait until Tony and Chet see this!" Joe exclaimed, when they were pulling back towards the boathouse.

"Speaking of Tony—there he is," Frank said. Their dark-haired classmate was standing on the dock, shouting and waving to them.

Joe, who was at the wheel, brought the *Sleuth* neatly alongside. He turned off the engine as Tony rushed up.

"Don't tell me this dreamboat is yours?" he demanded in amazement.

"Nothing but," Joe said proudly.

Tony and the brothers inspected the boat carefully, comparing her various features with the *Napoli*. They lifted the battens from the *Sleuth*'s cowling and admired the powerful motor underneath.

"She's neat all right," said Tony. "But I'll still promise you a stiff race in the *Napoli*!"

"We'll take you up on it after the *Sleuth*'s broken in," Joe returned, laughing.

Tony became serious. "Say, fellows, something happened today in connection with my dad's business that I want to tell you about. Your mother said you were down here," he explained.

"What's up?" Frank asked.

Tony's father was a building contractor and also had

a construction supply yard where Tony worked during the summer. "Today I went to the bank, just before it closed, to deposit the cash and cheques we took in this week." he said. "The teller discovered that one of the bills was a counterfeit!"

"A twenty-dollar bill?" Frank guessed.

"Yes. How'd you know?"

The Hardys related Chet's experience. Tony's dark brows drew together. "I'd like to get my hands on the guy making the stuff!" he said angrily.

"So would we!" Joe stated.

The Hardys learned that the head teller had told Tony he would make a report to the Bayport police and turn the bill over to the Secret Service. "Did he explain how he could tell that the bill was a fake?" Frank asked.

"Yes," replied Tony, and from his description the Hardys were sure that the bill had come from the same batch as the one passed to Chet.

"Think back, Tony," Frank urged. "Have you any idea who gave it to you—or your father?"

Tony looked doubtful. "Three days' trade—pretty hard to remember. Of course, we know most of the customers. I did ask Mike, our yardman, who helps with sales. He mentioned one purchaser he didn't know."

Frank, eager for any possible lead, carefully questioned Tony. The Hardys learned that three days before, just at closing time, a faded green truck had driven into the Prito supply yard. "Mike remembers there were no markings on the truck—as if the name might have been painted out."

"Who was in it?" Joe prompted.

"A young boy—about fourteen—was with the driver. Mike says they bought about fifty dollars' worth of old bricks and lumber. The boy paid him in assorted bills. One was a twenty. Our other cash customers had given smaller bills."

"What did the driver look like?" Frank probed.

"Mike said he didn't notice—the fellow stayed behind the wheel. There was a last-minute rush at the yard, so the boy and Mike piled the stuff into the back of the truck. Then the driver gave the boy money to pay the bill."

Frank and Joe wondered the same thing. Had the man driving the truck passed the bogus bill deliberately? If so, was he the one who had fooled Chet? "It seems funny he'd go to so much trouble to dump one phoney twenty-dollar bill," Joe said.

Frank agreed, and added, "Besides, what would a person in league with counterfeiters want with a pile of old bricks and lumber?"

He turned to Tony. "Did Mike notice anything in particular about the boy?"

"He was tall and thin. Mike thinks he was wearing a striped shirt."

Frank and Joe exchanged glances. "Could be Ken Blake!" Joe declared. Briefly, the Hardys explained their first encounter with the boy.

"He might have been helping pick up the load for Elekton," Frank reasoned. "But why would a modern plant want second-hand building material? And why wouldn't they have the purchase billed to them?"

"What's more," his brother put in, "why didn't the

driver get out and help with the loading? Unless, perhaps, he wanted to stay out of sight as much as possible."

"Too bad Mike didn't notice the truck's licence number," Tony said. "Naturally he had no reason to at the time."

"Was there anything unusual about the truck besides the fact it wasn't marked?" Frank asked his chum.

Tony thought for a moment. "Mike did say there was a bike in the back. He had to move it out of the way."

"Ken rides one," Joe remarked.

"Well, Dad will be glad if you two pick up any clues to these counterfeiters," Tony said. "He's hopping mad at being cheated, and Mike feels sore about it."

"We'll keep our eyes open for that green truck," Frank assured him. "The whole business sounds suspicious—though the bill could have been passed accidentally."

"Let's question Ken Blake," Joe proposed.

He and his brother housed the *Sleuth*, and the three boys started homeward. On the way they continued to speculate on the counterfeiting racket.

"Let me know if I can help you detectives," Tony said, as he turned into his street.

"Will do."

That evening, when it grew dark, Frank and Joe told their mother and aunt that they were going out to do some investigating. Before they left, the boys had a chance to speak to their father in private about Tony's report of the counterfeit bill and green truck and their own hunches.

Mr Hardy agreed that the purchase of lumber and bricks seemed odd, but he felt that until more positive evidence could be obtained, it was best not to approach Elekton officials on the matter.

"I guess you're right, Dad," said Frank. "We might be way off base."

The detective wished them luck on their sleuthing mission. The boys decided to make the trip in the *Sleuth*. They rode their motorcycles down to the boathouse, parked them, then climbed aboard the new boat. Joe took the wheel and soon the sleek craft was cutting across the bay towards the mouth of Willow River.

When they entered it, Joe throttled down and carefully navigated the stream. Meanwhile, Frank shone his flashlight on the wooded banks.

"There's the cave—ahead!" he whispered.

Joe ran the boat astern a few yards and Frank dropped anchor. The brothers waded ashore, carrying their shoes and socks.

When they reached the mouth of the cave, Joe said, "Let's investigate this place first."

They went into the cave and moved forward to the tunnel. One glance told them that the tunnel had become impassable—it was filled with water.

"Must have been the cloudburst," said Frank, as they emerged from the cave. "We'll have to wait until the ground dries out. At least we can take a look through the woods and the area around the mill for clues to the bowman."

Shielding the lenses of their flashlights, so that the light beams would not be easily detected by anyone lurking in the vicinity, the boys began a thorough search of the wooded section. As they worked their way noiselessly uphill among the trees, the only sound was the eerie rattling the wind made in the leaves and branches.

Frank and Joe shone their lights beneath shrubs and rocks, and even crawled under some fallen trees. They found nothing suspicious. They were approaching the edge of the woods and could see the outline of the mill beyond. The old wheel creaked and rumbled.

Suddenly Frank whispered hoarsely, "Look! Here's something!"

Joe joined his brother, and together they examined the leather object Frank had picked up.

"An archer's finger guard," he said.

"It may be a valuable clue to the arrow warning," Joe said, as Frank pocketed the guard. "Let's go up to the mill," he proposed. "Maybe the men there have seen something suspicious."

As the boys crossed the clearing towards the gate-house, they saw that it was in darkness.

"Probably everyone has gone to bed," Frank remarked.

For a moment the brothers stood wondering what to do next. "Something's missing," Joe said, in a puzzled voice. "I have it! The mill wheel has stopped turning."

"Maybe it was switched off for the night," Frank observed.

The boys were eager to question the occupants, but decided not to awaken them.

"Let's walk round the mill," said Frank, "and look through the woods on the other side."

The boys had just passed the north corner of the

building when, with a creaking groan, the wheel started to turn again.

"There must be something wrong with the mechanism," Frank deduced. "The wheel hasn't been used for so many years that adapting it to work the generator may have put a strain on it."

"We'd better let the men know it's acting up," Joe said.

The boys retraced their steps to the mill door. As they reached it, the wheel stopped turning.

Frank and Joe stood staring off to their left where the mass of the motionless wheel was outlined against the night sky.

"Spooky, isn't it?" Joe commented.

Frank nodded, and knocked on the door. There was no response. After a short wait, he knocked again—louder this time. The sound echoed in the deep silence of the night. Still no one answered.

The Hardys waited a little longer. Finally they turned away. "Must be sound sleepers," Joe commented. "Well, maybe they'll discover what's wrong tomorrow."

Frank and Joe were about to resume their search for clues when they heard a loud crashing noise from the woods which bordered Willow River.

The boys dashed ahead to investigate. Entering the woods, they made their way stealthily forward, flashlights turned off. Silently they drew near the river.

After a few minutes they stopped and listened intently. The sound was not repeated.

"Must have been an animal," Joe whispered.

Just then they heard a rustling sound behind them

and turned to look. The next instant each received a terrific blow on the back of the head. Both boys blacked out.

·9·

Tracing a Slugger

WHEN Frank regained consciousness, his first thought was of his brother. He turned his throbbing head and saw that Joe was lying next to him.

"Joe!" he exclaimed anxiously.

To his relief, Joe stirred and mumbled, "W-what happened?"

"Someone conked us on the head—"

Frank broke off as he became aware of a gentle rocking motion. He sat up. Was he still dizzy or were they moving? When his mind and vision cleared, he knew they were certainly moving.

"Hey!" he said. "We're on the *Sleuth!*"

Astonished, Joe raised himself and looked around. They were indeed aboard their boat—lying on the foredeck and slowly drifting down Willow River towards the bay. The anchor lay beside them.

"A fog's rolling in," Frank said uneasily, observing white swirls of mist ahead. "Let's start 'er up before visibility gets worse."

The boys wriggled into the cockpit and Joe pressed the starter. It would not catch. While Joe stayed at the controls, Frank climbed to the foredeck and lifted the cowling from the engine. He quickly checked to see if the distributor wires were in place. They were. There did not seem to be anything visibly wrong with the engine, but when he lifted the top off the carburettor, he found it empty.

A quick check on the petrol tank revealed the cause of the trouble. The tank had been drained.

"Fine mess we're in," he mumbled. "What was the idea?"

"The man who hit us on the head can answer that one," Joe said bitterly. "He sure did a complete job—even took both our oars!"

"We'll have to tow her," Frank said tersely, "to make more speed and guide her."

While Joe stripped to his shorts, Frank quickly led a painter through one of the foredeck fairleads.

"Take this painter," Frank said, handing Joe the rope. "Make it fast round your shoulder and swim straight ahead. I'll unhinge one of the battens and use it as a paddle and try to keep her straight. In a few minutes I'll change places with you."

The Hardys knew that keeping a dead weight like the *Sleuth* moving in a straight line would be a tough job. However, with Joe swimming ahead and Frank wielding the batten, they managed to make fairly steady progress.

It was slow, back-breaking work, and before they reached the bay, the boys had changed places three times. Their heads were pounding more than ever from the physical strain. Also, the fog had grown so dense that it was impossible to see very far ahead.

Frank, who was taking his turn in the water, did

not know how much longer he could go on.

Suddenly Joe shouted from the boat, "There's a light! Help! Help! Ahoy! Over here!" he directed at the top of his lungs.

Gradually the light approached them. Frank clambered back into the *Sleuth* as a Harbour Police boat, making its scheduled rounds, pulled alongside.

"You're just in time!" Frank gasped to the sergeant in charge. "We're exhausted."

"I can see that. You run out of petrol?" the police officer asked.

"Worse than that. Foul play," Frank replied.

"Tough luck," the sergeant said. "You can tell your story when we get to town."

The officer gave orders to his crew, and a tow-line was put on the *Sleuth*. The boys were given blankets to throw round themselves.

When the two crafts reached the Harbour Police pier, the boys went inside and gave a full account of what had happened to them and asked that the report be relayed to Chief Collig.

"We'll give you some petrol," said the sergeant who had rescued the boys. "Then do you think you can make it home alone?"

"Yes, thank you."

A half-hour later the boys, tired and disappointed, cycled home. Their mother and aunt gasped with dismay at the sight of the weary boys in the water-sodden clothing. Joe and Frank, however, made light of the evening's experience.

"We ran out of petrol," Joe explained, "and had to swim back with the *Sleuth*."

Aunt Gertrude sniffed sceptically. "Humph! It must have been some long ride to use up all that fuel!" She hustled off to make hot chocolate.

Mrs Hardy told the boys that their father had left the house an hour before and would be away overnight working on his case. Again Frank and Joe wondered about it. And did the attack tonight have any connection with either case?

After a hot bath and a good night's sleep, Frank and Joe were eager to continue their search for clues to the bowman, the counterfeiters, and the writer of the first warning note to Mr Hardy.

Breakfast over, Frank and Joe went to the lab and dusted the archer's finger guard. To the brothers' delight they lifted one clear print.

"We'll take this to Chief Collig on our way to the paper company in Bridgeport," Frank decided.

Just before they left, Chet telephoned. "Guess what!" he said to Frank, who answered. "I have an appointment at Elekton to see about a job!"

"How'd you do it?" Frank asked, amazed. "You sure work fast."

Chet laughed. "I decided to telephone on my own," he explained. "The man in the personnel office told me there might be something available on a part-time basis. How about that?"

"Swell," Frank said. "The vacancy must have come up since yesterday."

"Funny thing," Chet added. "The personnel manager asked me if I had applied before. I said No, though the guard had phoned about me yesterday. The manager said he didn't remember this, but that somebody else in the office might have taken the call."

Chet became more and more excited as he talked about the prospect of getting a job in the Elekton laboratory. "I'm going to make a lot of money and—"

"Don't get your hopes up too high," Frank cautioned his friend. "Elekton is such a top-secret outfit they might not hire anyone on a part-time basis for lab work. But you might get something else."

"We'll see," Chet replied optimistically.

"Joe and I have something special to show you," Frank told him. "After you have your interview, meet us at the north end of the Bayport waterfront."

Chet begged to know why, but Frank kept the news about the *Sleuth* a secret. "You'll see soon enough," he said.

"Okay, then. So long!"

The Hardys hopped on their motorcycles and rode to police headquarters. They talked to Chief Collig in detail about the attack on them, and left the bowman's fingerprint for him to trace.

"Good work, boys," he said. "I'll let you know what I find out."

Frank and Joe had decided not to mention to him the green truck and its possible connection with the counterfeiters until they had more proof.

The boys mounted their motorcycles and rode to Bridgeport. They easily located the Quality Paper Company, and inquired there for Mr Evans, the sales manager, with whom they had talked the day before.

When Frank and Joe entered his office and identified themselves, Mr Evans looked at the brothers curiously. But he was most co-operative in answering their questions.

"No," Mr Evans said, "we don't sell our star watermark paper to retail stores in this vicinity. All our purchasers are large industrial companies. Here is a list." He handed a printed sheet across the desk to Frank.

The boys were disappointed not to have obtained any individual's name. Nevertheless, Frank and Joe read the list carefully. Several names, including Elekton Controls Limited, were familiar to them. The warning note could have come from any one of thousands of employees of any of the firms.

"I guess there's no clue here to the man we want to locate," Frank said to Mr Evans.

The boys thanked him. As they started to leave, he called them back.

"Are you boys, by any chance, related to Mr Fenton Hardy?" he asked.

Joe, puzzled, nodded. "He's our father. Why?"

"Quite a coincidence," Mr Evans said. "Mr Hardy was here a little while ago."

"He was!" Frank exclaimed in surprise. The brothers exchanged glances, wondering what mission their father had been on.

"Maybe I shouldn't have mentioned Mr Hardy's visit," Mr Evans said.

"That's all right," Joe assured him. "If Dad had wanted the visit kept secret, he would have told you."

When the boys were outside again, Frank said, "I

hope Dad will be home. I'd like to find out what brought him here."

Frank and Joe rode directly home and were glad to see Mr Hardy's car in the driveway. The boys rushed into the house.

They found the detective in his study, talking on the telephone. The boys paused next to the partly open door.

". . . . the same eight-and-one pattern, I believe," their father was saying . . . "Yes—I'll be there . . . Goodbye."

Frank knocked and the boys entered the room. Mr Hardy greeted them warmly. He was startled when Joe told him, "We know where you've been this morning, Dad."

"Were you two shadowing me?" the detective joked.

"Not exactly." Frank grinned, and explained why they had visited the Quality Paper Company.

"Good idea," said the detective. "Did you learn anything?"

"No," Joe replied glumly, then asked suddenly, "Dad, did you go to Quality Paper in connection with he warning note on the arrow?"

Mr Hardy admitted that he had gone there to investigate the watermark. "I believe I did find a clue to confirm a suspicion of mine. But I'm not sure yet where it will lead."

The boys sensed that their father's trip had been linked to his secret case. "If it was to help us on the counterfeiting mystery, he would say so," Frank thought. "And he hasn't mentioned Elekton, so I guess he doesn't suspect any of that company's employees."

Mr Hardy changed the subject. He looked at his sons quizzically. "What's this I hear from Aunt Gertrude about you boys coming home last night half dead?"

The boys explained, omitting none of the details. "We didn't want to alarm Mother and Aunt Gertrude," Frank said, "so we didn't tell them about the attack."

Mr Hardy looked grim and warned his sons gravely to be extra cautious.

"There's one bright spot," he added. "The print you found on that finger guard. It could be a big break."

During lunch the detective was unusually preoccupied. The boys tried to draw him out by questions and deductions about the counterfeiting case. He would say very little, however, and seemed to be concentrating on a knotty problem.

A little later the boys rode their motorcycles straight to the boathouse and parked at the street end of the jetty. "Chet ought to show up soon," Joe remarked.

As the brothers walked towards the boathouse, Frank commented on his father's preoccupation during luncheon.

"I have a hunch Dad's assignment is even tougher than usual," he confided. "I wish we could help him on it."

Frank seemed to be only half listening and nodded absently.

"What's the matter with you?" Joe laughed. "I'm talking to myself!"

Suddenly Frank stopped. He grasped his brother's arm firmly.

"Joe!" he said. "We may have found a clue in Bridgeport this morning and didn't realize it!"

10

The Sign of the Arrow

"WHAT clue do you mean, Frank?" Joe demanded eagerly.

"Elekton's name was on that list Mr Evans showed us this morning."

"Yes, I know. But Dad didn't seem excited over that."

"Well, I am," Frank said. "Put two and two together. Every time we've been near the Elekton area, something has happened. First, the warning on the arrow, then the attack last night."

"Of course!" Joe said. "I get you! Someone who has access to the company's paper supply could have sent the warnings, and knocked us out. But who? An employee of Elekton?"

"That's the mystery," said Frank. "Is the person trying to get at Dad through us? And which of the cases is this mysterious person connected with—the counterfeit case, or Dad's secret one?"

"Then there's the bike," Joe recalled. "Someone from the company could easily have taken it from the storage area under the mill at night when the guard and maintenance man were inside the gatehouse."

"Joe," said Frank slowly, "we're theorizing on the

case having a connection with Elekton. Do you think Dad is too, even though he didn't tell us? The Elekton name may have been the clue *he* found at Quality Paper!"

Joe snapped his fingers. "My guess is that Dad is doing some detective work for Elekton! That would explain why he can't say anything. Elekton *is* doing top-secret space missile work."

"It's possible," Frank speculated, "that Elekton retained Dad because of the chain of sabotage acts in plants handling similar jobs for the government."

"Sounds logical," Joe agreed. "I guess Dad's main assignment would be to ward off sabotage at Elekton. No wonder he is so anxious to find out who sent the warnings."

Just then Chet arrived in the Queen and leaped out. "I have a job!" he announced to Frank and Joe. Then he looked a bit sheepish. "It's—er—in the cafeteria, serving behind the food counter. The cafeteria is run on a concession basis, and the people working there aren't as carefully screened as the plant employees."

Joe grinned. "It's not very scientific, but think of the food! You'll be able to eat anything you want."

Chet sighed, and did not respond with one of his usual humorous comebacks. A worried expression spread over his face. He shifted from one foot to the other.

"What's on your mind?" Joe prodded. "Not nervous about the job, are you?"

Chet shook his head. He dug into his pocket and pulled out a piece of white paper. "I *am* nervous about this—another warning note! It was on the seat of my car when I came out after the job interview." He handed the note to Frank.

Unfolding it, Frank read aloud, " '*You and your pals watch out!*' " There was no signature on the boldly printed note, but at the bottom was the crude drawing of an arrow.

Chet gulped. "Must be that arrow shooter. He's keeping tabs on all of us!" he said.

Frank and Joe studied the note intently for a minute, then Frank asked Chet, "Where did you park?"

"Near the front entrance. The guard at the mill told me to go in that way to reach the personnel office." Chet smiled faintly. "Boy, was *he* surprised when I told him I had an appointment."

The Hardys were more convinced than ever that their unknown enemy must somehow be linked with the Elekton company. "We'll compare this note with the others," Frank said. "But first, Chet, we'll show you something to cheer you up."

The brothers led their friend into the boathouse. "Feast your eyes!" Joe grinned. "This is our surprise."

Chet gasped when he saw the *Sleuth*. "Wow! She's really yours?"

"You bet! How about a ride?"

Eagerly Chet accepted. As the Hardys refuelled from the boathouse tank, they told Chet about the adventure they had had the previous night.

"You suspect there's a connection between somebody at Elekton and the counterfeiting?" Chet guessed.

"That's right," Frank replied.

He then told Chet about the Pritos having received a

counterfeit bill. "We think," said Joe, "the boy in the panel truck who gave Mike the counterfeit twenty *might* have been Ken Blake."

"Ken Blake again," Chet commented. "Funny how he keeps turning up."

The Hardys agreed. As Frank steered the *Sleuth* into the bay, Joe suggested, "Let's run up Willow River to the mill. That'll give you a good chance to see how the boat rides, Chet, and also we can stop to question the guard and maintenance man, and Ken Blake. They might have seen some suspicious people in the area."

"I should've known this would turn into a sleuthing trip." Chet sighed. "Oh, well, I'm with you if we can learn anything about the counterfeiters."

When Frank had the *Sleuth* well away from shore and out of the path of other craft on the bay, he pushed the throttle for more speed and steered the boat towards the mouth of the river.

The *Sleuth* responded like a thoroughbred. The stern sat back in the water and in a second it was planing wide open across the bay.

"How do you like this?" Frank called from the cockpit.

"Terrific!" Chet yelled back enthusiastically.

Frank now swung the wheel back and forth to show his friend how stable the boat was. Then he said, "Joe, take the wheel and show Chet your stuff!"

The brothers changed places and Joe made a wide circle to port, with the *Sleuth* heeling beautifully. Then he headed for the river's narrow mouth.

"Better slow down!" Frank warned him.

Obediently Joe began to ease the throttle. The

Sleuth did not respond! And there was no lessening of the roar of the engine.

Quickly Joe turned the throttle all the way back. Still there was no decrease in speed.

"Something's wrong!" he shouted. "I can't slow her down!"

11

Sinister Tactics

"WHAT do you mean you can't slow down?" Chet yelled. "Turn off the engine!"

"Joe can't," Frank said grimly. "He has the throttle to *off* position and we're still travelling at full speed."

There was no choice for Joe but to swing the *Sleuth* into another wide, sweeping turn. It would have been foolhardy to enter the river at such speed, and Joe knew that under the circumstances he needed lots of room to manœuvre. The motorboat zoomed back into the middle of the bay. It seemed to the boys that suddenly there was far more traffic on the bay than there had been before.

"Look out!" Chet yelled. Joe just missed a high-speed runabout.

He turned and twisted to avoid the small pleasure boats. The young pilot was more worried about endangering these people than he was about colliding with the larger vessels, which were commercial craft.

"Keep her as straight as you can!" Frank shouted to Joe. "I'll take a look at the engine and see what I can do with it."

Frank stood up and leaned forward to open the cowling in front of the dashboard, as the boat leaped across the waves in the bay.

"Watch out!" Chet yelled, as Frank almost lost his balance.

Joe made a sharp turn to avoid cutting in front of a rowboat containing a man and several children. Joe realized that the wash of the speeding *Sleuth* might upset it.

"If those people are thrown overboard," he thought, "we'll have to rescue them. But how?" Fortunately, the boat did not overturn.

Frank quickly lifted the cowling from the engine and stepped into the pit. He knew he could open the fuel intake and siphon off the petrol into the bay, but this would take too long.

"I'll have to stop the boat—right now!" he decided.

Frank reached down beside the roaring engine and pulled three wires away from the distributor. Instantly the engine died, and Frank stood up just as Joe made another sharp turn to miss hitting a small outboard motorboat that had wandered across their path.

"Good grief!" Chet cried out. "That was a close one!"

Even with the *Sleuth*'s reduction in speed, the other boat rocked violently back and forth as it was caught in the wash. Frank grasped the gunwale, ready to leap over the side and rescue the man if his boat overturned.

But the smaller craft had been pulled round to face the wash. Though it bounced almost out of the water, the boat quickly resumed an even keel.

The lone man in it kept coming towards the *Sleuth*. As he drew alongside, he began to wave his arms and shout at the boys.

"What's the matter with you young fools?" he

yelled. "You shouldn't be allowed to operate a boat until you learn how to run one."

"We couldn't—" Joe started to say when the man interrupted.

"You should have more respect for other people's safety!"

Frank finally managed to explain. "It was an accident. The throttle was jammed open. I had to pull the wires out of the distributor to stop her."

By this time the outboard was close enough for its pilot to look over the *Sleuth*'s side and into the engine housing where Frank was pointing at the distributor.

The man quickly calmed down. "Sorry, boys," he said. "There are so many fools running around in high-powered boats these days, without knowing anything about the rules of navigation, I just got good and mad at your performance."

"I don't blame you, sir," said Joe. Then he asked, "Do you think you could tow us into the municipal dock so that we can have repairs made?"

"Glad to," said the man.

At the dock, the Hardys and Chet watched while the serviceman checked the *Sleuth* to find out the cause of the trouble. Presently he looked up at the boys with an odd expression.

"What's the trouble?" Frank asked. "Serious?"

The mechanic's reply startled them. "This is a new motorboat and no doubt was in tiptop shape. But somebody tampered with the throttle!"

"What!" Joe demanded. "Let's see!"

The serviceman pointed out where a cotter pin had been removed from the throttle group. And the tension spring which opened and closed the valve had been replaced with a bar to hold the throttle wide open, once it was pushed there.

The Hardys and Chet exchanged glances which meant: "The unknown enemy again?"

The boys, however, did not mention their suspicions to the mechanic. Frank merely requested him to make the necessary repairs on the *Sleuth*. Then the trio walked back to the Hardys' boathouse.

Several fishermen were standing at a nearby wharf. Frank and Joe asked them if they had seen anyone near the boathouse.

"No," each one said.

The three boys inspected the boathouse. Frank scrutinized the hasp on the door. "The *Sleuth* must have been tampered with while it was inside. Unless it was done last night while we were unconscious."

There was no sign of the lock having been forced open, but near the edge of the loose hasp there were faint scratches.

"Look!" Joe pointed. "Somebody tore the whole hasp off the door and then carefully put it back on."

Frank looked grim. "I'm sure this was done by the same person who attacked us last night, and sent us the warnings."

"You're right," said Joe. "This is what Dad would call sinister tactics."

Again both brothers wondered with which case their enemy was concerned. There seemed to be no answer to this tantalizing question which kept coming up again and again.

Chet drove the Queen back to the Hardys', and the

brothers rode their motorcycles. When they reached
the house they went at once to the lab with the note
Chet had found in his car.

They dusted it for fingerprints but were disappointed
again. There was not one trace of a print. The boys
found, however, that the paper was the same as that
used for the previous warnings.

"Well," said Joe, "I vote we go on out to the mill."

The boys went in the Queen. Chet had just brought
his car to a stop on the dirt road when Joe called out,
"There's Ken Blake trimming the grass over by the
mill-race. Now's our chance to talk to him."

The three jumped out. Ken looked up, stared for a
second, then threw his clippers to the ground. To the
boys' surprise, he turned and ran away from them,
along the stream.

"Wait!" Frank yelled.

Ken looked over his shoulder, but kept on running.
Suddenly he tripped and stumbled. For a moment the
boy swayed on the bank of the rushing stream. The next
instant he lost his balance and fell headlong into the
water!

At once the Hardys and Chet dashed to the water's
edge. Horrified, they saw that the force of the water
was carrying the boy, obviously a poor swimmer,
straight towards the plunging falls!

12

An Interrupted Chase

FRANK, quick as lightning, dashed to the mill-stream and plunged in after Ken Blake. The boy was being pulled relentlessly towards the waterfall. In another moment he would be swept over the brink of the dam!

With strong strokes, Frank swam towards the struggling boy. Reaching out desperately, he managed to grasp Ken's shirt.

Joe jumped in to assist Frank. The two boys were buffeted by the rushing water, but between them they managed to drag Ken back from the falls.

"Easy," Frank cautioned the frightened youth. "Relax. We'll have you out in a jiffy."

Despite the weight of their clothes, the Hardys, both proficient at lifesaving techniques, soon worked Ken close to the bank. Chet leaned over and helped haul him out of the water. Then Frank and Joe climbed out.

To their relief, Ken, though white-faced and panting from exhaustion, seemed to be all right. The Hardys flopped to the ground to catch their breath.

"That was a whale of a rescue!" Chet praised them.

"You bet!" Ken gasped weakly. "Thanks, fellows! You've saved my life!"

"In a way it was our fault," Joe replied ruefully.

"You wouldn't have fallen in if we hadn't come here. But why *did* you run away when you saw us?"

Ken hesitated before answering. "Mr Markel—the guard at the gatehouse—said you wanted to talk to me. He warned me about talking to outsiders, because of the strict security at Elekton."

Joe nodded. "We understand, Ken. But," he added, "we have something important to ask you, and I don't think you will be going against company rules if you answer. Did anybody use your bike the night before last to deliver a message to our house?"

"Your house?" Ken sounded surprised. "No. At least, not that I know of."

Joe went on, "Did you buy a pedal in Bridgeport to replace the one missing from your bike?"

Ken again looked surprised. "Yes. It was gone yesterday morning when I came to work. I suspected someone must have used my bike and lost the pedal. When I couldn't find it around here, Mr Markel sent me to Bridgeport to buy a new one."

It was on the tip of Frank's tongue to ask the boy if he had seen any person in the area of the mill carrying a bow and arrow. But suddenly Mr Markel and the maintenance man came dashing from the mill.

"What's going on here?" the guard demanded, staring at the Hardys and Ken, who were still dripping wet.

Briefly, Frank told the men what had happened. They thanked the brothers warmly for the rescue, and the maintenance man hustled Ken into the mill for dry clothes. He did not invite the Hardys inside.

Frank and Joe turned to Mr Markel, intending to

question him. But before they could, a horn sounded and a shabby, green panel truck approached the plant gate.

The guard hurried over to admit the truck and it entered without stopping. Suddenly Joe grabbed Frank's arm. "Hey! That truck's unmarked—it looks like the one Tony described."

The brothers peered after the vehicle, but by this time it was far into the grounds and had turned out of sight behind one of the buildings.

"I wonder," Joe said excitedly, "if the driver is the man who gave the Pritos the counterfeit bill!"

The boys had noticed only that the driver wore a cap pulled low and sat slouched over the wheel.

"If this truck's the same one, it may be connected with Elekton," Frank said tersely.

Both Hardys, though uncomfortably wet, decided to stay and see what they could find out. They hailed Mr Markel as he walked back from the Elekton gate.

"Does that truck belong to Elekton?" Frank asked him.

"No, it doesn't," the guard answered.

"Do you know who does own it?" asked Joe.

Mr Markel shook his head regretfully. "Sorry, boys. I'm afraid I'm not allowed to give out such information. Excuse me, I have work to do." He turned and went back into the gatehouse.

"Come on, fellows," Chet urged. "You'd better not hang around in those wet clothes."

The Hardys, however, were determined to stay long enough to question Ken Blake further, if possible.

"He'll probably be coming outside soon," said Joe.

"Frank and I can dry out on the beach by the cave. It won't take long in this hot sun."

Chet sighed. "Okay. And I know what I'm supposed to do—wait here and watch for Ken."

Frank chuckled. "You're a mind reader."

Chet took his post at the edge of the woods, and the Hardys hurried down to the river's edge.

They spread their slacks and shirts on the sun-warmed rocks. In a short while the clothing was dry enough to put on.

"Say, maybe we'll have time to investigate that tunnel before Chet calls us," Joe suggested eagerly.

He and Frank started for the cave, but a second later Chet came running through the woods towards them.

"Ken came out, but he's gone on an errand," he reported, and explained that the boy had rushed from the mill dressed in oversize dungarees and a red shirt. "He was riding off on his bike when I caught up to him. I told Ken you wanted to see him, but he said he had to make a fast trip downtown and deliver an envelope to the Parker Building."

"We'll catch him there," Frank decided.

The three boys ran up the wooded slope and jumped into the Queen. They kept on the main road to Bayport, hoping to overtake Ken, but they did not pass him.

"He must have taken another route," Joe said.

At the Parker Building there were no parking spaces available, so Chet stopped his jalopy long enough to drop off Frank and Joe.

"I'll keep circling the block until you come out," Chet called as he drove away.

There was no sign of Ken's bicycle outside the building. The Hardys rushed into the lobby and immediately were met by a five o'clock crowd of office workers streaming from the elevators. Frank and Joe made their way through the throng, but saw no sign of Ken.

Joe had an idea. "Maybe he was making the delivery to Mr Peters, the name I saw on the Manila envelope I picked up the other day. Let's see if Ken's still in his office."

The boys ran their eyes down the building directory, but Mr Peters was not listed. The brothers questioned the elevator starter, who replied that so far as he knew, no one by the name of Peters had an office in the building.

Joe asked the starter, "Did you notice a boy wearing dungarees and a bright red shirt in the lobby a few minutes ago?"

"Sure," was the prompt reply. "Just before the five o'clock rush started. I saw the boy come in and give an envelope to a man waiting in the corner over there. The man took the envelope and they both left right away."

"I guess he must be Mr Peters," Frank said.

"Could be," the starter agreed. "I didn't recognize him."

As the Hardys hurried outside, Joe said, "Well, we got crossed up on that one. Let's get back to the mill. Ken will have to drop off the bike."

The brothers waited at the kerb for Chet. In a few minutes the Queen pulled up. "All aboard!" Chet sang out. "Any luck?"

"No."

When Frank told Chet they were returning to the

mill, their good-natured friend nodded. "It's fortunate I bought these sandwiches," he said, indicating a paper bag on the seat beside him. "I had a feeling we'd be late for supper."

Joe snapped his fingers. "That reminds me. I'll stop and phone our families so they won't hold back supper for us."

After Joe had made the calls and they were on their way again, he told Frank and Chet that Mr Hardy had left a message saying he would not be home until after ten o'clock.

As the Queen went down the side road past the Elekton buildings, Frank thought, "If Dad *is* working for Elekton, he might be somewhere in the plant right this minute."

The same possibility was running through Joe's mind. "Wonder if Dad is expecting a break in his secret case."

As Chet neared the turn into the mill road, a green truck zoomed out directly in front of the Queen. Chet jammed on his brake, narrowly avoiding a collision. The truck swung round the jalopy at full speed and roared off towards the highway.

"The green truck we saw before!" Joe exclaimed. "This time I got the licence number, but couldn't see the driver's face."

"Let's follow him!" Frank urged.

Chet started back in pursuit. "That guy ought to be arrested for reckless driving!" he declared indignantly.

The Hardys peered ahead as they turned right on to the main road, trying to keep the truck in sight.

Suddenly the boys heard a tremendous *bo-o-om* and felt the car shake.

"An explosion!" Joe cried out, turning his head. "Look!"

Against the sky a brilliant flash and billows of smoke came from the direction of Elekton. Another explosion followed.

"The plant's blowing up!" Joe gasped.

13

Sudden Suspicion

THE roar of the explosion and the sight of smoke and flames stunned the three boys for a moment. Chet stepped on the brake so fast that his passengers hit the dashboard.

"Take it easy!" urged Frank, although he was as excited as Chet.

All thoughts of chasing the mysterious green truck were erased from the Hardys' minds.

"Let's get as close as possible," Frank said tersely, as Chet headed the car back towards the plant. "I'd like to know what—"

Frank broke off as a series of explosions occurred. The brothers sat forward tensely.

As the Queen drew near the main entrance, the boys could see that the flames and smoke were pouring from a single building at the north-east corner.

"It's one of the labs, I think," said Frank.

Quickly Chet pulled over and parked, and the boys hopped out of the jalopy. The series of explosive sounds had died away, but the damage appeared to be extensive. Most of the windows in the steel-and-concrete building had been blown out by the force of the blast.

Smoke and flames were pouring out of the blackened

spaces where the windows had been. As the boys ran towards the front, the roof of the west wing caved in. The rush of oxygen provided fuel for a new surge of flames that reached towards the sky.

"Lucky this happened after closing time," Chet murmured, staring wide-eyed at the fire. "There might have been a lot of injuries."

"I hope no one was inside." Joe exchanged worried glances with his brother. Both shared the same concern. It was for their father.

"I wish we could find out whether or not Dad's at Elekton," Frank whispered to Joe.

At this point the boys heard the scream of sirens. Soon fire trucks and police cars from Bayport pulled up at the front gate. The Hardys saw Chief Collig in the first police car. They rushed up to him and he asked how they happened to be there.

"Sleuthing," Frank answered simply. Without going into detail, he added, "Joe and I aren't sure, but we have a hunch Dad may have been—or still is—here at Elekton. All right if we go into the grounds and look round?" he asked eagerly. "And take Chet?"

The officer agreed.

By this time the guard had opened the wide gate, and the fire apparatus rushed in. Some of the police officers followed, while others took positions along the road and directed traffic so that it would not block the path of emergency vehicles.

As the boys rode inside with the chief, Joe asked him, "Any idea what caused the explosion?"

"Not yet. Hard to tell until the firemen can get inside the building."

When they reached the burning structure, Chief Collig began directing police operations, and checking with the firemen. As soon as they seemed to have the flames under control, the firemen entered the laboratory building to look for any possible victims of the explosions.

The Hardys and Chet, meanwhile, had searched the outside area for Mr Hardy, but did not see the detective.

"Maybe we were wrong about Dad's coming here," Joe said to his brother, more hopeful than before. "Dad probably wouldn't have been in the lab."

The brothers went back to Chief Collig, who told them he had not seen Fenton Hardy. Just then the fire chief came up to the group.

"I'll bet this fire was no accident," he reported grimly to Collig. "The same thing happened in Indiana about two months ago—and that was sabotage!"

Frank and Joe stared at each other. "Sabotage!" Joe whispered.

A startling thought flashed into Frank's mind and, drawing his brother aside, he exclaimed, "Remember what we overheard Dad say on the phone? 'The same eight-and-one pattern. I'll be there.' "

"And two months equal about eight weeks," Joe added excitedly. "That might have been the saboteurs' time schedule Dad was referring to! So maybe the explosion at Elekton was set for today!"

Frank's apprehension about his father returned full force. "Joe," he said tensely, "Dad might have been inside the lab building trying to stop the saboteurs!"

Deeply disturbed, the Hardys pleaded with Chief

Collig for permission to enter the building and search for their father.

"I can tell you're worried, boys," the officer said sympathetically. "But it's still too risky for me to let you go inside. It'll be some time before we're sure there's no danger of further explosions."

"I know," Frank agreed. "But what if Dad *is* in there and badly hurt?"

The police chief did his best to reassure the brothers. "Your father would never forgive me if I let you risk your lives," he added. "I suggest that you go on home and cheer up your mother in case she has the same fears you do. I promise if I see your dad I'll call you, or ask him to."

The boys realized that their old friend was right, and slowly walked away. Frank and Joe looked back once at the blackened building, outlined against the twilight sky. Wisps of smoke still curled from the torn-out windows. It was a gloomy, silent trio that drove to the Hardy home in the Queen.

Frank and Joe decided not to tell their mother or aunt of their fear, or to give any hint of their suspicions. When the boys entered the living-room, both women gave sighs of relief. They had heard the explosions and the subsequent news flashes about it.

Aunt Gertrude looked at the boys sharply. "By the way, where have you three been all this time? I was afraid that you might have been near Elekton's."

Frank, Joe and Chet admitted that they had been. "You know we couldn't miss a chance to find out what the excitement was about," Joe said teasingly, then added with an assurance he was far from feeling,

"Don't worry. The fire was pretty much under control when we left."

To change the subject, Frank said cheerfully, "I sure am hungry. Let's dig into those sandwiches you bought, Chet!"

"Good idea!" Joe agreed.

"Are you sure you don't want me to make you something hot to eat?" Mrs Hardy asked.

"Thanks, Mother, but we'll have enough." Frank smiled.

Chet called his family to let them know where he was, then the three boys sat down in the kitchen and halfheartedly munched the sandwiches. Aunt Gertrude bustled in and served them generous portions of deep-dish apple pie.

"This is even more super than usual," Chet said, trying hard to be cheerful.

The boys finished their pie, but without appetite. When they refused second helpings, however, Aunt Gertrude demanded suspiciously, "Are you ill—or what?"

"Oh, no, Aunty," Joe replied hastily. "Just—er—too much detecting."

"I can believe that!" Miss Hardy said tartly.

The evening dragged on, tension mounting every minute. The boys tried to read or talk, but their concern for the detective's safety made it impossible to concentrate on anything else.

Eleven o'clock! Where *was* their father? Frank and Joe wondered.

"Aren't you boys going to bed soon?" Mrs Hardy asked, as she and Aunt Gertrude started upstairs.

"Pretty soon," Frank answered.

The three boys sat glumly in the living-room for a few minutes until the women were out of earshot.

"Fellows," said Chet, "I caught on that you're sure your dad is working on an important case for Elekton, and it's a top-secret one—that's why you couldn't say anything about it."

"You're right," Frank told him.

Chet went on to mention that his father had heard of various problems at Elekton—production stoppages caused by power breaks, and, before the buildings were completed, reports of tools and equipment going missing.

"This ties in with our hunch about the secrecy of Dad's case," Frank said. "The company must have suspected that major sabotage was being planned, and retained Dad to try and stop it."

Talking over their speculations helped to relieve some of the tension the boys felt and made the time pass a little faster as they waited for news of Fenton Hardy.

"I wonder how the saboteurs got into the plant?" Joe said, thinking aloud. "Both the gates are locked and well guarded. It seems almost impossible for anyone to have sneaked in the necessary amount of explosives—without inside help."

A sudden thought flashed into Frank's mind. He leaped to his feet. "The green truck!" he exclaimed. "It was unmarked, remember? It could have been carrying dynamite—camouflaged under ordinary supplies!"

"That could be, Frank!" Joe jumped up. "If so, no

wonder it was in such a rush! I'll phone the chief right
now and give him the truck's licence number."

Frank went with Joe to the hall telephone. As they
approached the phone, it rang. The bell, shattering the
tense atmosphere, seemed louder than usual.

"It must be Dad!" exclaimed the brothers together,
and Chet hurried into the hall.

Frank eagerly lifted the receiver. "Hello!" he said
expectantly.

The next moment Frank looked dejected. He replaced the receiver and said glumly, "Wrong number."

The Hardys exchanged bleak looks. What *had*
happened to their father?

14

Prisoners!

THE Hardys' disappointment in discovering that the telephone call was not from their father was intense. Nevertheless, Joe picked up the receiver and dialled police headquarters to report the truck's licence number.

"Line's busy," he said.

Joe tried several more times without success. Suddenly he burst out, "I can't stand it another minute to think of Dad perhaps lying out there hurt. Let's go back to Elekton and see if we can learn something."

"All right," Frank agreed, also eager for action, and the three rushed to the front door.

Just as they opened it, the boys saw the headlights of a car turning into the driveway.

"*It's Dad!*" Joe barely refrained from shouting so as not to awaken Mrs Hardy and Aunt Gertrude.

The detective's saloon headed for the garage at the back of the house. Heaving sighs of thankful relief, the boys quietly hurried through the house into the kitchen to meet him.

"Are we glad to see you, Dad!" Frank exclaimed as he came into the house.

His father looked pale and dishevelled. There was a

large purple bruise on his left temple. He slumped wearily into a chair.

"I guess I'm lucky to be here." Mr Hardy managed a rueful smile. "Well, I owe you boys an explanation, and now is the time."

"Dad," Joe spoke up, "you *are* working on the sabotage case for Elekton, aren't you?"

"And you were in the lab building during the explosions?" Frank put in.

"You're both right," the detective replied. "Of course I know I can depend on all of you to keep the matter strictly confidential. The case is far from solved."

Mr Hardy was relieved that Frank and Joe had kept their fears for his safety from his wife and sister. He now revealed to the boys that for the past several hours he had been closeted with Elekton's officials. Suspecting that the saboteurs had inside help, the detective had screened the records of all employees. He and the officials had found nothing suspicious.

"I'll submit a full report to the FBI tomorrow morning, and continue a search on my own."

When Joe asked if the eight-and-one pattern referred to the saboteurs' schedule, his father nodded. "In the other plants, the sabotage took place eight weeks plus one day apart.

"In each of those plants," the detective went on, "the damage occurred right after closing time. Figuring the schedule would be exactly right for an attempt on Elekton in a couple of days, I started a systematic check of the various buildings. I planned to check daily, until the saboteurs had been caught here or elsewhere. At my request, one company security guard was assigned to assist me. I felt that the fewer people who knew what I was doing, the better. That's how I ruined the saboteurs' plan in Detroit.

"Nothing suspicious occurred here until today when I took up a post in the section of the building where the experimental work is being conducted. After all the employees had left, and the dim night-lights were on, I went towards the east lab wing to investigate."

Mr Hardy paused, took a deep breath, and continued, "Just as I reached the lab, I happened to glance back into the hall. Things started to happen—fast."

"What did you see, Dad?" asked Joe, and all the boys leaned forward expectantly.

The detective went on, "Hurrying down the hall from the west lab were two men in work clothes, one carrying a leather bag. I knew there weren't supposed to be any workmen in the building. I stepped out to question them, but the pair broke into a run and dashed past me down the stairs."

"Did you see what either of them looked like?" Frank asked.

"I did catch a glimpse of one before they broke away. He had heavy features and thick eyebrows. But just as I was about to take off after them, I smelled something burning in the east lab and went to investigate. The first thing I saw was a long fuse sputtering towards a box of dynamite, set against the wall.

"I didn't know if it was the kind of fuse that would burn internally or not, so I took my penknife and cut it close to the dynamite. Professional saboteurs don't usually rely on just one explosive, so I started for the west wing to check the lab there."

Mr Hardy leaned back in his chair and rubbed the bruise on his temple. In a low voice he said, "But I didn't make it. I was running towards the hall when there was a roar and a burst of flame. The explosion lifted me off my feet and threw me against the wall. Though I was stunned, I managed to get back to the east wing. I reached for the phone, then blacked out.

"I must have been unconscious for some time, because when the firemen found me and helped me out of the building, the fire had been put out."

"You're all right now?" asked Frank.

"Yes. It was a temporary blackout from shock. What bothers me is that I had the saboteurs' pattern figured out—only they must have become panicky and moved forward their nefarious scheme by two days."

Joe looked grim. "I wish we'd been there to help you capture those rats!"

Chet asked Mr Hardy if he would like a fruit drink. "I'll make some lemonade," he offered.

"Sounds good." Mr Hardy smiled.

As they sipped the lemonade, Frank and Joe questioned their father about his theories.

"I'm still convinced," said Mr Hardy, "that one of those men works in the plant. How else would he have known when the watchman makes his rounds and how to disconnect the electronic alarms? But I *can't* figure how the outside accomplice got in—those gates are carefully guarded."

At this point Frank told his father about the green truck. "We suspected at first it might be connected with the counterfeiters. Now we have a hunch the saboteurs may have used it."

Fenton Hardy seemed greatly encouraged by this possible lead. Joe gave him the licence number, which Mr Hardy said he would report to Chief Collig at once.

When Mr Hardy returned from the telephone, he told the boys the chief would check the licence number with the Motor Vehicle Bureau in the morning and by then he would also have some information about the print on the archer's finger guard.

The next morning after breakfast Frank said he wanted to take another look at the warning notes.

"Why?" Joe asked curiously, as they went to the file.

Frank held up the "arrow" warning, and the one received by Chet. "I've been thinking about the printing on these two—seems familiar. I have it!" he burst out.

"Have what?" Joe asked.

"This printing"—Frank pointed to the papers—"is the same as the printing on Ken's envelope addressed to Victor Peters. I'm positive."

Excitedly the brothers speculated on the possible meaning of this clue. "I'd sure like to find out," said Joe, "who addresses the envelopes Ken delivers, and if they're always sent to Mr Peters in the Parker Building. And why—if he doesn't have an office there. And who *is* Victor Peters?"

"If the person who addresses the envelopes and the sender of the warnings are the same," Frank declared, "it looks as though he's sending something to a confederate, under pretence of having work done for Elekton. I wonder what that something could be?"

"At any rate," Joe added, "this could be a link

either to the counterfeiters or to the saboteurs. Which one?"

The boys decided to go out to the mill again, in the hope of quizzing Ken Blake. Just then their father came downstairs. Frank and Joe were glad to see that he looked rested and cheerful.

Mr Hardy phoned Chief Collig. When the detective hung up, he told his sons that the licence number belonged to stolen plates and the fingerprint to a confidence man nicknamed The Arrow.

"He's called this because for several years he worked at exclusive summer resorts, teaching archery to wealthy vacationers, then fleecing as many of them as he could. After each swindle, The Arrow disappeared. Unfortunately, there's no picture of him on file. All the police have is a general description of him."

Frank and Joe learned that the swindler had a pleasant speaking voice, was of medium height, with dark hair and brown eyes.

"Not much to go on," Joe remarked glumly.

"No, but if he *is* working for Elekton, he must be pretty shrewd to have passed their screening."

Mr Hardy agreed, and phoned Elekton, requesting the personnel department to check if anybody answering The Arrow's description was employed there.

The brothers then informed their father about the similar lettering on the warnings and Ken's Manila envelope.

"A valuable clue," he remarked. "I wish I could go with you to question Ken." The detective explained that right now he had to make his report of the explosion to the nearby FBI office.

When he had left, Frank and Joe rode off to the mill on their motorcycles.

At the gatehouse the guard had unexpected news. "Ken Blake isn't working here any more," Mr Markel said. "We had to discharge him."

"Why?" asked Joe in surprise.

The guard replied that most of the necessary jobs had been done around the mill grounds. "Mr Docker—my co-worker—and I felt we could handle everything from now on," he explained.

"I see," said Frank. "Can you tell us where Ken is staying?"

Markel said he was not sure, but he thought Ken might have been boarding in an old farmhouse about a mile up the highway.

When the brothers reached the highway, they stopped. "Which way do we go? Mr Markel didn't tell us," Joe said in chagrin.

"Instead of going back to find out, let's ask at that petrol station across the way," Frank suggested. "Someone there may know."

"An old farmhouse?" the attendant repeated in answer to Frank's query. "There's one about a mile from here going towards Bayport. That might be the place your friend is staying. What does he look like?"

Frank described Ken carefully. The attendant nodded. "Yep. I've seen him ride by here on his bike. A couple of times when I was going past the farm I noticed him turn in at the farm road."

"Thanks a lot!" The Hardys cycled off quickly.

Soon they were heading up the narrow, dusty lane, which led to a ramshackle, weather-beaten house. The brothers parked their motorcycles among the high weeds in front of it and dismounted.

"This place seems deserted!" Joe muttered.

Frank agreed and looked around, perplexed. "Odd that Ken would be boarding in such a run-down house."

Frank and Joe walked on to the creaky porch and knocked at the sagging door. There was no answer. They knocked again and called. Still no response.

"Some peculiar boarding-house!" Joe said. "I wouldn't want a room here!"

Frank frowned. "This must be the wrong place. Look—it's all locked up and there's hardly any furniture."

"I'll bet nobody lives in this house!" Joe burst out.

"But the attendant said he has seen Ken riding in here," Frank declared. "Why?"

"Let's have a look," Joe urged.

Mystified, Frank and Joe circled the house. Since they were now certain it had been abandoned, they glanced in various windows. When Joe came to the kitchen he grabbed Frank's arm excitedly.

"Somebody *is* staying here! Could it be Ken?"

Through the dusty glass the boys could see on a rickety table several open cans of food, a carton of milk, and a bowl.

"Must be a tramp," Frank guessed. "I'm sure Ken wouldn't live here."

In turning away, the young detectives noticed a small stone structure about ten yards behind the house. It was the size of a one-car garage. Instead of windows, it had slits high in the walls.

"It probably was used to store farm equipment," Frank said. "We might as well check."

They unbolted the old-fashioned, stout, wooden double doors. These swung outwards, and the boys were surprised that the doors opened so silently. "As if they'd been oiled," Frank said.

"No wonder!" Joe cried out. "Look!"

Inside was a shabby, green panel truck! "The same one we saw yesterday!" Joe exclaimed. "What's it doing here?"

The boys noticed immediately that the vehicle had no number plates. "They were probably taken off," Frank surmised, "and disposed of."

Frank checked the glove compartment while Joe looked on the seat and under the cushion for any clue to the driver or owner of the vehicle. Suddenly he called out, "Hey! What's going on?"

Joe jumped from the truck and saw with astonishment that the garage doors were swinging shut. Together, the boys rushed forward but not in time. They heard the outside bolt being rammed into place.

"We're prisoners!" Frank exclaimed.

Again and again the Hardys threw their weight against the doors. This proved futile. Panting, Frank and Joe looked for a means of escape.

"Those slits in the wall are too high and too narrow anyway," Frank said, chiding himself for not having been on guard.

Finally he reached into the glove compartment and drew out an empty cigarette package he had noticed before. He pulled off the foil. Joe understood immediately what his brother had in mind. Frank lifted the truck's hood and jammed the foil between the starting wires near the fuse box. "Worth a try," he said. "Ignition key's gone. If we can start the engine—we'll smash our way out!"

Joe took his place at the wheel and Frank climbed in beside him. To their delight, Joe gunned the engine into life.

"Here goes!" he muttered grimly. "Brace yourself!"

"Ready!"

Joe eased the truck as far back as he could, then accelerated swiftly forward. The truck's wheels spun on the dirt floor and then with a roar it headed for the heavy doors.

15

Lead to a Counterfeiter

C-R-A-S-H! The green truck smashed through the heavy garage doors. The Hardys felt a terrific jolt and heard the wood splinter and rip as they shot forward into the farmyard.

"Wow!" Joe gasped, as he braked to a halt. "We're free—but not saying in what shape!"

Frank gave a wry laugh. "Probably better than the front of this truck!"

The boys hopped to the ground and looked around the overgrown yard. No one was in sight. The whole area seemed just as deserted as it had been when they arrived.

"Let's check the house," Joe urged. "Someone *could* be hiding in there."

The brothers ran to the run-down dwelling. They found all the doors and windows locked. Again they peered through the dirty panes, but did not see anyone.

"I figure that whoever locked us in the garage would decide that getting away from here in a hurry was his safest bet."

"He must have gone on foot," Joe remarked. "I didn't hear an engine start up."

The Hardys decided to separate, each searching the highway for a mile in opposite directions.

"We'll meet back at the service station we stopped at," Frank called as the boys kicked their motors into life and took off towards the highway.

Fifteen minutes later they parked near the station. Neither boy had spotted any suspicious pedestrians.

"Did you see anybody come down this road in a hurry during the past twenty minutes?" Joe asked the attendant.

"I didn't notice, fellows," came the answer. "I've been busy working under a car. Find your friend?"

"No. That farmhouse is apparently deserted except for signs of a tramp living there," Joe told him.

The Hardys quickly asked the attendant if he knew of any boarding-house nearby. After a moment's thought, he replied:

"I believe a Mrs Smith, who lives a little way beyond the old place, takes boarders."

"We'll try there. Thanks again," Frank said, as he and Joe went back to their motorcycles.

Before Frank threw his weight back on the starter, he said, "Well, let's hope Ken Blake can give us a lead."

"If we ever find him," Joe responded.

They located Mrs Smith's boarding-house with no trouble. She was a pleasant, middle-aged woman and quickly confirmed that Ken was staying there for the summer. She was an old friend of his parents. Mrs Smith invited the Hardys to sit down in the living-room.

"Ken's upstairs now," she said. "I'll call him."

When Ken came down the Hardys noticed that he looked dejected. Frank felt certain it was because of losing his job and asked him what had happened.

"I don't know," Ken replied. "Mr Markel just told me I wouldn't be needed any longer. I hope I'll be able to find another job this summer," he added. "My folks sent me here for a vacation. But I was going to surprise them—" His voice trailed off sadly.

"Ken," Frank said kindly, "you may be able to help us in a very important way. Now that you're not working at the Elekton gatehouse, we hope you can answer some questions—to help solve a mystery."

Frank explained that he and Joe often worked on mysteries and assisted their detective father.

Ken's face brightened. "I'll do my best, fellows," he assured them eagerly.

"Last week," Joe began, "a shabby, green panel truck went to Pritos' Supply Yard and picked up old bricks and lumber. Our friend Tony Prito said there was a boy in the truck who helped the yardman with the loading. Were you the boy?"

"Yes," Ken replied readily.

"Who was the driver?" Frank asked him.

"Mr Docker, the maintenance man at the mill. He said he'd hurt his arm and asked me to help load the stuff." Ken looked puzzled. "Is that part of the mystery?"

"We think it could be," Frank said. "Now, Ken— we've learned since then that one of the bills you gave the yardman is a counterfeit twenty."

Ken's eyes opened wide in astonishment. "A—a counterfeit!" he echoed. "Honest, I didn't know it was, Frank and Joe!"

"Oh, we're sure you didn't," Joe assured him. "Have you any idea who gave Docker the cash?"

Ken told the Hardys he did not know. Then Frank asked:

"What were the old bricks and lumber used for, Ken?"

"Mr Docker told me they were for repair work around the plant. After we got back to the mill, Mr Markel and I stored the load in the basement."

"Is it still there?" asked Frank.

"I guess so," Ken answered. "Up to the time I left, it hadn't been taken out."

The Hardys determined to question Markel and Docker at the first opportunity. Then Frank changed the subject and asked about the day of the picnic when Joe thought he had seen Ken at the window.

"I remember," the younger boy said. "I *did* see you all outside. I never knew you were looking for me."

"When we told Mr Docker," Frank went on, "he said Joe must have been mistaken."

Ken remarked slowly, "He probably was worrying about the plant's security policy. He and Mr Markel were always reminding me not to talk to anybody."

"During the time you were working at the Elekton gatehouse, did you see any strange or suspicious person near either the plant or the mill grounds?" Frank asked.

"No," said Ken in surprise. Curiosity overcoming him, he burst out, "You mean there's some crook loose around here?"

Frank and Joe nodded vigorously. "We're afraid so," Frank told him. "But who, or what he's up to, is what we're trying to find out. When we do, we'll explain everything."

Joe then asked Ken if he had seen anyone in the area of the mill with a bow and arrow.

"A bow and arrow?" Ken repeated. "No, I never did. I sure would've remembered that!"

Frank nodded and switched to another line of questioning. "When you delivered envelopes, Ken, did you always take them to Mr Victor Peters?"

"Yes," Ken answered.

The Hardys learned further that Ken's delivery trips always had been to Bayport—sometimes to the Parker Building, and sometimes to other office buildings in the business section.

"Did Mr Peters meet you in the lobby every time?" Frank queried.

"That's right."

"What was in the envelopes?" was Joe's next question.

"Mr Markel said they were bulletins and forms to be printed for Elekton."

"Were the envelopes always marked confidential?" Joe asked.

"Yes."

"Probably everything is that Elekton sends out," Frank said.

"Sounds like a complicated delivery arrangement to me," Joe declared.

Ken admitted that he had not thought much about it at the time, except that he had assumed Mr Peters relayed the material to the printing company.

Frank and Joe glanced at each other. Both remembered Frank's surmise that the bulky Manila envelopes had not contained bona fide Elekton papers at all!

"What does Mr Peters look like?" asked Joe, a note of intense excitement in his voice.

"Average height and stocky, with a sharp nose. Sometimes he'd be wearing sunglasses."

"Stocky and a sharp nose," Frank repeated. "Sunglasses." Meaningfully he asked Joe, "Whom does that description fit?"

Joe jumped to his feet. "The man who gave Chet the counterfeit twenty at the railroad station!"

The Hardys had no doubt now that the mysterious Victor Peters must be a passer for the counterfeit ring!

16

A Night Assignment

GREATLY excited at this valuable clue to the counter-feiters, Frank asked, "Ken, who gave Mr Markel the envelopes for Victor Peters?"

"I'm sorry, fellows, I don't know."

The Hardys speculated on where Peters was living. Was it somewhere near Bayport?

Joe's eyes narrowed. "Ken," he said, "this morning we found out that sometimes you'd ride up that dirt road to the deserted farmhouse. Was it for any particular reason?"

"Yes," Ken replied. "Mr Markel told me a poor old man was staying in the house, and a couple of times a week I was sent there to leave a box of food on the front porch."

"Did you ever see the 'poor old man'?" Frank asked. "Or the green panel truck?"

The Hardys were not surprised when the answer to both questions was No. They suspected the "poor old man" was Peters hiding out there and that he had made sure the truck was out of sight whenever Ken was expected.

The brothers were silent, each puzzling over the significance of what they had just learned. If the truck was used by the counterfeiters, how did this tie in with its being used for the sabotage operation at Elekton?

"Was The Arrow in league with the saboteurs? Did he also have something to do with the envelopes sent to Victor Peters?" Joe asked himself.

Frank wondered, "Is The Arrow—or a confederate of his working at Elekton—the person responsible for the warnings, the attack on us, and the tampering with the *Sleuth*?"

"Ken," Frank said aloud, "I think you'd better come and stay with us for a while, until we break this case. Maybe you can help us."

He did not want to mention it to Ken, but the possibility had occurred to him that the boy might be in considerable danger if the counterfeiters suspected that he had given the Hardys any information about Victor Peters.

Ken was delighted with the idea, and Mrs Smith, who knew of Fenton Hardy and his sons, gave permission for her young charge to go.

As a precaution, Frank requested the kindly woman to tell any stranger asking for Ken Blake that he was "visiting friends."

"I'll do that," she agreed.

Ken rode on the back seat of Joe's motorcycle on the trip to High Street. He was warmly welcomed by Mrs Hardy and Aunt Gertrude.

"I hope you enjoy your stay here," said Mrs Hardy, who knew that Frank and Joe had a good reason for inviting Ken. But neither woman asked questions in his presence.

"Your father probably will be out all day," Mrs Hardy told her sons. "He'll phone later."

While lunch was being prepared, Frank called police headquarters to give Chief Collig a report on what had happened at the deserted farmhouse.

"I'll notify the FBI," the chief said. "I'm sure they'll want to send men out there to examine that truck and take fingerprints. Elekton," the chief added, "had no record of any employee answering The Arrow's description."

"We're working on a couple of theories," Frank confided. "But nothing definite so far."

After lunch the Hardys decided their next move was to try to find out more about the contents of the envelopes Ken had delivered to Peters.

"We could ask Elekton officials straight out," Joe suggested.

His brother did not agree. "Without tangible evidence to back us up, we'd have to give too many reasons for wanting to know."

Finally Frank hit on an idea. He telephoned Elekton, asked for the accounting department, and inquired where the company had its printing done. The accounting clerk apparently thought he was a salesman, and gave him the information.

Frank hung up. "What did they say?" Joe asked impatiently.

"All Elekton's printing is done on the premises!"

"That proves it!" Joe burst out. "The set-up with Ken delivering envelopes to Peters isn't a legitimate one and has nothing to do with Elekton business."

Meanwhile Ken, greatly mystified, had been listening

intently. Now he spoke up. "Jeepers, Frank and Joe, have I been doing something wrong?" he asked worriedly.

In their excitement the Hardys had almost forgotten their guest. Frank turned to him apologetically. "Not you, Ken. We're trying to figure out who has."

Just then the Hardys heard the familiar chug of the Queen pulling up outside. The brothers went out to the porch with Ken. Chet leaped from his jalopy and bounded up to them. His chubby face was split with a wide grin.

"Get a load of this!" He showed them a badge with his picture on it. "I'll have to wear it every day when I start work. Everybody has to wear one before he can get into the plant," he added. "Even the president of Elekton!"

Suddenly Chet became aware of Ken Blake. "Hello!" the plump boy greeted him in surprise. Ken smiled, and the Hardys told their friend of the morning's adventure.

"Boy!" Chet exclaimed. "Things are starting to pop! So you found that green truck!"

Suddenly Joe noticed a strange look cross his brother's face.

"Chet," Frank said excitedly, "did you say *everybody* must show identification to enter Elekton's grounds?"

"Yes—everybody," Chet answered positively.

"What are you getting at, Frank?" his brother asked quickly.

"Before yesterday's explosion, when we saw the gate guard admit the green truck, the driver didn't stop— didn't show any identification at all!"

"That's true!" Joe exclaimed. "Mr Markel doesn't seem to be the careless type, though."

"I know," Frank went on. "If the green truck was sneaking in explosives—what better way than to let the driver zip right through."

Joe stared at his brother. "You mean Markel deliberately let the truck go by? That he's in league with the saboteurs, or the counterfeiters, or both?"

As the others listened in astonishment, Frank replied, "I have more than a hunch he is—and Docker too. It would explain a lot."

Joe nodded in growing comprehension. "It sure would!"

"How?" demanded Chet.

Joe took up the line of deduction. "Markel himself told Ken the envelopes were for the printer. Why did Docker say Ken wasn't at the mill the day I saw him? And what was the real reason for his being discharged?"

"I'm getting it," Chet interjected excitedly. "Those men were trying to keep you from questioning Ken. Why?"

"Perhaps because of what Ken could tell us, if we happened to ask him about the envelopes he delivered," Joe replied. Then he asked Ken if Markel and Docker knew that Joe had picked up the envelope on the day of the near accident.

"I didn't say anything about that," Ken replied. The boy's face wore a perplexed, worried look. "You mean Mr Docker and Mr Markel might be—crooks! They didn't act that way."

"I agree," Frank said. "And we still have no proof.

We'll have to see if we can find some—one way or another."

The Hardys reflected on the other mysterious happenings. "The green truck," Frank said, "could belong to the gatehouse men, since it seems to be used for whatever their scheme is, and *they* are hiding it at the deserted farmhouse."

"Also," Joe put in, "if Victor Peters is the 'old man,' he's probably an accomplice."

"And," Frank continued, "don't forget that the bike Ken used was available to both Docker and Markel to deliver the warning note. The arrow shooting occurred near the mill; the attack on us in the woods that night was near the mill. The warning note found in Chet's car was put there after Markel told him to go to the front gate. The guard probably lied to Chet the first day we went to the mill—he never did phone the personnel department."

"Another thing," Joe pointed out. "Both men are more free to come and go than someone working in the plant."

There was silence while the Hardys concentrated on what their next move should be.

"No doubt about it," Frank said finally. "Everything seems to point towards the mill as the place to find the answers."

"And the only way to be sure," Joe added, "is to go and have a look around it ourselves. How about tonight?"

Frank and Chet agreed, and the boys decided to wait until it was fairly dark. "I'll call Tony and see if he can go with us," Frank said. "We'll need his help."

Tony was eager to accompany the trio. "Sounds as if you're hitting the root of the mystery," he remarked, when Frank had brought him up to date.

"We hope so."

Later, Joe outlined a plan whereby they might ascertain if Peters *was* an accomplice of Docker and Markel, and at the same time make it possible for them to get into the mill.

"Swell idea," Frank said approvingly. "Better brush up on your voice-disguising technique!"

Joe grinned. "I'll practise."

Just before supper Mr Hardy phoned to say that he would not be returning home until later that night.

"Making progress, Dad?" asked Frank, who had taken the call.

"Could be, son," the detective replied. "That's why I'll be delayed. Tell your mother and Gertrude not to worry."

"Okay. And, Dad—Joe and I will be doing some sleuthing tonight with Chet and Tony to try out a few new ideas *we* have."

"Fine. But watch your step!"

About eight-thirty that evening Chet and Tony pulled up to the Hardy home in the Queen.

Ken Blake went with the brothers to the door. "See you later, Ken," Frank said, and Joe added, "I know you'd like to come along, but we don't want you taking any unnecessary risks."

The younger boy looked wistful. "I wish I could do something to help you fellows."

"There *is* a way you can help," Frank told him.

At that moment Mrs Hardy and Aunt Gertrude came into the hall. Quickly Frank drew Ken aside and whispered something to him.

· 17 ·

Secret Signal

WITH rising excitement, Frank, Joe, Chet and Tony drove off through the dusk towards the old mill.

Chet came to a stop about one hundred yards from the beginning of the road leading to the gatehouse. He and Tony jumped out. They waved to the Hardys, then disappeared into the woods.

Joe took the wheel of the jalopy. "Now, part two of our plan. I hope it works."

The brothers quickly rode to the service station where they had been that morning. Joe parked and hurried to the outdoor telephone booth nearby. From his pocket he took a slip of paper on which Ken had jotted down the night telephone number of the Elekton gatehouse.

Joe dialled the number, then covered the mouthpiece with his handkerchief to muffle his voice.

A familiar voice answered, "Gatehouse. Markel speaking."

Joe said tersely, "Peters speaking. Something has gone wrong. Both of you meet me outside the Parker Building. Make it snappy!" Then he hung up.

When Joe returned to the Queen, Frank had turned it round and they were ready to go. They sped back towards the mill and in about ten minutes had the jalopy parked out of sight in the shadows of the trees where the dirt road joined the paved one.

The brothers, keeping out of sight among the trees, ran to join Chet and Tony who were waiting behind a large oak near the edge of the gatehouse grounds.

"It worked!" Tony reported excitedly. "About fifteen minutes ago the lights in the mill went out, and Markel and Docker left in a hurry."

"On foot?" Joe asked.

"Yes."

"Good. If they have to take a bus or cab to town, it'll give us more time," Frank said.

Tony and Chet were given instructions about keeping watch outside while the Hardys inspected the mill. The brothers explained where the Queen was parked, in case trouble should arise and their friends had to go for help.

Frank and Joe approached the mill cautiously. It was dark now, but they did not use flashlights. Though confident that the gatehouse was deserted, they did not wish to take any chances. As they neared the building the Hardys could see that the shutters were tightly closed. Over the sound of the wind in the trees came the rumble of the turning mill wheel.

The Hardys headed for the door. They had just mounted the steps when the rumbling sound of the wheel ceased.

In the silence both boys looked around, perplexed. "I thought it had been fixed," Joe whispered. "Seemed okay the other day."

"Yes. But last time we were here at night the wheel

stopped when we were about this distance away from it," Frank observed.

Thoughtfully the boys stepped back from the mill entrance to a point where they could see the wheel. They stood peering at it through the darkness. Suddenly, with a dull rumble, it started to turn again!

Mystified, the Hardys advanced towards the gatehouse and stopped at the entrance. In a short while the wheel stopped.

"Hm!" Joe murmured. "Just like one of those electric-eye doors."

"Exactly!" Frank exclaimed, snapping his fingers. "I'll bet the wheel's *not* broken—it's been rigged up as a warning signal to be used at night! When someone approaches the mill, the path of the invisible beam is broken and the wheel stops. The lack of noise is enough for anyone inside to notice, and also, the lights would go out because the generator is powered by the wheel."

The Hardys went on a quick search for the origin of the light beam. Frank was first to discover that it was camouflaged in the flour-barrel ivy planter. Beneath a thin covering of earth, and barely concealed, were the heavy batteries, wired in parallel, which produced the current necessary to operate the light source for the electric eye.

The stopping and starting of the wheel was further explained when Frank found, screened by a bushy shrub, a small post with a tiny glass mirror fastened on its side.

"That's the complete secret of the signal!" he exclaimed. "This is one of the mirrors a photo-electric cell system would use. With several of these hidden mirrors, they've made a light-ring around the mill so that an intruder from any side would break the beam. The barrel that contains the battery power also contains the eye that completes the circuit."

"I'll bet Markel and Docker rigged this up," Joe said excitedly. "Which means there must be something in the mill they want very badly to keep secret! We must find a way inside!"

The Hardys did not pull the wires off the battery connection, since they might have need of the warning system. Quietly and quickly the brothers made a circuit of the mill, trying doors and first-floor windows, in hopes of finding one unlocked. But none was.

"We can't break in," Joe muttered.

Both boys were aware that time was precious—the men might return shortly. The young sleuths made another circle of the mill. This time they paused to stare at the huge wheel, which was turning once more.

"Look!" Joe whispered tensely, pointing to an open window-shaped space above the wheel.

"It's our only chance to get inside," Frank stated. "We'll try climbing up."

The Hardys realized it would not be easy to reach the opening. Had there been a walkway on top of the wheel, as there was in many mills, climbing it would have been relatively simple.

The brothers came to a quick decision: to manœuvre one of the paddles on the wheel until it was directly below the ledge of the open space, then stop the motion. During the short interval which took place between the stop and start of the wheel, they hoped to climb by way of the paddles to the top and gain entrance to the mill.

Joe ran back through the beam, breaking it, while Frank clambered over a pile of rocks across the water to the wheel. It rumbled to a stop, one paddle aligned with the open space above. By the time Joe returned, Frank had started to climb up, pulling himself from paddle to paddle by means of the metal side struts. Joe followed close behind.

The boys knew they were taking a chance in climbing up the wet, slippery, mossy wheel. They were sure there must be a timing-delay switch somewhere in the electric-eye circuit. Could they beat it, or would they be tossed off into the dark rushing water?

"I believe I can get to the top paddle and reach the opening before the timer starts the wheel turning again. But can Joe?" Frank thought. "Hurry!" he cried out to his brother.

Doggedly the two continued upwards. Suddenly Joe's hand slipped on a slimy patch of moss. He almost lost his grip, but managed to cling desperately to the edge of the paddle above his head, both feet dangling in mid-air.

"Frank!" he hissed through clenched teeth.

His brother threw his weight to the right. Holding tight with his left hand to a strut, he reached down and grasped Joe's wrist. Joe locked his fingers on Frank's wrist, and let go with his other hand.

Frank swung him out away from the wheel. As Joe swung himself back, he managed to regain his footing and get a firm hold on the paddle supports.

"Whew!" said Joe. "Thanks!"

The boys resumed the climb, spurred by the thought

that the sluice gate would re-open any second and start the wheel revolving.

Frank finally reached the top paddle. Stretching his arms upwards, he barely reached the sill of the opening. The old wood was rough and splintering, but felt strong enough to hold his weight.

"Here goes!" he thought, and sprang away from the paddle.

At the same moment, with a creaking rumble, the wheel started to move!

The Hidden Room

WHILE Frank clung grimly to the sill, Joe, below him, knew he must act fast to avoid missing the chance to get off, and perhaps be crushed beneath the turning wheel. He leaped upwards with all his might.

Joe's fingers barely grasped the ledge, but he managed to hang on to the rough surface beside his brother. Then together they pulled themselves up and over the sill through the open space.

In another moment they were standing inside the second floor of the building. Rickety boards creaked under their weight. Still not wishing to risk the use of their flashlights, the Hardys peered around in the darkness.

"I think we're in the original grinding room," Frank whispered, as he discerned the outlines of two huge stone cylinders in the middle of the room.

"You're right," said Joe. "There's the old grain hopper." He pointed to a chute leading down to the grinding stones.

Though many years had passed since the mill had been used to produce flour, the harsh, dry odour of grain still lingered in the air. In two of the corners were cots and a set of crude shelves for clothes. Suddenly the boys' hearts jumped. A loud clattering noise came from directly below. Then, through a wide crack in the floor, shone a yellow shaft of light!

"Someone else must be here!" Joe said in a low voice.

The Hardys stood motionless, hardly daring to breathe, waiting for another sound. Who *was* in the suddenly lighted room?

The suspense was unbearable. Finally the brothers tiptoed over and peered through the wide crack. Straightening up, Frank observed, "Can't see anyone. We'd better go and investigate."

Fearful of stumbling in the inky darkness, the boys now turned on their flashlights but shielded them with their hands. Cautiously they found their way to a door. It opened into a short passageway which led down a narrow flight of steps.

Soon Frank and Joe were in another small hall. Ahead was a partially opened door, with light streaming from it.

Every nerve taut, the young sleuths advanced. Frank edged up to the door and looked in.

"Well? What is it?" Joe hissed. To his utter astonishment, Frank gave a low chuckle, and motioned him forward.

"For Pete's sake!" Joe grinned.

Inside, perched on a chipped grindstone, was a huge white cat. Its tail twitched indignantly. An overturned lamp lay on a table.

The Hardys laughed in relief. "Our noise-maker and lamplighter!" Frank said, as the boys entered the room.

"The cat must have knocked over the lamp and clicked the switch."

Although the room contained the gear mechanism and the shaft connected to the mill wheel, it was being used as a living area by the present tenants. There were two overstuffed chairs, a table, and a chest of drawers. On the floor, as if dropped in haste, lay a scattered newspaper.

"Let's search the rest of the mill before Markel and Docker get back," Joe suggested. "Nothing suspicious here."

The Hardys started with the top storey of the old building. There they found what was once the grain storage room. Now it was filled with odds and ends of discarded furniture.

"I'm sure nothing's been hidden up here," Frank said.

The other floors yielded no clues as to what Docker and Markel's secret might be.

Frank was beginning to feel rather discouraged. "Maybe our big hunch is all wrong," he muttered unhappily.

Joe refused to give up. "Let's investigate the cellar. Come on!"

The brothers went into the kitchen towards the basement stairway. Suddenly Joe gave a stifled yell. Something had brushed across his trouser legs. Frank swung his light around. The beam caught two round golden eyes staring up at them.

"The white cat!" Joe said sheepishly.

Chuckling, the Hardys continued down into the

damp, cool cellar. It was long and narrow, with only two small windows.

Three walls were of natural stone and mortar. The fourth wall was lined with wooden shelves. Hopefully, Frank and Joe played their flashlights into every corner.

"Hm." There was a note of disappointment in Joe's voice. "Wheelbarrow, shovels, picks—just ordinary equipment."

Frank nodded thoughtfully. "That seems to be all, but where are the old bricks and lumber that Ken said were stored here?"

"I'm sure the stuff was never intended for Elekton," Joe declared. "More likely the mill. But where? On a floor? We haven't seen any signs."

Thoughtfully the boys walked over to inspect the shelves, which held a varied assortment of implements and tools. Frank reached out to pick up a hammer.

To his amazement, he could not lift it. A further quick examination revealed that all the tools were glued to the shelves.

"Joe!" he exclaimed. "There's a special reason for this—and I think it's camouflage!"

"You mean these shelves are movable, and the tools are fastened so that they won't fall off?"

"Yes. Also, I have a feeling this whole section is made of the old lumber from Prito's yard."

"And the bricks?" Joe asked, puzzled.

His brother's answer was terse. "Remember, this mill was used by settlers. In those days many places like this had hidden rooms in case they were attacked by Indians—"

"I get you!" Joe broke in. "Those bricks are in a secret room! The best place to build one in this mill would have been the cellar."

"Right," agreed Frank. "And the only thing unusual here is this shelf set-up. I'll bet it's actually the entrance to the secret room."

"All we have to do is find the opening mechanism," Joe declared.

Using their flashlights, the boys went over every inch of the shelves. These were nailed to a backing of boards. The Hardys pulled and pushed, but nothing happened. Finally, on the bottom shelf near the wall, Frank discovered a knot in the wood. In desperation, he pressed his thumb hard against the knot.

There was the hum of a motor and, as smoothly as though it were moving on greased rails, the middle section of shelves swung inward.

"The door to the secret room!" Frank exclaimed excitedly.

Quickly the boys slipped inside the room and shone their flashlights around. The first thing they noticed was the flooring—recently laid bricks. Frank snapped on a light switch beside the entrance.

The boys blinked in the sudden glare of two high-watt bulbs suspended from the low ceiling. The next instant both of them spotted a small hand-printing press.

"The counterfeiters' workshop!" they cried out.

On a wooden table at the rear of the room were a camera, etching tools, zinc plates, and a large pan with little compartments containing various colours of ink. At the edge of the table was a portable type-writer.

Frank picked up a piece of paper, rolled it into the machine, and typed a few lines. Pulling it out, he showed the paper to Joe.

"This is the same machine as was used to type the warning note Dad got!" Joe exclaimed excitedly. "The counterfeiters must have thought he was on their trail."

"And look over here!" exclaimed Frank, his voice tense. A small pile of twenty-dollar bills lay among the equipment. "They're fakes," he added, scrutinizing the bills. "They're the same as Chet's and Tony's."

Joe made another startling discovery. In one corner stood a bow, with the string loosened and carefully wound around the handgrip. A quiver of three hunting arrows leaned against the wall nearby.

Excitedly Joe pulled one out. "The same type that was fired at the girls," he observed. "This must belong to The Arrow!"

"Docker matches his description," Frank pointed out enthusiastically. "He could easily have coloured his hair grey."

The Hardys were thrilled at the irrefutable evidence all around them. "Now we know why Markel and Docker rigged the mill wheel—to give a warning signal when they're working in this room!"

"Also, we now have a good idea what was being sent to Peters in the envelopes—phoney twenty-dollar bills!"

"Let's get Dad and Chief Collig here!" Joe urged,

stuffing several of the counterfeits into one of his pockets.

As the boys turned to leave, the lights in the secret room went out. Frank and Joe froze. They realized the mill wheel had stopped turning.

"The signal!" Joe said grimly. "Someone is coming!"

· 19 ·

Underground Chase

THE Hardys knew this was the signal for them to get out of the secret room—and fast! As they hurried into the cellar, the lights came on again. With hearts beating faster, they started for the stairway. But before the boys reached it, they heard the mill door being unlocked, then heavy footsteps pounded overhead.

"Docker!" a man's voice called. "Markel! Where are you!"

The Hardys listened tensely, hoping for a chance to escape unseen. When they heard the man cross the ground floor and go upstairs, Joe whispered, "Let's make a break for it!"

The boys dashed to the steps. They could see a crack of light beneath the closed door to the kitchen. Suddenly the light vanished, and the rumble of the mill wheel ceased.

The Hardys stopped in their tracks. "Somebody else is coming!" Frank muttered. "Probably Docker and Markel. We're trapped!"

Again the brothers heard the mill door open. Two men were talking loudly and angrily. Then came the sound of footsteps clattering down the stairs to the first floor.

"Peters!" The boys recognized Docker's voice. "Where in blazes were you? We waited for you as long as we could."

Frank and Joe nudged each other. Victor Peters *was* in league with the gatehouse men!

"What do you mean? I told you I'd meet you here at eleven," snarled Peters.

"You must be nuts!" retorted Markel. "You called here an hour ago and said there was trouble and to meet *you* at the Parker Building."

Peters's tone grew menacing. "Something's fishy. I didn't phone. You know I'd use the two-way radio. What's the matter with you guys, anyway?"

"Listen!" Markel snapped. "*Somebody* called here and said he was you. The voice did sound sort of fuzzy, but I didn't have a chance to ask questions—he hung up on me. I thought that maybe your radio had conked out."

The Hardys, crouched on the cellar stairs, could feel the increasing tension in the room above. Docker growled, "Something funny *is* going on. Whoever phoned must be on to us, or suspect enough to want to get in here and snoop around."

"The Feds! We'll have to scram!" said Markel, with more than a trace of fear in his voice. "Come on! Let's get moving!"

"Not so fast, Markel!" Docker barked. "We're not ditching the stuff we've made. We'll have a look around first—starting with the cellar."

The men strode into the kitchen. Below, Frank grabbed Joe. "We've no choice now. Into the secret room!"

Quickly the brothers ran back into the workshop. Frank pulled the door behind him and slid the heavy bolt into place.

Tensely the brothers pressed against the door as the three men came downstairs into the basement. Frank and Joe could hear them moving around, searching for signs of an intruder.

"I'd better check the rest of the mill," Docker said brusquely. "You two get the plates and the greenbacks. Go out through the tunnel, and I'll meet you at the other end. We'll wait there for Blum to pay us off, then vamoose."

"We're in a fix, all right," Joe said under his breath. "What tunnel are they talking about?"

"And who's Blum?" Frank wondered.

The boys heard the hum of the motor that opened the secret door. But the bolt held it shut.

"The mechanism won't work!" Markel rasped.

"Maybe it's just stuck," said Peters.

The men began pounding on the wood.

"What's going on?" Docker demanded as he returned.

"We can't budge this tricky door you dreamed up," Peters complained.

"There's nothing wrong with the door, you blockheads!" Docker shouted. "Somebody's in the room! Break down the door!"

In half a minute his order was followed by several sharp blows.

"Oh, that's great!" Joe groaned. "They're using axes!"

"We won't have long to figure a way out," Frank said wryly.

"Way out!" Joe scoffed. "There isn't any!"

Frank's mind raced. "Hey! They said something about leaving through a tunnel! It must lead out from here."

Frantically the Hardys searched for another exit from the secret room. They crawled on the floor, and pried up one brick after another looking for a ring that might open a trap door.

"Nothing!" Joe said desperately.

All the while the men in the cellar kept battering away at the door. "Good thing that old lumber is such hard wood," Frank thought. "But they'll break through any minute."

"Look!" Joe pointed. "Over there. Under the bench!"

Frank noticed a shovel lying beneath the worktable. The boys pushed it aside and saw that the wall behind the table was partially covered with loose dirt. On a hunch, Frank grabbed the shovel and started to dig into the dirt.

"This dirt might have been put here to hide the entrance to the tunnel!" he gasped.

"It better be!" His brother clawed frantically at the dirt.

At the same moment there was a loud splintering noise. The Hardys looked round. A large crack had appeared in the bolted door.

One of the men outside yelled, "A couple more blows and we'll be in."

Frank dug furiously. Suddenly his shovel opened up

a small hole in the crumbly dirt. Joe scooped away with his hands. Finally there was a space big enough for the boys to squeeze through. Without hesitation, Frank wriggled in, then Joe.

From behind them came a tremendous crash and the sound of ripping wood. Markel's voice shouted, "Into the tunnel! After 'em!"

The Hardys heard no more as they pushed ahead on hands and knees into the damp darkness of an earthen passageway.

Joe was about to call out to his brother when he became aware that someone was crawling behind him. "No room here for a knockdown fight," he thought, wondering if the pursuer were armed.

The young detective scrambled on as fast as he could in the narrow, twisting tunnel. He managed to catch up to Frank, and with a push warned him to go at top speed.

"Somebody's after us!" Joe hissed. "If only we can outdistance him!"

The underground route was a tortuous, harrowing one. The Hardys frequently scraped knees and shoulders against sharp stones in the tunnel floor and walls. They had held on to their flashlights, but did not dare turn them on.

"This passageway is endless!" Frank thought. The close, clammy atmosphere made it increasingly difficult for his brother and he to breathe.

Joe thought uneasily, "What if we hit a blind alley and are stuck in here?"

The boys longed to stop and catch their breath, but they could hear the sounds of pursuit growing nearer, and forced themselves onward faster than ever.

Frank wondered if Chet and Tony had seen the men enter the mill and had gone for help.

"We'll need it," he thought grimly.

Suddenly the brothers came to another turn and the ground began to slope sharply upwards.

"Maybe we're getting close to the end," Frank conjectured hopefully.

Spurred by possible freedom, he put on a burst of speed. Joe did the same. A moment later Frank stopped unexpectedly and Joe bumped into him.

"What's the matter? Why have you stopped?" he barely whispered.

"Dead end," reported his brother.

Squeezing up beside Frank, Joe reached out and touched a pile of stones blocking their path. The boys were now able to hear the heavy breathing of their pursuer.

"Let's move these stones," Frank urged.

Both Hardys worked with desperate haste to pull the barrier down. They heaved thankful sighs when a draught of fresh air struck their faces.

"The exit!" Joe whispered in relief.

The brothers wriggled quickly through the opening they had made and found themselves in a rock-walled space.

"It's the cave by the river, Joe!" Frank cried out. "Someone put back the rocks we removed!"

The boys clicked on their flashlights and started towards the entrance of the cave.

"We beat 'em to it!" Joe exclaimed.

"That's what you think!" came a harsh voice from the entrance.

The glare from two flashlights almost blinded the Hardys. Docker and Markel, with drawn revolvers, had stepped into the cave.

· 20 ·

Solid Evidence

FOR a second the two armed men stared in disbelief at Frank and Joe. "The Hardy boys!" Docker snarled. "So you're the snoopers we've trapped!"

There was a scuffling in the tunnel behind the boys. A stocky man, huffing and puffing, emerged from the tunnel. The Hardys recognized him instantly: the counterfeit passer, Victor Peters.

The newcomer gaped at the Hardys. "What are *they* doing here?"

"A good question!" Markel snapped at his accomplice. "You told us on the two-way radio you'd locked 'em up with the truck."

Peters whined, "I *did*. They must've broken out."

"Obviously." Docker gave him a withering look.

Frank and Joe realized that Peters had not returned to the old farmhouse.

Docker whirled on them. "How *did* you escape?"

The boys looked at him coldly. "That's for you to find out," Joe retorted.

"It's a good thing Markel and I decided to head 'em off at the cave," Docker added angrily. "Otherwise they would have escaped again."

The Hardys could see that the men were nervous and edgy. "I'm not the only one who made a mistake," Peters growled. "I told you a couple of days ago to get rid of that kid Ken when these pests started asking about him, and then found the tunnel. We could have thrown 'em off the scent!"

While the men argued, the Hardys kept on the alert for a chance to break away. Markel's eye caught the movement, and he levelled his revolver. "Don't be smart!" he ordered. "You're covered."

Peters continued his tirade against his confederates. "Docker, you should've finished these Hardys off when you put 'em in the boat that night! And you"—Peters turned on Markel—"*you* could have planted a dynamite charge in their boat instead of just monkeying with the throttle."

The Hardys, meanwhile, were thankful for the precious minutes gained by the men's dissension. "Tony and Chet might come back in time with help," Joe thought.

Simultaneously, Frank hoped that Ken Blake had carried out his whispered instructions.

Docker glanced nervously at his watch. "Blum ought to be here," he fumed.

"Who's Blum?" Frank asked suddenly. "One of your counterfeiting pals?"

Docker, Markel and Peters laughed scornfully. "No," said Markel. "We're the only ones in our exclusive society. Paul Blum doesn't know anything about our—er—mill operation, but it was through him we got the jobs at the gatehouse. The whole deal really paid off double."

Docker interrupted him with a warning. "Don't blab so much!"

Markel sneered. "Why not? What I say won't do these smart alecks any good."

Joe looked at the guard calmly. "Who paid you to let the green panel truck into Elekton?"

All three men started visibly. "How'd you know that?" Markel demanded.

"Just had a hunch," Joe replied.

The former guard regained his composure. "We'll get our money for that little job tonight."

Frank and Joe felt elated. Paul Blum, whom these men expected, must be the sabotage ring-leader! "So that's what Markel meant by the deal paying off double," Frank thought. "He and Docker working the counterfeit racket on their own—and being in league with the saboteurs."

Frank addressed Markel in an icy tone. "You call blowing up a building a 'little job'?"

The counterfeiters' reactions astonished the Hardys. "*What!*" bellowed Peters, as Docker and Markel went ashen.

Joe snorted. "You expect us to believe you didn't *know* explosives were in that truck?"

Victor Peters was beside himself with rage. "*Fools!*" he shrilled at Docker and Markel. "You let yourselves be used by saboteurs? This whole state will be crawling with police and federal agents."

The gatehouse men, though shaken, kept their revolvers trained on the Hardys. "Never mind," Docker muttered. "Soon as Blum shows up we'll get out of here and lie low for a while."

Frank and Joe learned also that Docker and Markel actually were brothers, but the two refused to give their real names.

"You, Docker, are known as The Arrow, aren't you?" Frank accused him.

"Yeah. Next time I'll use *you* boys for targets!" the man retorted threateningly.

The Hardys kept egging the men on to further admissions. Docker and Markel had been approached several months before by Blum who tipped them off to good-paying jobs at the Elekton gatehouse. Docker had cleverly forged references and identification for Markel and himself.

As soon as he and Markel had obtained the jobs, Blum had instructed them to buy the truck second-hand in another state, and told them only that Markel was to lend Blum the truck on a certain day when notified, let him through the gate, then out again soon after closing time. The guard would be handsomely paid to do this.

When Markel and Docker had become settled in the mill, the two had discovered the secret room and tunnel, which once had a been settlers' escape route. The men had wasted no time in setting it up for their counterfeiting racket, and often used the nondescript green truck to sneak in the required equipment.

"Who rigged up the electric-eye signal?" Frank queried.

"My work," Docker replied proudly.

As the boys had surmised, Peters, an old acquaintance of theirs, was "the old man" at the deserted farmhouse. When the boys had left the mill that morning

Docker had radioed Peters, telling him that if the Hardys showed up at the farm, he was to trap them.

"No doubt you planned to finish us off when you came back," Joe said.

Peters nodded.

Frank said to Docker, "I must admit, those twenties are pretty good forgeries. The police think so too."

The counterfeiter smiled in contempt. "Your fat friend sure was fooled."

He explained that his skill at engraving, which he had learned years ago, had enabled him to make the plates from which the bills were printed.

"Which one of you rode Ken's bike and left the typed warning for our father?" Frank asked.

"I did," Markel replied promptly.

"Why? He wasn't involved with the counterfeiting case."

"We thought he was when we overheard a company bigwig say Fenton Hardy was 'taking the case.' "

"Yeah," Docker said. "I wasn't kidding when I sent the warnings—on paper and by phone."

He had acquired some sheets of bond paper from Elekton on a pretext; also the Manila envelopes used to deliver the bogus money to Peters. Docker admitted he had "unloaded" the counterfeit twenty at Prito's yard by mistake.

Peters broke in abruptly. "We'd better get rid of these kids right now!"

The three men held a whispered conference, but Docker and Markel did not take their eyes from the Hardys. Suddenly the boys' keen ears detected the put-put of an approaching motorboat.

One thought flashed across their minds—Chet and Tony were bringing help. But in a few minutes their hopes were dashed! A heavy-set, dark-haired man peered into the mouth of the cave.

"Blum!" Markel said.

"Who are these kids?" Blum asked, squinting at Frank and Joe.

"Their name is Hardy—" Docker began, but Blum cut him short.

"Hardy!" he said sharply. "Listen—I just gave Fenton Hardy the slip at the Bayport dock. He was on a police launch."

"We've got to move fast!" Markel urged. "Docker and I caught these sons of his snooping. Pay us what you promised and we'll scram."

Blum looked disgusted. "Stupid amateurs! You let kids make it so hot you have to get out of town?" The heavy-set man pulled out his wallet. "Here's your cut for letting me into the plant," he continued scornfully. "I'm glad to get rid of such bunglers."

"It's not just these kids that made it hot for us!" Docker stormed. "If we'd known you were going to blow up that lab, we never would've got mixed up with you."

The Hardys noticed that Paul Blum appeared startled at Docker's words.

Frank spoke up boldly. "Sure. We all know you're behind the sabotage. Who pays *you* for doing it? And who's *your* inside man at Elekton?"

Blum glared, then in a sinister tone replied, "You'll never live to sing to the cops, so I'll tell you. Several countries that want to stop United States progress in missiles are paying me. My friend in the plant is a fellow named Jordan."

The saboteur revealed that his accomplice had first carried out smaller acts of sabotage, the ones which Chet had heard about from his father. It had been Blum himself who had driven the truck into the grounds and placed the dynamite in the laboratory. "Jordan and I gave your father the slip then, too!"

"You guys can stand here and talk!" snapped Peters. "I'm going. You'd better take care of these Hardys." He backed out of the cave and raced off.

The counterfeiters discussed heatedly whether "to get rid" of Frank and Joe immediately or take "these kids" and dispose of them later.

"That's your worry!" Blum said. "*I'm* taking off!"

"Oh, no, you're not. You can't leave us in the lurch." Markel waved his gun meaningfully.

At that instant there was a crashing noise outside the cave. The three men swung around.

This was all the Hardys needed. They hurled themselves at their captors, forcing them backwards on to the rocky beach. From the woods they heard Chet yell, "Here we come, fellows!"

Frank had tackled Blum, and Joe was wrestling with Docker on the beach.

Tony Prito yelled, "Got you!" as he took a flying leap at Markel and brought him to the ground.

The older men, though strong, were no match for the agile Hardys and the furious onslaught of Chet and Tony. Finally the struggle ended.

The saboteur and counterfeiters were disarmed and lined up before the cave, their arms pinioned behind them by Joe, Chet and Tony. Frank took charge of the revolvers.

"Good work, you two!" he said to his friends.

Chet, out of breath, grinned proudly. "I'm glad Tony and I stuck around when we saw these guys running through the woods."

Now Frank turned to the prisoners. "Okay. March!" he ordered.

But before anyone could move, footsteps were heard approaching through the woods. A moment later Chief Collig and another officer appeared. With them, in handcuffs, was Victor Peters.

"Chief! Are we glad to see you!" Joe exclaimed.

The chief stared in amazement at the boys and their captives. "I got your message from Ken Blake," he told Frank. "Looks as if you have your hands full!"

"Oh, we have!" Joe grinned, then, puzzled, he asked his brother, "What message?"

"Just before I left the house I told Ken to call Chief Collig if we weren't back by eleven, and tell him where we had gone."

While Blum and the counterfeiters stood in sullen silence, the four boys learned that Ken had called the chief just minutes after Fenton Hardy had left in the police launch in pursuit of Paul Blum.

"When we reached the mill we met this crook running out of the woods." Chief Collig gestured towards the handcuffed Peters. "I recognized him from Chet's description. When we found phoney money on him, he told me where you were, hoping to get off with a lighter sentence."

"You rat!" Docker's face contorted with rage.

At that moment the group became aware of a police launch churning towards them, the beam from its searchlight sweeping the water. In the excitement, no one had heard the sound of its engine.

"Dad!" cried the Hardys, spotting the detective's erect figure standing in the bow. Soon the launch was beached, and Mr Hardy, with several officers, leaped ashore.

"Well," Mr Hardy said sternly when he saw Blum, "you won't be escaping again."

The captured lawbreakers were handcuffed and put aboard the launch. Mr Hardy looked at his sons and their friends proudly. "You've done a yeoman's job—on both cases, yours and mine," he said.

After the police cruiser had departed, Frank and Joe led their father and the others into the mill cellar and showed them the secret room.

"This is all the evidence you need against the counterfeiters, Chief," said Mr Hardy. "I can see there are plenty of fingerprints on this equipment. We know some will match the one on the finger guard. Besides your evidence, boys, Ken's testimony should be more than enough to convict them."

"What about Jordan, Blum's confederate at Elekton?" Frank asked.

Mr Hardy smiled. "He was my big prize and I'm glad to say he is in jail!" The detective explained that further sleuthing had led to Jordan—and through him, Paul Blum. Mr Hardy's first break had come when he learned that one Elekton employee had seen Jordan going towards the laboratory building at closing time on the day of the explosion.

A police guard was assigned to watch the counterfeiters' workshop and its contents. Then the four boys, Mr Hardy and the chief left the mill. Outside, they paused and looked back at the turning wheel.

Frank laughed. "Its signalling days are over."

"Sure hope so," Chet declared firmly. "No more mysteries for a while, please!"

Tony chuckled. "With Frank and Joe around, I wouldn't count on it."

His words proved to be true. Sooner than even the Hardy boys expected, they were to be called upon to solve another mystery—*The Shore Road Mystery*.

Now Joe turned to their plump friend. "Good thing you bought that microscope, Chet. We started to look for nature specimens and dug up the old mill's secret!"